LETHAL MERCY

Also by Harry Lee Kraus, Jr.

Stainless Steal Hearts

Fated Genes

LETHAL MERCY

Harry Lee Kraus, Jr., M.D.

CROSSWAY BOOKS • WHEATON, ILLINOIS
A DIVISION OF GOOD NEWS PUBLISHERS

This is a work of imagination. None of the characters found within these pages reflect the character or intentions of any real person. Any similarity is coincidental.

Lethal Mercy

Copyright © 1997 by Harry Lee Kraus, Jr.

Published by Crossway Books
        a division of Good News Publishers
        1300 Crescent Street
        Wheaton, Illinois 60187

Cover design: Cindy Kiple

First printing, 1997

Printed in the United States of America

Library of Congress Cataloging-in-Publication Data
Kraus, Harry Lee, 1960–
   Lethal mercy / Harry Lee Kraus, Jr.
      p.   cm.
   ISBN 0-89107-921-1
   I. Title.
PS3561.R2875F3 1996
813'.54—dc20   · 96-38742

06	05	04	03	02	01	00	99	98	97
15	14	13	12	11	10	9	8	7	6	5	4	3

For my parents
Harry and Mildred Kraus
in honor of their golden wedding anniversary

PROLOGUE

OCEAN SANDS WELLNESS FACILITY

JAKE Hampton's hand trembled as he stroked his wife's cheek for the last time. Moments before, Sarah, whose freckled complexion appeared almost plastic in the dim light, had choked on her final breath, the terminal indignant event in an agonizing fight against breast cancer. Jake tearfully looked away. The serenity of the resort atmosphere and the cool breeze coming off the nearby Atlantic provided a sharp contrast to the turmoil boiling within him. How could it have come to this?

He instinctively pulled his hand away and gently touched Sarah's swollen abdomen. There he monitored the violent kicks of his yet to be born daughter, who ceased all movement a full two minutes after her mother's last heartbeat. Jake choked back a sob of emotion. His dreams seemed as dead as the body beside him.

Tears clouded his vision as anger, confusion, and guilt prodded him to action. *Flee this place of death!* He looked around the well-furnished, comfortable suite. This is what she wanted, wasn't it? She wanted it to end! Jake stopped suddenly and looked up, toward the open sliding door leading to the balcony overlooking the ocean beyond. Had he seen someone?

He froze momentarily and watched the curtains fluttering with the midnight breeze. *It's just the wind, Jake,* he chided himself. He quickly returned to the task at hand, picking up a twenty cc syringe and a small vacuum-sealed tube of blood, pushing them deep into his pants pocket.

Jake looked back at his wife again but couldn't prevent his thoughts from screaming once more, *Away from this place!* Away from this place where fate had crushed his dreams—away from the empty shell that had once housed the vibrant life of his only love.

A chill warned him to stop again. Was someone watching him? He shook his head and stumbled to the open door. He would leave the way he came—quietly, via the beach—and hopefully go unnoticed by the militant hospital security. "Fools!" he muttered under his breath. "They probably won't find her for hours."

He slipped into the night air and paused on the narrow balcony, closing the door behind him. There he stopped, intentionally staring at the blackness of the ocean beyond, away from the lighted patient rooms, to restore his night vision. Coming in had been easy enough. That it had been too easy was an option he'd failed to consider. He'd only seen one guard, who was busy talking to a patient undergoing rejuvenation treatment in an oxygenated pool.

Now he reviewed his plan. First, climb off the balcony to the rocks below, then along the hedge that stretched to within a hundred feet of the sand, then over the bushes, then a short sprint to the—

Another chill!

◆　◆　◆

One hundred yards away, the facility's director walked out of a plush office opening onto an expansive balcony where his guest waited. He spoke in hushed tones. He was aging but healthy; prosperous beyond his dreams, but working more than he'd like.

His guest, his nephew by marriage, sat sipping an herbal tea and looking at the ocean beyond, lost in his own sea of memories. Tonight, like so many nights before, the man would review the events that had forced his brilliant career into oblivion. He'd come here to relax. Why did his uncle insist on stirring the bitterness that choked him?

The director grew impatient. He wanted an answer. Slowly he stepped between the railing and his nephew, the cardiac surgeon, Dr. Michael Simons. "Well, Michael, what do you think?"

The surgeon shifted in his chair but did not speak, merely staring at the moon's reflection on the waves below.

The director, whom everyone knew as Dr. D, spoke again. "Could you see retiring to this view every evening?"

Simons shifted again.

"If it's the money, I can easily see our profits from your affiliation lifting us to well over—"

"It's not the money. It's just that—" He paused and stood nervously. "I'm a surgeon, for heaven's sake!" He shook his head. "I don't belong here!" He looked at the white-haired man who'd married his mother's sister. Not wanting to hurt him, he softened his voice. "I trained too long to give it up . . . for this."

The older man stiffened. He knew it wouldn't be easy to convince Michael to come aboard. He had been skeptical himself at the beginning. That was before the money started to flow, of course. Since then he had found it increasingly easier to turn his back on conventional medical teaching and pursue these lucrative "alternative therapies."

"It was hard for me to accept in the beginning, too, Michael. But eventually I found that the patients who really believed were better, you know? That's what counts, isn't it?"

"And I suppose you would forego your salary for the patient's benefit?"

The jab stung.

"I have to live. I've made more money here than I ever could in my family medical practice. When reimbursements went down, I couldn't resist—"

"I can! And I will!" Simons sat down again.

"Look, I respect your surgical skills, Michael. But I also know how difficult it has been for you since leaving Taft University." He decided to play hard. "The reputation you earned there hasn't been easy for you to shake. It's time to face life and deal with the hand you've been dealt."

The cardiac surgeon cringed. Once he had stood on the top of the academic world. He chaired a major pediatric surgery program at a respected university. He edited prestigious journals. He pioneered work in pediatric heart surgery. But all that was before his career was sidelined by a zealous resident, Matt Stone, who uncovered Simons's unethical research practices. Although Simons had not permanently lost his rights to practice, the reputation had stuck, and since that time he'd explored and been denied seven academic positions. Most recently, he'd sought work at a private institution attempting to set up a new pediatric heart program, only to find there the very surgeon who had derailed his academic career a few years before!

He heaved a sigh and tried to focus his energy. Every time he reviewed the situation, his anger toward Dr. Matt Stone escalated. Stone, a general surgeon, had trained under Simons at Taft University. It was Stone who called his research into question and uprooted his brilliant career. And now Stone seemed to be the only roadblock to his joining one of the most prestigious pediatric surgery practices in the southeast, Valley Surgeons for Children. If it hadn't been for Stone . . .

Dr. D brought him back to the present. "At least think about it. Once I get a replacement back home, I'll be here full-time myself. With your credentials, we can keep the FDA at bay indefinitely. The patients are here, the money is here . . ." He faced the younger man and softened. "Look, Michael, these therapies may not be as exciting as cardiac surgery, but at least I'm making a living." He heaved a sigh of his own. "Just think about it."

The two stood quietly looking at the ocean. The beach seemed quiet. They thought little of the lonely midnight jogger running along the surf. Resort life always produces weird schedules.

◆ ◆ ◆

Jake stood on the small balcony outside his wife's room and shivered. He shook his head, trying to suppress the dread he sensed. What was it about this place? Certainly he had been around death enough not to react like this. Yes, but those times were the deaths of others, patients he cared about but didn't love, at least not like this. Not like his Sarah—

Another wave of fear interrupted his thoughts.

Why was he afraid? What did he fear? He paused a moment longer, staring at the black ocean, unable to pinpoint the source of his discomfort. The urgency remained. *I've got to get out of here!* He studied the terrain below and selected a large, flat rock that would lie only a foot or two below his feet if he hung from the ledge. Slowly he eased himself over the rail. He could feel the syringe in his pocket as he twisted his leg into the air.

Suddenly he was flying, falling. *Was I pushed?* Jake's mind whirled. The world turned as his feet were hopelessly trapped in a vine growing on the balcony's railing. *I don't remember that plant. . .*

Confusion, anger, and guilt instantly gave way to searing pain, blackness, and coma as he struck his head on the rocks below.

Surgeon Jake Hampton wouldn't remember anything until he awoke the next day at Beach Memorial Hospital. The events of that night wouldn't be immediately clear, clouded by his own anguish and by the closed head injury from his fall.

The police would fill him in on the details.

CHAPTER

1

DR. Jake Hampton downshifted his Isuzu Trooper and turned up Main Street, heading for his office in downtown Taylorville. It had been six months since Sarah's death, but still Jake saw her everywhere. There, by the statue of George Washington in the front of City Hall, next to the playground at her old school, sitting in the Trooper beside him . . . It seemed like her memory was inescapable. He squinted at a pretty woman with auburn hair sitting in a convertible at the bank drive-in window and sighed. She sure looked like Sarah.

Six months. Might as well have been six years. Jake winced. *I see her everywhere, and yet when I try to picture her in my mind, the image is cloudy. If only I could wipe away the fog . . . I need to remember.*

It had only been three months since Jake moved home. Taylorville, everybody's hometown, a cozy place without a concrete skyline, where the only things higher than a three-story building were the southern pines that lined the streets and provided the cones for the annual Evergreen Festival. He hoped that coming home would be his ticket to remember . . . and to forget.

It had only been four months since the grand jury decided he wouldn't be tried for the double murder that seemed to capture the South—an outspoken pro-life physician accused of assisting his pregnant wife to die. It was the stuff of tabloids and slick city lawyer talk. Jake wanted to get away from all of that. He wanted nothing except to practice general surgery and get on with life with his son Kyle—a life he wanted desperately to be predictable and boring.

Leaving Grantsville and his big-city surgical group partnership certainly hadn't been in the plans six months ago. He had everything. But of course that was before the illness, before the pregnancy, before the cancer that slowly stole the life away from his Sarah and changed everything. Even after Sarah's death, Jake thought little of running. He didn't even know how to escape. But then the good Dr. William Dansford made him aware of the opening in Taylorville and encouraged him to come and take a look.

One look was all Jake needed. One office. One hospital. A school for Kyle within a short bus ride of the greatest old Victorian house that had appeared on the market the week before. Everything seemed perfect. Life away from the big city would be better. There would be time to heal. Time to mend. Time to learn to know Kyle again. Time to remember . . . and to forget.

Taylorville. Tree-lined streets, a court square, two parks, a bus station, a new shopping mall in the west end, a county hospital, and southern loyalty. The kind of people who would stick by you if you were in trouble. *Just the kind of patients I need,* thought Jake. But as it turned out, they were also the kind of people who were just a little suspicious of a newcomer, even if Dr. Willie did say he's a local boy.

Jake tapped his fingers on the dash. He'd been stopped at the only traffic light on Main Street, just a block south of his red-brick office. Actually it was Willie's office, or at least that's what everybody said. *Not for long,* sighed the young surgeon. *In another year Willie will be fishing out his retirement, and I'll be the only act in town.* He looked at the lunchtime crowd milling around The Taylorville Pub. "We'll see who you go to for help when he's gone," Jake whispered to the nameless diners.

The light changed, and Jake pulled away and turned into the spacious parking lot. He found a space near the back door and checked his watch. Two minutes to spare.

Jake smiled at his office staff but frowned when he saw his messages. Two were from Sharon Isaacs, a guidance counselor at Kyle's elementary school. Dr. Hampton looked at his nurse and pulled the yellow note off his desk. "Great. This lady has met my son one time and already she has him labeled." His nurse wasn't listening, but he went on anyway. "She wonders if I've ever had him evaluated for A.D.D.—attention deficit disorder." He crumpled the yellow paper and threw it in the trash for an imaginary audience. "Two points."

He walked up the hall, still muttering as he picked up the first patient's chart from a rack outside the exam room. "I'm the doctor around here. I am certainly able to spot a disorder in my own family. Who does she think she is?" He came to a sudden stop as the irony of his statement hit him for the first time, and his conscience launched an attack of its own. *Wasn't it you, good doctor, who missed your wife's cancer?* He cringed and looked up to see if his nurse was watching. She wasn't. He coughed nervously and loosened his tie. He opened the door to the exam room. Time to work!

With serious demeanor and a plastic smile to hide his turmoil, Dr. Hampton entered the small room. "Mrs. Little." He extended his hand. "How are you today?"

◆ ◆ ◆

Outside, a shadowy figure slipped from behind the dumpster and slid into Jake's unlocked Trooper. Once inside, he paused, resting in the plush driver's seat, and adjusted the side mirror to his satisfaction. With his face expressionless, he examined his pimpled complexion in the rearview mirror, then turned it away to examine the parking lot around him. No one in sight. He gripped the wheel and depressed the clutch, shifting the transmission through an imaginary hill-climb, leaving black grease on the handle as he interrupted his playful car-noises to mutter an expletive and some instructions. He looked around and nodded his head to his own spoken command. He was alone.

He inhaled deeply, as if sampling the air might gift him with some strange insight, pausing with his breath held tightly until he thought his lungs would burst. He exhaled slowly, trying not to spit. He continued his dialogue and opened the glove-box, a move he had suggested to himself. "Go slow," he urged. "We've got all the time we need."

His clothes smelled of sweat, french fries, and fried fish, a witness to his daily labor with deep-fat frying. Slowly he sifted through the contents of the glove compartment. Mostly he was silent, but occasionally he grunted an approval or a question. He looked behind the driver's seat and found a half dozen samples of an ulcer medication, which he recognized and pocketed. After a systematic search of the vehicle, he sat for a moment or two in the backseat, then shifted so he could see himself in the rearview mirror. "There," he whispered as he viewed his uneven front teeth. His calm countenance did not betray his thoughts. "An eye for an eye, Dr. Hampton," he warned. He watched his own tongue protrude between his front teeth. ". . . and a tooth for a tooth."

He exited into the daylight. No one had seen him, a trait that remained his trademark and his greatest asset. He loped down Taylorville's Main Street with his green army jacket pulled tightly around him, muttering to himself, a small notebook concealed beneath the long front jacket flap.

◆ ◆ ◆

Two blocks away, Dr. William Dansford gripped the hand of a tearful mother as he turned to leave. "Don't worry, Maggie. Rachel's gonna be fine." His warm smile matched the strength of his handshake.

The young mother nodded and bit her lip. "Thanks, Dr. Willie." She blew her nose. She used the name by which everyone knew the respected physician. "Thanks a lot."

As the white-haired generalist turned to go, the husband spoke up. "Uh, doc . . . you know times have been tough for us lately. I'll pay you when I can. I—"

The old doctor shook his head. "You just worry about getting that little one to eat. We won't worry about the bills. You can see I've never missed a meal," he added with a smile while patting his generous waist.

As he walked away, the father called out again, "Thank you, Dr. Willie. Thanks a lot." The doctor pretended not to hear and walked briskly to the hospital's main entrance to leave.

Willie Dansford. The name was synonymous with medical care in Taylorville. He did it all, from pediatrics to geriatrics, from setting broken bones to fixing hernias. Dr. Dansford was Taylorville health care. He did it for love, he did it for pride, and occasionally he did it for money. Oh, make no mistake, he made a fine living; but lately, as costs increased and the local economy sagged, he saw more and more patients like his last one—Rachel Edwards, uninsured, with unemployed parents. He might get a Christmas card. If he was lucky, he'd get a load of firewood or a fruit basket. Somehow, however, he did it all, and mostly with a smile, and apparently with sufficient financial gain. The no-payers didn't seem to sour Willie's day.

Dr. Dansford practically skipped up the sidewalk to his car. With Jake in the office, he could take the afternoon off. Five minutes later his wife Deloris met him at the door of their stately brick home.

"You're home early." She offered a kiss that he accepted.

Willie smiled. "Just like I told you, Dee." He smiled and loosened his tie.

She frowned. "I suppose you're going to tell me it's all due to that new doctor of yours."

"Exactly." He paused. "I'd never be home at this hour if he weren't covering the office. You know that as well as I."

Dee shook her head. She had been skeptical from the beginning. Right in the middle of the investigation of Sarah Hampton's death, Willie started talking about recruiting Jake Hampton! "It's ludicrous!" Dee had shouted. "He's perfect," Willie had countered. "No one else will come. We've been looking for years. The people will accept a local . . . Just watch."

Dr. Dansford was right of course, just like he was about most things. No one was interested except Jake. The depressed local economy and a dozen new managed health-care contracts made practice in Taylorville and other small towns a risky venture. He needed someone with other reasons to come. Someone with nothing to lose . . . and everything to gain. He needed someone with surgical skills who was willing to see an occasional family-practice patient. He needed Jake Hampton, and from every appearance Jake needed Willie, someone willing to give him a fresh start, someone with a solid reputation that could get him off on the right foot.

Dee sighed, willing to put the small battle aside for the moment. She knew better than to argue with Willie. He'd win, and she'd end up apologizing. She didn't really mind. She trusted the man and loved him as much now as she did when they'd married twenty-five years before. "How about some lunch?"

He picked up the mail. "I grabbed a reuben at the hospital deli."

His wife raised her eyebrows.

He continued, "It's really gotten better since they put in the new sandwich line." He put down the bills and threw a second stack of envelopes into the trash. "Want to go with me down to the country club?"

Her expression changed again. She tried not to show her irritation. "Not today. I'm going into town to get my hair cut."

"Oh, come on." Willie smiled and gently placed his hands on his wife's shoulders. "You look gorgeous just like you are." His eyes met hers. "You could swim in the new pool."

Dee squirmed. Willie tightened his grip. They both laughed.

She stood her ground. "Not today. You go ahead. I'll make supper. We can eat on the deck."

Willie exaggerated a frown. "I may be late."

Deloris Dansford turned away. "I can wait. I'll have a snack if I get hungry."

He kissed the back of his wife's head. "I'll hurry." He turned, then added. "Georgio has arranged a foursome." He checked his watch. "We tee off in fifteen," he said, turning to go.

In a moment, with his hand on the door, his wife eyed him suspiciously. "Aren't you going to change?"

He looked at his clothes. "At the club, my dear . . . at the club." With that, he disappeared, the screen door slammed, and Dee winced and watched him go.

◆ ◆ ◆

The young mother eyed Dr. Hampton and clutched the sleeping infant in her arms. "Perhaps if I brought him back to see Dr. Willie . . ."

Jake sighed with frustration. He could see he wouldn't win this one. The young woman continued, "If he feels as you do, then we can schedule the surgery."

The surgeon nodded and opened the door. "Please see the receptionist. She can give you another appointment." He forced a smile, his lips closed over his tightly clenched teeth. "I'll be glad to see Joey again next week, after Dr. Dansford has had a chance to speak with you." With that said, he stepped into the hall. His eyes met Lucille's, the only nurse Dr. Dansford had ever had.

She grabbed his hand. He didn't mind. She was old enough to be his mother and knew enough to keep her doctors out of trouble. She knew everyone in Taylorville, and everyone knew the untiring nurse. "Give it some time. They'll come around."

Jake shook his head. Taylorville!

Lucille continued, "Once you've mended a few of these families, they'll see. You know Taylorville. They don't trust a newcomer, but once you're in—"

"But I'm not a newcomer!"

"You've been gone a long time." She patted his hand. "When you left, we didn't even have a drugstore in this town." She walked down the hall to the next exam room. "Just give it some time."

He mumbled something about being the only board-certified surgeon who needed a grandfatherly family doctor to approve his recommendations, then sighed again. He shoved the thought aside and grabbed another chart. He'd lose himself in his work. All right! Gallstones and abdominal pain!

◆ ◆ ◆

Laurie Simpson opened the refrigerator in search of cold pop. Her normally styled hair had been hastily pulled back and covered by a western bandanna. At the front, where the cloth touched her forehead, sweat had darkened the red print.

"Another cola?" Her mother, Jody Simpson, looked incredulous.

"This kid is wearing me out!" She opened the can and sat down at the wooden kitchen table.

Mrs. Simpson looked onto the backyard, where Kyle Hampton continued doing cartwheels at a dizzying pace. "He does seem to have a lot of energy."

Laurie rolled her eyes. "He's been doing that for thirty minutes." She sighed. "I'm not sure I should have taken this job. He goes from one thing to the next so quickly." She joined her mother at the window. "This is the first thing he's stuck to for more than a few moments."

"At least it's consistent money," her mother reassured. "Dr. Hampton said he can give you all the hours you want."

"I'll never make it to my senior year of high school if I keep up this pace," Laurie moaned.

"You'll never make it to college unless you stick to a job for more than a week!" her mother countered.

"Mom! I couldn't keep that other job. Band practice always meets—"

Jody Simpson smiled and interrupted, "I've heard it before. Just give this kid a chance. He's been through a lot, from what I hear . . ."

◆ ◆ ◆

Two blocks south of the railroad tracks, the deserted Taylorville judicial complex decayed without a hint of town remorse. In actuality, the town had fought over the building of a newer complex in Grantsville, since more than forty of the townspeople were employed there. But now, with that battle long lost and with most of the old employees either relocated or in different jobs, the jailhouse sat forgotten, a "For Sale" sign the only indication that anyone in Taylorville even knew the place existed.

That situation seemed perfect for the old brick jail's only resident. Of course, no one knew he was there, and that's how he preferred it. He rarely entered the facility during daylight hours, wanting to preserve the anonymity with which he lived. But today was different. He felt "in touch." The voices were telling him of his power again. No one would see him today. He could come and go as he wished. Jake was working. He wouldn't hurt him today.

His green army coat caught on the edge of the window latch as he squeezed through, leaving behind a few threads to go with the growing collection. As he dropped to the floor, the smell of old human urine struck him, reminding him that it was time to go again. He'd once read that his medication could cause urinary retention. Since then, he had compulsively emptied his bladder every few hours, afraid the medicine would cause him to lose the ability completely if he didn't continue his private routine. He'd begun by using the commodes in the cells of the east wing of the complex, as the lack of running water in the facility made urinating in his own cell appalling, even to him. Now, if he didn't have time to use the large bushes out front, he used the commodes in the basement. He would never do more than urinate. Anything else would have to wait until he got to work at McDonald's.

He meandered the halls, talking to himself, speaking aloud to the guards as he remembered them. He felt safe here. At home. After all, it had been his home once, but that was long ago . . . after the bombing and before the decision that he should be at the hospital.

The hospital. How he hated that place! The sameness was worse than at the jail. At least at the jail the food was hot. At the hospital they always "protected" him from hot foods, which were dangerous for him, they said—he might try to burn himself. They had little understanding of his delusions and cared even less. Finally, after the state scaled back its funding, he found himself on the street. Now he lived in an apartment on Third Street in Taylorville, close to the railroad tracks. But more and more often he lived here . . . especially when his paranoia made him run.

The bombing. The one climactic moment in his life when he felt that justice had been served. Surely God would forgive him for killing the one who had killed his son! He would smile whenever he remembered the sight of the clinic burning to the ground. Few occasions since that time had filled him with such a feeling of power, fairness, retribution.

Now, as he reflected back on his visit to Jake Hampton's Trooper, he grinned. *That feeling will be mine again. How fortunate for me that you have come back*, he pondered, a thin smile creeping across his face.

He climbed to the first floor and into the old sheriff's office. There he jumped to the top of a gray metal desk. He gently dislodged the ceiling tile and reached into the blackness above. With practiced swiftness he brought out a bulging shoe box and reseated the ceiling tile. Slowly he returned to his old cell on the third floor. There he would go over the past again, reading and rereading the documents he'd collected. There he would plan the future.

Justice would be served. He would have it no other way.

CHAPTER
2

JAKE always felt like a kid when he was in his mom's house. It didn't really bother him that she continued to mother him. In fact, right now he thought he could use it. The elderly woman put a plate of hot chocolate-chip cookies in front of him and handed him a tall glass of milk. "Take them home to Kyle. I can't really eat this stuff anyway," Phyllis Hampton huffed. "Dr. Willie would have a cow if he saw me eatin' this!"

Jake nodded and wondered if Dr. Willie was as much a part of Taylorville as he seemed to be. He inhaled a moist cookie and picked up a second. "Thanks." Other than "Hello," it was the first thing Jake had said since stopping at his mother's after work. That was the one thing he'd missed when he lived in Grantsville. His father had died two years before, and his mom lived alone in the same white house on Taylorville's Main Street that he grew up in. Now that he'd moved back and his social calendar seemed barren, he visited her house often.

She looked at her son with wrinkled brow. Jake looked tired, his tie loosened and his collar unbuttoned. His blond hair was graying at the temples and thinning on the top, a characteristic he'd inherited from his father. "How are you doing?"

Jake mumbled distractedly, "Fine."

Phyllis grasped his hand. "Jake, I mean it. I'm eighty years old. You stop in here nearly every day. I can tell that things aren't right." She paused. "Is it Sarah?"

He stiffened and offered no reply.

"Kyle?" Phyllis persisted.

"I don't know." Jake began to pace. "I just don't know."

"It hasn't been easy for you. I mean . . . I know . . ." She paused, looking at her son. "Has anything cleared up for you yet? Can you remember anything?"

Jake heaved a long sigh. Shaking his head, he continued pacing. "Nothing. I remember seeing her face, then . . ." He wiped a tear from his eye. ". . . then nothing—nothing until I woke up at the hospital."

His mother poured a cup of tea. "It will come to you. I've been praying."

The young surgeon bit his lip. He'd prayed too. A thousand times. A thousand prayers . . . but no understandable answer. Where was God now? He slowly looked up until his eyes met those of his aging mother's. "Do you think I killed her?"

"Please don't use that word, Jake." She looked away and stopped talking.

"I want to know what you think, Mom. I come here every day hoping to remember, hoping something in my memory will open up."

"Maybe you loved her so much that you didn't want her to suffer."

"Is that what you think? That I helped her die?"

"Would that really have been so bad?" She shuffled over to a picture of Jake's father, Samuel Hampton. "When Sam suffered, there were so many nights I just prayed that God would take him." She looked at Jake. "Is that really any different?"

"You're avoiding my question."

"I—I don't really know, Jake." Her voice stammered with a hint of Parkinson's disease. "But it doesn't matter to me."

He shook his head. "It matters to me." He looked at the picture of his father. "He taught me to stand on principle." Jake fumbled with his hands. "This has been a hot area of controversy, Mom . . . and people know I was outspoken on the issue. Now it looks like I caved in under pressure."

Phyllis forced a thin smile and changed the subject. "You'd better go after Kyle. It's almost 6:30."

Her son nodded and picked up the plate of cookies. When he reached the door, his mother asked, "Do you talk about her to anyone else?"

Jake answered with a shake.

"Why don't you talk with one of your old doctor friends? They would understand so much better than I. Maybe the issues would clear up a little and you'll stop torturing yourself."

He thought for a moment. He didn't really have anyone else to talk to. "I could talk to Dr. Willie, but he's so busy—"

"Why don't you call one of your residency friends? Who was that Christian boy? The one you told me about . . . He went to Africa or some such place. What about him?"

"Matt. Matt Stone." Jake smiled at the mention of his friend's name. Maybe that was a good idea. "Maybe I'll call him." He reached for the door.

"Say hi to Kyle."

"Bye, Mom."

"Bye."

◆ ◆ ◆

"Put your hand here." Linda Stone's green eyes were dancing. So apparently was the baby within her.

Matt leaned over his wife, who was nestled in her favorite old lounge chair. He gently touched her lower abdomen. "Whoa! This guy's playing soccer in there!"

"This *guy?*" Linda smiled. "What if this *girl's* playing soccer?"

Matt did his best to look studious and felt for the next kick. "No, it's a boy all right. Some things a father just knows." He returned a smile.

Linda laughed, then stopped as the child kicked again, under her right rib cage. "We'll see, Dr. Stone, we'll see."

He went over and collapsed on a flowered couch. "I hope the beeper stays quiet tonight. I can't stand too many more nights like the last two."

Matt Stone worked as a staff surgeon at Crestview Women's and Children's Health Center. He had come eight months ago, planning to stay for only two months. Two turned into four when the surgeon he was replacing went on extended leave, and four turned into a commitment for a year when Linda's obstetrician put her on bed rest. Looking for another job without Linda seemed silly to Matt, and so they stayed and made plans to solidify their future after their son was born. At least that's what Matt said.

Matt had trained at Taft University where he finished one year behind

Dr. Jacob Hampton. He and Jake had been almost inseparable at one time, with the pressures of surgery residency welding a secure bond. They found common ground in their love of general surgery and their mutual Christian faith and once spoke of practicing together after leaving the university.

That, however, was before Jake went on to join a successful group in Grantsville, before Matt met and fell in love with Linda Baldwin, before Matt squared off in a fight for his job with Dr. Michael Simons, and before the Stones accepted an assignment in East Africa working as medical missionaries. Now, with experiences and time separating them, the once inseparable friends found their recent communication limited to a card at Christmas.

Matt had followed Jake's recent ordeal with interest but had not been personally involved, not wanting to pry where he wasn't asked. He knew as much as anyone who was following the media's interpretation. Sarah Hampton had died suddenly at a ritzy alternative health facility of an apparent drug overdose. Her husband, an outspoken pro-life surgeon, was found unconscious on the ground outside her balcony. Because conventional medications were not allowed at the facility, speculation grew that Dr. Hampton had assisted his wife in death, then jumped in anguish in a pitiful attempt at taking his own life. Others pointed to his apparent displeasure at his wife's seeking help outside conventional medicine as a sore spot that goaded Hampton into shortening his wife's life. Even some zealous pro-life advocates watched the case closely and vocally declared that he should be charged with not one death but two, as Sarah's child was nearing legal dates for viability. Dr. Hampton maintained the flimsiest of defenses: amnesia for the event. No known witnesses came forward. The clinic, wanting to move beyond the controversy, did not push for further investigation, but the stigma of guilt hovered. Eventually Jake remained unconvicted, except in his own mind where he alone served as a stern judge over his actions.

When Jake left Grantsville for a new start, he was only an hour's drive from his old friend. Matt suppressed the desire to visit him, however, thinking it was too soon to interfere. Little did he know how helpful he could have been. Schedules, work pressures, and Matt's recent involvement in helping another surgeon through a personal crisis all made it easier for Matt to quiet the gentle voice urging his support of yet another friend in trouble.

Matt looked up at Linda. "What's for dinner?"

"Look in the refrig. I'm resting, remember?" She smiled.

Matt smiled and stumbled toward the kitchen, mumbling, "Maybe a Twinkie will take the edge off for a while."

Some things never change.

◆ ◆ ◆

Frank Grimsted rented a one-bedroom apartment across from the only McDonald's in Taylorville. He now felt more comfortable in the deserted jailhouse, so he didn't come to his apartment but once a week to check his mail. Today his mail would hold a second notice for a prescription change, representing a slow reduction in his antipsychotic medication. After the first such lowering, Frank's paranoia had intensified. After the second, he began frequenting the jail and hearing the voices again. After the third, he moved in to stay. The jail was safe. The jail was home. Dr. Hampton couldn't get him there.

He took off his grease-stained T-shirt and flung it onto the cell's concrete floor. He carefully lit a small kerosene heater. Then he slowly opened his shoe box and began reviewing the items he had stored there. As he read, he muttered to himself. He sorted a variety of articles into small stacks and placed them on top of a stained mattress. In one, articles about an abortion clinic bombing, now nearly fifteen years old. In another, a handful of articles about Sarah Fields, soon to be Sarah Hampton. In another, the small town paper's followings of a local boy's successful completion of medical school, residency, and practice. In another, articles on Sarah's death and the controversy that followed. Once all of the papers were in neat piles, he removed the final item in the box—a tattered 5 x 7 photograph from his high-school prom. Frank Grimsted and Sarah Fields—the couple everyone thought would be the class's first marital bond.

Frank's thoughts were interrupted momentarily by a rhythmic beeping from his wristwatch. Time to urinate again. Frank regretted leaving the papers in the open but couldn't resist the overwhelming compulsion. He slipped off the bed and traveled quickly and quietly to the basement, where he went to the farthest cell. A pungent aroma slapped him. *Man, I wish there was running water in this place!*

Back in his own room, Frank again picked up the tattered photograph. That was a happier time for Frank Grimsted . . .

◆ ◆ ◆

"Frank! Where are you taking me?" Sarah giggled again. "I'm going to trip if you don't slow down!" She walked through the tall, wet grass with an awkward gait. Her prom date continued, undaunted by the grass that had soaked his tuxedo pants. He pulled her along with a tight grip.

"It's just ahead." Frank smiled.

"The only thing I see is an old barn." The moon illuminated a deserted structure rising from the edge of the grassy field.

"Exactly."

Sarah resisted and stopped walking. "I'm not going in there. It's spooky."

Frank tugged her hand. "Come on. It's OK."

Sarah stood her ground. "No way." She giggled nervously. Frank pushed his face against hers. She was about to speak again when he kissed her noisily.

"Come on," he whispered. "We'll be alone." He kissed her again. He turned and walked a few steps away.

Sarah began to plead. "Don't make me stand out here by myself. It's dark!"

"Come on!" He returned and took her hand again. "I'll stay with you." Now his eyes were doing the pleading. He looked toward the looming barn. "Come on." He kissed her passionately.

Sarah softened. "Stay with me."

He pulled her toward the entrance of the barn. "I've fixed it up special for us."

Once inside, he struggled to light a Coleman lantern. Soon the lamp cast a series of eerie shadows in the drafty palace. Frank had spent hours transforming the deserted barn. In the center of the wooden plank floor, candles decorated a linen-covered table. On the floor a bottle of champagne cooled in an ice-bucket.

Sarah's eyes widened. "Frank!"

He picked up the bottle and struggled with the cork. After a few moments, a *pop!* rewarded him. He picked up one of two plastic cups. It was all he could afford after paying his brother for the champagne. He tried to pour it properly. "To us."

"To us."

Sarah coughed on the first swallow. Then she laughed. Frank laughed too and quickly emptied his first glass.

"Frank!"

"I'm OK." He laughed again. "I just need something to keep me warm." He looked down at his pants. "I got pretty wet coming through the weeds."

"Me too." She shivered and held up her hands to the lantern.

"Here." Frank moved close and sat next to her on an old covered apple crate. He placed his arms around her and pulled her close. "I'll keep you warm."

Sarah sipped the cool liquid. "This stuff burns."

"It's good." He poured additional champagne into their glasses. "It's supposed to be that way."

She looked unconvinced but giggled nervously to cover her doubt. "Mom thinks I'm spending the night at Sherry's."

Frank, whose mother had died when he was only five, nodded. "My pop could care less."

She kissed his neck. Frank responded.

Soon he led her to a padded loft where he had stored blankets and sleeping bags. He wasn't interested in talking anymore.

"Frank—" She could feel her forehead tingling from the alcohol. "I've never—"

He smothered her mouth with his and interrupted her sentence. "Don't worry." Sarah yielded to his pressure and collapsed onto an old quilt.

The moon filtered its light through the cracks in the weathered building. The wind picked up a mournful melody as it followed a meandering path through the wood slats.

Sarah winced.

The wind gusted again.

In the shadows of the loft, it was too dark for Frank to see her tears.

◆ ◆ ◆

Frank stood up and grabbed a clean shirt. Almost time for work. He stuffed the papers back into their holding place and began muttering. He pushed his toothbrush into his pants pocket. He would brush his teeth and wash his hair in the bathroom before work.

A few moments later, he stood on the old metal desk in the sheriff's office and dislodged the ceiling tile. He carefully put the box in to the left where he always kept it. He compulsively felt to the right.

He felt the cold metal. *Yes, everything is in place*, he thought confidently. He replaced the tile.

Now, off to work. I could use a fish sandwich today.

CHAPTER
3

THE following morning found Jake Hampton sitting in a small waiting area outside the school counselor's office at Taylorville Elementary. It wasn't often that Jake found himself waiting for others. He didn't really mind. He didn't have any cases scheduled in the O.R. and didn't have any clinic patients to see until that afternoon.

The office, decorated in tile and light yellow paint, seemed exactly as he remembered it as a kid. After a moment Sharon Isaacs walked in. "Dr. Hampton?"

Jake stood. Sharon was slender but solid. She was wearing a casual exercise outfit that complemented her muscle tone. She appeared to be in her thirties. Her hair was pulled back, and she wore no jewelry except a small pair of gold post earrings. She wore a pair of Nike running shoes, the same ones she had worn during her last marathon. Jake was taken aback. He scanned her fingers. No rings. He accepted her handshake. "Ms. Isaacs?"

"That's me." She saw his surprise at her outfit. "It's for the kids," she explained, opening the door to her office. "I used to wear a dress like any other professional. Then one day when I didn't have a chance to change, I ended up at work like this. The difference in my relationship with the kids was noticeable immediately." She paused and held her hand out to an empty chair. "I've dressed like this ever since."

She sat down in a chair next to Jake's, intentionally avoiding sitting at her desk and putting the old metal office table between them. She opened Kyle's folder. "Thanks for taking time from your busy schedule to see me."

Jake nodded.

"Kyle is a very active boy."

Jake nodded again.

"I'll get right to the point."

"Please do." Jake liked her style. Crisp. On the edge. Nothing in the shadows. *She'd make a good surgeon*, he mused.

"I want to get Kyle tested for attention deficit disorder. He shows all the classic signs. In addition, I think he is hyperactive."

Sharon noticed an almost imperceptible rising of Jake's eyebrows. She continued, "I would like to get Dr. Willie to see him. He handles all of our medications for A.D.D. here, and I think Kyle may be able to benefit from his services."

Dr. Willie. Was there anything he didn't treat?

Jake looked up again, his mind snapping back to the present as Sharon shifted in her seat. He shrugged his shoulders. "OK." He trusted Dr. Dansford. He wouldn't have come here if he didn't. His anxiety had eased after he heard his name. "OK, sure," he repeated. "What do I have to do?"

"Just make the appointment for Kyle. I assumed that you'd want to arrange it because of your working relationship. I'll send him a copy of our file here. He'll use it in his assessment." She smiled.

Jake relaxed another notch. He had come ready to defend himself. After all, he was the physician around here, and he should be able to recognize when his own son needed help, shouldn't he? At least that's what he'd thought. But Sharon's manner had disarmed him in little time. He returned her smile.

Sharon stood. Jake found himself wishing the meeting hadn't gone so fast. Only moments ago he would have been delighted to get away. Now he found himself lingering momentarily in the presence of a very persuasive individual. *There is something magnetic about you*, he thought. *Not a model, mind you, but cute . . . No, that's not it. It's not something physical . . . She's certainly pleasant.* He looked around the small office. She had several colorful posters. Not the routine "Just say no" fliers, but large pictures, mostly of athletic events. On the desk was a smaller, framed edition of a popular essay entitled, "Footprints in the Sand." His eyes lit up.

"Are you a Christian?"

She followed his eyes to the small frame on her desk. "That's what keeps me going." She looked up. "What about you?"

"Oh, me too." He hesitated. "I guess I don't always feel like it, but I do believe." He shuffled his feet, then turned toward the door. "I'll get that appointment with Dr. Willie. Kyle will like him." He paused again. "I know I do."

"He's an old softy. He always has time for one more work-in. You're privileged to be associated with him."

Jake opened the door. "Thanks."

"Say, Dr. Hampton—"

"Call me Jake."

Sharon swallowed. "OK, Jake." She lowered her voice. "The school board won't let me talk about it too loud, but I've been praying for Kyle." She hesitated. "I'll be praying this all works out."

Jake felt a knot in his throat. "Thanks," he squeaked. "Me too." He turned and walked into the tiled hallway, passing an elementary-sized water fountain.

"Me too," he whispered, and he prayed that would be true.

◆ ◆ ◆

Things could never move fast enough for Michael Simons, M.D. He had been waiting six months for the new state license, controlled substance application, and contract negotiations with Valley Surgeons for Children. They didn't seem to understand how valuable he really was. He sighed as he heaved another request for credentials onto the top of his desk. This seemed like the last hoop, but he was losing hope that the approval process would ever end. The form requesting hospital privileges at Crestview Women's and Children's Health Center had been filled out months ago. Who was responsible for this new delay?

An answer came to Simons's mind and grew into near-obsessive proportions: Matt Stone. Regardless of the truth or falsehood of his beliefs, Simons was convinced that his old resident had persuaded the surgeons at Crestview to hold things up. *He just can't let go, can he? It would have been easier to follow my uncle down to Ocean Sands and practice there!*

Simons shook his head and scoffed at the thought. *As if alternative health therapy—coffee enemas and fruit drinks—could ever bring the excitement that heart surgery provides! What a way to make a living!*

Every time Dr. Simons called for an update on the status of his privileges at Crestview, he received the same answer: "The committee has to meet one more time. We will call you."

With each passing week, Simons began to fume even more as his paranoia grew. He was convinced he was the target of a one-man conspiracy to bar him from medical practice. *It has to be Stone. No one else there knows anything about my research at Taft University! No one else would savor getting me back for the way I treated him.*

Simons sat at his desktop computer and began typing a letter to the credentialing committee at Crestview. His fingers worked as deftly on the keyboard as they did in the O.R. *If something doesn't break for me soon, someone's going to pay,* he reflected. *And I'm going to enjoy watching it.*

In a few minutes he lifted his hand to his throbbing teeth. He hadn't even noticed how tightly he was clenching them.

◆ ◆ ◆

That afternoon Jake saw twelve patients in the office. Only one patient refused to see him and rescheduled with Dr. Willie, and only one other asked him to check his advice out with his associate. *That's two fewer than my last clinic day,* Jake mused as he slid into his desk chair. *Earning public favor at Taylorville is more difficult than I ever dreamed. At least Dr. Dansford seems to understand. He's been so supportive, so kind. If he weren't willing to give me a chance . . .*

Just then Willie Dansford stuck his head through the doorway. "Tough day?"

Jake looked up at the gentle man. "Just following big footprints, I'm afraid."

Willie laughed. "Give it some time, Jake. You're a good doctor. These people will learn. You'll see. If I trust you, they will trust you, right?"

The younger doctor shrugged his acknowledgment. He knew that what Willie thought was as important as gold in Taylorville. "Hey, I've fought tougher battles," he responded. "I'll stick with it. Don't worry."

"I just don't want to lose you back to those big-city doctors. We need you here." He chuckled. "Just give it some time."

As Jake looked at the chart on the desk, Willie spoke again. "Join us for supper tonight, Jake? Deloris is making her award-winning meat loaf and mashed potatoes."

"Man, that sounds great, but I think I'll spend some time alone with Kyle. We both need it." He stood and walked nervously to the window. "Say, would you look at Kyle sometime? The school counselor is convinced he has A.D.D. and wants him evaluated." He looked at Dr. Dansford. "I was kind of reluctant to admit it, but maybe I'm just too close to him to see that he needs help."

"I'd be glad to see him. Just have Amy put him on the books." He turned to go. "Don't ever be reluctant to ask me about your family, Jake. I'd do the same for you. I never play doctor to my Deloris. Never have. I've always made her call a doctor up in Harristown or Jones City. She doesn't like it, but I always thought it would be best."

Jake nodded. He had been kicking himself for months for not finding his wife's breast cancer. Who would trust a doctor who missed his own wife's cancer?

"If you change your mind about the supper, just come on over. We're flexible."

"Thanks, Willie."

With that, the older doctor disappeared, leaving the office otherwise deserted. The office staff had whisked out at 5:01 P.M., pleased that Dr. Dansford wasn't running the clinic that day. When he saw patients, the staff rarely got home by 7.

Jake sat back down and stared at his empty hands. His conscience compelled him to review his troubled situation again. "Did I kill her, Lord? I have to know." He spoke audibly but softly. "If not me, who? Herself?" He paused, eyes open. "How did she get the drugs? She didn't want to take any treatment because she was so concerned about hurting the baby. Why would she change at the end and commit suicide?" Jake shook his head. Nothing added up. Nothing made sense.

He fumbled with his hands. There were no answers today either. He sighed with frustration. *Maybe I should call Matt Stone. It certainly couldn't hurt to talk this thing through with a brother.*

He picked up the phone and dialed directory assistance. In a few minutes he called his old friend.

◆ ◆ ◆

Matt was just coming in the front door when the phone rang. Linda appeared to be napping on the couch. "Don't get up," he said softly. "I'll get it." He picked up the phone. "Hello."

"Hello. Matt?"

He recognized Jake's voice immediately. "Jake!"

Jake smiled and began chatting nervously. "Hi, old friend. What's up?"

"We're doing fine. I've been thinking about you. I wasn't sure if I should call."

"I understand. I've had some pretty heavy things going down. You've probably followed the story."

"I think everyone around here has, Jake." He paused. "We've been praying for you."

"I knew you would be. That's one reason I called. I thought maybe we could talk sometime. I'm kinda out here on my own . . . no one real close to talk to. I've moved back close to my mother, but I think maybe I need someone a bit closer in background, if you know what I mean."

"Sure, Jake, sure." Matt found himself wondering if his friend needed to confess killing his wife.

Silence followed for a moment as Matt tried to shake the vision of Jake forcing his pregnant wife to die.

"How are things going anyway?"

"I'm trying to rebuild, Matt. A great guy, Willie Dansford, opened his practice to me here in Taylorville. I'm taking over the surgical side of his general practice."

"That's great."

"It's been slow going business-wise. I think the community needs time to see that I'm OK."

Matt nodded even though Jake couldn't see. Jake went on, "I don't really mind it, though. I can use the time sorting through Sarah's death." He hesitated. "The problem is, I can't remember what happened that night. The police have their opinion, the media has theirs . . . Everyone seems to have reached a judgment except me." He paused again. "I guess that's one reason I called. I hoped that working through some of this with someone I trust might help me remember."

Matt wanted to be supportive, but he wasn't so sure this was a good idea. "I don't know, Jake. I'm no professional . . . Uh, I mean . . . what if you do remember something and . . . I mean—"

"You mean, what if I remember something I don't want to know . . . something you don't want to know?"

"Something like that." Matt paused. "What if your amnesia is a protective mechanism?"

"I hit my head, Matt. I think the amnesia is post-traumatic."

"But what if it's some sort of post-traumatic stress reaction or something? Don't you think maybe you should talk this out with a professional counselor?"

Jake sighed. "Maybe you're right. Maybe I shouldn't have called."

Matt felt rebuked. "Look, Jake . . ." He stopped again when he saw Linda's glare. "Maybe I'm the one out of line here. I'm your friend."

More silence.

Matt continued, "If you can't talk to me, who can you talk to?"

Jake laughed nervously, out of relief. "Maybe I can come up sometime? I'd like to see Crestview. You guys carry quite a reputation in this state."

"Hey, I'm only a temporary here. After Linda has the baby, we're moving on."

"The baby?"

"I forgot I hadn't told you. She's due in a few weeks."

Jake thought back to his Sarah, the way he knew her at the last— happy and pregnant. "Congratulations."

"Thanks." Matt had twisted the phone cord unbelievably during his pacing. He consciously started reversing the small circle he had been following, so he could get the cord back to normal. "When are you free for a visit?"

"I'm on this weekend, but what about next?"

"Good with me. I've got to cover the E.R., but it's usually not that bad for me."

"Great."

The two talked on for a few minutes, making plans and joking about old times. Finally Matt advised, "Say, Jake, have you ever tried journaling about your life with Sarah? Writing always helps jog my memory."

"I'm not much of a writer." He paused. "I guess it couldn't hurt."

"Just a thought."

Jake looked at his watch. "I've got to pick up Kyle. See you next Saturday then?"

"Looking forward to it."

"Me too. Bye."

◆ ◆ ◆

Friday night at the Taylorville McDonald's was bedlam. Taylorville High had a game, and there wasn't any other place to go, unless you wanted to drive all the way to Jones City to see a movie or go to the mall. Frank fried hamburgers until he had counted sixty-one: nineteen quarter pounders and forty-two other patties, one each for the singles, two for the double hamburgers and Big Macs. On his own break, he consumed double fries and two fish sandwiches and drank a large Coke. He locked himself in a bathroom stall to urinate and take his medicine where no one would see.

He watched the football team members sitting around the crowded tables while he cooked and later while he mopped before closing. There were cheerleaders, too. Each one seemed to be hanging on to the arm of a muscled young ball player. The guys ordered one or two burgers. The girls usually ordered fries. He watched the cheerleaders the most, but carefully so Gladys, his manager, wouldn't see and so the customers wouldn't get uncomfortable.

The cheerleaders reminded him of Sarah. He listened to them laugh, and that reminded him of her too. She never seemed to stop giggling when he was around. She said he made her laugh. She was the last person to feel that way.

Sometimes he thought back to the final time they were together in this very McDonald's. He hadn't been laughing then.

He would have given anything to make it work out differently.

◆ ◆ ◆

Sarah looked up and bit her trembling lower lip. McDonald's wasn't crowded. Gladys, just a worker then, was mopping up. Sarah stayed quiet until she pulled the mop bucket back into the kitchen.

Sarah finally forced it out. "I'm pregnant."

Frank's heart sank. "What?" He looked around. For once he was glad they were alone. "Does anybody else know?"

"I told Sherry."

"Your parents?"

"I'm not stupid." The tears welled up again.

Frank thought about how his own father would react. *He's gonna kill me.* Frank's father wasn't known for his compassion. He was prejudiced, white, and southern and proud to be all three. When he drank, he talked about moving out of their "nigger-infested neighborhood." Once when an unmarried black female became pregnant, he told Frank that God would judge her for her wicked lack of self-control. It wouldn't matter to him that Sarah was white. She was wicked scum if she had sex out of wedlock, and God would see to it that she was justly punished.

Frank didn't know what to say, though he knew he would have to take responsibility. Abortion was out of the question. If he knew one thing about God's judgment, it was that people who had abortions were eternally damned. His father had taught him that too. Frank's father, Larry Grimsted, lived in a black-and-white world, and this was definitely black.

Finally, after sizing up the situation for another minute, he made a bold proclamation. "Let's get married."

Sarah looked around. "Frank . . ."

"What? I'm serious!"

"I'm not stupid." Sarah spoke without raising her voice. "We can't . . ."

"I'll get a job. I can go to Jones City to the quarry. Dad said they'd always have room for me there."

"Frank, they just laid off fifty people!"

"But Dad said—"

"Was he sober?"

The words stung. Sarah regretted them immediately but didn't retract them. She felt like lashing out and was glad she did.

"Sarah!"

She kept her voice low. "Can you take me to Grantsville? They have a clinic for women up there. It will only take four hours and will cost me two hundred dollars."

"You can't be serious!"

She knew she was. "I can't have a baby. I'm going to Leesburg State in the fall, and I can't give up my scholarship."

Frank couldn't believe his ears. If word ever got out that he had fathered a child . . . and that it had been aborted . . . If Larry Grimsted's grandchild was killed in an abortion clinic and he ever found out . . . Worse yet, if God found out, Frank would be damned for sure! "Sarah, you can't do this! You've got to reconsider!"

"I'm not asking your permission. I don't need it. In Grantsville, they don't even require my parents' approval. All they need is the money."

"Why are you telling me all this then?"

"Because you're the father. You should know." She paused. "I thought you'd want to know, that's all."

His eyes widened. "Don't do this!"

Sarah wiped her eyes. "You got me into this, and I'm going to get myself out of it."

"Sarah, there's a better way. Let's get married."

"No."

He pleaded with his eyes. "We'll be damned if we kill our baby. Don't do this!"

"Stop it, Frank. It's legal, remember?" Frank looked so afraid. "Since when did you get religious?"

"You know I believe in God."

"You haven't seen the inside of a church for years."

"That doesn't mean—"

"Enough, Frank. Maybe I shouldn't have told you." She raised her eyebrows but not her voice. "I thought maybe I could count on you for some of the money, but I'll manage on my own." She stood up.

"Don't walk out on me like this. I'm part of this too," he pleaded.

She departed without saying another word.

◆ ◆ ◆

Frank finished the floor after the last of the celebrating Taylorville Knights finished eating. He always liked Friday nights. Gladys let him stay late and lock up. Sometimes he would sit in the dark and watch the teenagers who hung out in the parking lot after the place closed. He was closing the cash register when his wristwatch chirped again. Bathroom time. He hesitated, then obeyed his compulsion. *You can't be too careful about your bladder function when you're on medication,* he told himself. *It's OK to pay attention to necessary details. You're taking good care of yourself, aren't you, Frank?*

CHAPTER
4

ON Saturday, Jake finally wrestled Kyle into bed at 9:30. He walked across the creaky kitchen floor to the refrigerator where he took out a Diet Pepsi and drank from the forty-eight ounce bottle. Sarah never liked that much, a fact that Kyle reminded him of whenever he caught him. Jake could almost hear her speaking when Kyle scolded him.

He sat down at the old wooden table and opened a yellow legal pad. "Matt said writing it down might help, Lord," he whispered in a prayer. "Help me remember."

He stared at the blank pages for a full five minutes, not knowing where to start or how to begin. Finally he closed his eyes and began to recall . . .

◆ ◆ ◆

Sarah had been so excited about this baby that she sent Jake flowers. They were at the main O.R. desk when he finished a gall bladder removal.

"Thanks, team. Nicely done." Jake pulled off his sterile gown and gloves and wadded them into a ball. He looked at the anesthesiologist, Chuck Westwood. "Thanks, Chuck."

He washed his hands, grabbed the chart, and headed to the recovery room and the waiting room beyond. There he talked to the patient's family and headed back to the O.R. desk to check the schedule. That's when he saw the flowers. Pat, the head nurse, smiled. Jake assumed the flowers were for her. "What's the occasion, Pat? Harold want to go to the track again?" He laughed.

"Hey, these aren't mine. They're for you."

"Me?" He looked incredulous. "No way. Patients never send me flowers. A thank you note maybe, but never flowers." He sniffed the long-stemmed red roses. "My wife's favorite. Maybe I'll just change this card and give them to her," he said with a wink.

"Too late. They're from Sarah. She dropped 'em off herself while you were doing that last case."

The card read, "Congratulations, Daddy." Jake felt a rush. They had been trying to expand their family ever since Kyle was two. That was eight years ago. An infertility workup had revealed nothing. It must just be a matter of God's timing, they assured themselves.

Now their waiting for another baby would come to an end! Jake smiled and whistled to himself, walking toward the changing room.

Pat called out behind him, "What's the occasion?"

"Oh, nothing. My wife just loves me, that's all." Jake knew he couldn't share the news yet. There would be plenty of time for that. He just hoped his wife's obstetrician, who practiced at the same hospital as he did, could keep the secret tight.

The next three weeks were filled with excitement and anticipation. They enjoyed their love for each other without the pressure of having to make another baby. Jake found himself calling Sarah for updates two or three times a day, sending her notes, even running errands for her when he could. He also spent more time with Kyle.

Sarah, normally comely, became radiant. She did all the right things. No coffee, no artificial sweeteners, no medicines. She faithfully took her vitamins and watched her weight. She couldn't have been happier. Finally she was having another baby. Finally her prayers had been answered. Finally she would hold a baby in her arms again.

◆ ◆ ◆

Jake's memories seemed to stop whenever he tried to write them down. He looked at his paper. All he had written was: "She was happier than she'd ever been before."

◆ ◆ ◆

The following morning, Jake took Kyle to his mother's at 7, promising to make rounds and meet them at her church by 10. He almost kept his promise but then answered an E.R. call and gladly did an appendectomy on a classmate of Kyle's. It seems everyone is labeled somehow, and to this patient Dr. Jake Hampton was merely "Kyle's dad."

He managed to slip onto the back bench of Taylorville Community Church just before the closing hymn. He stretched his neck to see his mother . . . sitting in the third bench all the way to the right. *Of course,* he realized, *the same place as for the last sixty-five years.* Kyle sat next to her and stared out the window. *He's in his own world, somewhere out there, entertaining himself,* Jake reflected.

That's when Jake saw her, sitting two rows ahead of him, on the far left. He held up his hymnal in her direction, so it wouldn't be so obvious that he was trying to get a better look. Yes, it was her . . . Sharon Isaacs. Wouldn't she be surprised to see Kyle sitting so still? She seemed to be sitting with an older man. Her father perhaps? Jake hadn't seen any rings when he visited her the other day. *Boy, she looks as nice in that dress as she did in that sports—*

The song ended, and Jake hoped no one had noticed his distraction. After the service, he joined his mother and Kyle and filed out the rear of the church with everyone else to shake the pastor's hand. Jake managed to get one more look at Sharon Isaacs as she put on her coat in the lobby, but all he managed was an "Oh, hi" since Kyle had started hopping down the sidewalk on one foot toward the car. Jake smiled sheepishly and chased after his son. *Great timing!*

◆ ◆ ◆

Dr. D spent Sunday morning going over charts at the Ocean Sands Wellness Facility. He signed each one for billing purposes and to add some professionalism to the record. The "M.D." after his signature would encourage the insurance companies to pay the claims. He glanced at the first chart, a Mary Brazwell. She was sixty-two, admitted for detoxification for arthritis. She was put on a strict juice fast and a series of thrice daily coffee enemas for cleansing.

Many of the facility's regimens for healing operated on the same theory: clean the gastrointestinal tract and liver of toxins, and the body will heal itself. They pushed the clean-out program on most of their cancer patients and those with other chronic diseases. It mattered little to the director that the National Institutes of Health had studied the remedies thoroughly and found them no better than no treatment at all. All that mattered was reimbursement. If insurance companies didn't pay, the patients were expected to produce out of pocket. Most of them did.

Mary exercised daily in the ozone rejuvenation pool. The exercise benefited her health-wise and added eighty dollars a day to her stay. By the end of three weeks, Mary had put out $3,700 and went home tanned and with less arthritic pain in her hips. In another week her testimonial would appear in ads across the Southeast.

Dr. D signed the second chart. Harold Geiser had sought an alternative to bypass surgery for debilitating chest pain. He was treated with a low-fat diet, chelation therapy, and, of course, daily trips to the oxygen pool. He left two weeks later six pounds lighter and $2,800 poorer and with a new commitment to fat-free living. He died six months later, two months after his published testimonial.

Dr. D made quick work of his signatures and sighed. *If only I could get Michael to join me. Once here, he'd see just how much sense all of this makes,* he reasoned. He closed the last folder and rubbed his neck, hoping to alleviate his headache. He grabbed his keys and headed for the facility's pharmacy. There he found what he needed. In the midst of the vitamins and herbs, he kept an assortment of other medications that he used rarely. They watched the room closely and kept it locked to keep patient access to a minimum. He couldn't have people seeing everything now, could he?

The therapies at Ocean Sands stressed natural cures for the most part. Prescription medications were frowned upon and were used only at the discretion of Dr. D, mostly as an adjunct to other therapies that got the credit for the medicine's benefit. Most of the time the patient was unaware of Dr. D's pharmaceutical addition. He tried to minimize this, of course, but enjoyed "enhancing the ability of the natural cures to heal." If he had to do this without patient knowledge, so be it. That mattered nothing to him.

He popped two Tylox, a strong oral narcotic, and decided to stroll the beach. The sea air and the medication would do wonders for his demeanor, and it would give him a chance to look for a few shark's teeth for his collection.

◆ ◆ ◆

Because his Haldol dosage had been lowered, Frank's paranoia intensified. Now just checking his mail was an adventure. His mailbox was on the ground level of a two-story apartment building. He first scouted the area and approached only after he was sure it was uninhabited. He knew Hampton might try to strike at any time, and from what he'd read, mail-bombs were a favorite tool for most vigilantes. So he felt he could never be too careful. His slot was the second to the right. He thought of pouring water over it, in hopes of shorting out any electronic device, but he feared that might cause an explosion somehow. He finally resorted to duct-taping his mail key onto the end of a broom and standing at a distance to open his box. He knew that might look silly, but who cares about looks when there are mail-bomber kooks on the loose? Once, when somebody came out of her apartment, he just started sweeping, like he cleaned the hallway every day.

He waited until Neal got his mail. Neal was always the first, showing up at his box on the heels of the mailman. Frank always watched from the McDonald's across the street. Once Neal was out of the way, he would have at least thirty minutes before Ms. Thompson left for work. She always retrieved her mail on the way out. It was during this time, once a week, that Frank would make his move.

Today he quickly scampered across the street. Good—the hallway was empty. He carefully inspected his box, then felt it for heat. He wasn't sure why, but he thought that a careful person would do this. He pulled the broom out of its hiding place behind the stairs, then stood back and inserted the key. He carefully shielded his eyes before turning it. Slowly. Carefully. No explosion. Relief flooded him again. No suspicious packages. Just a bill from Sears. He shoved the letter into his greasy pants pocket and quickly hid the broom again. He felt confident and safe because he had acted so fast.

He was glad to be alive, but he continued to wonder where and when Hampton might try to strike. As he walked back across the street, he mumbled to himself, "Murderer. I'll see that justice is served . . . just like with my son's killer. Murderers have to pay. An eye for an eye, Daddy always said."

Fear was the primary reason he stayed away from his apartment. *That's where he'd expect me to be*, he strategized. He walked along, clutching his green army surplus jacket. *Besides, the jail isn't so bad, especially since I got the kerosene heater.*

It was daylight, so he walked only as far as the railroad tracks before heading off into the bordering woods. He picked his way through the trees, listening as he went. He traveled as far as the field just beyond the old judicial complex before pausing to wait for nightfall. He didn't want to cross the open field in the daytime if it could be helped.

Soon, however, a steady, cold drizzle ruined his plans, and he headed for the bushes outside the jailhouse. No one was likely to be out in this weather anyway, he figured.

Once inside, he opened a can of pork and beans and ate them along with a swig of water from his old Boy Scout canteen. Then he returned to his ritual reading of his shoe box's contents. Gently he lifted an ad from the Grantsville Women's Health Clinic. "The people who killed my son," he mumbled. His heart rate quickened in response to the memory.

Because Sarah refused to talk to him, he had followed her in his brother's car.

◆ ◆ ◆

Sherry stalled the car again. "You didn't tell me your mom's car was a stick."

"I didn't know it would matter," Sarah responded with a frown. The car jerked ahead two feet and stalled again. "Give it some gas!"

Sherry started the engine, pressed the accelerator, and let out the clutch. The tires responded with a squeal. They shot out of the school parking lot and into the street.

Sarah giggled. "Are you sure you don't want me to drive?"

"I'll be OK," Sherry answered. "Besides, I'm going to have to drive you home, remember? I better get in some practice while I can."

"Great." Sarah coughed nervously. "You'll get me killed, and then I won't need this procedure after all."

"Sarah!"

"Just kidding, Sherry. Don't have a fit. Just keep your eyes on the road." They approached Taylorville's only stop sign and lurched to a stall. Sherry restarted the engine. Sarah coached, "Now give it some gas, and ease out the clutch slowly this time."

Two hundred feet behind, Frank Grimsted followed in his brother's black Camaro. He kept his distance until he was sure they were headed for Grantsville. He thought momentarily of trying to run them off the road but abandoned that idea because he didn't want anyone getting hurt. *What am I supposed to do now?* he wondered. *It's not like she'll listen to reason.*

A dozen different ideas ran through Frank's already stressed mind. He hadn't really known what he would do to stop her from having the abortion. He just knew he had to try or face damnation for sure. Force her off the road? He'd already rejected that idea. Pass her and then slow down? No. She'd likely just pass him back. Pass her, then pull off, and wave her down? No. She'd never stop if she knew it was Frank. He didn't know what to do. *I guess I'll have to disable the car somehow.*

He tapped the steering wheel. "If I could only get their car keys," he mumbled to himself. He thought for a few minutes longer, then passed a sign—"Grantsville, 20 miles." It seemed to urge him to do something, even if he didn't have a complete plan. *First, get them to stop,* he plotted. *I have to make them stop!*

He sped up and flashed his lights on and off, on and off. He raced to within a few feet of Sherry's rear bumper and blared the horn.

Sherry lurched. "What's that nut doing?" She waved her hand. "Go around!"

Sarah looked back. "That's Jerry's car." She squinted. "It's Frank!" She cursed. "How'd he know about this?"

Sherry weaved across the center yellow line. "Idiot!" She pressed on the accelerator.

The black Camaro responded, staying right on her bumper. Frank beeped the horn again. "Pull over!" he yelled, not knowing if they could hear him.

Sherry began to brake.

"Don't stop!" Sarah pleaded. "He's acting crazy!"

Sherry punched the gas pedal again.

The Camaro hugged the bumper.

Sherry weaved again, her right tires spraying gravel from the road's shoulder, hoping to cloud Frank's vision and convince him to give up the chase. He didn't.

A turn was coming up, so Sherry hit the brakes. Frank did the same, missing the other car by inches. "Sarah, I've got to stop. I'm not a good enough driver to get away from him." Sherry was the one who was pleading now.

Frank began to yell.

Sherry manipulated the curve but slowed down even further. "I'm pulling over."

"Please!" Sarah looked back. They could hear Frank screaming. "You can't stop. Sherry—he's crazy!"

"I have an idea." Sherry stopped the car but avoided the soft shoulder. Frank pulled to a stop behind her and got out.

"Sarah!" Frank lunged at the driver's door just as Sherry floored the accelerator. Frank's body rolled off the back of the moving car and onto the pavement. Dazed, he stood up and brushed himself off.

He quickly resumed the chase. It took him a minute or two to catch them, though he was traveling in excess of eighty miles per hour.

Just then another set of lights joined the chase. A state trooper behind the Camaro flipped on his siren.

Frank looked in his rearview mirror. "Great! Just great!"

"Sarah! Police!" Sherry cried.

"Pull over, Sherry. He can help us." Sarah looked relieved. She slowly uncurled her white fingers from around her shoulder harness.

Sherry pulled over. Frank came to a stop just behind Sherry.

The trooper eyed Frank cautiously. Frank looked the part of a drugged teenager. His eyes were wide, and his clothes were dirty. He immediately launched into a tirade. "Officer! We've got to stop them!"

"Step out of the car!"

In the blink of an eye Frank found himself facedown on the hood of the Camaro. The officer made quick work of searching him, then led him to the back of his car. Frank's screams were silenced by one command of the large officer. "Quiet!"

Once Frank was in the officer's car, Sherry and Sarah told him the story. "He was chasing us. We pulled over, and he tried to jump in our vehicle to stop us."

Officer Shifflet checked Sherry's driver's license. "You should be in school."

"My friend has an appointment to see a doctor in Grantsville. I'm taking her." Sarah quickly produced an appointment card.

The state trooper studied the situation for a moment longer before warning the girls and letting them go. He was anxious to search the Camaro for drugs.

Frank began cursing his misfortune. This officer was certainly interfering with the last hope of saving his and Sarah's baby. *Maybe he's part of the conspiracy!* Frank's thoughts spun wildly, on the brink of control. *Maybe God is punishing me already!*

The officer made quick work of a vehicle search and ticketed the confused young man. He thought twice about taking him to the hospital to be tested but decided against it when the boy calmed down. After half an hour Frank pulled away, dejected and convinced of a cosmic plot against him and his son or daughter.

Frank's fixation on the abortion precipitated a quick unraveling of his thought processes. Within two weeks he slid into his first psychotic episode and was hospitalized in Jones City since Taylorville Hospital didn't have a locked psychiatric ward and wasn't equipped to deal with violent patients.

Fortunately for Sarah, no one ever spoke of the events of that day. She did get a letter from Larry Grimsted, Frank's father, who blamed his son's illness upon Frank's wickedness. She wasn't sure if he knew about the abortion.

Mr. Grimsted was rarely seen in public after Frank entered the hospital. It was as if a cloud of shame pushed him from relating with anyone except the owner of the local grocery/department store.

Sarah moved on, hoping the memory of that regrettable day could be locked up forever. After all, Sherry was the only other person who knew, except for Frank, and Frank was locked away where he could do no more harm.

◆　◆　◆

It was Thursday before Jake had another chance to sit down with his yellow legal pad and his memories. He wanted to get something in writing before talking to Matt Stone on Saturday. At least it would look like he'd tried.

He positioned himself in his favorite chair and looked at the page in front of him. He'd written so little last time, he wondered if journaling was really going to help. He sighed, then contemplated where to begin. With the events surrounding Sarah's death? With his suspicions about her treatment at Ocean Sands? No, he needed to start before that. He wrote the word "CANCER" in capital letters at the top. It was the cancer that changed everything. Sarah had been so happy until then.

◆ ◆ ◆

It was the evening of the dedication of the new hospice wing at Grantsville General Hospital. Dr. Jacob Hampton, general surgery attending, was making final preparations for a speech. The event, hosted by the hospital auxiliary was a black-tie extravaganza, the finale of over two years of fund-raising and community support.

"Members of the auxiliary, staff members, physicians . . ." Jake cleared his throat and began again after straightening his bow tie in the mirror. "I'd like to give a special welcome to the hospital auxiliary, led by Mary Blevins . . ." He turned toward the bathroom, where steam was still coming from behind the shower door. "Do you think I should welcome the chairman of the fund-raising committee by name?"

Sarah replied with a muffled, "What?"

It was futile to ask her anything with the shower on. Jake continued on his own. Sarah wasn't paying attention to him anyway.

Sarah's left breast was getting increasingly sore. *I guess it just goes with the pregnancy*, she assumed. *I haven't been pregnant for so long, I probably just forgot what it's like*. She smiled when she thought about her new baby. A little breast tenderness was a small price to pay for such happiness. Her hand went instinctively to a spot in the lateral upper left breast. As she massaged it gently, she noted a small dimpling of the skin. Her breasts had always been lumpy. That was nothing new. Her doctors called it "fibrocystic disease." She had dealt with that since she was twenty.

As she explored the area with her fingertips, she tried to reassure herself. *Must be another cyst*. She shuddered with a ripple of anxiety. *I'll ask Dr. Kramer about it when I go for my next checkup*.

The evening was beautiful. Jake's message was brief, and his unabashed pro-life philosophy was received without much controversy in that setting. This was about life and a celebration of it, from birth until death. This was about leaving the timing of death in God's hands. "We stand willing to provide comfort and relief from suffering and to provide a natural setting for death to occur when it is inevitable that medicine will not cure," he concluded.

The hospital president cut a yellow ribbon. A triple-layer cake was served. A reception, followed by a tour of the facility, capped the well-planned and well-attended event.

Sarah remained distracted. Outwardly, she appeared calm. Inwardly, a gnawing anxiety about her breast discomfort began to rise.

The following morning she made an appointment with Dan Kramer, her gynecologist. She shared none of this with Jake. *It's probably nothing,* she hypothesized. *There's no use in both of us being afraid. Besides, he's never found anything worrisome about my breasts before.*

Two days later Sarah grimaced during her exam. "It's probably just this fibrocystic condition I've always had. I've read it can worsen during pregnancy."

Dr. Kramer continued his exam in silence. He concentrated on an area of firm tissue in the upper outer breast quadrant. "There?" He couldn't hide his concern. "The skin is retracted here. That's not too common with cysts, Sarah."

"I was afraid of that." Sarah squelched a sob. "What do I do now?"

"I want you to see a surgeon." He picked up her folder. "Would you like to see one of Jake's partners?"

She thought of Jake's associates, Richard Dearborn and Stanley Leslie. She knew them so well. "I don't know."

"There are other practices in town. There's Dave Kennel's group." He paused. "I've heard good things about him."

Sarah thought for another moment. How would it look if she went to her husband's competition? "No," she responded. "I'd better stick to my husband's practice." She bit her lip. "I'd rather Jake not be bothered with this yet."

Dan Kramer squinted. "Sure. This is between us." He completed a form on the front of her chart. "I'll have the front office make you an appointment. I'm sure they can work you in."

"Nothing like connections," Sarah added, attempting a smile.

Two days later Sarah went through the same routine. This time Jim Barber did the exam, followed by a needle aspirate of a firm mass just beneath the dimpling in the skin. Sarah cried, not from physical pain but from fear. The concern in Jim's voice didn't reassure her.

"What if it's cancer?"

"We can talk about that when we get the cytology report, Sarah."

"I want to talk about it now." She stiffened and got right to the point. "What will we do about the baby?"

"The baby?" Jake hadn't told his partners about the pregnancy, and up until this moment Sarah hadn't mentioned it either. Jim was used to getting referrals from the obstetricians, but most of the patients weren't pregnant.

"We just found out three weeks ago. We've been trying for a long time."

Dr. Barber cleared his throat. "We will have to take that into account for sure, but—" He paused. "Our main concern will be your treatment. If we can keep you healthy, the baby will do OK."

That seemed to satisfy her for the moment. It wasn't until she was home with Jake later that evening that she told him the news, then broke down completely. Deep down, she already knew. She didn't need to wait for the cytology report. She had seen it in Dan Kramer's face, then in Jim Barber's, then in Jake's. But even before that, when she found the mass in the shower, she knew. The pathologist's report of the needle test would only substantiate what she most dreaded: ductal carcinoma.

When her worst fears were confirmed, the words rang in her ears like a cymbal. "It's cancer."

She would fight the cancer, but she had already made up her mind that she would accept absolutely no treatment that could harm her baby. She had been given a great gift, and she believed it was her right to protect it.

She had cancer. CANCER. Sarah had been so happy. But cancer changed everything.

◆　◆　◆

His beeper brought Jake back to the present. He looked at the number. Taylorville Hospital emergency room. He dialed the number.

"Emergency room."

"This is Dr. Hampton. I was paged."

"Hold for Dr. Bateman."

The emergency room physician explained the problem, a pneumothorax in an eighteen-year-old male. A ruptured air sack had caused his lung to collapse. A chest tube inserted between the ribs would evacuate the leaking air and allow the lung to reexpand.

"I'll be right in." It wasn't a major procedure, but it was a chance for Jake to perhaps gain a little more credibility in Taylorville.

Within a few minutes he was looking at the chest X-ray of Tom Larrs, scheduled to be the center on that year's Taylorville High School basketball team. Jake went over the X-ray findings with Tom and his parents and explained the needed procedure. Reluctantly they agreed.

Jake instructed Debbie, an E.R. nurse, to sedate the patient. "Give Fentanyl, fifty micrograms, IV now."

Carefully, Jake painted the boy's chest with a betadine solution.

Deb called out a blood pressure reading. "B.P. 128 systolic."

"Good. Give the Versed. Titrate up to five milligrams, IV. I want him pretty sleepy."

In another three minutes Tom Larrs slept peacefully. He grunted when Jake injected a local anesthetic, then fell back asleep. The surgeon made a small incision in the right chest at the fifth intercostal space. He deepened the incision into the chest cavity, where he was rewarded with a hiss of air under pressure. "The pneumothorax has been relieved." He quickly worked to slide a chest tube into the pleural space outside the right lung. He secured it with a suture and dressed the wound. The tube was connected to a collection chamber placed next to the stretcher.

As he finished up, Dr. Bateman stuck his head in the doorway. "Hey, I've got another one for you before you go." He handed him a chart. "Someone you did an appendectomy on a few days ago."

Jake looked at the chart. "Thanks."

After he talked to Mr. and Mrs. Larrs, he dictated a short note and went to Room C to find his other patient. It was Bobby Henson, a classmate of Kyle's. He had just been released two days earlier. Jake entered the room, where Bobby sat in his mother's lap. He wasn't sure who was holding whom tighter. "Hi. I didn't expect to see you so soon."

The mother looked at the father, who spoke first. "We didn't expect to see you either."

"What's the problem?"

Mrs. Henson spoke up. "His incision is red and sore. I think it's going to burst."

Bobby cried. His father said consolingly, "Now, now, Bobby, it will be all right."

"Let's take a look." Bobby reluctantly got up on the stretcher. Sure enough, the wound had become infected and needed to be opened for drainage. Jake frowned. "There's an infection. We're going to have to open the wound."

"I thought so," the father responded.

Jake looked around. "I'll need to collect a few items. I'll ask the nurse to give him something for pain and sedation."

"You plan on doing this right here?" Mrs. Henson looked concerned.

"Sure. It will only take a few seconds, OK?" Jake turned to leave.

"That's not OK." The father stiffened. So did Jake. "I want Dr. Willie to see my boy. We had wanted him to do Bobby's surgery to begin with. We settled for you, and now look what we got. I ain't settlin' no more."

Dr. Hampton cringed inside. "This infection is easily managed. Sometimes these things happen. About one in twenty cases of appendicitis have to be treated in this way. It doesn't mean anything was done incorrectly. He's just one of the unlucky ones."

Mr. Henson wouldn't hear him. "We don't believe in luck, Mr. Hampton," he stated flatly after emphasizing the "Mr." "We believe in skill. And we're asking for the skill of Dr. Willie."

"Look," Jake almost pleaded, "I work with Dr. Willie. We are associates in the same medical practice. He's not on call today. I don't know if they'd even be able to find him."

"If not, we'll take Bobby to see him tomorrow."

"The infection could spread. I would caution against waiting."

The father sneered. Jake didn't like it, but he knew it was time to back off. "I'll see if they can get Dr. Willie."

The E.R. nurse found Dr. Willie at home. Jake apologized and explained the situation to his associate.

"Don't worry about it, Jake. Tell them I'll be right in."

Two minutes later Jake Hampton jumped in his Isuzu Trooper. "It's not fair, Lord," he whispered. "They need to give me a chance." He struck the steering wheel with his palm. "Even my hometown isn't sure I can be trusted."

He started the Isuzu and headed out of town. He didn't have a destination. He just needed to drive . . . and to pray.

CHAPTER
5

Partly because the patient was Jake's kid, and partly because a thorough examination was what was needed, Dr. Willie spent two hours with Kyle the following afternoon. After reviewing the school reports, performing a routine history and physical exam, and doing an extensive interview and psychological testing, Willie sat down to review the diagnostic criteria for attention deficit hyperactivity disorder in children.

He read from *DSM-III-R*, the psychiatric manual. "Hmm, let's see . . . 'Often fidgets with hands or feet or squirms in seat' . . . yes . . . 'has difficulty remaining in seat when required to do so' . . . yes . . . 'often shifts from one uncompleted activity to another' . . . yes again . . . 'has difficulty playing quietly' . . . yes . . . 'often talks excessively' . . . yes . . . 'often interrupts' . . . yes . . . 'often loses things necessary for tasks or activities at school or home' . . . yes again." Willie closed the manual. It was a textbook diagnosis. He went to his bookshelf and pulled out a volume on A.D.D. to give to Jake. He knew education and understanding are key to effective treatment. *After he's read this, we'll think about some medication. Jake has to be convinced,* he concluded to himself.

He sat back down and dictated a full report. "Show a copy to Dr. Hampton," he concluded and set the Dictaphone back in its cradle.

◆ ◆ ◆

Two blocks away, Jake ordered a Big Mac and a side salad. Kyle wanted a cheeseburger and fries. Patties number fourteen and fifteen, according to Frank who kept compulsive mental records of such things.

Jake and Kyle sat down to eat, and Frank frequently glanced their way. *He acts like he doesn't even know me,* Frank thought. He watched as Jake and Kyle bowed for prayer before eating. He watched as they talked about their day. He watched as Kyle tossed french fries in the air, proudly catching them in his mouth.

Frank gritted his teeth. "Fine," he muttered, heading for the bathroom. "You've got your son. You don't even know what happened to mine." He was mindful to keep his face covered as he passed in easy view of the Hamptons. He didn't want to be detected. *You can't be too careful about these things,* he reminded himself.

Once in the bathroom, he shut and locked the single stall. He took out his Haldol and dry-swallowed the pill. He didn't want to be seen taking his medication. *That would give Gladys grounds for getting rid of me,* he mused. He prided himself on the work he did and didn't want to lose his job. He'd experienced that only once in his life, and he was determined that it would never happen again. *That was a long time ago,* he told himself. *Things are different now. Even Dad might be proud of me this time.* He had gotten this job on his own . . . not like that first one down at the quarry in Jones City. His dad had landed that one for him. How could he forget?

◆ ◆ ◆

"I can't just lie to them, Dad!" Frank pleaded. He didn't want to anyway. He was sure God was keeping score.

"This is different, son," his dad bellowed. "You're not lying. You're just not telling them everything. The foreman won't mind if you're on medication. Just do a good job, and he won't care about anything."

"What about this one?" He held up the job application to his father and read, "Hospitalizations." He pitched the paper onto the kitchen table. "I'm sure they'll hire me if I tell them about my Jones City Hospital admission," he stated sarcastically. "And what about this one? 'Mental illnesses.' Do you want me to just ignore that one too?" He held his head in his hands. "What if they find out about the schizophrenia?"

"It's our secret, son! I won't have other people knowin' about private family matters!" He cursed. "Can't you see? You're fine now! The medication has everything under control, right? It's like the doctor told us, it's a matter of confidentiality. No one has to know this stuff! It's not their business." His father opened a beer. "Besides, all they want to know is that you're a good worker." He gulped down half of the contents of the brown bottle. "Besides," he chuckled, "they can't have just any old kook handling all those explosives."

Somehow Frank didn't find his father's words too comforting. He again looked at his dad.

"Give me that thing. I'll fill it out for you. I'll take it down to Ray tomorrow. I've got to go to Jones City to get a load of wood anyway." He ripped the application out of his son's hand. "Don't you worry about it. I'll do the applyin' around here."

Putting a simple diagnosis on a form for Frank Grimsted would have been a challenge for even the most educated mental health professional. Frank had been characterized as paranoid schizophrenic, with an unusual mix of homicidal and religious idea formations; but he also had a strong sense of self-preservation. The combination was rather unusual. He had complex obsessive, compulsive features seen in other personality disorders and had intelligence scores that were well above average. He was predictably paranoid when off medication and became fixated on momentous events in his life, especially those having to do with the girlfriend he had during his first major psychotic breakdown.

Once his father had the application, Frank never saw it again. His father even signed it for him and wrote "National Honor Society member" at the bottom. As if Ray the foreman could care. Oh, Frank was in the National Honor Society all right, but of course his father omitted his son's psychiatric history. *Oh, well,* Frank figured, *God can't hold me responsible for my dad's deceptions.*

◆ ◆ ◆

Frank unlocked the stall and peered slowly around the corner. The Hamptons had left. *Good,* he exulted. *It's time for me to clean the tables anyway.*

◆ ◆ ◆

The next afternoon found Michael Simons lounging at the pool at Ocean Sands Wellness Facility.

"Care for a drink?"

Simons eyed the young man who held a pitcher of orange-colored liquid. The man, dressed in a clinical uniform, explained, "It's a natural fruit juice blend, with aloe juice and amino acid powder."

The cardiothoracic surgeon turned up his nose. His reply was clearly sarcastic. "Sounds simply yummy."

The attendant poured Simons a glass and left it on a table beside him.

The director, Dr. D, held up his glass for a refill. "Thanks, Calvin."

"I'd really hoped that your visit might signal a change of heart, Michael. I'm still interested in bringing you on here if you're agreeable." He sipped his fruit cooler. "You could work wonders for our cardiac rehab program."

"I suppose you think I buy all this chelation stuff?"

Dr. D looked around and lowered his voice. "I would only expect that you wouldn't speak against it publicly. It wouldn't be good for business. I don't care what private beliefs you have."

"That wouldn't work. I'm not into repressing my professional opinions, for any reason. Anyway, I'm jumping through the last hoop in hopes of setting up a new pediatric heart program at Crestview."

"The same program you've been 'about to establish' for six months?" Dr. D raised his eyebrows.

Simons sighed. "The same."

After a few minutes of uncomfortable silence, Simons picked up the drink beside him. He sipped it cautiously. "Not bad," he added setting it aside.

"So what's the holdup? I thought you'd be back in the O.R. by this time. You must be tired of writing by now."

"I never tire of writing. My textbook's almost finished. If it weren't for that, I'd be completely insane by now. I do miss the theater though." Simons always called the operating room "the theater."

"So what's in your way?"

Michael Simons sighed again. "I don't have a good explanation for it. I can only assume that one of my former residents who is now on staff at Crestview has it out for me." He paused. "We went head to head when I was at Taft. I tried to have him removed for incompetence, and he's hated me ever since."

"Matt Stone?"

"Exactly." He paused. "I guess I told you the story."

"Of course." Dr. D shook the ice in his glass. "Plus I've checked you out for myself, Michael. I really want you here—you know that. From what I've heard, Stone didn't act out of hatred to you. He acted out of a conviction that your research method of using aborted fetal hearts was wrong from a moral standpoint. I would doubt that he carries any personal vendettas against you."

"You *have* done some checking," Simons said, impressed. "But remember, I went after him hard. I wanted him out of the way completely. Even a man with moral convictions doesn't like his career stomped on. He could be carrying a heavy grudge."

"I suppose it's possible."

"Possible? I've sensed it. It is something I *know*. There's no other explanation for the slow treatment I've been given. The surgeons at Crestview and Valley Surgeons for Children say they want me. My credentials speak for themselves. It's only the whim of some privilege-granting committee that stands in my way." He looked at his uncle and took another sip of the fruit beverage. "Matt Stone must have influenced the committee in some way. Why else would it be taking so long?"

"So what are you going to do?"

"Nothing rash. The upper hand never comes to someone who rushes fate."

"What do you mean?"

"There is within each of us great untapped power to transcend these mundane problems. The ability to overcome this obstacle is certainly within my reach." He gulped his drink more quickly, then looked away at the pool. "I only need to listen." He quieted himself, then added a question. "Do you believe in destiny?"

"Perhaps." Dr. D paused. "I'm not sure I'm following you."

"The proper opportunity will present itself. When it comes, so will an answer."

The director squinted. "Stone will get his due?"

Simons answered with silence and stared into the dancing reflections on the surface of the pool.

Later Michael did speak again, but in the form of a question of his own. "What about your situation here? Is the investigation about Mrs. Hampton's cancer death over?"

"What do you know about that?"

"Only what I saw in the paper. It seems everyone has forgotten about it now."

"There was no real investigation of our facility, Michael. The situation was pretty open and shut, fortunately so for us. It seems the only investigation of Ocean Sands was by the one who had the most to gain out of getting the suspicions cast away from himself."

"Jake Hampton?"

"Sure. In the eyes of the police he was the guilty party. He certainly had the know-how and the motive."

"Motive?"

"It was well-known that he despised his wife for seeking care here and for promoting our facility. It made his own practice look bad."

"Maybe he just didn't want his wife to suffer . . . Maybe it was mercy."

"Most of us can do without that kind of mercy."

"Don't give me that. I know you've been an advocate of physician-assisted suicide. You're involved with the local chapter of Mercy Physicians. I've seen the newsletter."

"OK, so I'm for it, but I'm not for the way it appears to have happened in Dr. Hampton's case. If he helped his suffering wife die, fine. But . . ." He raised his voice. "But don't do it and then deny it or say you don't remember."

Simons remained silent.

Dr. D responded to his silence. "Why do you ask about Jake Hampton?"

"He was a resident of mine. I'm curious, that's all."

"You knew him?" Dr. D seemed startled that his nephew might know Jake personally.

"Does that alarm you?"

The director hesitated. "Of course not." He paused again. "I just hate to see someone you trained undergo such misfortune."

"So he has stopped questioning your facility?"

Dr. D hesitated one more time. Finally he answered with the same question Simons had posed a few minutes earlier. "Do you believe in destiny, Michael?"

Simons didn't answer. His uncle didn't expect him to.

Dr. D stood, laughed heartily to cover the seriousness of the moment, and headed for a stroll on the beach. "Go for a walk?"

"The exercise will do me good."

◆ ◆ ◆

Jake Hampton sat on a stool interviewing a new patient. The female, forty-two years old, had been referred for evaluation of a breast lump. Jake ran through the list of routine questions for each new patient with this problem.

"Any breast diseases in your mother?"

"She had a biopsy. It wasn't cancer, though."

"Good," Jake responded. "Do you have any sisters?"

"Two."

"Any breast disease in them?"

"Not that I'm aware." The patient paused. "But Susan lives in Portland, and we'd never know she was alive if it weren't for Christmas cards."

"How old were you when you first started having menstrual periods?"

"Oh me." The patient smiled. "Twelve years old, I think."

"How old were you when you became pregnant?"

"Let's see, Jim is twenty, so . . . I must have been twenty-one when I got pregnant."

"Any earlier pregnancies that ended in miscarriage or abortion?"

"No." The patient answered stiffly, then asked, "Why do you need to know that?"

Jake paused as a memory flooded his brain. His hand trembled slightly. He collected himself and answered, "All of these items help us classify our patient's risk of developing breast cancer. We have discovered a higher incidence of breast cancer in females who wait a long time before having their first pregnancy and also in women who have had an abortion."

His reaction to her question was unexpected. He had heard the question before. His Sarah had asked him that very thing. It was that memory that came so abruptly into his mind. Sarah, like many other women, wanted to know why it was necessary to pry so deeply into their intimate past. He wasn't sure if they gave him honest answers half the time anyway. He remembered that Sarah hadn't.

◆ ◆ ◆

Sarah was weeping again. It seemed to Jake as if her joy about the baby had been completely destroyed by the cancer. It not only robbed her body—it robbed her soul.

Jake went to her and put his arms around her waist. He didn't need to speak. He just needed to be there. Around her on the kitchen table were books—books on prenatal development, books on breast cancer . . . and books on miracle cancer cures.

"It's my fault, isn't it, Jake?"

Jake pulled his head away in surprise. "What do you mean?"

"Why did Jim need to know about the abortion?"

"Did you tell him?"

Sarah bit her lip. "I didn't want him to know. I didn't know it might be important."

"It doesn't really matter, Sarah. We only ask that question because it helps us predict a woman's risk profile, that's all."

"That's all?" She picked up a book from the kitchen table. "It says that abortion significantly increases the incidence of breast cancer." She looked away.

"Look, honey, it's all past. We've dealt with it." He tried to discern his wife's thoughts. "It has nothing to do with today."

"It has everything to do with it, Jake." She let her old remorse flow over her again. "I killed my baby, remember?" She squeezed her fists. "Now I'm reaping what I sowed."

"Sarah, the abortion was a long time ago. God forgives. We left that old Sarah at the cross years ago."

She shook her head. The condemnation she felt was oppressive and dark. It wouldn't lift with simple reassurance from Jake. "I'm obligated to take the judgment God has rendered."

"Don't punish yourself like this, Sarah. God's judgment *has* been rendered—you're forgiven." He sighed, sensing she couldn't hear it.

"For so many years I shoved it away, Jake. I didn't want to deal with it. I denied that what I did was wrong." She paused and walked to the sink. She leaned low and placed her head in her hands. "Then when I came to Christ, and I faced who I really was and what I'd done, I thought his forgiveness was too good to be true . . . all my sins washed away, no more penalty." She heaved a sob. "Yes, it's true, he's forgiven me . . . But I still need to face the natural consequences of what I've done. My sin might be gone, but the judgment for my actions is being born out here and now."

"It's not hopeless, Sarah. There is surgical and medical treatment."

"You're talking like a surgeon, not like my husband."

"Sarah, I'm concerned. As your husband and as a doctor."

"I'm obligated to accept my fate."

"What do you mean?" Now Jake sounded alarmed. "Aren't you going to fight?"

"Of course, I'll fight." She looked at the stack of books and straightened up. "But from everything I've read, the therapies that fight the cancer will also threaten the baby."

"If we don't save your life, the baby won't live either, Sarah."

She stiffened. "I killed one baby, can't you see!" She moaned with deep anguish. "That's why I'm in this fix now. It's because of what I did!" She glared at her husband. "I'll not do anything to harm this baby. Not after what I did before. Never again."

Jake would remember that look for many months. And it would be the image he would remember best for weeks after she was dead.

He shook his head. "Sarah . . ."

She spoke only three more words to him that day.

"Sarah," he said softly, reaching for her shoulder.

"Leave me alone!"

CHAPTER
6

JAKE spent part of Friday morning making lists for Kyle. From what he'd read from the literature Willie had given him, organization was a key to helping those with A.D.D. stay on track. He made one list for his bedroom and one for the bathroom. Each had a list of items to check off before Kyle could leave the room.

One of the big areas of struggle Kyle had at home was following through on the mundane tasks his father asked him to do. In the bathroom, for instance, he constantly left the towel off the rack or the toothpaste tube uncapped or the soap in the sink. His new checklist ended with things like, "Turn out the light." Kyle's initial response was favorable. Jake hoped this would work.

After making the lists, Jake took Kyle to school and went to the hospital for rounds. One of the pluses of not being very popular yet was having the luxury of spending a little extra time with each patient and at home. He only had one scheduled procedure that day, a colonoscopy, a procedure whereby a thin, flexible, illuminated tube is steered through the lower bowel in order to make diagnosis or remove polyps.

He did the procedure on an eighty-year-old male with an iron deficiency from an unknown cause. He sedated the patient and introduced the "scope." Unfortunately, Jake found an obvious colon cancer in the right colon. He did biopsies for confirmation and made plans to admit the patient for surgery on Monday. Fortunately for Jake, the man seemed to like him, and he didn't lose another case to Dr. Willie.

After his procedure, Jake picked up his lunch and headed for Kyle's school. The administration and teachers encouraged parents to eat with their children when possible. That gave the parents a positive feeling of being involved in the school and gave the teachers a chance to meet them. As he prepared to leave the hospital, Jake shoved a copy of Dr. Dansford's workup of Kyle in his briefcase. He thought the school office might want it. Besides, he might get to see Sharon Isaacs that way.

In another ten minutes Jake was sitting with twenty-four fifth graders. Kyle was exalted to the guest of honor since his dad was eating with him. He couldn't have been happier. The table was little and the noise level just slightly less than an O'Hare runway. *Oh well*, Jake thought with a smile, *I can tolerate anything for thirty minutes.*

After lunch Jake approached Sharon's office. As he entered, an older man exited—apparently the same man who had been with Sharon in church last Sunday. The man hugged her quickly and kissed her cheek. "Bye, love," he whispered.

Sharon seemed surprised to see Jake.

You didn't expect anyone to walk in on you, did you? Jake accused silently. He tried to hide his feelings. "Hi."

"Hi," she responded.

"I brought you a copy of Dr. Dansford's workup."

"Thanks." She accepted the copy and smiled.

"It looks like you were right." He paused. "Maybe I owe you an apology."

She looked at him curiously.

"I was upset at first." He shuffled his feet. "I guess offended is a better word. It's my pride, really. I didn't want anyone seeing anything I didn't see first myself, especially in my own son."

"I didn't pick up on that." Her smile returned. "It's OK."

Jake looked around. "I hope I wasn't interrupting anything just now."

"Oh no. My dad was in town visiting and stopped by to say good-bye."

Her dad! Jake chided himself. Of course.

"Can I ask you a personal question?"

He squinted. "Sure."

"Where's Kyle's mom?" She paused. "I mean, Kyle's completely silent on the issue, and her name isn't on our records. Are you divorced?"

"Kyle's mother died of breast cancer."

"I'm sorry. I didn't know. I—"

Jake interrupted her. He found it refreshing for someone to actually not know, or at least suspect, how she died. "Are you not from this area? Her death was quite a media event around here."

"I'm from California. I just moved here two weeks before Kyle started attending Taylorville Elementary."

That explained a lot. She had to have been dropped here from outer space, or California, or . . . heaven, Jake thought with a smile. Everybody else sure seemed to know all about him.

"Do you have family here? What would bring you all the way to Taylorville? Certainly not the salary." He chuckled.

"Not the salary." She gently laid Kyle's workup on her desk. "My father works for the government and was transferred to D.C. I just wanted to be closer to him, that's all."

"But D.C.'s still three hours by—"

"Closer," she responded quickly, "but not too close."

Jake smiled. He shuffled his feet again. "I'd better run."

"Will Dr. Willie be starting Kyle on medication?" Sharon shifted the conversation back to business.

"Probably. He wanted me to get a handle on organizing him without medication, if I could, first."

"Believe me, he knows what he's doing. I've worked with all kinds of psychiatrists with A.D.D. students in California. His workups beat theirs hands down."

Jake nodded. He turned to go. "See ya."

"Sure."

Jake walked swiftly to his Trooper. On the seat was a crinkled Zero candy wrapper. *That's odd—Sarah's favorite candy bar. I haven't eaten one of these in months.*

Behind the big oak tree in the middle of the school playground, Frank Grimsted paused for a snack. He clung to the candy as tightly as he did his old memories. The white chocolate mashed against his palm and created a sticky mess.

◆ ◆ ◆

A few minutes later Frank slid through the window into the basement of his new "home." The cool weather seemed to have made the aroma less intense. He paused, inhaling through his nose, thankful for the change. He headed straight for the sheriff's office, where he opened the ceiling tile again. The time was drawing near, he sensed. He had started doing inventory every day. His shoe box was there. His father's old .38 was there . . . and the box of explosives. He did his entire inventory by feel. One, two, three . . . twelve sticks in all. *That should be enough*, Frank concluded. *That should be fine*.

Frank had learned to use dynamite in the Jones City quarry. He was always very careful and even compulsive about the rules. His father was right. He was a good worker. That's all his foreman seemed to care about. At least until Frank's second dip out of reality.

◆ ◆ ◆

Ironically, it had been the blasting that stressed him the most. At first he fit in easily, but the paranoia gradually crept upon him again. He began to eat alone. Then he started avoiding the quarry's water supply, certain it had been contaminated. With no water, he avoided taking his medication. Without his medication, reality and fantasy began to blur. The blasts became God's fury. The dust became his own guilt. The more he heard and the dustier he became, the more he was convinced of his wickedness and his inability to stop Sarah's abortion. He had to take action, to get even. If he could only silence the voices!

He began to formulate a plan. He would destroy those who had destroyed his child. That would silence the blasts of God's wrath.

Every day for a dozen days he took a single stick of dynamite home in his lunch box. Every day for a dozen days he prayed he wouldn't get caught.

On the thirteenth day he skipped work and drove his brother's Camaro to Grantsville. At noon he carried out his plan.

He carried his supplies in a J.C. Penney shopping bag. Wearing his nicest clothes, he looked just like a frazzled shopper. He stumbled into the waiting room at the Grantsville Women's Health Clinic holding his stomach. He looked at the women lining the room. "I need a bathroom." He belched and moved his hand over his mouth.

The receptionist stood. "Are you OK?"

"I'm sorry. I think I'll be all right. I just need a bathroom." He looked white as a sheet. In truth, he was petrified. But he was on a mission . . . a mission from God, he believed.

He belched again. "Sorry."

"Right this way." She led him to a small facility at the back of the waiting room.

"Thanks."

He closed and locked the door. He had practiced this hundreds of times. In just moments he had wired the dynamite and lit the fuse. He figured he'd need twenty seconds to get to the front exit. He let the fuse burn for two minutes, then left the bathroom, closing and locking the door behind him. He burst across the waiting room like the wild man that he was. He jumped over an empty chair, then noticed a young girl with auburn hair sitting next to the door.

"Sarah!" he screamed. The girl looked up. It wasn't her, but he grabbed her anyway and bolted for the door. "Come on!" He'd just reached the doorway when the bomb exploded. He immediately found himself facedown on the asphalt lot beside the clinic. Muffled screams erupted, and glass and bricks rained on the cars all around him. When he stood, blood trickled from a cut over his left eye. He felt no pain. He had succeeded. He would now be free.

◆ ◆ ◆

Frank rubbed his left eye, stirred by the fresh memory of his victory. He pinched his eyebrow, leaving a small bruise. It had been numb ever since he fled from the parking lot that day.

◆ ◆ ◆

Matt Stone entered the small apartment, easing open the door quietly, in case Linda was napping. Not the case today. Linda was in the kitchen, listening to her favorite Mozart symphonies at a level she could *feel*. As she worked, she intermittently directed the music with whatever happened to be in her hand . . . first a spoon, then a cake-turner, then an eggbeater.

Matt slipped in under the cover of the Mozart. He stood in the doorway admiring her for a moment. *Never more beautiful*, he thought. "Is it loud enough for you?"

Linda shrieked. "Matt! You scared me!"

He smiled sheepishly and pecked her cheek. "Sorry."

"I saw the doctor today." She beamed. "No more bed rest."

"So I figured. Either that or you'd die if you had to eat my cooking one more time," he joked.

"Very funny." She turned the light on to view a cake in the oven.

"What's the occasion?"

"Your friend's coming tomorrow, remember?"

"Jake. Of course."

"I'm going to the hospital Monday for an ultrasound."

"What for?"

"Mostly routine. I guess they just want to check for progress. There certainly haven't been any more contractions."

"Can I come? I want to see my boy." He smiled.

"You may come and see the baby, Matt." She paused. "But I've already told them I don't want to know the baby's gender."

"I've already told you that anyway."

"Right. How could I forget?"

Matt helped her set the table. In a few minutes the plates were filled with ham-and-broccoli quiche and salad. Matt looked over the meal. Yep, Linda was back on the job.

After dinner Matt pushed back from the table.

"I've been thinking about Jake."

"I thought so." Linda sighed. "You've been pretty quiet."

"I guess I'm not so sure about all this. I mean, what if talking it through does bring his memory back? What if he remembers helping Sarah die? Are we sure that's the kind of stuff we want to dig through?"

"You know him better than I do, Matt. He's your friend. You always spoke so highly of him. I never met him until our wedding."

"So what are you getting at?"

"Just that if you're such good friends, don't you think helping him through this, no matter how painful, is what you should do?"

Matt remained quiet for a few moments. "I guess so. I guess so," he repeated. "It's been so long, really. Maybe things have changed. Maybe Jake has changed, I mean."

"Maybe you've changed."

Matt assumed a confused expression. Linda explained, "Maybe you're afraid your feelings toward Jake will be different if you find out he's as guilty as the media has speculated. Do you think your friendship could handle that?"

Matt was silent. Finally he got up from the table and cleared the dishes. "We'll just have to see," he eventually replied. "We'll just have to see."

◆ ◆ ◆

If Sarah carried one obsession throughout her cancer treatment, it was the safety of her unborn child. It was as if the idea of hurting the baby somehow magnified the remorse she felt about her abortion. She became, Jake recalled, completely intolerant of even hearing about therapies that might have side effects for the baby. As a result, her cancer went untreated and, because of her high estrogen level during the pregnancy, spread at an alarming rate.

Some would not agree that her cancer went untreated. More accurately, she refused all conventional therapies. Jake tried to remember the first time she talked about accepting treatment.

Jake looked at his wife as she dressed. He could see that the skin over the left breast was beginning to redden. He held his tongue. They had talked about it so many times, he knew he needed to be silent.

"I saw the obstetrician today," Sarah reported, slipping on her blouse. "He says the baby is doing fine."

Her denial was only too sad. Jake sighed. He couldn't resist trying again. "Honey, I spoke to the oncologist today. He—"

"Jake, stop," she interrupted. "I've made up my mind about this. No surgery. No radiation. No chemotherapy. When the baby's born, I'll take all the treatment they can dish out."

Jake shook his head. "Sarah, you might be dead!"

"Look . . . God gave me this baby, and I'm going to protect it. That's my job." She looked at her husband. "I know this is hard on you, and I know you love me, but you've got to understand . . . I failed my first baby,

Jake. I'm not going to fail this one." She paused. "If it makes you feel any better, I asked the obstetrician about speeding up the baby's maturity with steroids. That way, maybe I can be induced early and have the baby at seven and a half or eight months without harming him or her. Then I can get on with my treatment."

Jake raised his eyebrows. "What did he say?"

"He said it sounded promising."

"That's a start," Jake mumbled under his breath.

Sarah went over to a stack of magazines on the dresser. "Jake, what would you think if I checked this out?" She handed him a flyer on the Ocean Sands Wellness Facility. "It's located about an hour from here. It says here that they specialize in cancer prevention and treatment without medicine."

Jake read the pamphlet and remained silent.

"Listen to what the director says . . ." Standing beside him, she read from the caption of a color photograph. "'We at Ocean Sands augment the body's own ability to fight cancer cells by proper nutrition and detoxification.'"

"Sarah, this stuff is a bunch of—"

"He's board-certified, Jake. It says so right here!" she interrupted.

"That doesn't mean anything—"

"Then why did you pursue it so passionately?"

"That's different. Besides. there's no proof that any—"

Sarah grabbed the flyer from his hand and turned it over. "Look at this . . . Testimonials of cancer patients who were cured at their facility."

"Sarah, that's just—"

She began to cry. "I simply want to get well, Jake." She slumped onto the bed. "I just can't do it your way." She looked at him, her eyes pleading. "Can't you see that?"

"Honey, you can't expect me to endorse something like this. It's . . . it's—"

"It's worth a try," she added, completing the sentence for him. "It can't hurt."

"Sarah . . ." He didn't know what else to say.

Jake looked at his wife. She needed treatment.

She was starting to cry again. She used to be so happy.

The cancer had changed everything.

CHAPTER
7

Raining glass, bricks, drywall, and dust filled the air. Screaming voices pierced the midday traffic noise. Confusion ruled. Frank stumbled to his feet and wiped off his clothes. Blood flowed from the laceration above his left eye. He saw the girl with the auburn hair lying a few feet away. She wasn't moving. Frank looked closer. Yes, she was breathing. She moaned, and he looked away. Two men jumped from the back of a pickup truck that had been stopped at the traffic light in front of the clinic.

"Are you OK?" A stocky man in blue jeans seemed winded.

Frank responded, "Just a little cut." He pointed at the girl. "She needs some help."

The other man looked at Frank. "Here," he said. "Hold this over your eye." He handed Frank a white cloth.

Just then a woman struggled through the front window of the clinic. "Somebody call 9-1-1!" Another woman could be heard screaming repetitively, "Ginny! Ginny! Ginny!" "Help us!" someone else shouted.

The front door pushed open. Two women in dirty white uniforms appeared.

The whole scene blurred as Frank squinted from beneath the makeshift bandage held against his eye. The dust began clearing as a siren wailed in the distance. Additional help arrived from the shopping center next door.

Frank slipped away to his brother's Camaro, parked a block to the north. He pulled out just as the first of numerous police vehicles arrived at the scene.

Instead of driving away, he wanted to stick around and watch them bring out the bodies. He wanted to see the doctor who had killed his child—now dead in retribution for his evil act. He drove back in front of the clinic and stopped. No one was in charge. He could see the girl with the auburn hair. She was standing now, crying, and holding her arm. "Sorry," Frank whispered, then smiled. "I kind of saved your life, didn't I?"

Overall he felt euphoric. It had been so easy. Just like at the quarry. Shortly the first ambulance arrived. *Maybe now they'll bring out the victims*. He waited a minute longer, then pulled away. *I suppose I'd better move along*, Frank reasoned. *It might take hours to find them all*. He laughed.

He was hungry. He hadn't eaten before because he was so nervous. He looked at himself in the rearview mirror and decided against stopping at McDonald's. When he got to Taylorville, he went to the hospital emergency room. He told them he'd cut his eye at the quarry, though he was still wearing his dress clothes. They made quick work of suturing up his wound.

It wasn't until Frank was leaving that the Taylorville Hospital was notified about the explosion in nearby Grantsville. The E.R. was placed on alert for possible overflow casualties. That's when a suspicious nurse grabbed Frank Grimsted's chart and called the quarry. Her suspicions were correct: they hadn't had an accident that morning. In fact, Frank Grimsted hadn't even shown up for work. She called the police.

Twenty minutes later, as Frank ate a peanut butter and jelly sandwich, a strong knock announced visitors. He naively opened the door to face two city police officers.

"Mr. Frank Grimsted?"

Frank nodded. Busted!

In another ten minutes they led him to the back of the patrol car. He looked at the sun. He wouldn't see it again as a free man for more than fifteen years.

◆ ◆ ◆

Frank felt obligated to go over the memory of the bombing in detail. He wouldn't make the same mistakes again. He got up from his bed and put on his clothes. He wanted to be out early, to learn Jake Hampton's weekend routine. He slipped on his army coat and stuffed a day-old donut and a Zero bar in his pocket.

The light was just beginning to break when Frank settled into position behind a tall hedgerow beside Jake's house. Jake lived on the end of a cul-de-sac, so no one could see Frank from this position. He, however, had a view of Jake's bedroom window and of the front door. He settled down, peered between the scratchy bush branches, and unwrapped a Zero bar.

A minute later Jake's bedroom light came on. Frank checked his watch and recorded the time on a page of notebook paper. Six minutes later he entered another time as Jake appeared to get the morning paper. A full hour later, just as Frank thought the numbness in his backside might be permanent, he made his last entry for the morning as Jake left the house with a sleepy child in tow.

After Jake's Trooper sped out of view, Frank stood and brushed himself off. His pants were damp from the morning dew. He stretched for a moment and waited until the feeling returned to his tingling feet. Then he went to Jake's mailbox and stuffed the crinkled Zero bar wrapper into it. "There," Frank mumbled. "Just to let you know I've been watching."

Slowly he sauntered back up the road, trekked out of the neighborhood, and walked onto Main Street. He stopped at the 7-Eleven store and bought coffee, not speaking to the talkative cashier. He went to McDonald's and picked up his paycheck, then went on to the bank. Finally he went back to the jail to rest until he could check his mail back at his apartment. He checked his watch. Neal wouldn't get his mail for another hour. Then he'd have thirty minutes to get his before Ms. Thomson left for work. That should be enough time, even with the extra precautions he needed to take to detect a possible mail-bomb.

◆　◆　◆

Jake stood nervously at his friend's front door. He was alone. Kyle was spending the day with his grandmother. After a knock, Jake heard footfalls inside. The door swung open, and Matt Stone smiled.

"Jake."

"Hi, Matt. Long time no see."

"Too long," Matt said, giving his friend a bear hug. "Too long."

He looked at Linda. Matt continued, "Jake, you remember Linda."

"Hi, Jake. Good to have you here." Linda smiled.

"We'd been trying to pin down exactly how long it's been," Matt commented.

"The last time I saw you, you were leaving the church on your wedding day."

"Has it really been that long?"

Jake nodded. Matt took his coat. "Have a seat."

The three friends caught up on old times, commiserated about surgical training, and laughed. Before lunch Matt took Jake for a tour of Crestview Women's and Children's Health Center where Matt worked. After lunch, the trio converged on the little front room to talk.

The Stone baby was frisky today, and Linda was feeling a new kick every few minutes. "Oooh." She looked at Matt. He raised his eyebrows in a question. "Another soccer game, that's all."

Matt came over and placed his hand on his wife's abdomen. "Wow." Jake smiled.

Matt looked at Linda. "This is wild. Mind if Jake feels this?"

Linda rolled her eyes. "I'm getting used to it."

Jake joined the two already gathered around the recliner chair. In a moment he too felt a strong kick. Jake suddenly paled and looked away. He withdrew his hand as a flash of memory flooded over him. His eyes filled with terror, and he was far, far away.

Matt looked at his friend. "Jake?"

Jake paused for a moment longer before speaking. "Oh man . . . I just had my first memory of Sarah's death. I remember putting my hand on her swollen abdomen to feel our baby just as she died. The baby was quite active for a moment or two after . . . after Sarah was gone. I guess he wasn't getting oxygen, and he struggled for a moment before . . ." His voice choked. ". . . before he died."

"Can you remember anything else?"

Jake closed his eyes and strained. He waited. Finally, he shook his head. "Not a thing," he stated flatly. "Not a thing." He sighed in defeat.

He walked over to the couch and sat down. "It's always the same. I remember only going to see her . . . and then nothing. Nothing until I woke up with a headache the next day. It surprised me when the nurses told me she was gone." He looked at his friends. "By the time a policeman came to talk with me, I knew what he was going to say. The surprise was being charged with helping her die."

Matt and Linda nodded. What could they say?

Jake continued, "At first they said I must have murdered her. Then later they accused me of physician-assisted suicide and said I'd tried to kill myself too." He shook his head. "In the end, it didn't seem like they had enough evidence to make any charges stick . . . so it all got dropped."

"So there's been no relief from your own search?" Linda inquired thoughtfully.

"Not much. I try to get lost in my work or in working things out for Kyle." He paused. "But this is always cooking on the back burner. I can't escape it." He sighed heavily. "I have to know. Even if I did it, I have to know."

"Is it possible, Jake?" Matt asked. "I mean, you and I used to talk about these things. I remember that you were definitely against physician-assisted death."

"The police knew I was too. But they thought this story was different—they'd figured I'd been hardened by seeing my wife suffer so much."

"Some people would say such a step wouldn't be so bad, Jake," Linda stated, doubting the validity of the argument she was suggesting. "Some would even see your motivation as love." Such an idea disturbed Linda, especially after all she had done to speak out for life on the abortion issue. She was just trying to help Jake to consider all the angles and find the truth about his wife's death.

Jake froze. Linda's words brought an angry knot to the pit of his stomach. He shook his head. "I—I just don't buy that suggestion. It has a ring of humanitarian concern to it, but I don't think I could ever really believe it."

"Do you feel guilty for what happened, Jake?" Matt queried with obvious concern.

"Yes." He nodded slowly.

"Even if you don't know whether it's true? You've already passed sentence on yourself." Matt paced the living room. "Why not reserve judgment until your memory returns?"

"The guilt isn't just for her death, Matt. It's complicated, but . . . I feel guilty for not picking up on the cancer myself." His eyes were on the floor in front of him. "I'm her husband. I'm a surgeon. I should have known."

"How could you have detected what Sarah didn't recognize herself?" Linda interjected. "She was a smart woman, Jake."

"But I'm a doctor. I should—"

"It was *her* body, Jake! No one could have known it more intimately!" Linda surprised Jake with her forcefulness. "How did you find out?" she asked more softly.

"She didn't tell me until after she had seen her obstetrician and a surgeon, one of my partners. Of course, at that point she let me examine her. I was worried right away. I should have been able to feel it. I should have picked it up sooner."

Matt shook his head. "You were her husband, Jake, not her doctor. When you touched her, you were her lover, not her examiner. There's a difference." He paused. Jake was still staring at the floor. "You've already mentioned that she was able to hide it from you until she had time to see two physicians. That's because it wasn't your job to examine her. You weren't her doctor."

Jake nodded. "Maybe you're right . . ."

"Besides, none of us is perfect. Give yourself a break." Matt stopped pacing.

"It's called forgiveness, Jake. God's not standing over you with a club. He loves you. It seems to me that you need to forgive yourself for not knowing about the cancer," Linda added.

"I know you're right. I've just been so obsessed by this whole thing . . ."

"Would you be open to praying together about this?" Matt put his hand on Jake's shoulder.

"Sure."

"Let's do it."

And that's just what they did.

◆　◆　◆

Later that afternoon, with his mind refreshed, Jake headed down curvy Route 31 toward Taylorville. He didn't feel like rushing, and he continued his review of Sarah's fight, searching for a glimpse of light that would bring resolution to his thinking.

◆ ◆ ◆

"I can't believe I'm doing this," Jake continued, looking at his wife.

"Believe it, Dr. Hampton." Sarah smiled. "It's not like it will contaminate your reputation just to look at the facility."

Ocean Sands Wellness Facility. It sounded more like a resort than a hospital. "That's because it is," Jake would argue later. Over forty acres of prime ocean frontage, three buildings, a perimeter of grass with the quality of any groomed golf course, surrounded by a massive stucco wall that housed the facility's secretive interior from anyone on the outside. The only way in was by invitation, through the guarded gate at the facility's main entrance. To walk in by way of the beach was cumbersome because of two canals bordering the north and south edges of the property, isolating the hospital on a tongue of warm, sandy soil. At extreme low tide, Jake learned, one could skip across the salty puddles left by the receding ocean and enter the grounds from the south. It was the only way in, other than the gate, unless you came by boat.

Jake drove up under a covered entrance. He followed the instructions on a small sign. From the outside, there was no indication they were in the right place. He spoke clearly into an aluminum grid after pushing the red button. "Hello?"

"How may I help you?" The voice came from the same grid.

"I'm Jake Hampton. My wife Sarah and I are here for a tour. She called and spoke to your receptionist."

"Ah, yes, Dr. Hampton. Good to have you here. Drive straight ahead. The gate will open."

He followed instructions again. A video camera mounted in a palm tree on Jake's left recorded the whole thing. They drove the Isuzu Trooper into the lush grounds. Grass, flowering bushes, and palms abounded. "I wonder how they get everything to grow so well this far north?"

In a few moments they were joined by a parking host and surrendered their vehicle to the valet service. Then they met Ms. Tucker, their tour guide, a former patient of the facility.

"So glad to have you with us." She extended a tanned hand.

Sarah smiled and looked around. "This doesn't look like a hospital—"

"Exactly. Most hospital environments promote illness. We prefer wellness."

Jake responded, "I didn't even see a sign. I wasn't sure we were at the right place. If it weren't for the instructions—"

"Exactly," Ms. Tucker interrupted again. "Security is very important to our facility. The nature of many of our techniques makes us the object of much skepticism, Dr. Hampton. Certainly you can appreciate the need for the utmost privacy for our patients?"

Jake and Sarah nodded. Ms. Tucker continued, "Some of our patients are well-known. They prefer the added benefit of anonymity."

"Of course." Jake nodded again.

She gave them a forty-five minute tour, then accepted a folder of Sarah's medical records from Jake. "Dr. D will review these. If he feels you are an acceptable candidate, we will be in touch."

"Can I talk to the medical director?"

"I'm sorry, Dr. Hampton, but he isn't in today. He has another busy private practice that prevents him from being here full-time." She paused. "A pity really. He enjoys his work here so much and has so much to offer."

"I see," Jake mumbled.

"I know he is looking into getting additional help. He's currently interviewing a world-renowned cardiothoracic surgeon for heart consultations. I can't really say more, except to say that we are really fortunate to have a visionary like Dr. D to lead us."

"So our next step is to just go home and wait?" Sarah asked.

"I'm afraid so, Mrs. Hampton. It won't be a long wait, though. Dr. D usually comes by quite late. He'll make a decision in a day or two. Then we'll call."

With that, she extended her hand again, signaling an end to their tour/interview. Jake and Sarah left, Jake full of skepticism over unproven techniques, Sarah full of hope that something might yet give her a fighting chance.

◆ ◆ ◆

"It's about time," Simons whispered under his breath. Then, loudly enough for the other phone party to hear, "Thanks, George. I'll have a full cardiothoracic pump team assembled for practice runs within a week. I've had a great team on standby for three months now."

Simons talked briefly with George Latner, M.D., an associate in Valley

Surgeons for Children, associated with Crestview Women's and Children's Health Center. They had just gotten full clearance from Crestview, and the heart program was a go. Now Simons needed to assemble a team so he could start the new pediatric cardiothoracic surgery service. Crestview already stood out as the best regional hospital to receive non-cardiac surgery and obstetrical and pediatric care. Now, with Simons's expertise, pediatric heart surgical care would be elevated to a whole new level.

The surgeon sighed. It had been a long six months. First a regional certificate of need by the state, then application for state licensure, then hospital privileges . . . His mind turned again to Matt Stone. *You couldn't stop me this time, could you, Stone?* Simons smiled. It would be good to get his hands back into the O.R. He smiled faintly. *Even if I might have to cross paths with my old buddy.* He laughed out loud. It was good to be back.

CHAPTER
8

FRANK looked around the cold room and scuffed his tennis shoes on the floor. He remembered the first time he sat in this very cell. It was the night of the bombing. His body was imprisoned, but his spirit was free. He had sought righteous vengeance, and he had been successful! They put him in this holding room until they could firm up the case against him, which didn't take them long. They rounded up Ray, his foreman, who did a quick inventory of the dynamite stock. "Yes, there is some missing," he reported. A search of Frank's home netted more convicting evidence: fuses and a pamphlet on the clinic he'd bombed. The final blow was the personal testimony of the girl with the auburn hair. Her identification linked Frank to the scene of the crime.

◆　◆　◆

"Line up." The deputy's words were stern.

Frank filed in along with five other men of similar build and age.

The lights were shining brightly. A window in the back of the room appeared to be a mirror. "Turn to your left . . . OK, turn back to the right."

In the back of the room, Stephanie Gardner bit her trembling lip. Her sister, Rachel, had been killed in the bomb blast. She twisted her auburn hair with her fingertips. She was only seventeen. "That's him. The third from the left."

The detective looked back at the sergeant. "OK."

"Tell 'em to file out," the sergeant barked, pressing on an intercom. He released the switch. "He's our man."

"Grimsted."

"Grimsted," the sergeant repeated. "Must be some kind of religious nut."

"I'd like to find this guy in a dark alley. What a punk!" the detective sneered.

◆ ◆ ◆

The deputy pushed Frank into a small holding room. The room was small but smelled of body odor and urine. Other than a small cot, the room's only other item was a sticky commode in the corner. "Enjoy yourself."

"Hey, I'm hungry!"

"Breakfast is at 8."

"What about supper? I haven't had anything to eat since noon."

"Hard of hearing? Breakfast is at 8."

Frank sulked on the cot, cursing audibly. After a moment he laid down. In another ten minutes he forgot about his empty stomach and concentrated on his victory. By midnight he was euphoric, convinced he would be forgiven because of the righteous retribution he had executed. He couldn't sing, and he didn't know half the words, but he tried anyway—"I'm so glad Jesus set me free! I'm so glad Jesus set me free!"

By morning he was hoarse and tired. He fell asleep just before breakfast was served.

◆ ◆ ◆

Frank smiled at the memory. He knew he had acted correctly. At least he had done what the voices had instructed. He wondered why the voices stayed quiet for so long. But now, with his new dosage, the voices were back, and with more volume than before. *Maybe it's all according to a great cosmic plan*, Frank thought as he prepared his simple supper. *After all, who would ever have imagined that Jake Hampton would come back here to Taylorville—to me—after all this time.* He had been fixated on the Hamptons for so long that Jake's move convinced him even more of the doctor's ill intentions toward him. And the more he studied it all, the more he understood what his role was to be. *That's what the doctor keeps telling me, right? That I'm supposed to listen to discover my role?* "Listen and understand the circumstances around you, Frank. When a job is made for you, you'll know it right here." He remembered the physician putting his hand on his chest. "When the situation is made clear, you should act on your impulses." Wasn't that what he'd been told?

He smiled again and put a can of pork and beans on a small electric burner. After a few minutes he ate in silence, straight from the can. He had dishes back at his apartment, but getting them here wasn't easy, especially when he had to make all the trips in the dark. Plus there was always the concern about a bomb in his building. All that made trips to his house something to be avoided except when absolutely necessary. When he finished the beans, he unwrapped another Zero bar. He allowed himself two a day. It was his favorite, ever since Sarah introduced him to them.

His watch alarm sounded, signaling the end of his supper and telling him it was time to search for a new bathroom. As he walked away, he wondered again at his fortune—Jake Hampton within striking distance after all these years. His stomach churned at the thought. *Who will strike first, Jake? Who will strike first?*

◆ ◆ ◆

A week later Dr. Simons found himself "back in the saddle again." With his team assembled, he began. "Knife." It was not a request. He wouldn't say please.

The instrument was gently placed in his fingers. He glided the blade over the skin and easily parted the flesh beneath. He spread the soft tissue above and below the sternum, to free up the bone. "Saw." The blade deftly parted the breastbone into equal halves.

"Pickups . . . scissors . . . stitch . . . stitch." His fingers blurred as he tied a knot. "Pursestring . . . scissors." As he spoke, his scrub nurse placed each instrument in his outstretched palm. "Cannula." He slid the cannula into the superior vena cava and tied a pursestring suture around it to hold it secure. "Aortic cannula." He repeated the maneuver on the patient's aorta.

"Venous lines to you." He spoke in the direction of his pump tech, the woman operating the cardiopulmonary bypass machine that would pump and oxygenate the blood during cardiac arrest so the delicate surgery could be accomplished. He unclamped the line leading from the patient's heart. "We're on bypass."

"On bypass, 10:22," the technician called out mechanically.

The patient, a two-year-old beagle, served as a teaching aide to help the team get oriented to their tasks before opening the new heart program to humans.

After an hour, the team had created and patched an atrial septal defect (a hole between the top two chambers of the heart) and created a shunt between the pulmonary artery and the subclavian artery. All in an hour. All for practice. In the end the patient was carried out in a plastic bag.

"Good work, team." Simons took off his gloves. "A little rusty for our first pump run, but we'll be there in another week." He looked at the pump technician, Susan Bellamy. "Nicely done."

He walked down the hall into the doctors' changing room. He had forgotten just how much he loved the O.R. This was definitely his forté.

Matt Stone was just taking off his white coat, preparing for a hernia repair. His eyes met Simons's. It was their first contact since Matt's residency. "Hi, Dr. Simons."

Simons nodded.

"I heard you might be coming on board." Matt stepped toward the older surgeon and held out his hand.

Simons ignored it.

Matt shuffled his feet and closed his hand into a fist at his side. "Crestview can use a good cardiothoracic surgeon. It's good to have you aboard."

Michael Simons sneered. "How long will you be around?"

"Another month anyway. Linda, my wife, is due to have a baby almost anytime. After that, we'll look for a more permanent position."

"Interesting."

Matt didn't know what else to say. Simons was pure ice.

"Dr. Stone?" a female voice called from the doorway. "We're ready for you in O.R. 6."

Relieved, Matt looked at Simons before stepping away. "See you around."

The meeting was awkward at best, unpleasant at worst. Matt shrugged off the bad vibes. *What can he do to me now?* Matt asked himself. *I'm not his resident anymore.*

He shook his head and walked into O.R. 6.

◆ ◆ ◆

As Jake remembered it, Sarah never had a negative word to say about Ocean Sands. From the moment she received her acceptance letter, she started feeling stronger. It was the greatest placebo effect he could remember.

The weather was warm when the letter came. It was a Saturday. Sarah had been waiting for the mailman all morning.

"It's here!" Sarah waved the letter and walked toward the house. She tore the letter open, with Jake looking on. She scanned the letter and smiled, then handed it to her husband.

Jake was the first to speak. "The director didn't even sign it."

"Yes, but it says he reviewed my case. He thinks they can help me."

Jake shook his head. "Look, Sarah, the first trimester will be over soon. Surgery during the second trimester isn't very risky—"

"Jake Hampton, let me do this my way!" Sarah was uncharacteristically firm. "None of your colleagues will guarantee me anything when it comes to our baby. At least the Ocean Sands facility understands my feelings about that!"

He could see the futility of arguing with her. He could only sit back and watch. At a minimum he maintained a hope that she would make it to delivery and then accept some legitimate treatment. The trouble was, he wasn't sure *he* could make it that long. He moaned and then asked with a sigh, "When do they want you?"

"Monday."

"Great."

"Can you take me?" Sarah sounded a bit sheepish after her strong statement a moment before.

Jake sighed again. "Why not?" He looked at his wife. She seemed slimmer than he ever remembered. "Do I get a choice?"

"I could take a cab."

"Never mind. I'll take you." He shook his head again. "I can get Denny to cover for me for a half day. That way maybe I can meet this mysterious Dr. D."

Sarah nodded. She wanted to meet him too.

◆ ◆ ◆

Kyle squirmed in his seat. Dr. Willie chuckled. Carefully he wrote out the prescription. "You're a big boy for your father to let you come back here all by yourself."

The redheaded young man smiled. "I've been going to doctor visits without my parents ever since Mom died."

Willie nodded thoughtfully. "I want you to start taking these pills— one small tablet twice a day. We'll work our way up to three times a day."

"Will they make me smarter?"

"You are already too smart." The doctor winked. "Smarter than me anyway. These pills will help you concentrate." He looked at his young patient eye to eye. He knelt on one knee and held the boy by the shoulders. "Do you understand what that means?"

"Help me pay attention?"

"Exactly."

"Pay attention, huh? Dad always says I'm too poor to pay anything."

"Your dad is joking, Kyle."

"I know."

Dr. Willie handed his young patient the prescription. "One pill twice a day. Got it?"

"Two pills once a day. Got it!" Kyle said with a smirk.

"I'll get you!"

Kyle opened the exam door. His father was waiting.

Dr. Dansford looked at Jake. "I'm starting the Ritalin. We'll start low. Only five milligrams twice a day. Then we'll slowly go up, watching for things like insomnia or loss of appetite."

"Gotcha." Jake turned to go. "Thanks. It's never easy being on this side of the stethoscope. I wasn't good at it with Sarah, and I doubt I'm much better with this character," he added, rubbing Kyle's thick wavy hair. "Thanks for making it as easy as you have."

"Glad to do it."

"See you in the morning."

"Say, Jake, I was thinkin' of taking off a few days next week. Can you cover my patients on Thursday and Friday?"

"Sure, Willie. I'd be glad too. Your patients might all hold their breath till you come back though."

Willie laughed.

Kyle tugged on Jake's coat. "Let's go!"

"Where are we going to eat?"

"McDonald's!"

"OK, but next time I'm choosing." Jake headed for the exit after winking at Dr. Willie. "Thanks again."

The older doctor waved. "Get out of here, you two."

◆ ◆ ◆

At Bridgewater University Medical Center, a radiologist, Dr. Tom Beale, picked up a videotape from a stack entitled "O.B. review." The tapes had already been interpreted by an obstetrician and forwarded to the Radiology Department for confirmation. He looked at the front of the tape: "Fetal ultrasound. Linda Stone, baby, confirmation of dates." He popped the tape into the V.C.R., then watched as the head, hands, fingers, and toes were scanned. The perineum was next. *A little boy. Can't miss that one.*

The abdomen and chest were next. The technician had turned on the doppler probe—a color probe. Flow away from the transducer was red; flow toward the transducer showed up on the screen as blue. When he looked at the heart, something caught his eye. "Hmmm," he whispered. "We need a better view of this." He frequently talked to himself while he read films. He picked up the Dictaphone. "Dictation. Fetal ultrasound. Baby of Linda Stone. Indications: confirmation of dates. Code as written. New paragraph. Sonographic views of the fetus confirm date approximately thirty-eight weeks gestation. Spine, upper and lower extremities, head and abdomen appear normal. Normal amount amniotic fluid. Genitalia is masculine. There is some concern for a ventricular septal defect as seen by a shunt between the ventricles. A formal cardiac ultrasound for confirmation is recommended. Copy of this to Dr. Kramer. End." He thought for a moment and then added, "Also send a copy of this report to Dr. Lucille Morra, pediatric cardiologist. Thanks."

Dr. Beale set the handset down again. He read the obstetrician's interpretation: "Normal." "I hope I'm wrong about this one," he whispered to himself. "I hope I'm wrong."

He ejected the tape and started the process over again with the next tape in the stack.

◆ ◆ ◆

After dinner at McDonald's, where unknown to them they ate burgers thirty-one and thirty-two of Frank's evening shift, the duo headed home.

Kyle looked at his father. "Thanks for dinner."

"Sorry I don't cook as much as Mom did. Maybe when you get older you can learn with me."

"I can make scrambled eggs," Kyle added. "Mom used to let me make 'em on Saturdays."

Jake pulled into the driveway and stopped at the mailbox. He pulled out the mail—and a crinkled Zero wrapper. "Kyle, did you put this in here?"

Kyle wrinkled his nose. "No."

"Listen to me, Kyle, this is important. This is the second one of these I've found in the mailbox." He squinted at his son, trying to read his mind. "You're not joking with me, are you?"

"Why would I joke?"

"Maybe you think I wouldn't like you eating candy—I don't know." Suddenly Jake felt foolish for doubting his son. He shook his head. "It's just kind of weird—I'm starting to find these all over." He paused and slipped the Trooper into gear. "They were Mom's favorite."

"I know," Kyle responded. "She used to give them to me in my lunch."

"Oh." Jake nodded. He was still learning about the thousand little things Sarah did that made her so special.

"Why would someone put Zero bar wrappers in our mailbox?"

"I don't know, son."

Kyle got a funny look on his face and became silent. When Jake stopped and took off his seat belt, Kyle didn't move. Jake looked at his son curiously. "What are you thinking?"

"Maybe it's Mom."

"Maybe what's Mom?"

"Maybe Mom is trying to contact us . . . give us a sign that she's OK . . . that she still eats Zero bars in heaven or something."

"I don't think so, sport. Besides, you know Mommy is OK. She's in heaven with Jesus. We talked all about that before, remember?"

"How do you know it's not her? You said yourself that they're her favorite!" Kyle hopped out of the vehicle.

"Kyle, people who have died don't try to communicate with us like that."

The boy wasn't satisfied. "I saw it in a movie once."

"Great. Now the movies have more influence over you than I do." Jake chuckled.

Kyle wasn't laughing. "I still say it could be a sign."

His father shook his head. "Come on in, sport. You need to finish your homework, plus tonight is bath night." They walked together into the house.

Kyle groaned and skipped off to do his homework. Jake sat down with the mail: two bills, some pizza coupons, and a letter from the Pin Oak Society. *Hmmm,* Jake wondered, *what could these guys want with me?* The Pin Oak Society had lobbied heavily for right-to-death legislation to be introduced on the state ballot last November, Jake remembered. He read the letter with mixed interest. *Great!* Jake huffed. *They want me to speak at their next fund-raising dinner!* He reread part of the letter.

We are aware of your fight for cancer patients' rights to die in a chosen and dignified manner. Your public struggle with your wife's assisted suicide is a touching story that would interest our supporters . . .

"This is ridiculous!" He spoke out loud even though no one was in the room with him. "They seem to have me all figured out . . . as if I helped Sarah die!" The veins stood out on the sides of his temples. "I can't believe this!" He threw the letter aside.

"How can everyone else know what happened that night when I can't remember myself?"

Kyle walked in. "Who are you talking to, Dad?"

Jake spun around. "Uh, no one, Kyle." He was obviously startled. "I was just spoutin' off, that's all." He paused.

Kyle looked at him like he was infectious.

"Get your homework done, OK?"

"Sure."

Jake slumped into his easy chair. He shook his head. He hadn't had any more restored memories since his deja vu experience when feeling Linda Stone's baby kicking.

He closed his eyes and began to review. There was something about the Ocean Sands Wellness Facility that just didn't set right with him. More than just the exotic alternative natural therapies. But just what, he couldn't quite put his finger on. *Maybe it's just because that's where Sarah died,* he speculated. No, it was more than that. *Didn't I feel that way before?* Jake, struggling to remember, pulled out his yellow legal pad. Somewhere, sometime something had to give.

CHAPTER
9

ON the day Sarah's therapy started, Jake left with a sour taste in his mouth. And it wasn't just the green drink sample Sarah's nurse had given him. It was the attitude that if he wasn't going to think positively about the program, he wasn't welcome there. The administrator told him, rather forcibly, that if Sarah was to benefit from the program at all, she must be surrounded by support mentally, physically, and spiritually. She must not be allowed to be in the presence of negative emotions or thoughts. Such negative forces would prevent her from benefiting from the positive energy that flowed throughout the complex. In fact, the Ocean Sands staff reserved the right to censor all visitors who might detract from the positive energy force. How else could they be responsible for Sarah's healing? "And right now," the administrator had insisted, "you are exhibiting a negative attitude. I'll kindly ask you to leave."

Jake looked at Sarah.

Sarah looked back at Jake, her eyes pleading. "Please, Jake, this place is my only hope," she stated flatly. "You promised."

Jake looked away and sighed. He kissed her and then looked sternly at the administrator, who returned the glare.

"Bye, Jake."

"I'll see you in a week."

"Come with a positive attitude," the administrator warned. "The changes should be obvious by the end of one week."

With that, she nodded at Sarah. "Come with me. We have a lot to accomplish today." Sarah followed obediently, casting a glance over her shoulder at Jake, still standing in the lobby. Sarah offered a timid wave and passed out of sight down a long corridor.

Jake walked to the reception desk. "I would like to see the medical director."

"Sorry, Mr. Hampton, Dr. D doesn't come on Mondays. I can make an appointment for you later this week if you'd like to discuss your wife's progress."

"Don't bother," he said with a sigh. "I have to work. And it's *Dr.* Hampton." He turned to face the front entrance. "Thanks anyway."

Sarah went down a hallway and up the stairs. She would have a room on the second floor. Her room assignment would be the same on each of her subsequent visits. The attendant in her room was dressed in basic clinical white.

The attendant showed her a daily schedule. "Here's what's in store. Your nurse will be around shortly to check you in." The young lady smiled. "Enjoy your stay."

Sarah wrinkled her brow. "Do you know how long I'll be here?"

"Most folks' first visit is twenty-one days. More for some, less for others. Your nurse will fill you in on the details." With that, the attendant was gone.

Sarah looked around the room. She was drawn to the balcony and pushed open the door. The salty air greeted her. What a view! *Jake was right*, she thought. *It does seem more like a resort.* She was leaning on the railing when her nurse came in.

"Ms. Hampton?"

"Hi." Sarah offered her hand.

"I'm Susan Rolan. I'll be your nurse during the day shift." She held a clipboard and a lengthy set of questions. "I need to complete your initial assessment before your treatment begins."

"When will I see the doctor?"

"Probably not until the day after tomorrow. He usually comes late in the day."

Sarah nodded.

"We keep him informed. He already knows your history from the papers we received from your gynecologist."

"Oh."

"I'll need to ask you a ton of questions. You should sit down and be comfortable."

For the next hour the nurse took a detailed history. Everything was covered, right down to eating practices, cooking habits, exercise history, family history, drug use, childhood medical history, menstrual history, personality profile, attitudes toward health and wellness, and even a detailed bowel history. Sarah was relieved when it was finally over. She was convinced that they were thorough, if nothing else.

Next, they went through the daily schedule. She was to be initiated into the detoxification plan, a vigorous attempt to rid her body of the toxic buildup from which she undoubtedly suffered. She would be on a juice fast with high-colonic irrigations four times a day, along with twice-daily coffee enemas.

"For starters, we need to get your colon clean. Then we'll introduce the first coffee enema to help stimulate your sluggish liver and gallbladder into action. It's the liver's job to detoxify us. We are just helping the body get back to the way it was intended to function."

"Coffee? As in caffeine?" Sarah squinted.

"Exactly," Susan replied.

"But I'm pregnant. I've been avoiding all caffeine."

"We won't let you drink it either," she explained. "This is different. It's to help stimulate the liver." She spoke slowly and distinctly, as if repeating the information might make some sense of it all.

Sarah nodded.

"I'll help you the first few times. Then you'll get the hang of it and will be able to do most of the colonic irrigation therapies yourself."

Sarah wrinkled her nose. The idea of giving herself an enema didn't excite her.

"You'll get used to it. You'll feel so clean. When you see what comes out, you'll understand the necessity of it all." She opened the top drawer of an oak dresser. "Here," she said, handing Sarah a pair of cotton sweats. "Put these on. I'll be back to help with your first irrigation in a moment."

She looked at the sweats. On the pocket were the words, "Ocean Sands," above a small embroidered ocean wave. Very artistic and tasteful.

Five minutes later Susan arrived with a large plastic container and a series of rubber tubes. "Come in here," she said, motioning toward the large bathroom. "It's time to get started."

◆ ◆ ◆

Frank lay still on the stained mattress. When he was quiet, he could hear the voices better. He was beginning to understand. He knew the time to act was drawing closer. But something held him back. Things were not quite ready. He must be careful. Fate could strike him at any moment.

Things were comfortable for Frank here. Not like in the hospital. He tried to remember back. He could still remember being taken to the state institution. They had a special place for violent offenders. They considered him violent because of the bomb. He thought that was odd. He was only doing what God had commanded. He was merely a tool of revenge. If people live their lives as they should, they have nothing to fear.

The day he left was cold. He had made friends in the jail. The deputies even joked with him after a while. The only one he didn't like was the chaplain. He acted like he pitied Frank. He didn't want to be pitied. He didn't mind the jail. In fact, he wanted to stay there. He had heard bad things about the state hospital. He feared he would starve if the food was as bad as others said.

His lawyer had arranged it all. He said Frank was insane, hearing voices, hearing divine proclamations. *Well then, Moses and Jesus were crazy too*, Frank postulated. *I'm just a tool.*

The court-appointed psychiatrist said Frank was schizophrenic, but that his paranoia was the only thing characteristic of his diagnosis. It seems that Frank had definite mental pathology that the doctors couldn't easily fit into one diagnosis. They asked for another opinion, and more assessments were tossed around. The prosecution hired their own physicians, but they couldn't agree. The only thing they all agreed on was that Frank wasn't fit to stand trial. "He is certifiably crazy," his lawyer stated flatly to the media and to anyone else who suggested he be held accountable for his crime.

It became clear that he wouldn't serve jail time beyond however long it took them to secure a locked room in the state mental hospital.

The day he was taken to the state hospital, Frank cried. He remembered because his tears nearly froze on his cheeks as he passed through the prison yard on the way to the van. He didn't *feel* sick. He wanted to stay. Yes, he'd committed crimes. But he felt they were justifiable crimes. He only killed the one who had killed his child. The voice demanded an eye for an eye, and Frank had merely obeyed.

His father was there when he arrived at the hospital. It was a rare show of concern, one of a handful of times that Frank recalled when his dad actually showed some interest in his son's well-being. It would be one of the last times Frank saw him.

"Can you take off the leg-irons? He won't run away." Larry Grimsted looked at his son with shame.

"When the hospital docs sign him in, we'll take off the restraints," the deputy responded. "Policy."

Frank kept his eyes on the ground in front of him. He didn't want his father to be upset. After a few minutes the magic signatures were obtained, and the deputy unlocked the leg-irons. Frank was free . . . sort of. He looked around the lobby of his new home. Actually it would be the last time he saw the lobby for another sixteen months. For the orientation and for the majority of his "treatment," he would be confined to a locked ward.

Larry grabbed his son's arm. "They said they can help you, son."

"I know what I did. I don't need their help."

A psychiatric attendant stepped forward. "Mr. Grimsted," he said, speaking to Frank's father, "we really didn't expect you today. We need some time to get Frank adjusted. We have visiting hours on weekends and on Thursday afternoons."

Frank kept his eyes on the floor. Larry released his arm.

Frank looked at him and spoke only two more words during his father's brief visit. "Bye, Dad."

Larry Grimsted walked away, shaking his head. He felt like a failure. He had allowed his son to fall into wickedness, and now it looked like Frank had reaped what he'd sown. Larry looked back once as they led his son down a long corridor. At the end the large door into the locked ward squeaked eerily and then slammed shut and emitted an electronic note— the ominous sounds of a newcomer being let onto the ward.

As they led Frank to his room, he watched the people he would get to know over the next months and some over the next few years. They stared at him with hollow eyes—some with the blankness that comes with overmedication, some with the paranoia that comes with the necessity of analyzing everything everyday.

"You must be Frank!" The squeaky voice of a wan, male teenager spoke. "I read about you, man." The boy spit on the floor after he spoke and was quickly reprimanded by an attendant.

"Richard!"

"Fresh boy. Fresh meat!" The deep voice came from a darkened patient room next to the one they had assigned to Frank.

Frank looked worried.

"Don't worry 'bout that," the attendant cautioned. "He talks like that to everyone."

Frank looked at the bed and the small desk in his room. The door couldn't be locked from the inside. Again he liked the jail a lot better.

He always would.

◆ ◆ ◆

Frank shut out the memory. It was time to eat. He had to work tonight anyway. Maybe he could just go early and cook burgers number one and two for himself tonight.

◆ ◆ ◆

Linda Stone was delighted that her bed rest restrictions had been lifted. She spent the afternoon running errands. She went to the Post Office and then to the grocery store. When she arrived home, she noticed how tired she was. As she opened the door, the phone was ringing.

"Hello, Stones' residence."

"Hello. Linda?"

"Yes."

"Dr. Kramer here. I've been trying to reach you. I'm glad to catch you at home."

Linda's countenance stiffened. "Is something wrong?"

"I don't think so. We just need you to come back for another ultrasound. There is something we need to check further."

Linda wanted specifics. "What do you mean, something you need to check?"

"Well, it could be nothing," Dr. Kramer stated vaguely. "I looked at the ultrasound myself and saw nothing but a healthy baby."

"Then what's the problem?"

"No problem, really. It's just that the radiologist reviewing the film thinks we need to look more closely at the baby's heart with a special ultrasound—maybe even get the pediatric cardiologist to come by and look at it."

"Pediatric cardiologist?" Linda's stomach felt queasy. "My baby has a heart problem?"

"Not for sure, Linda. We just need to run another test. He's probably overcalling it just to be safe. Like I said, I didn't see anything—"

"When can we do this?"

"Can you come by tomorrow at 2? I can have the pediatric cardiologist here to review the video."

"I'll come over now if we can do it today."

"There's no need to rush. Remember, this baby's not even born yet. If they did find something, we probably wouldn't need to do anything right away."

His words did little to comfort her.

"OK." Linda sat down. "Where do I go?"

"Go to the main radiology reception desk. Check in by 1:45 P.M. I'll see you there."

"OK," Linda mumbled.

Click.

She actually felt far from "OK." She just didn't know what else to say. It wasn't like anything had definitely changed, but the news had swung her mood from high to low in a matter of seconds. Linda paced the floor for a moment as the plans for a romantic dinner for two evaporated. She definitely didn't feel like cooking.

She felt very tired. She looked at the clock. Two P.M. *Matt will be in the O.R. until at least 4,* she figured. *Maybe I'll feel like cooking if I take a nap.* She walked into the bedroom and lay down on the bed. Instinctively she placed her hand over her lower abdomen. When she felt the kicks, she began to cry. "Be well, little one. Be well," she wished aloud. She closed her eyes and tried not to think about the situation and what it might mean. She just wanted the test to be over so she would know. She looked at the clock again. She'd have to wait twenty-four hours. It would seem like an eternity. She had to know. She just had to.

◆ ◆ ◆

Sharon Isaacs looked at the progress report on Kyle Hampton. Solid improvement in three categories. "Chalk another one up to Dr. Willie," she whispered, even though she was alone. "And me," she added with a smile.

She pushed the folder aside but kept staring at it on and off all afternoon. Her mind kept wandering back to Kyle's father. *I wonder what he meant about Kyle's mother's death being quite a media event around here. Is he just referring to his own prominent standing in the community? He doesn't seem the arrogant surgeon stereotype. He seems . . . well, nice.* She tried hopelessly to focus on another child, another problem, but her mind kept returning to Jake Hampton.

Was he disappointed when he saw my father kiss me good-bye? She thought she had detected a slight look of concern. *He tried to hide it, but wasn't he relieved when I told him that was my dad?*

She smiled, then cautioned herself. Part of the reason she'd come this far east was to escape the feelings of a broken engagement. She couldn't allow herself to hope . . . Not yet.

She looked at the clock. She thought the teachers looked forward to the three o'clock bell as much, if not more than, the kids. Knowing she only had a few minutes, she packed her briefcase and straightened her desk. She liked to stand in the hallway after the final bell. It gave her a chance to say good-bye to her favorite students, and her presence always helped calm the rowdies. When she got to the door, she surrendered to her impulses, returned to the desk, and opened Kyle's folder one more time. She copied his home phone number and slid it into her briefcase. *Never know when I might need a doctor*, she justified. She grabbed her case just as the final bell unleashed the elementary masses.

Kids swirled around her, walking fast, wanting to run. Loud voices, footsteps, locker-slams, laughter, and squeals were followed quickly by an odd quiet as the halls emptied as quickly as they had filled.

She walked slowly to her car, a ten-year-old Honda Accord. She freed her brown hair from a ponytail as she walked. Shaking it out, she mentally cast off the day. It was a practice she'd tried for a decade, without much success. No matter how hard she tried, the kids' problems always ended up at home with her—in her heart and in her prayers. That was the kind of person she was made to be.

On the way home, she stopped at the Taylorville YMCA. It was the one luxury she allowed herself on her starting salary. In California she had eight years' experience going for her. Here in Taylorville she had to start at ground zero. Some of her friends called her crazy. Sometimes she wondered if they were right. But it was her life, right? And she had prayed about this, hadn't she? She reminded herself of that fact every time she was tempted to pack up and head west again. She just couldn't. A still small voice had spoken. She had followed the peaceful leading of the Holy Spirit, hadn't she? Whenever she questioned her move, she waited to sense whether the peace was still there. She paused at the door of the Y. Yes, she assured herself, the peace was still there. God had led her here for a reason, though just what it was, she wasn't sure. She sighed. *I'm sure if I stay here long enough, I'll find out.*

Right now, it was time for a swim. After twenty laps in the pool, she would think about Jake again.

CHAPTER
10

"Here's your morning cleansing regimen." The nurse smiled as she handed two small vials to Sarah.

Sarah, who never considered herself much of a breakfast person, wrinkled her nose. "What is it?"

"Olive oil and grapefruit juice," the nurse stated as if everyone was certainly aware of the health benefits to be gained from such a combination.

Sarah wiped her eyes and looked at the nurse suspiciously. "You've got to be kidding. How about one of those fruit punches I saw the patients drinking down by the oxygen pool?"

"Sorry. They're here for a different reason. Come on," she encouraged. "I do this myself." She patted Sarah on the shoulder patronizingly. "Drink this, and then I'll need you to lie on your left side for twenty minutes with your right knee drawn up to your chest. This will open your gallbladder passageway and allow for the dissolution of the thick bile and gallstones by the olive oil and grapefruit juice."

The sleepy cancer patient nodded. It would take her a few days to be convinced of the benefits of the unusual drink.

She swallowed the contents of the two small glasses with a shudder. "Ugh!"

"OK, on your side now." The nurse grabbed Sarah's right leg under the knee. "Like this. That's good." She walked to the door. "Stay on your side like that for twenty minutes. I'll be back to check on you. This will help clear your liver of the toxins."

Sarah nodded lamely.

"A liver can't be expected to fight cancer if it's as clogged as the colon."

"Sure."

"Breakfast and your first colonic after this." The energetic nurse bounded out of the room.

Breakfast? Sarah questioned. *I wonder what constitutes breakfast on a juice fast?*

Sarah lay still for the required time. An Olympic-sized cramp was creeping into her hip just as the nurse returned.

"You can straighten out now," she said, placing an eight-ounce glass of green liquid on the table. "Why don't you go to the bathroom, then drink this while I prepare for your first high-colonic enema irrigation of the morning?"

Sarah looked at her incredulously. How could anyone be so cheery about an enema?

She looked at the drink. "What is this?"

"Breakfast. It's a mixture of barley and wheat grasses, kelp, and distilled water. You get to drink this four times a day."

"Kelp? That's seaweed, isn't it?" Sarah wrinkled her nose again.

"You'll get used to it." The nurse looked at Sarah with compassion. "Look, they've written you up for a strict, no-holds-barred type of fight here. Working together, we are going to beat that cancer! But it is imperative that you get detoxified so your immune system can begin functioning normally."

Sarah nodded as if she understood. "I guess I really don't have a choice."

The nurse didn't hear her anyway. She was already in Sarah's bathroom preparing the colonic irrigation.

Sarah gagged down the green drink. "Oh, God, help me," she prayed with more urgency than in a very long time.

◆ ◆ ◆

Willie smiled when he saw the name of the next patient on the chart in the door-rack. Bob Rivers, Taylorville's mayor. Willie knew him as a friend, golf partner, and political ally. He grabbed the chart and headed into the room. "What's up, Bob?"

"Hi, doc." He reached out his hand and flashed a thousand-dollar smile.

"How are you?"

"I couldn't be much better, Willie." He smiled, then looked at the floor. "But of course I wouldn't be here if I didn't have a little problem." He grabbed his lower abdomen. "I think I have a hernia. I tried to stack a load of wood yesterday, and I felt something give way. Lizzie says I've got a hernia for sure."

"One way to tell," Willie stated with a professional air. "Let's take a look."

The mayor lowered his pants. Willie did the exam. "Turn your head and cough."

Bob Rivers cooperated.

"Uh-huh."

"What's uh-huh?"

"Uh-huh, you have a hernia."

Willie asked a stream of questions about other symptoms and his overall health status.

"OK, Willie, I give—what's all this mean? Do I need surgery?"

"Sure, you do. And I know just the man for the job."

The mayor eyed his friend suspiciously but didn't speak.

"Jake Hampton."

"Now wait a minute, Willie. I came in here to see you, and I don't want to go under unless you're on the other end of the knife!"

The doctor shook his head. "You wait a minute, Bob. This is exactly what Dr. Hampton has been trained to do. It's right up his alley. He's the one with the board certification in surgery, not me."

"I don't care about any piece of paper, Willie. I know your reputation around here."

Willie shook his head again. "You pull a lot of weight in this town, Bob. A case like yours could be just what Jake needs."

"So that's what this is about—"

"Look," Willie said firmly, interrupting him, "I brought Jake to this town because he needed a new job, a new start . . ." His voice trailed off. He looked at his friend's blue eyes. "The truth is, if I can't sell him on this practice, I'm shot. I'm getting old and a little tired. I'm getting desperate to find someone to sell to. No one's biting, Bob. I've had this practice up for sale for over five years. I just can't compete with all the big managed-care jobs these guys are snatching up. No one wants to go to the Taylorvilles anymore. Everyone wants big money." He paused and lowered his voice. "Look, friend, I'm asking this as a favor to me. I wouldn't ask you to do it if I thought he wasn't qualified. He's a good kid. He's a qualified surgeon. If the town sees that you trust him, well, then . . . maybe they'll trust him, too. Maybe then he'll stay and buy me out."

"Come on, Willie, we're talking about my health here. You can't believe this kid's your only chance on retirement."

"How long's it been since we played golf at Templeton Greens together? Nearly eight years as I remember it. I met Dr. Nevins there. He was the first to come and look, and the first to decline my offer to buy."

"Has it been that long?"

"Afraid so, my friend." He looked up. "Will you do it? It's only a hernia, Bob. What can go wrong?"

Bob sighed. "I'll think about it."

Willie smiled. "Just call and I'll make you an appointment to see him. I'm sure he'd be honored." He extended his hand. "Thanks."

The mayor huffed but didn't refuse. "Sure," he said with a sigh, putting on his pants.

◆ ◆ ◆

Frank was on break again. He'd cooked twenty-two quarter pounders and fifty-one regular patties and had fried thirteen fish sandwiches. He didn't like the thirteen part. He would fry a few more by the end of his shift just so his totals wouldn't include the number thirteen. *You can never be too careful about these things,* he remembered as he headed to the bathroom. He locked himself in the stall and dry-swallowed his medication. His doctor had lessened his medication again. Maybe he was finally getting better. He could only hope.

When he was again in front of the mirror, he stared at his pale complexion. *I need more sun.* His mind stumbled as he looked at his reflection. His tongue explored the missing space in the middle of his front teeth. He remembered losing the tooth at Central State Hospital during the shock therapies.

◆ ◆ ◆

"Where's the anesthesia resident?" Dr. Dave Foley, the chief resident in psychiatry at Central State, was obviously ticked. He looked at his watch again.

It was difficult getting an anesthesia resident to the state mental facility, impossible to get the attending. They were needed on Monday, Wednesday, and Friday mornings for the electric shock therapy. More and more often, the anesthesia residents found excuses not to go. They hated the place. It was a scary place at worst, an inconvenience at best.

"Has anyone called the U? They should be here by now if they are going to grace us with their presence," Dr. Foley said as he flexed his fist. "I'm not going to wait much longer."

The psychiatric intern, Jim Maley, eyed his superior suspiciously. "What do you think we should do? Call Dr. Eagle and tell him it's off?"

"Not on your life. I need his recommendation for my psychiatric fellowship. What's he going to think if I can't line up a few successful shock therapies?"

"It's not our fault the anesthesia guys don't want to be here. You should see 'em the first time they come into this place. They walk around more like zombies than do our frontal lobotomy patients. They're scared."

"Who's on this morning's list?"

"Just Frank and Mrs. Leno."

"Hmmm." The chief resident scratched his brown beard. "Do we have the drugs?"

"Sure, but—"

"Get them. I've seen 'em push this stuff a thousand times. Let's get started." He looked around. "Where's Frank?"

A large African-American attendant pushed Frank Grimsted forward in a wheelchair. Since coming to Central State eight months before, Frank had become more and more despondent. He didn't fit the typical schizophrenic diagnosis. Now, because of his depression symptoms, the psychiatrist had concluded he was "schizoaffective." The shock therapies were given every two or three days. He had been given six. They planned six more.

Frank looked at Dr. Foley. "Not again. I don't want this again."

"Got to do it, Frank. You don't have a choice."

"I don't want it!"

"Start the IV," Dave ordered the intern.

Jim Maley looked back with eyes that said, "All right!"

They wrestled Frank to a stretcher. "Hold your arm still, Frank. We need to start the IV."

Frank held still for a moment, then jerked when the intern stuck him with the needle.

"Ow!"

"Hold his arm down!" Dave shouted at the attendant.

The intern made fast work of securing the IV. "There."

"Give him some Valium. Make him sleepy."

"No!"

The intern shoved the syringe into the IV and injected the sedative.

In a few minutes Frank was sleeping.

They placed electrodes on both sides of his forehead to supply the shock. An EKG monitor was attached via three chest leads, and a nurse wrapped a blood pressure cuff around Frank's ankle. They would blow up the cuff to keep the paralyzing agent from reaching the foot. That way, the only part of the body to twitch during the electric shock would be Frank's foot. The rest of him would be paralyzed and thus unable to seize. A nurse would watch the foot and time the seizure to be sure the shock was adequate.

Once they were all ready, Dr. Foley put an oxygen mask over Frank's face. He then drew up two medications—a muscle relaxant (a paralyzing agent) and a short-acting barbiturate (to keep the patient asleep). After injecting the barbiturate, he spoke to the nurse. "Blow up the blood pressure cuff."

The nurse responded and inflated the cuff on Frank's right ankle.

The intern stuffed some rolled gauze into Frank's mouth. Although he would be paralyzed, his jaw would still clamp down because of direct stimulation of the muscles by the electric shock.

"Give the succinylcholine now."

"How much?"

"The anesthesia guy always just gives a few cc's."

The intern shrugged and obeyed.

The chief resident looked at the monitors. "All clear." The team stepped away from the stretcher. Dr. Foley adjusted the pulse width, duration, and voltage, then pressed a second button to activate the shock. "Time."

The nurse recorded the time. "Nine forty-one."

Foley watched the instruments. "Here he goes."

Frank's jaw began tightening down. His arms began to twitch. In another second, his whole body began to tighten. He had stopped breathing.

The intern's eyes widened.

"How much did you give him?" Dr. Foley shouted at the intern.

Frank's torso contorted into a tight bend. He looked like he would bend over double.

"Just what you told me!"

"He hasn't had enough paralyzing agent! Grab him! The clonic phase of the seizure is about to start—"

Dr. Foley's words were interrupted by the onset of a violent thrashing of arms and legs. Frank's arms rebounded off the stretcher rails, and he bloodied the nurse's nose with a sharp kick. The gauze between his teeth tumbled to the floor. Frank clenched his teeth tighter and tighter as the electric stimulus produced a grand mal style seizure pattern.

Frank helplessly bit through his tongue. Defenseless against the seizure, he clenched his teeth again, fracturing his right front incisor. Blood sprayed from the socket of his broken tooth.

Foley cursed. The attendant rode Frank like a rodeo horse. After thirty long seconds, it was all over. Frank was bleeding from the mouth, and his left arm hung at an awkward angle. The EKG leads were detached and twisted.

The intern looked at his chief resident. "Is he alive?"

"Of course he's alive, stupid!" Foley scoffed.

"He's not breathing."

Dr. Foley slid his fingers to the side of Frank's trachea. He still had a pulse. "Bag him until the Pentothal wears off. He'll start breathing on his own in a few minutes. He always has before."

The intern snapped, "The anesthesiologist has always been here before!"

"Just bag him." Foley's eyes could have cut a hole in the younger intern. "When he wakes up, send him over to the university E.R. Tell them he fell down the stairs and cut his tongue." He looked at Frank's arm. "Better have this X-rayed."

With that, the chief resident headed for the door. When he reached the treatment room door, he called back to the nurse, "Cancel the next appointment, Alice. Tell Dr. Eagle I refused to let the anesthesiology resident continue after what he did to Frank." He winked.

The nurse remained silent.

The intern started to sob.

Frank took a breath. At least he was going to be OK.

◆ ◆ ◆

The memory made Frank shudder. Without thinking about it, he rubbed an old fracture site on his left arm. He looked at his watch. Break was almost over. Time to fry some more fish patties.

◆ ◆ ◆

Linda was silent for the entire trip to Bridgewater University Medical Center.

Matt drove across the Nickel Bridge, named for an old toll. Finally Linda broke the silence. "What if the radiologist is right?"

"And?"

"And our baby has this . . . this VSD or whatever." Linda made a face to make fun of the medical term.

"A ventricular septal defect, from what I've read, can even close on its own. It doesn't necessarily mean surgery."

Linda rode on in silence for another minute before speaking. "I just pray that they're wrong." She rubbed her tummy. "The baby acts so healthy. It doesn't seem possible that something could be wrong."

"Let's pray so." Matt turned toward Bridgewater University. The medical complex was located just north of the main campus. He parked in a parking deck and opened the door for Linda. He asked her about a medical student they knew who attended Bridgewater University. "Have you told Mary Jacobs about this?"

"No. I was hoping there would be nothing to tell."

"Right." Matt felt for his wife's hand and walked toward the medical complex. "Just think, the next time I bring you here might be the big day."

Linda nodded. She had been so excited about that prospect in the past. Now her anxiety over the baby's health had crowded her excitement onto a back burner.

They took the elevator and found the Radiology Department. There Linda signed the registry and sat down to wait. In a few minutes a technician called her name. "Linda Stone?"

Linda and Matt stood together.

"Come this way."

They entered an exam room. Linda was given a flimsy patient gown. The tech. pointed to a curtain. "Please remove your top. You can change over there."

Linda slipped behind the curtain to change. In a minute she came out, wearing the light beige gown. "Is it me?" She held up her hands and attempted to cover her nervousness with humor.

Matt smiled. "It's you."

"Ms. Stone, please lie down on this stretcher." The technician patted her hand on the thinly padded bed. Linda obeyed. "I'm going to get started. Dr. Kramer ought to be here any minute." She spread the cold slime onto Linda's abdomen. "A little cool gel here," the tech reported mechanically.

As she began to scan, Matt whispered a prayer. "Make it OK, God." Then he paused. "Help us to accept your way."

Two minutes later Dr. Kramer arrived with a breathless pediatric cardiologist in tow. The doctor, a female who appeared about fifty, had eyes that seemed to sparkle, even in the dimly lit procedure room. "Hi, Linda. This is Dr. Lucille Morra. She's a children's heart specialist. I wanted her to look to see if everything is OK."

The tech. immediately surrendered the probe to Dr. Morra, who skillfully and gently guided it across Linda's slick abdomen.

"Hello, baby." Dr. Morra talked as she would to any of her infant patients. "We need to see your heart." She scanned for a minute. "You're such a good, baby, yes, you are. Look at your fingers. Look at your smile," the cardiologist continued. "Such a nice baby."

Dr. Morra's voice calmed Linda. She enjoyed looking at the screen, seeing her baby.

"Here's your heart." Dr. Morra looked at the tech. "Turn on the doppler please."

The rhythmic swishing sound of the heartbeat drowned out Dr. Morra's chatter.

She raised her voice. "Here's the right ventricle. Here's the left." She studied carefully and looked at Dr. Kramer. "VSDs are hard to see before birth, because the pulmonary vascular resistance is so high that nothing much crosses the shunt." She continued focusing on the screen. "Ooh, here it is."

Dr. Kramer squinted.

Linda held her breath.

Matt stared at Dr. Morra.

Dr. Morra studied the screen and for the first time remained silent.

"There . . . With the color probe doppler, it's clearer now," Dr. Kramer announced.

Dr. Morra nodded. "Dr. Beale was right."

Linda bit her lip.

Matt spoke first. "Now what?"

Dr. Morra looked at Matt. "The baby won't have any trouble while it's in utero. After birth, babies with VSDs can be asymptomatic or very symptomatic, depending on how big the shunt is. We'll just have to wait and see."

Linda frowned. Dr. Morra continued, "Most of these are very treatable, Mrs. Stone. It's not often that we pick one of these up before birth."

"Can't you just fix it?" Linda asked.

"Not now. The baby gets all the oxygen it needs straight from your bloodstream. After birth we'll monitor the baby to see how serious it is."

Linda didn't seem satisfied, so Dr. Morra continued, "If the baby needs surgery, it's not usually right away. Some babies have VSDs that close on their own."

Matt looked at the pediatric cardiologist. "From what I understand, if you wait too long to operate, the pulmonary vascular resistance will rise and make a successful operation impossible."

Dr. Morra's eyes widened. Dr. Kramer explained, "Matt's a surgeon. He's been doing his reading."

Dr. Morra smiled. "Of course, but we'll monitor the baby closely, so that's not likely to happen." Matt nodded. She continued, "But you're right. We don't want to wait too long or the pulmonary vascular resistance can rise to a level where successful surgery is not a possibility."

Matt gripped Linda's hand. "So we just have to wait and see."

Lucille Morra nodded. "I'm afraid so. There's nothing else to do at this point." She looked at Dr. Kramer. "So when's this one due?"

"Anytime." He smiled.

"I'd be glad to come to the delivery. That way if there are any problems, I'll be right on it."

"Thanks, Lucille."

Linda swallowed hard. Nothing to do but wait, she thought. A perfect time for faith.

◆ ◆ ◆

Later that evening Jake joined Willie and some of his friends for poker. The atmosphere was casual. As he came in Willie's front door, the older doctor made introductions. "Jake, this is Ed Lakeford. He lives across the street. He's an attorney with Lakeford and Lakeford, so you know he doesn't like to bluff." Willie laughed at his own joke. He looked at Ed. "Ed, this is Jake Hampton. He's the young cuss that's buying my practice." He winked at Jake. "Jake, this is Ned Upton. You've probably seen him around the hospital. He runs the Medical Records Department."

Jake shook their hands. "Nice to meet you."

Ned smiled. "We wanted someone named Fred to take Larry's place, but I'm sure you'll do fine."

Ed shook his head as it started to sink in. "Ned, Ed, and Fred. Very funny." He looked at Jake. "You sure you know what you're doing? Willie Dansford can lie through his teeth. You'd better run while you can, son."

Jake didn't back down. "Right."

The four men trudged to a downstairs den and closed the door. "Here," Willie said, passing out the cigars. "It's kind of a tradition. None of us smoke except on poker nights, once a month."

"Let's see," Ned counted, "that means we've smoked about three hundred of those horrible stogies in this very room."

Jake didn't smile and held up his hand. "No thanks." He coughed nervously and shifted in his seat.

"Come on, Jake." Willie chided. "One's not gonna hurt."

"I don't think so." *You're serious about this. You really smoke these things?*

"Suit yourself."

Ed laughed. "He'll be smoking in a minute whether he wants to or not," he added, blowing a thin stream of smoke into the air.

Jake eye the trio pensively. It was only too obvious that these men had played together for a long time. He was starting to wonder whether this had been such a good idea. *Oh, well,* he thought, *I've been wanting to be a bit more friendly with Willie. He's sure done enough for me.* He watched Willie light his cigar. *Do I really know you?*

The atmosphere quickly thickened. Curls of blue smoke filled the air above a card table situated in front of a burning fire. Willie dealt.

Ned groaned.

Ed flashed a thin smile.

Willie was silent.

Jake made it obvious he was a novice as he took his time sorting his cards.

Ed opened the bids by throwing two red chips on the table. Ned eyed him. "I'll call," he said slowly, tossing in an identical bid.

Willie tossed in his chips without speaking. Jake did the same.

"How long you been in town, Jake?" Ned asked.

"Just over six weeks now."

Ned nodded. Ed threw two cards on the table. "I'll need two."

"I'll take one."

"I'll take two."

"Three for me," Jake added.

Ned looked at Ed, trying to read his mind and come up with a winning strategy.

Willie passed out the new cards. "Jake's working out real well. For a while there I thought I would never be able to quit."

Jake shrugged. "It's been a slow start."

Ed threw two more red chips on the table.

Ned folded.

"It will just take some time." Willie said. "I fold."

Jake tossed two more chips in the ante.

Ed added a chip to the pile and squinted. "What's gonna take time?"

Jake looked at Willie. He wasn't sure how much to tell these new acquaintances. Willie chuckled. "He's just experiencing a little of the

Taylorville shutout. They're afraid of the new doctor until he proves himself. That's all."

Jake threw one more chip on the table.

Ed folded. Jake opened his hand. He had a pair of twos and a pair of aces.

"Two pairs!" Ned scoffed as he looked at the three threes in his own hand.

Jake pulled the chips into his corner and looked at Willie. "Deal?"

Willie dealt another hand, then cracked the top of an aluminum beer can. After all, he wasn't the on-call doctor. Ned and Ed did the same.

Jake eyed them with growing anxiety. *Great. First cigars, now this. What have I gotten myself into?*

They played fifteen more hands. Ned won three, Ed won two, Willie took four, and Jake won six.

"Beginner's luck." Willie smiled thinly.

"If it was only so good on the job."

"Stop worrying, Jake. I'm telling you, this town will warm up." Willie looked at him squarely.

By now Ed was growing irritated from losing so much to Jake. He slurped his third beer. "Maybe it has something to do with all the rumors going 'round, Willie."

Willie cast him a concerned glance and ignored the comment.

Jake looked at Ed. "What rumors?"

"About your wife." He glared at Jake. "Is it true?"

Jake looked at Willie. Willie looked back at Jake. "Give him a few beers, and he just spouts off. Ignore him."

"Is what true?"

"Did you help your wife commit suicide?" Ed cast a glance at Willie and defended his question. "Hey, we're all friends. You know we talk about anything here. Nothing hidden. Nothing's off-limits."

Ned chuckled. "Except your first wife."

Jake looked uncomfortable.

Willie glared back at Ed. "Ease up, Ed! You hardly know Jake. He's a good kid. He had good reasons for whatever he did."

Jake stood. "Is that what you think? That I helped my wife die?" He dropped his cards on the table. "And that's the end of it? That maybe it was the right thing to do . . . that it's OK as long as I had a good reason?"

Willie softened his voice. "Look, Jake, I'm sorry he brought it up. It doesn't matter to me. I don't really care what went on."

Ned tried to make light of the tension. "I wanted to kill my first wife," he said casually. "Even bought a shiny new shotgun for the occasion."

Ed raised his voice. "Come on, Ned. Be serious."

"Let's play cards," Willie offered.

Jake shook his head. They had definitely touched a nerve. "Look, Ed, thanks for your honesty, but I can't really answer your question."

"You don't have to, Jake," Willie urged. "It doesn't matter."

"But it does matter," Jake insisted. "It matters to me." He walked over to a walnut bookshelf. "I don't really know," he confessed. "I still can't remember how she died."

Willie looked alarmed. *Interesting.* "You really can't remember?"

Jake tapped his head. "Nothing here. Not yet."

"So you just assumed the accusations were true?" Willie probed.

"Not entirely. There's something crooked about the hospital she was treated in."

Willie raised his eyebrows. "What do you mean? You can't believe the hospital had something to do with her death?"

"I—I don't really know," Jake stuttered. "I've said too much. Maybe I'd better get on home."

Willie thought he'd better let it drop. He looked at Ned and Ed. "What about you guys?"

"I guess I'll go back to my Gloria."

"I'd best take off too."

Willie studied the younger doctor. *He really doesn't remember! I can tell he feels guilty about it. I've never seen him react so strongly before.* He didn't speak as Jake stacked the cards. He watched in silence as Jake repackaged the game. *If this town will accept him,* Willie mused, *maybe his guilty conscience will obligate him to buy me out after all and stay right here where I want him.*

CHAPTER
11

ON Sunday morning it was Sharon Isaacs who sat in the back and strained her head to see who was sitting beside Jake Hampton. *It's just his mom*, she concluded and tried to concentrate on the sermon. A few minutes later she watched his head nod and snap upright again. Jake rubbed the back of his neck. *He must be tired*, Sharon observed. *Maybe he was out late doing surgery. That must be exciting.* After a few more minutes she heard the shrill call of his pager. He leaned over, whispered something to his mother, and slipped out. She caught his eye just for a moment as he was leaving. She smiled. *Did he smile back? Did he see me? I think so. Pay attention, Sharon*, she scolded herself. *The preacher's almost finished.*

Jake never returned to the service. Sharon talked to Kyle, who explained that his dad had to go to the emergency room.

"Can you join us for dinner?" Phyllis Hampton grasped Sharon's hand. "You're new in town, and I've been meaning to ask."

"Well, I—" Sharon was taken aback. "Sure." She smiled at Kyle. "As long as it's all right with Kyle."

"We're just having stew. I'm too old for fancy entertaining." Phyllis took Sharon's arm. "Help me get through this crowd, and you can follow us home."

◆　◆　◆

Jake looked at the stately gentleman on the E.R. stretcher—Bob Rivers, mayor of Taylorville. "How long have you known about this hernia?"

"Only for a couple of weeks. I saw Willie in the office just the other day. He confirmed my fears."

"When did it get tender?"

"Started last night. I was unloading my golf clubs. I think the hernia has been stuck out ever since."

"Any vomiting?"

"Twice, early this morning."

"Mind if I take a look?" Jake pulled up the patient gown and gently palpated the man's abdomen. A tender bulge protruded. "Have you tried pushing it back?"

The mayor frowned. "Tried. Hurts too much."

Jake pushed gently. No movement. "We'll need to fix this."

"Now?"

"Afraid so, mayor. There's a chance your intestine is caught in the hernia. If we wait, the intestine could die."

"Willie warned me about that."

Jake thought he would make a suggestion before Mayor Rivers did. "Do you want me to call Dr. Willie?"

The patient sighed in disgust. "No. Just fix me up, boy. I guess if Willie can trust you, so can I."

Jake nodded. "I'll call in a team."

Forty-five minutes later Bob Rivers, mayor of Taylorville, put his trust in Dr. Jake Hampton.

With adequate anesthesia underway, Jake thought about an old prayer. *God, as much as is possible, in your sovereignty, use my hands as instruments of healing.* It was a prayer Jake had whispered hundreds of times since his internship back at Taft University.

He entered the O.R. with his hands dripping. The nurse handed him a sterile towel to dry himself. He then put on a sterile gown and gloves and placed sterile drapes around the border of the patient's exposed abdomen.

Jake glided the knife over the skin of the right groin. The hernia was tense and contained a knuckle of small intestine. It was deeply cyanotic—the tight neck of the hernia sac had cut off the blood flow to that segment of bowel. Jake looked up at the scrub nurse assistant. "We're going to have to do a small bowel resection. This segment of intestine has had it."

"Get me the bowel instruments," the scrub nurse barked at the circulating nurse.

"I'll need a G.I.A.," Jake said, referring to a special instrument designed for cutting the intestine and stapling the ends closed in one action.

"G.I.A.," the nurse echoed.

The circulator brought in the needed supplies. Jake made quick work of removing a short segment of intestine and repairing the mayor's hernia.

"Closin' music." Jake smiled. The circulator turned on a C.D. of Twila Paris.

He worked for seven more minutes, then stood back and asked for the bandage. "House dressing please." He walked to the door. "Thanks a bunch, everybody." He looked at the anesthesiologist. "Thanks, Craig. I'll have the chart with me in the recovery room."

When he finally arrived at his mother's house to pick up Kyle, Sharon Isaacs had just left.

◆ ◆ ◆

George Latner pushed the large stack of papers to the center of his desk. It might take him all weekend to clean off his desk, but he was determined to do it. Since losing his senior partner and founder of Valley Surgeons for Children, the paperwork was the one thing George found easiest to postpone. The problem was, it kept piling up and seemed to cry out for attention louder and louder each time he passed his burdened desk.

"I guess I can get one of the clerks to file this away," he muttered to himself as he picked up an application folder on Michael Simons. The folder was thick, and a few papers dropped to the floor as he threw the file into his Out box. George muttered a curse and bent over to pick up the papers. One of them, a recommendation letter, had come from an unlikely source: Matt Stone. As the only surgeon around who had worked with Simons firsthand, George had asked him to write down his thoughts. What Stone wrote was lengthy, detailing a conflict that arose between the two surgeons during Stone's residency. Stone disagreed with Simons's personal ethical stand on the issue of research using aborted fetal tissue. But when it came to an analysis of Simons's surgical skills, Stone had nothing but praise for his old adversary. "If even his enemies hold him in this kind of respect, we can overlook his past problems with questionable research ethics," Latner had told his partner, Mark Davis.

George quickly shoved the letter back into Simons's file. "Let's hope Matt Stone was right about this guy. I can use some help around here," George muttered.

It was Stone's letter, in fact, that clinched Simons's new position. This, of course, was unknown both to Matt Stone and Michael Simons. If Simons had known, it would have saved him a mountain of misery.

◆ ◆ ◆

George Latner wasn't the only one catching up on paperwork. Dr. D reviewed the file in front of him: Sarah Hampton, breast cancer, dead at age thirty-five. *Everything seems in order here*, he concluded. He checked the med sheets and IV records. *Good, no record of the chemotherapy, no record of any narcotic use*. He closed the file and opened a walnut case behind him. He found what he wanted and poured himself a small glass of the spirited liquid. As he sipped, he thought back to the days before Sarah Hampton's death. *Come to think of it*, he thought, *we haven't gotten any recent letters from Jake either. And if ol' Frank is predictable, I won't ever have to worry about Jake keeping people away from Ocean Sands. We're just getting started, after all. A few more months like the ones we've been having, and I won't have to keep up my family practice at all*. He chuckled to himself and filed Sarah's chart. *When did I first see her anyway?*

◆ ◆ ◆

"Sarah . . ." The nurse, Susan Rolan, nudged her gently. "Wake up, honey. Dr. D is here today. I'll take you to him so he can examine you."

Sarah squinted at the sunshine as the nurse opened the drapes. "Oooh. I was dreaming about my baby. I dreamed I had a little girl."

"Do you have any kids now?"

"One boy—Kyle. He's a handful too."

"Why don't you wear your sweats?" Susan put them on a wicker chair in the corner. "I'll be back in a few minutes to take you up to Dr. D's."

Sarah dressed and went to the bathroom. This was the first morning she wasn't greeted with the olive oil/grapefruit therapy. *Maybe my gall-bladder has been sufficiently cleansed*, she speculated hopefully.

Unfortunately, Susan arrived two minutes later with the olive oil and grapefruit juices. "Let's just put these here until you return. You won't have time to properly position yourself after the juices, to assist your gallbladder drainage."

Sarah nodded. "I had hoped I might be done with that."

"You'll be doing this every morning." Susan smiled. "I do it myself. Nothing like it, you know?" She watched Sarah brushing her hair. It seemed like a lot was coming out in the brush. "Come on. I'm sure you'll love Dr. D."

She led her patient to a small exam area just off the main building's lobby—right next to Dr. D's office, Sarah thought.

An older physician came in smiling. He had white hair and looked about thirty to forty pounds overweight. Not exactly the proper picture of wellness, Sarah mused.

Dr. D. was pleasant and thorough. As he examined her, Sarah watched his face. His brow wrinkled. *He's worried.* The thought was not comforting.

The director sighed. He could see that the cancer was spreading to the axillary lymph nodes. She had a suspicious lump under her arm, in addition to erythema or reddening of the skin over the breast cancer. He tried not to frown, but he felt the perspiration on his hands and forehead. *Her cancer is out of control. It must be hormonally sensitive and growing rapidly due to her pregnancy*, he reasoned silently. *She needs an abortion!*

He tried to approach the subject gently. "Mrs. Hampton, your cancer is acting aggressively. I'm afraid it is responding to the high levels of estrogen in your body due to the pregnancy. Have you thought of the possibility of ending the pregnancy to improve your chances of cure?"

Sarah stiffened. "I will not have an abortion, if that's what you mean. That's why I'm here. I didn't want any conventional therapy that might do harm to my baby."

Dr. D pursed his lips and nodded his head without speaking. *She expects this clinic to come through in an impossible situation.* He looked over her record again. His eyes stopped on the information he saw there. *Her husband's a surgeon. Great! That's all I need!* He sighed again. *Ocean Sands*

Wellness Facility is fighting to take patients away from conventional medical physicians, and now, thanks to a patient who will certainly die of her illness, I may not be able to avoid proving that they're right and we're wrong. This case could be a lightning rod that brings disaster down on our heads.

"We will certainly do our best." He looked at Sarah with real concern, both for her health and for the reputation of his facility. He sighed again. "We will need to intensify your regimen. If we are to win—" He paused, as if thinking. "If we are to win, and I think we can, we will need to repair your immune system and activate all of your natural defenses."

"What more can we do?"

"We may have to consider some natural IV therapies, chelation therapy, hydrogen peroxide therapy perhaps. For now we will continue your diet and detoxification plan. He extended his hand. "We are here for you. Keep fighting, Mrs. Hampton."

With that he excused himself, and Susan Rolan escorted Sarah back to her room.

The director walked to his office and sat down. *This case could be a real turning point for us,* he reflected. *If the treatment fails, her surgeon husband is likely to try to close us down.* He paused. *If, however, I can show him that our therapies really work . . . that would certainly mean a boost to our facility.* He squeezed his fist. *But how? Sure, our natural therapies have some validity. But in cases like this, where the disease is so aggressive and becoming advanced . . . it's going to be impossible to cure her with our detox plan!* He went to his balcony and looked at the ocean. Slowly a strategy came into focus. He walked to his bookshelf and pulled out his *Physician's Desk Reference.* He needed some drug information, and he knew just where to find it.

◆ ◆ ◆

Frank spent Sunday afternoon compulsively sorting and resorting the clippings and articles he kept in his shoe box. He had collected most of the material during his days at Central State Hospital. They didn't like him cutting things from the newspaper there, and they wouldn't let him handle sharp instruments, so most of the articles had irregular, torn edges. He had collected anything and everything he could on Sarah. Some things made him proud—her graduation picture, an announcement about her job as a teacher, and so on. But some things made him angry—the wedding announcement and the picture of her with Jake, a picture of Kyle and his father at the fair down in Grantsville, and other items. He spent hours looking over the pictures, captions, and brief articles, long since committed to memory.

Sometimes he would speak to her out loud. Sometimes, since the night she died, he thought the voices were calling him to join her. "Sarah, what shall we eat for dinner, honey?" He smiled as he imagined her coming to him and kissing him softly. "Shall we eat in?" He frowned. "Has something made you afraid? You know I'll protect you. It's not safe outside in the dark without me."

His wrist alarm interrupted his fantasy. Bladder time again. He slowly trudged off to the basement to find an unused spot.

Crash! He heard glass dropping onto the concrete floor. *Somebody's coming! It must be Jake!* He heard laughter. *They'll see my stuff!*

Frank crept back toward the source of the noise. *I've got to get my box!* His mind was screaming. *Can't let them find me. Can't let them know I'm here.* He crept to the edge of a concrete wall. He could hear faint voices.

"I'm not going in there."

"Chicken." A skinny, blond youth slipped through the window and looked back at his companion who knelt at the window ledge. "Lenny's chicken!"

"I am not!" He stuck his head in the window. "Sheesh! It smells like something died in there!"

The first voice laughed. "Maybe they did. They probably forgot someone who was in solitary confinement when they moved the jail." He held his hands up like he was shaking an invisible set of iron bars. "Let me out of here. Somebody left me here! Ahhhhh!"

"Shut up, Todd," the second youth ordered. "I'm still not coming in."

"Suit yourself. I'm just going to look around."

"You're crazy. If anyone catches you, you're dead meat!"

Todd Gifford shrugged off his friend's taunts. If he could explore an abandoned jailhouse, it would be worth a fortune in bragging rights down at the middle school. He rounded the corner and started down a long hall. He was alone. It was frighteningly quiet. All he could hear was his own footsteps. It smelled bad. It smelled real bad down toward the end.

Frank watched the young man. *Is he looking for something? Is he look-*

ing for me? Frank flopped his head around the corner from the stairwell where he was hiding. *Jake must have sent him! How did he know where I was?*

"Let me out of here!" the youth screamed. "Ahhhhh!"

Frank jumped. But the boy was only taunting his friend.

"Come back, Todd!" Lenny called from outside. "I'm leaving!"

"Ahhhh!" The boy laughed. He was getting closer to Frank. Frank would have to do something. Todd would see him soon.

Frank slammed his body against the boy, knocking him into the far wall. His head hit the wall with a sickening thud. His yelling ceased, and his body fell limp.

Lenny called again. "I'm leaving, Todd! See you later!" He turned and ran to his bicycle parked in the bushes. He kept talking to himself and to Todd, not knowing if his friend could hear him. "I don't care what you say, I'm outta here!"

Inside, Frank looked down at the silent youth. Somehow he found a twisted irony in the situation. "Just like Jake! He came to kill Sarah, and he ended up like this. Now he sends you after me, and you end up like this!" He laughed. "When will you get the hint, Jake?"

A motorist found Todd three hours later in the middle of the road near the railroad crossing, dazed but alive. He wouldn't remember a thing.

And Lenny was too afraid to tell. Lenny was a chicken.

◆ ◆ ◆

By the end of the day, Jake was exhausted. He had returned to see the mayor, only to find an aggressive reporter who wanted all the details. Jake deferred giving out any medical information except that which was issued in a formal media release by the hospital. He had to respect the confidentiality of the doctor/patient relationship. He wasn't being hard to get along with. He just felt the information needed to come from the mayor, not from himself.

Unfortunately, the reporter didn't take too kindly to Jake's silence and began a full assault on Jake's qualifications, training, background, and personal life. "Dr. Hampton, weren't you involved with a criminal charge down at the Ocean Sands Wellness Facility a few months back?" the young reporter asked calmly, with an attitude that said, *I've got you where I want you now.*

"That is something I'd rather not discuss," Jake stated flatly. "It has nothing to do with the mayor or his case."

"Then you're not denying it?"

"It's a matter of public record, I suppose." Jake sighed. "I would like to state that all charges were found groundless, and I wasn't asked to stand trial." Jake wanted to glare at the reporter but didn't want to anger him further. He sulked silently instead. *I thought this operation might be a positive turning point in my acceptance in this community. Instead, it's just a chance for the media in this town to rehash my past. Now it will be even harder to earn respect here.*

"What were the original charges, Dr. Hampton?"

"I'd prefer not to discuss it."

The reporter had done his homework. It really hadn't been that hard. The local papers had covered the stories about Jake. "How do you feel about physician-assisted suicide, Dr. Hampton?"

Jake winced every time the reporter repeated his name. It was as if he was mocking his title. He sighed again and collected his thoughts. The reporter seemed insistent that he make a comment.

"Dr. Hampton?"

"I'm against it, OK?" Jake's eyes met the reporter's, who turned away to his notes. "I think it's wrong. No one has the right to take a life, not even their own. Only God gives life, and only God has the right to decide when it's over."

"May I quote you, Dr. Hampton?"

"Sure. Just get it right." Jake wasn't enjoying himself. "I'm against physician-assisted death. Look," he added, "this has nothing to do with my present involvement with surgery on the mayor. Please don't get distracted by these peripheral issues. It's been hard enough for me to convince the members of this town that I am a competent surgeon."

The reporter backed down. "Thanks for your time."

In a few minutes Jake was back home, wishing he was anywhere but Taylorville. *Maybe I would have had better success staying in the big city. At least there, there are enough other scandals going on that people would soon forget about me.*

Jake smiled at the baby-sitter, who told him that Kyle was already in bed. After she collected her books and left, Jake checked in on Kyle. He tousled his son's wavy red hair and smiled. Kyle's hair was the one thing that reminded Jake of Sarah so much.

When he finally laid his own head against a pillow, sleep was elusive. He was haunted by vague memories of Sarah's final moments. It seemed like just when he started getting over it all, something brought it all rolling back again—like that arrogant reporter. Jake stared at the ceiling. He could remember placing his hands on Sarah's abdomen, feeling the baby kicking . . . He squeezed his eyelids. *Why can't I remember more?* He rubbed the back of his head, where the first hint of tension was beginning to throb. *What if my fall wasn't an accident? If I didn't help Sarah die, who did?*

Maybe Dr. Willie is right. What was it he said? "You can't believe the hospital had something to do with her death?" That does sound absurd, doesn't it?

Jake looked at the clock and rubbed his eyes. He turned on the light and looked at the Bible on his nightstand. The cover was dusty, clear evidence that he hadn't read it lately. He shook his head. "I've let this thing consume me, Father. I'm even ignoring you," he whispered. *Maybe I need to return to doing the things I know to do. Perhaps I should concentrate on my son rather than on figuring out the past.*

He opened the leather-bound book in his hand. It had a good feel to it. He opened to the inscription written by Sarah the first year of their marriage, a tough year: "In every thing give thanks: for this is the will of God." It was a quote from 1 Thessalonians, one of Sarah's favorites. She always seemed to know and do the will of God: giving thanks.

"Thank you, Lord, for opening the door for me to come back to Taylorville." Jake's words flowed from trembling lips. They surprised even himself.

CHAPTER
12

LINDA winced. The contractions were coming every eight minutes. So far she had been able to walk through the contractions but knew she would want an epidural anesthetic if things got much worse. "That was definitely stronger," she said, looking at her watch, "and it lasted almost thirty seconds." She looked at Matt. He looked worse than she did. Neither of them had slept much. For half the night Linda had tossed and turned. For the other half, she'd paced the small apartment. "Maybe it's time to head for Bridgewater."

"I'll get the suitcase." Matt stood up and walked to the front closet. He paused to smile at the mirror that hung by the closet door. "Hmmm. Maybe I should pack my razor. I could use a shave."

"You're going to need more than that by the time we're through. Dr. Kramer told me the first one can take longer."

"Longer than what?"

"Longer than our next one, silly."

Matt opened the door. "Let's concentrate on one at a time." He held up his hand. "After you, Mama."

"I can't believe the time is finally here."

"Believe it. It's been a long nine months."

Matt helped her into the car. The drive would take thirty minutes. The happy day had finally arrived.

◆   ◆   ◆

Sharon Isaacs recoiled when she saw the morning paper.

MAYOR UNDERGOES SUCCESSFUL SURGERY
Former Murder Suspect Performs Emergency Operation

Bob Rivers, Taylorville's mayor, underwent surgery to correct a hernia and an associated bowel obstruction. The operation, performed by a new surgeon in Taylorville, Dr. Jacob Hampton, took ninety minutes and was completed yesterday morning without apparent complication. The mayor is listed in satisfactory condition this morning. Dr. Hampton moved to Taylorville recently in the wake of a scandal in which he was alleged to have participated in his wife's suicide. The mayor is expected to recover . . .

Jake? Sharon shook her head. *He's definitely not going to like seeing this,* she realized. *So that's what he meant about Kyle's mother's death being a media event. Probably wouldn't have even made the papers in California.*

She prayed for Jake as she sipped her morning cup of decaffeinated coffee. She had wanted to ask him more about his wife the other day when she inquired about Kyle's mom. Once she found out she was dead, however, she didn't want to pry. Now, with the morning's paper glaring an ugly headline about him, her curiosity reached new levels. How could she find out more about this man?

She ate a quick breakfast and dressed for work. Today would be a casual sweat outfit with matching top and pants. On the way out she folded the paper under her arm. *Maybe someone at work knows more about Jake Hampton than I do,* she thought as she headed for her Honda.

◆   ◆   ◆

Frank spent a sleepless night in his own apartment, across from McDonald's. He slept with the light on and a loaded .38 by his bed. He would have to wait for a few days before returning to the jail. Of course, it wasn't safe here at the apartment either, he'd convinced himself. Anyone could look up his address and find him. When he finally got to sleep around 4 A.M., he awoke shortly thereafter, convinced that the voices had warned him of his need to be alert. He had to formulate a plan. He had to stay out of the public eye for a few days at least.

He got up before 6 A.M., driven from his bed by his paranoid delusions and by his hunger. He scoured the kitchen and found a few cans of pork and beans and a can of cheesy, cartoon-shaped pasta. That would do for breakfast and lunch, he figured. He would have to conserve his food in case it wasn't safe to leave for a few days. At 7 he called his manager at McDonald's, announcing he was sick and wouldn't be in until later in the week.

Frank couldn't risk being seen by the boy whom he'd jumped at the jail. He knew he'd seen him before. Frank was sure the youngster was looking for him but wasn't sure how much he knew about Frank. His frightened thoughts ran in circles at a dizzying pace. He brought all he needed for survival into the kitchen. His sleeping bag, the food, and his shoe box were all within reach. He sat down in the middle of the floor and prepared to wait. He trained the pistol on the front door. *It's only fourteen feet from here. I was always accurate up to twenty-five feet before I went into the hospital.*

◆ ◆ ◆

Jake saw the headlines while he was making breakfast for Kyle. He dropped the cereal box in his hand. "What . . . !" His cheeks paled as he read through the brief article. He threw the paper aside. "Great! That's all I need!"

"What's all you need, Dad?" Kyle was dressed and ready for breakfast. The reminder list on his door was working.

Jake shook his head and looked at his son. He poured him a bowl of cereal, then sat down in front of him. "Son, do you remember how in Grantsville some people thought I had something to do with Mom's dying?"

"They thought you killed her," he said slowly. Eleven-year-olds usually cut straight through the mud.

Jake jerked his head back. "Err, well, yeah, that's essentially it, isn't it?" He looked at his son, amazed at how easily he dealt with the matter. "Well, there's a story in the paper this morning about me operating on the mayor. It says I did a good job."

"That's good, isn't it, Dad? I know you're a good surgeon." He crunched his cereal. "The best."

"That's just the good part, Kyle. It also tells everyone in Taylorville that I was once suspected of murdering your mom."

"But that's not true. You didn't kill her!"

"I know that, Kyle." He paused. "But some people thought that I might have . . . and that makes me a suspect in their eyes. All the article really says is that I was a suspect, not that I did it."

"Why, Dad?"

"Why what, Kyle?"

"Why did they think you did it?" His eyes looked moist.

"Because I was there when she died, and no one really expected her to die so soon. After my bump on the head, I couldn't remember what I was doing there, so some people just assumed I caused Mommy's death."

"I say that's stupid."

Jake nodded his head. *This kid really has a way of cutting to the bottom line.* "Look, Kyle, I just wanted you to know about the article, in case some of the kids at school begin to tease you about it or say bad things about me. Remember, it doesn't really matter what other people think or say. What matters is what we think about ourselves."

Kyle nodded his head. "I know, Dad. I know."

It wasn't until Jake had dropped Kyle off at school and was on his way to work himself that his words to Kyle dawned on him as important for himself. *What matters is what we think about ourselves.* He knew that in order to win his present struggles, he needed to take it a step further: *What really matters is what God thinks of us.* Jake nodded in agreement with his thoughts. *That's what really matters.*

That was a principle that Sarah had practiced with a passion the year before she died, Jake remembered. The kitchen, particularly the refrigerator door, and the bathroom, particularly the mirror, were plastered with little handwritten notes reminding Sarah of what God thought of her. "I am his righteousness," she had written on one, "I am God's child" on another, and "I am salt and light" on a third. She just didn't seem to care what others thought, especially in the final few months. Jake could remember several disagreements because of his concerns over what other people would think. But it didn't seem to affect Sarah at all.

◆ ◆ ◆

Sarah was finally home from Ocean Sands Wellness Facility. Her first admission had been twenty-four days. For Jake and Kyle, it seemed twenty-four months. Her color was back as well. She was smiling again.

Her skin had changed, and the size of the lump had clearly regressed. Something good was definitely up. Sarah thought the Lord was answering their prayers through Ocean Sands' therapy. Jake thought the Lord was answering their prayers *despite* Ocean Sands' therapy.

Her first morning back, Sarah rose early and drank her olive oil and grapefruit juice. She was lying on her left side with her right leg flexed against her chest when Jake came back from the bathroom.

"Are you having cramps?"

"No, silly. This is part of my therapy." Sarah rolled her eyes.

"What is the purpose of this?" Jake attempted to imitate her position.

"It opens the passageway to the gallbladder. It helps the liver cleanse itself from toxins so it can do its work."

"Just by lying in this position?"

"Every morning I spend twenty minutes like this, after drinking olive oil and grapefruit juice that will dissolve or prevent gallstones."

"Come on, Sarah, your bile duct has a sphincter that only opens when the body secretes a hormone, cholecystokinin. You can't open your gallbladder simply by lying down like this."

"Typical surgeon explanation."

He shook his head and sighed. It seemed all he was doing lately was making fun of the Ocean Sands regimens. And that was definitely counterproductive to good communication with Sarah. "I guess you can't argue with success," he conceded. He *was* pretty impressed that he could see an improvement after just three weeks of therapy.

Sarah saw her husband's positive comment as an opportunity to broach a new question. "The director wants me to appear in an ad for the facility."

"Absolutely not."

"What if I want to do it?"

"Sarah! What will the people in this medical community think if they know my wife has shunned conventional medical care for this quackery? I'll be the laughingstock of—"

"That's the point, isn't it?" she interrupted, raising her voice. "Your reputation is on the line, isn't it?" She glared at him, looking up from her curled position on the bed. "Wouldn't this be a small thanks to Ocean Sands for the help they've given me? Admit it, Jake—it seems to be working."

Jake didn't know what to say. "OK, it seems to be working, but I still don't want you on TV doing one of those silly testimonials. It's hard enough convincing some of the folks from the country not to turn their back on the care we offer. Now if they see that you, a surgeon's wife, has done it . . . Well, a lot of patients might leave the practice."

"I don't think you're being fair. You are too concerned with what everyone else thinks about you, Jake. What about what you think about yourself? What about what God thinks? Why should you worry so about everyone else?"

He shook his head. She did have a point. He sat down on the side of the bed. "I won't say you can't. It's your decision." He paused. "But you know how I feel."

Sarah groaned and strained to see the clock. "I hear you," she grunted. "Can you see the time from there?"

"Sure. It's five after 7."

"Good. Right on schedule. Can you brew some coffee?"

"Honey, no caffeine, remember?"

"It's not to drink, Jake. It's for my colonic treatment. Just because I'm out of the hospital doesn't mean I'm going to let down on my therapy. Not when it's just starting to work." Sarah rolled over onto her back. "Oooh."

"Are you OK?"

She got up and moved swiftly into the bathroom where she dry-heaved over the commode.

"How long has that been going on?"

"Just for the last two weeks. Dr. D warned me that after they intensified the regimen, I might experience some nausea. He said it's my body's way of getting rid of the poisons in my system."

"I see."

After a few deep breaths, Sarah got up again and started assembling her enema rig. Jake looked on with wonder. "Think I'll start the coffee," he added.

"I'll need at least three cups."

"I'll make a full pot." He walked toward the kitchen.

In five minutes the fresh-brewed coffee aroma penetrated the air. Jake loved coffee. He started his day with it every day. It was the one thing in the kitchen he could make perfectly. Sarah entered holding a canister of green powder. "Time for breakfast," she said with a smile.

She mixed three tablespoons of the powder in a tall glass of distilled water.

"I'm afraid to ask what's in it."

"So don't. You wouldn't believe me anyway."

Jake sniffed the mixture. "Whew! Potent stuff." He looked at it curiously. "OK, what's in it?"

"I thought you weren't going to ask." Sarah lifted her nose in the air. "Barley, wheat, and kelp mostly. Sometimes we even add in some desiccated liver."

"Gag!"

Sarah frowned. "How about a little support? I'm the one enduring this therapy. It's not all enjoyable, but it seems to be working." She held her nose and chugged down the liquid.

Jake made a face as he watched her. "What's it supposed to do?"

"It's full of vitamins. The chlorophyll in the grasses add oxygen to my body's cells to kill the cancer cells." She put the top on the canister. "In the last few weeks they've been adding something that turns my urine blue."

Jake nodded without speaking. He could remember vaguely learning of a chemotherapy drug that frequently turned the patient's urine blue. He excused himself and headed upstairs to dress. "I've got an eight o'clock case. I'll call you later to make sure things are going OK."

A few minutes later, Jake left the house. Sarah was mixing her morning coffee.

◆ ◆ ◆

Jake pulled into the hospital parking lot. He remembered the conversation well. It was one of the first things that made him wonder whether Sarah might be getting more than she bargained for from the Ocean Sands Wellness Facility. It wouldn't be the last.

♦ ♦ ♦

"Eight centimeters and complete," Dr. Kramer stated with a ring of anticipation. "If you want an epidural, it's now or never."

Linda answered immediately, "Yes. I want it yesterday."

Matt smiled and shook his head. He looked at Dave Kramer. "She's acting more like a surgeon all the time."

The obstetrician smiled. "I'll call the anesthesiologist."

A few minutes later Dr. Kohring came in carrying an epidural kit in a sterile blue wrapping. After introducing himself, he asked Linda to roll onto her side. He prepped her back with a sterile betadine solution. "You'll feel a little cold now."

He palpated her vertebra and pricked the skin with a local anesthetic. He then pushed a longer needle into Linda's back, keeping gentle pressure on the syringe plunger. When the needle-tip entered the epidural space, the plunger slid into the syringe without resistance. The doctor unconnected the needle, threaded a small epidural catheter into position, and taped it to her skin. "There," he stated quickly. "All done." He filled another syringe of clear liquid and injected it into the epidural catheter, then hooked the epidural up to a pump to deliver a small continuous dose of medicine. "We want you to be able to sense pressure, but not to have pain. If you lose all sensation, let your nurse know, and we'll adjust the medication."

Linda smiled. "I can already tell it's working."

Matt smiled and leaned back in the padded chair next to Linda's bed. For the next few minutes they rested. It had been a long night.

Two hours later they converted Linda's labor bed into a delivery table. The foot was removed, and stirrups were placed in position. It was time to push.

She pushed with a contraction. "Give me a strong push with this next one," Dr. Kramer coached, watching the uterine monitor. "Here it comes. Hold your breath and push. Good. Count through it. That's good . . . Relax. Good job. A few more like those and we ought to be done."

Matt gripped Linda's shoulder. "You're doing great."

Sweat beaded on Linda's forehead.

"Here comes another . . . Push, one, two, three, four . . . Good . . . Push . . . Six, seven, eight, nine, ten . . . Relax."

Matt looked up just as Dr. Lucille Morra slipped in behind Dr. Kramer. She was wearing sterile gloves and a gown.

The baby came with the next contraction.

"It's a boy!"

"Waaah!"

Dr. Kramer cut the cord and handed the baby to Dr. Morra. She carried the baby to a warm incubator and whisked him out of the room.

"Hey!" Matt looked puzzled.

"My baby!"

"Just a precaution." Dr. Kramer spoke evenly. "I asked her to take the baby for an exam."

Linda looked at Matt, her eyes wide. Matt shrugged. What could he do? He patted her shoulder. "Don't worry. They're just being careful." A smile spread over his face. "We have a son!"

"Just like you said."

"Mark Aaron Stone."

"After your brother."

Matt beamed. The name was a tribute to Matt's twin brother who had died of leukemia.

◆ ◆ ◆

Lenny Thompson and Todd Gifford sat in the treehouse in the Giffords' backyard. It had plywood walls and a roof and a trap door in the center with a rope ladder hanging down.

"Come on, Todd, you have to remember something."

The skinny youth shook his head. "Nothing. Not a thing."

"Do you remember going to the jail?"

"Yeah, sort of . . . and going inside."

"You kept screaming, like you were a prisoner left behind. Do you remember that?"

"No."

"Have you told your folks what I told you?"

"That we were in the jail? No way! My father would skin me alive if he knew."

"We've gotta tell someone. Maybe the police!"

"Right! Like they wouldn't tell our folks!"

"But what if whoever is in there is still there? What if it's a hideout for a gang or something?"

"You've been watching too much TV, Lenny. Get real."

"I'm serious. What if they *are* still there? And what if they think we know something? We could be in big trouble."

"I'm not telling my folks," Todd repeated. "And I'm not telling the police."

"Then what do we do? We can't just let it go. It could be a hideout for spies or Mafia guys or something."

"A jail?"

"It's perfect. No one would think to look there."

"So let's go back and check it out ourselves," Todd suggested, hoping Lenny wouldn't take him up on it.

"Now I know you've got brain damage. Look what happened the last time."

A small intercom, connected with the Gifford home, buzzed. It was Todd's mom. "Todd, Kyle's here from next door. I told Dr. Hampton he could stay here while he goes to the hospital."

"Great. Just what we need—a little kid running around." Todd pressed the intercom and sighed. "OK, Mom. Send him on out."

Just then Todd's eyes lit up. Lenny could tell his friend had just come up with some brilliant idea. "What are you thinking?"

"Maybe we could dare Kyle to go in there."

"Right! Like a little guy like that would do it."

"He'll do anything to be a part of our club." Todd smiled.

"He could get hurt." Lenny shook his head. "I don't like it."

"We could keep an eye on the situation. If anything happens, we'll call the police. They're only a few blocks away. Besides, what could happen?"

Lenny shook his head. "I don't know about this, Todd."

Kyle walked out of the house toward the old oak tree that housed the Gifford fort.

"Up here, Kyle! Hey, buddy, wanna join our club?"

CHAPTER
13

DR. D cared little about right-to-death legislation. What he did care about was building and preserving his little fortune gained from alternative health care. But Jake Hampton's open criticism of his facility had stirred him up in the wrong way. He couldn't stand anybody calling his methods into question. He would see to it that Jake Hampton was kept in the public eye, if for no other reason than to limit suspicion about Ocean Sands to the realm of normal skepticism. And soon, he hoped, the time would be right to silence Jake Hampton altogether. First, however, he needed to be sure the public knew the real Dr. Hampton. Then, once things were in place, he would release Frank to see to it that Jake Hampton was out of his life forever.

His contacts were formidable. He knew just whom to call.

"Pin Oak Society. Pam speaking. How may I help you?"

"I need Steve Smith. Is he in?"

"Please hold."

In a moment a bass voice came on the line. "Hello."

"Hello, Steve."

Steve recognized the director's voice. Dr. D had been active in the group Mercy Physicians, an organization that promoted patient autonomy in death, including physician-assisted suicide. "Hi, D. What can I do for you?"

"I'm calling about your upcoming push in the state legislature for the

Death with Dignity Act. I've got a case for you to highlight. Maybe even a new candidate to suggest for one of the Pin Oak Advance Awards for effort in promoting your cause."

Steve was suspicious. "What's in it for you?"

"Nothing," the director lied. "I just became aware of the case because the woman was a patient here."

"What've you got?"

"A tragic story really, but one that shows what a difference your kind of legislation would make. A young mother with metastatic breast cancer. Nothing could be done to ease her pain. Her husband was a doctor, and she practically begged him to take her life. Her suffering was unbearable. We tried everything we could at our facility. She didn't have a moment toward the end when she wasn't in constant pain."

"Too bad."

"Her husband gave her the medications to end her suffering, Steve, and you wouldn't believe the grief he has taken for it. If you thought people were spiteful toward Kevorkian, you should see how they treat this guy . . . like he's some murderer or something."

"Didn't I read about this case? I think we contacted him after the story came out." He paused. "I think we even considered this guy for a speaking engagement. Didn't he claim not to have done it?"

"Not exactly. Publicly, he claims not to have remembered. But he has to say that, don't you see? The small town where he now practices thinks what he did is akin to murder." He paused. "I think we could do this guy a favor if we were to highlight the case in such a way that everyone would see that his choice was the only merciful course of action available. It's exactly the kind of emotional case that will turn the tide of public opinion in your favor."

"Hmmm. Sounds intriguing."

"I can give you the details of the case from our records at Ocean Sands if you like. I'm sure Dr. Hampton wouldn't mind. He needs all the help he can get."

"Will you be available this weekend?"

"Sure. Just give me a call." The director walked out on his balcony with the cordless phone. "Say, don't you have your annual awards dinner coming up? This guy would make an excellent recipient. This case could do a lot to advance your concerns through the legislature."

"I'll send you a nominating sheet."

"Great. I'll see you this weekend."

◆ ◆ ◆

Linda held little Mark Aaron tenderly against her. Little, of course, is a relative term. He weighed in at exactly nine pounds, one ounce. So far all he wanted to do was sleep, a normal agenda for the first twenty-four hours after birth.

"He looks so normal." Linda spoke softly as she looked at her baby. "It's hard to believe there's anything wrong with him at all."

Matt nodded.

Dr. Morra smiled tenderly. "It's a large V.S.D." She paused. "I know he looks normal now, but in the next few weeks things will change. Remember, before birth most of the blood is shunted away from the lungs, because the baby isn't breathing. The pulmonary or lung circulation resistance is high at birth, but it will lower over the next few weeks. There isn't much of a harmful shunt of blood through the hole in the infant's heart right now, but when the resistance lowers, flow through the shunt will increase, and heart failure will be inevitable."

Matt nodded again and looked at Linda. "Do you understand?"

"I think so."

Matt spoke the question that was on both of their minds. "So what's next? Will you schedule surgery?"

"I can call the surgeons." She paused. "This is a highly specialized area. We have a team of pediatric cardiothoracic surgeons here, but . . ." She paused again and lowered her voice. "Maybe I shouldn't even mention this, since I am a part of this university, but since you're a surgeon, you should realize that you do have choices. You have the option of taking your baby somewhere else."

Matt squinted. He wasn't sure what she was trying to say.

Dr. Morra continued, "Don't get me wrong—we have qualified surgeons here, but I was made aware recently of another option. One of the world's experts in this very problem has just opened a practice nearby at Crestview Women's. That's where you work, isn't it?"

"Yes," Matt responded, uneasy at the turn this conversation had taken. "Are you speaking of Michael Simons?"

"Yes. I'm glad you know of him. I wouldn't even mention this as an option, but his experience in this area far surpasses our surgeons here at Bridgewater."

Linda gasped. "Dr. Simons?"

Dr. Morra smiled. "You know of him too? He's really wonderful, isn't he?"

"'Wonderful' isn't exactly the adjective I had in mind," Linda quipped.

Matt shot a look in Linda's direction.

The pediatric cardiologist looked puzzled, so Matt attempted an explanation. "I worked with Dr. Simons back at Taft University."

"Oh," Dr. Morra interrupted. "I understand that he's difficult to work with, and probably very demanding." She looked at Linda. "But he didn't build his reputation by being nice. He built it by being very good at what he does."

Matt remained silent and looked at Linda.

Linda's eyes widened. "He's evil!"

Matt looked at his wife with an expression that said, *We'll talk about it later!*

Lucille Morra looked surprised. "Of course, you have options. Surgery will not need to take place for a few weeks. You have some time to decide. I merely brought it up because it's not fair to not tell you of this option since he is so close by." She looked at her watch. "I need to run. I've scheduled Mark for an angiogram in the morning. I'm sure whoever operates will need it."

Matt nodded, and Dr. Morra excused herself.

Linda looked at Matt. "I will not have that man touch my child!"

Matt shrugged. "What if he can do it better than anyone else?"

The new mother wasn't interested in thinking this through with her intellect. Her heart had spoken first, and she didn't want to talk about it any further. She continued gazing at her infant and stroked the dark tuft of hair on the top of his head.

"Don't worry, little one, I won't let any harm come to you."

The baby grimaced with a little yawn.

"I'll protect you. Mommy loves you."

The discussion was definitely closed for now.

◆ ◆ ◆

Jake Hampton sat down at the mayor's bedside. He certainly didn't need to hurry. He'd already called his office, and many of his patients had canceled after reading the morning paper. Talk about unfair! Jake had fumed. *Oh, well, at least I can spend a little more time at the hospital with the patients I have there.*

"Any flatus yet?"

The mayor looked at him curiously.

Jake used the more common term. "Have you passed gas since your surgery?"

The mayor smiled. "Not yet."

"We ask all our bowel surgery patients that so we know when it's time to give them something to drink."

The mayor nodded. "Thanks." He pointed at the inflatable compression devices on his legs. "When can I get these off?"

"Today, if you're able to get up and walk quite a bit. They keep the blood from clotting in the calf veins."

Jake pulled up the patient gown to check the dressing. It was dry. He looked at the bedside chart. All the data was appropriate. "Everything seems to be going well. I should be able to start you on some liquids by tomorrow."

"I'm in no hurry. You did a good job." He paused, then picked up the *Taylorville Times.* "I guess you saw this." He dropped his eyes. "I'm awfully sorry. The guy that wrote this is always searching for dirt under the rug."

Jake attempted a smile. "I guess operating on famous patients has its price."

"Just the same, I'm going to talk to the editor, Jim Quail. He's a friend of mine. He saved my backside a few times during the last election when a zealous reporter tried to tie me to a scandal I had nothing to do with."

The surgeon nodded. Unfortunately, for many folks the damage had already been done. "I just hope it doesn't take Taylorville too long to decide I'm OK."

"I'll see what I can do," the mayor stated solemnly.

"Thanks," Jake responded, then returned to thinking about the mayor's recovery. "Have you been up and walking at all yet?"

"Only in the room."

"Good, but try to take a walk in the hall today."

"Fine." The mayor reached out his hand. "Thanks again, Dr. Hampton."

"Sure." Jake shook his hand. *It's no wonder this guy's a politician*, he observed. *He does his best to make you feel important.*

Jake exited and walked to the nursing station to document his visit in the patient record. He knew the dictum well: "If you didn't record it, you didn't do it." He noted the mayor's morning lab values and wrote a daily progress note.

He took the elevator to the third floor to visit an appendectomy patient on pediatrics. After rounds, he went to his office. Of ten scheduled patients, five failed to show. Of the five no-shows, three called and rescheduled with Dr. Willie.

By 4, Jake was finished and headed home. Getting home early was the one benefit of his unpopularity. He stopped by the Simpsons' to pick up Kyle.

When he got home, Kyle headed for his bedroom to do his homework. Jake pressed the Message Playback button on his answering machine.

"Hello, Dr. Hampton, er, uh, Jake. This is Sharon Isaacs. I—I'm just calling to say I've been praying for you today. I saw the article in the paper this morning and . . . well, I—I just wanted you to know I was upset. I know reporters can certainly get things twisted, and, well, I don't really know the story, and maybe you think I'm just butting in where I'm not welcome, but I know what it's like to be new in town, and I thought you could use a little prayer support. That's all." *Click.*

She was talking fast to get through before the tape ran out. *I can't believe she called me.*

The next message was from Matt Stone.

"Hey, Jake . . . Matt here. We had a son! Mark Aaron Stone, nine pounds, one ounce. Just wanted you to know. There's one other thing I need to talk to you about. I'm not at home because Linda is still in the hospital. I'll try to get ahold of you later. I need your advice about some surgery the baby needs. I'll explain later."

Jake shook his head. *I wonder what he's talking about.*

He walked to the kitchen and fixed a tossed salad. He was just about to start some grilled-cheese sandwiches when the phone rang.

"Hello. Hamptons'."

"Hi, Jake. Matt Stone here."

"Hey, Matt. I just got your message. Congratulations, Daddy."

"Thanks."

"How's Linda?"

"She's fine." He paused. "Jake?"

Jake squinted at the phone. "What's wrong, Matt?"

"It's the baby. He has a large V.S.D."

"Oh, man." Jake's voice was solemn.

"You won't believe this . . . Our pediatric cardiologist isn't recommending surgery at the university. She wants to refer us over to Michael Simons."

"Simons!" Jake let the words sink in. "Whoa!"

Matt sounded tired. "I've been thinking about this a lot. Simons is the best pediatric cardiothoracic surgeon around."

"Certainly from a technical standpoint, that's right." Jake paused. "But could you trust him, knowing he might be out for revenge?"

"That's what I'm trying to think through. I mean, I want what's best for my baby. He deserves the best surgeon around."

"Have you talked to Simons?"

"No. I want to think this through first."

"He might refuse. He might think it's too great a conflict for him."

"I doubt it. His pride wouldn't let him turn me away. Remember, he *knows* he's the best."

"I remember." Jake scratched his head. "When do you have to decide?"

"I've got a week or two before the baby is likely to need anything."

"Have you been praying?"

Matt paused to think. "We knew the baby had this problem before he was born. We found out last week. I must have asked God a million times to heal him, so he wouldn't need surgery, but . . ." His voice trailed off. "I guess I really haven't stopped to ask for help with this decision about Simons."

Jake continued to probe. "How's Linda with all this?"

"At first she would have nothing to do with the idea of Simons touching our baby, much less operating on him. Now she seems to be softening a little. I think maybe she could be convinced if she was sure Simons was better than anyone else."

"I'd give her some time." Jake found it a relief to think about someone else's problems for a change. "I'd like to come up to visit . . . to see the baby."

"We'd like that."

Jake pondered his new relaxed schedule. "Maybe I'll drive up tomorrow evening."

"We'd love to see you. You gotta see my son."

"Matt?"

"Yes?"

"I'll be praying."

"Thanks. I'll see you tomorrow."

"OK. See you then."

◆ ◆ ◆

Frank's kitchen was starting to look more like a campsite than anything else. Cans and candy wrappers were tossed in a corner, and a sleeping bag and a few utensils were gathered in a mound in the center. The kitchen table had been turned on its side to serve as a small barricade; the chairs had been stacked against the door. Frank was sure the boys would talk. And if they knew who he was, they would trace him to his apartment. For now, the jail seemed off-limits. He'd be all right as long as no one went snooping and found his stash of explosives in the ceiling. There was really no other place for him to go. It was too cold to stay outside. He'd thought of staying in the McDonald's—he had a key, but it was one of the few places that the Taylorville police patrolled after midnight. If the boys didn't squeal, he'd be OK here. He just needed to make it a few more days, he told himself.

He fingered the gun beside him and counted his ammunition again. He fingered the binoculars around his neck and looked at his barricade. It would take anyone a few minutes to break through, giving him enough time to make an exit out his back window if necessary. He had a rope tied around his waist just in case such a second-floor escape was needed. The hours went slowly, giving him plenty of time to think and to daydream. He tried to think of an explanation, in case the boys reported him, but his mind kept wandering to another time when he had needed to protect himself . . .

◆ ◆ ◆

"Where's Frank? It's time for his shock therapy." Dr. Dave Foley was grumpy as usual.

"The attendant should be bringing him anytime," Jim Maley, the intern, answered.

The attendant came jogging up the hall . . . without Frank. He looked breathless. "Dr. Foley! Frank's locked himself in his room. He won't come out."

"Just get the keys. They're in the office. Just ask Julie—"

"No, it's not that. I already tried that. He's barricaded himself in. He thinks we're abusing him once he's asleep."

The intern shrugged his shoulders. "I guess if I woke up with a missing tooth and a broken arm, I'd be suspicious, too."

The chief resident cast him a look that communicated, *Shut up!*

"Go get him, Maley," Dr. Foley demanded. "Talk him into surrendering."

Jim Maley shrugged again and walked down the hall to Frank's room. The door was unlocked. He pushed against it . . . hard. No movement. "Frank, this is Dr. Maley. Can you let me in?"

"Go away!"

"I'm here to help you, Frank."

Frank's tongue explored his fractured tooth. He rubbed the plaster cast on his arm. "What do you guys do to me when you put me to sleep for shock therapy?"

"We've been through this, Frank. It's normal to have a seizure when the shock is given. You just bumped your arm on the railing."

"The doctor at the university said both bones were broken. He said it looked like a football injury!" Frank pressed his face up to a small crack where Maley and the attendant had wedged the door open. "Explain that!"

"I've tried. Look, Frank, maybe we don't even need to do the shock therapy today. Let's just talk."

Frank looked at the door. He wouldn't let it open any further. His bed and a dresser were wedged between it and the far wall. "We're talking." Frank smiled thinly. He hadn't felt in this much control in weeks. He also hadn't been this paranoid. "I know what you're trying to do. You want to kill me. You want to find out where my girlfriend lives so you can take her away from me."

"We're here to help you, Frank."

"Go away."

"Frank, we're not leaving."

"And I'm not coming out." Another thought hit him. "I want to see my lawyer."

"Frank, you don't have a lawyer."

"Sure, I do. The court assigned one to me when I went to the jail. Call him."

"Be reasonable, Frank. You know where the phone is. You get three calls a week. You can call him yourself."

The chief resident arrived. "What's going on here, guys?" He looked at his intern and the attendant and then at Frank's door. It was only slightly ajar. He slid his fingers through the crack to push on the door.

Spotting a new enemy, Frank got a running start and slammed his weight against the door, crushing Dr. Foley's fingers.

"Ahhhhhh!" Dr. Foley's colorful language filled the corridor. "My hand! He pulverized my hand!"

"You pulverized my arm," Frank responded flatly. "An eye for an eye, huh, Dr. Foley?"

"Get Maintenance. Let's take this door off!"

Frank looked around the room. His time was running out. They were after him. "Let's talk." He pushed his face up to the crack again. "No more shock therapy."

"OK," the intern said. "Whatever you say."

The chief resident shot him a stern glance.

"I want it in writing."

"Call Maintenance!" Dr. Foley repeated, holding his left hand.

"On my way, Dr. Foley," the attendant responded as he ran toward the nursing station.

Foley spoke in a whisper to Maley. "Once we've got him, put him in the locked solitary padded room."

Maley nodded.

The whispering only inflamed Frank further. "I know you want to kill me. You want Sarah!"

The chief resident whispered again. "We're going to need some heavy sedation. Why don't you get the emergency drug box out of the office?"

Inside, Frank threw a small hand-held mirror to the floor. He picked up the longest glass shard and wrapped a T-shirt around the widest spot so he could hold it. Now he was armed. Just let them take off the door!

The chief resident tried to talk calmly to Frank. "Sarah is a nice girl, isn't she?"

Frank pressed his face to the crack again. "You've seen her, haven't you?"

The resident decided to go with it. "Sure, Frank. I've seen her. She's very pretty. We wouldn't do anything to harm her. We wouldn't do anything to hurt you either, Frank."

"You beat me up when I was put to sleep. You want my girl!"

"Your broken arm was an accident, Frank. You know that."

Frank gripped the glass in his hand—carefully, not too tightly, so it wouldn't cut through the cloth.

The psychiatric resident had leaned closer, to see if Frank would make eye contact. "This is an accident too," Frank shouted as loudly as he could. He spit in the resident's face.

"Frank!"

The resident moved quickly away from the door and wiped the spit from his face with the back of his hand.

The maintenance supervisor arrived with a large toolbox. In another minute he started tapping the pins out of the hinges on Frank's door.

Frank stood back, gripping the pointed glass shard. "Stay away!"

Two additional attendants arrived. They looked like professional tackles.

Two pins were removed, and Frank positioned himself behind the door. He needed the element of surprise. When the last pin was knocked free, the maintenance man rocked the door and slid it to the side. All that was visible was the bed and dresser. No Frank.

"Frank?" The chief resident looked ahead. "Come on out. We don't want to—"

Frank jumped through the doorway, bringing his weapon high over his head in a perfect arc, aimed at Dr. Foley's left temple.

The large attendant to Dr. Foley's left reacted first, bringing a stiff blow to Frank's abdomen, sending him back onto the bed. The glass brushed Foley's shoulder, driving a sharp edge into Frank's palm as he fell. In seconds the attendants and Dr. Maley each gripped a limb. Frank began to scream.

Dr. Foley emptied a large syringe of clear fluid deep into Frank's flailing left thigh.

"No. No! Noooo!"

Frank arched his back and spit. "Let me go!" He slipped his plaster cast away from the intern's grip.

Jim Maley attempted to shield himself. "Ow!" The cast glanced off his right hip before Maley could force it down again.

Frank begin to calm down slightly. His yelling became incomprehensible.

In another minute he was asleep.

◆ ◆ ◆

Jake waited until Kyle was in bed before he returned Sharon's call. He stretched out in his favorite chair and dialed directory assistance. There was a number for "S. Isaacs." *Has to be her*, he deduced. *I wish she'd included her number in her message.*

As he dialed her number, he found himself suddenly dry-mouthed. *Why should I be nervous?* he chided himself. *It's just a friendly phone call.* Had he always been this shy, or was this was one of the aftereffects of the terrible trauma he'd suffered? He wasn't sure.

One ring, two, three . . . "Hello."

"Hello. Sharon?" He knew it was her but asked anyway. It seemed a natural way to begin.

"Yes."

"This is Jake Hampton. I got your phone message. I wanted to call and say thanks." He suppressed the urge to get up and pace.

"I hope you don't think I'm too forward." She giggled with a hint of nervousness herself. "I guess I'm still a California girl at heart."

"No problem. I'm glad you called. Things have been a bit . . . well . . . hard lately." Jake stumbled over his words. "It's nice . . . nice to know you cared enough to pray."

"Sure." Sharon smiled and nodded her head. "I wish the media would stick to reporting facts and stay away from hurtful personal gossip."

Now Jake was nodding. "I wish that too. They make starting out in a small place like Taylorville even more difficult."

"It's certainly not Southern California, I assure you."

Jake laughed. "I'm glad of that. I've had enough big-town life for a while, and I was only over in Grantsville." He paused. "I guess you probably wondered what the article was talking about."

"Well, yes, but I figured that reporter just wanted to sell more papers with some flashy lines."

"You may be right." Jake paused again. "In a way what he reported is technically true, but the implication that I'm running from my past certainly isn't."

When Sharon stayed quiet, Jake continued, "I was accused of assisting my wife to commit suicide, but nothing stuck. They decided they didn't even have enough evidence to take me to trial."

"What is the truth, Jake?" True to form, Sharon cut right to the meat of the issue at hand.

"I—I'm not sure. It's a long story, really. I mean, I don't even think my wife committed suicide at all. She wanted to die, I know. She was suffering terribly from breast cancer, but she was pregnant, and her whole goal at the end was to carry the baby through to viability. I don't think she wanted to die, not until the very end when she knew it was inevitable."

Sharon listened silently, not knowing what to say.

"Look," Jake added, "I don't want to drag you into this, really. I've been pretty confused about it all myself."

"I'd like to hear it, Jake. Talking about it could do you some good."

"You sound a lot like another friend of mine. He's always bugging me to talk it through, to journal it, to face the past. Don't get me wrong, I want to. It's just . . . Well, it's a lot to unload on someone you barely know."

"Your friend sounds like a smart guy."

Jake raised his eyebrows and smiled. "Would you like to meet him?"

Sharon squinted at the phone. "Well . . . sure."

"He's up in Green Valley, about an hour from here. I'm going up tomorrow afternoon to see his new baby. I'd love to take you along. That would give us a chance to talk. That is, if you're serious about all this."

"I get off at 3. I'm free after that."

Jake smiled. "I'll pick you up. Where do you live?"

"Abington Apartments."

"Across from McDonald's?"

"You've got it. I'm in the second building, directly opposite McDonald's. Apartment C, top of the stairs, on the left."

"I'll pick you up at 3:30."

"OK. I'll see you then. Bye."

"Bye." Jake smiled.

As she hung up the phone, Sharon smiled too. "Thank you, God."

CHAPTER
14

D<small>R.</small> Simons settled into his desk chair and combed through his in-box. Start-up had been slow but was gaining ground. He had fixed a patent ductus arteriosis in a premature infant and did one Blalock-Taussig shunt. But he was still looking for his first pump case, a case that would require a cessation of the patient's heart, with the oxygenation and circulation being maintained by the cardiopulmonary bypass pump. It felt good to be back in clinical practice. Editing a new textbook had been hard work, but it was hardly a substitute for holding a knife in your hand.

He had tried to understand his slow start and kept telling himself it was only routine. But within him, his bitterness over his dismissal from Taft University still ate away like a cancer. Every time he looked at his empty schedule book, he found himself fighting the "if onlys." *If only I had been able to keep my fetal research a secret until the proper time . . . If only Matt Stone hadn't stuck his nose in my business . . . If only I could have discredited him in time . . . If only . . .*

If he'd learned one thing in his pursuit of excellence, it was perseverance. That virtue had seen him through more than a decade of surgical residency and a push upward through the academic ranks at Taft. Now he would persevere again. Somewhere, somehow he knew he would have his chance to be on top again. He sensed it in the quietness of his bedroom at night, when he closed his eyes and sought to release his untapped potential for immortal accomplishment. He knew he would succeed. He just knew! That was the air he walked in. The air of greatness belonged to him, and no one could prevent it.

He picked up a referral letter from a short stack of mail. *Hmmm, a letter from Bridgewater University. What could they want?* He checked the return address. "Lucille Morra, M.D., Chief, Division of Pediatric Cardiology." He shrugged and opened the letter.

It began nicely enough.

Dear Dr. Simons:

Welcome to the community. I hope this letter finds you adjusting to your new place without difficulty. We are certainly pleased to have a surgeon of your caliber and reputation within our referral area.

Dr. Simons looked up and smiled. *I like this Lucille already*, he thought, then continued to read.

I am referring a patient, Mark Aaron Stone, to you for evaluation of a large V.S.D. He was born two days ago, and I did the angiogram this morning and confirmed my fears. I suspect urgent surgery will be needed before the child succumbs to heart failure or develops intractable pulmonary hypertension. Thank you for your evaluation.

Sincerely,
Lucille Morra, M.D.

Ahhh, a pump case at last!
He looked at the postscript:

P.S. I suspect you may have run across the baby's father, Dr. Matt Stone, who is a surgeon at your facility.

This news hit Dr. Michael Simons head-on. Matt Stone's baby! Simons excitedly stood and began waving his arms in a maddening blur. His mind raced, and he paced back and forth over his newly decorated office, the only sound the creaking of the wood floor beneath him. *Matt Stone's baby is likely to die without an operation, is he? And now suddenly I am the one chosen to stand between certain death and probable life for this little Stone, am I?*

Simons began to whisper. "Interesting. Very interesting." He stopped talking for a moment as he turned around and headed back across the room. "Kind of ironic, isn't it, Michael?" he said to himself. "Look who Stone turns to when the chips are down."

His face became serious, almost eerie. He continued to whisper to himself as if someone nearby might hear his thoughts. "But this operation is very serious. The team is inexperienced. At any of a hundred points, critical errors determining the outcome could occur." He smiled thinly. "After all, I've not actually done an open-heart case in a few years. And yet, I am the expert. Who would say something bad about me? Even if things go awry, everyone would understand. No one would dare criticize us for trying."

He increased his pace. "What if we mixed the wrong concentration of potassium in the pump? What if we miscalculated the baby's volume? What if we operate too late and pulmonary hypertension kills the child anyway? What if air gets trapped in the heart and embolizes to the brain, causing the little Stone baby to have a massive stroke?"

He paused, imagining Matt Stone holding his severely demented infant. "I'm so sorry, Matt. What can I say? It was unavoidable," he whispered, almost like he was rehearsing for a play.

"What if we damage the electrical system of the heart while we are closing the septal defect? What if the baby rejects being weaned from the cardiopulmonary bypass machine? So many things could go wrong. We will have to warn the Stones of the possible hazards. We must make sure they are comfortably informed."

He chuckled at that thought. *Yes, I'll make sure you are comfortable . . . comfortable with this decision to put your child's life in my hands.*

His fingers trembled slightly as he held the referral letter in his hand. His forehead glistened. *What was it I said to D about destiny?* He thought back to their conversation at Ocean Sands: "The upper hand never comes to someone who rushes fate."

Simons went to the bookshelf, pulled off an O.R. atlas, and turned to a chapter entitled "Ventricular Septal Defects." He had written the chapter himself, the last year he was at Taft University. He spoke softly to himself again. "Look, Michael! You're the world's expert. No one questions your outcomes. No one." He smiled and sat down to review the chapter.

Yes, Simons believed in destiny. And he believed in opportunity.

And he believed in revenge.

◆ ◆ ◆

That night before Jake slept he again attempted to journal his last months with Sarah, encouraged by his conversation with Sharon to think that the exercise might actually be beneficial. The first thing he wrote was, "There were a few times in the last six months that I remember actually seeing her happy again."

◆ ◆ ◆

"Look, honey. Look what pretty things I picked out at the store!" Sarah's eyes were aglow with excitement.

Jake returned a smile, then shook his head in amazement. "What if it's not a girl? Ever think of that?" He planted a gentle kiss on his wife's cheek.

"I know it is." She smiled coyly.

"Did you have an ultrasound?"

"No."

"Then how—"

She put her finger up to his mouth. "It's just something we mothers know." She smiled thinly and lifted her head. "Remember when I was pregnant with Kyle? I told you he was a boy."

"OK, you're one for one. That doesn't mean this is a girl."

"Just wait and see."

"Actually, I hope it's a girl. A boy would look awfully cute in all those frilly dresses." Jake laughed.

Sarah laughed too.

She carefully folded the clothes into a neat stack. "Can you help me put up the crib?"

"Honey, it's still a few months—" He stopped when he saw his wife's eyes. The eyes that had melted him when they dated. He dropped his own gaze to the floor. "Sure," Jake said. "I think it's in the basement. I'll carry it up."

Sarah smiled. "I just want everything to be ready. When you come up, I have something else to show you."

Five minutes later Jake struggled to the top of the stairs with a dusty, wooden crib. "Ugh. This thing's heavier than I remembered."

"Ooh, it's filthy. I'll get a damp cloth." Soon Sarah had it cleaned up.

"What was it you wanted to show me?" Jake plopped down in a rocking chair in the nursery.

Sarah carried over a large sample book of wall coverings. "I've been thinking about a new border in here." She turned a few pages and pointed. "What do you think of these? They're so precious!"

Jake raised his eyebrows and patted her stomach. "It had better be a girl if you decorate with this."

"OK, OK," she said excitedly. "What about these puppies? They're so cute." She giggled. "I could put a border around the top and paint this wall a light blue to match."

Jake's eyes met hers. She continued, "Girls like blue too."

"Don't you think I should hire a painter?"

"Jake, I feel fine!" Sarah protested.

"But what about the fumes? Don't some say to avoid paint fumes during pregnancy?"

"I've already checked that out, Dr. Hampton," she retorted with a smile. "As long as the place is ventilated, I'll be fine." She stood and put her hands on her hips. "Besides, I want to do it."

She was irresistible when she demanded her own way. "Well . . ." Jake dragged out his response. ". . . OK."

Sarah put her arms around her husband. "Thanks," she said softly. "It will be my own little celebration of my healing."

Jake kissed her. He didn't need to say any more.

◆　◆　◆

Kyle stood at the bus stop with Todd and Lenny, several yards removed from a group of elementary school students. Although Kyle went to the elementary school and Todd and Lenny went to the middle school, their pick-up site was the same. It was the one time in the day that Kyle felt extra-special because he'd managed to make friends with the older boys. Kyle would stand with them, purposefully away from the other elementary school students, until his bus came.

"Mom says you're coming over after school." Todd looked at Kyle.

"Guess so. My dad's gotta go see a friend over in Green Valley."

"He's sure gone a lot, isn't he?" Lenny commented.

"Not as much as when we lived in Grantsville. He was always busy then."

Lenny scuffed his feet on the sidewalk. "I wish my dad would go away more."

"My dad's never home," Todd boasted. "He goes bowling a lot."

"Ever go with him?"

"No."

Kyle grunted and looked down the street. "That's my bus."

Todd squinted at the big yellow vehicle approaching. "Yep. That's 22."

"See ya after school."

"Remember, today is initiation day. Today's your chance."

Kyle looked down. "I—I don't know if I can come over."

"You're already coming over. Your old man is going to Green Valley, remember?"

"Yeah, but—"

"But nothing!" Todd responded. "If you want to be in, we have to do it when your dad's away." He looked down at the younger boy as the bus drove up. "Are you chicken, Kyle?"

"I'm not chicken!" Kyle jumped onto the bus.

Todd called after him, "See you after school. Don't forget!"

◆ ◆ ◆

Jake pulled up in front of Sharon's apartment at 3:30 sharp. If there was one thing surgical residency had taught him, punctuality was it. He was wearing jeans and a flannel shirt over a turtleneck. He sat in the car for a minute, not wanting to appear overanxious, just in case Sharon was watching. He used the time to pick up the trash in the car and stuff it behind the passenger seat. *Man*, he thought, *I'm going to have to talk to Kyle about throwing some of his trash away.* That's when he saw another Zero bar wrapper. *That's odd. I don't remember eating this. Must be Kyle. Maybe it helps him remember his mother*, he hypothesized.

Jake checked his appearance in the mirror for a final time and opened the door. A minute later, he was standing on the landing in front of Sharon's apartment.

◆ ◆ ◆

Frank moved stealthily to the front room and peered between the venetian blinds. He had heard a car and came to investigate. *Jake! You've found me!* He ran to the kitchen and retrieved his gun. Gripping the handle made him feel better. He watched as Jake sat in the driver's seat of his Isuzu Trooper. What was he waiting for? He saw him lean down. He was holding something. Frank strained to see. He lifted his binoculars to his eyes. A Zero wrapper!

My warning! You couldn't stay away, could you, Hampton? You killed my Sarah, and now you want me, don't you?

Jake walked from his vehicle to the sidewalk. Frank heard the front door, then steps. Hoping the barricade would hold, Frank positioned himself behind a recliner chair. *I should be able to get a shot off from here before he even knows I'm home.* He raised the gun and checked the chamber.

More steps. Then a knock. A faint knock. Frank moved silently to his door and stepped onto the couch that blocked the doorway. He peered through the peephole, fully expecting to see Jake's face.

Instead, he saw Jake's back. *He's at the wrong door! What a fool! He thinks I live in Apartment C.*

Frank paused and tried to anticipate his next move. Certainly his neighbor would redirect Hampton to the right apartment. *Should I stay and fight him off?* The voices hadn't been clear. There had only been a warning: *He is out to get you, Frank.* Should he escape through the window? He checked the rope around his waist. Everything was set.

Frank strained to see if his enemy was armed. *Arrogant, isn't he? Doesn't even seem to have a weapon,* Frank reasoned. *Must be hidden under his shirt.*

He made his decision. He would wait for Jake to turn and knock. Then he would shoot right through the door. He slipped off the safety, braced the pistol at chest-level, and waited.

He heard a door open.

◆ ◆ ◆

"Right on time!" Sharon smiled. "I'll be ready in a sec. I just need to grab my jacket."

Jake smiled too. Sharon was wearing jeans with a solid-colored blouse with a print vest. "Hi." He stepped inside. The apartment must have housed a hundred plants. The effect was like walking into a greenhouse. "Wow."

"Pardon the plants. I moved from a larger place." She shrugged. "I just couldn't decide which ones to part with, so . . ." She lifted her hands in the air. "So I brought them all." She smiled.

"I can't seem to keep a plant for more than six weeks max. I buy 'em— I kill 'em. Pretty simple, actually."

"I've loved plants since I was a little girl," Sharon offered. "It's therapy."

"Ready?"

"Let's go."

The two stepped out onto the landing.

◆ ◆ ◆

Frank prepared to fire. He waited for the knock.

◆ ◆ ◆

Jake and Sharon descended the steps.

◆ ◆ ◆

Frank cocked his head. *Steps on the stairs? He's chickening out?* He moved to the peephole again and saw Jake opening the door for Sharon. He scratched his head and watched the Trooper drive away.

A thin smile crept onto Frank's face. "He thinks he can get to me through my neighbor, huh? I've got news for him."

Frank moved back to his nest in the kitchen, scratching his head. *Hmmm,* he murmured silently, suddenly contemplating his physical state, *it's been days since I've had a shower. Maybe I should go over to McDonald's to clean up. No, my manager might see me and wonder why I'm not at work. Maybe running the faucet here will be OK. It shouldn't make that much noise. Not that it makes much difference anyway, now that Jake knows I'm here.*

He began talking to himself aloud. "How long have I been hiding here? Since Jake knows I live here, and the police haven't come for me yet, maybe I'd be better off back at the old jailhouse."

◆ ◆ ◆

Jake and Sharon drove along for a few minutes, quickly moving through the small town and out onto the county route that would take them to Green Valley. Bridgewater University sat just to the south of the Wanoset River, which ran east toward the ocean.

They exchanged small talk for a while, both asking and answering questions about their day's activities and the weather. Once they were on the open road, Sharon began to probe deeper.

"So what really brings a dark, mysterious, young surgeon to Taylorville?" She looked at him, admiring his profile for a moment before adding, "Are you really running, Jake, like the reporter implied?"

"Hmmm. Got about two weeks?" Jake shifted in his seat and kept his eyes on the road.

Sharon remained quiet.

"Am I running? I'm not sure. I've asked myself that about a hundred times. I came here because I thought the Lord was leading me, you know?" He glanced at Sharon. She seemed OK with that concept. "I wanted to get away from Grantsville. I just couldn't get Sarah, my wife, out of my mind." He paused. "And of course there was the controversy about her death—the accusation that I gave her an intentional overdose to help her die. I thought I had lost the respect and trust of my patients. There was so much public attention . . . Well, I didn't like it at all. The whole mess was crushing me. Then Dr. Willie called out of the blue and offered me a job in Taylorville. It seemed like a dream come true. I welcomed the chance to return to my hometown. And getting Kyle closer to his grandmother seemed like a good thing—especially since Sarah was gone."

Sharon kept looking at Jake but didn't reply.

Jake continued, "So am I running? I wanted to believe my move to Taylorville was more like seeking a sanctuary, a place where Kyle and I could find some healing of our own."

"What did happen to Sarah?"

Jake looked at her as if trying to discern whether she was ready for his story. His face took on a pained expression. "This is the crazy part of the whole story. I don't really remember the moment she died. I know I was there. That much I do remember." He paused and cast another glance in her direction to check her reaction. She appeared interested but quiet. He sighed. "Sarah found a breast lump early in her pregnancy. Did I tell you she was pregnant?"

Sharon shook her head.

"Anyway, she had it checked out. She went to one of my partners without even telling me. It was as if she didn't want me to worry. Once she showed me, I couldn't believe how quickly it seemed to have developed. For a long time I kicked myself for not having found it myself." He paused.

Sharon nodded.

"Anyway, it was very aggressive. It soon involved the overlying skin and lymph nodes. She was determined to wait to get any therapy until after the baby was born."

Sharon nodded again, with increased understanding. "She didn't want to harm the baby."

"Exactly." Jake slowed to let a car pass. "She was convinced she had brought it all on herself . . . almost as if she thought God had planned her cancer as a form of punishment or something." He looked at Sharon. No reaction. He continued, "She'd had an abortion when she was a teenager—before she was a Christian. She knew having an abortion had increased her risk of developing breast cancer, and so she just accepted it, like she was reaping what she'd sown."

"What did you think?"

"I told her that I thought it was history, all covered by the blood of Jesus and forgiven." He looked at Sharon, trying to see if she understood. "I didn't condemn her. I'd known all about the abortion, even before we married." He heaved a heavy sigh. "But Sarah wouldn't let it go. She became all the more determined that she wouldn't harm another baby. She just seemed so fixated on the fact that she'd killed her first baby . . . There was no way she'd let me talk her into any more therapy."

"Wasn't there any therapy that wouldn't affect the baby?"

Jake shrugged. "It was all a matter of degrees, I guess. But as long as the physicians couldn't guarantee absolute safety to the baby, she wouldn't go for it."

"So she . . ." Sharon opened her mouth in disbelief. "She just let it grow?"

"There's more to the story. Somehow she got information about an alternative medicine hospital—the Ocean Sands Wellness Facility. She ordered their literature, then talked to the staff. All the guarantees that conventional physicians wouldn't give her, they handed out like it was a sure thing." Jake shook his head in disgust.

"I heard about a lot of that stuff in Southern California. Most patients there go to Mexico to get the unapproved treatments."

"Sarah really wanted to do something, and this seemed to make sense to her. It all seemed to focus on detoxifying her body to allow it to fight the cancer naturally." He glanced at his passenger and decided to go on. "She was really into it . . . juice fasts, kelp supplements, saline intervenous flushing, coffee enemas . . . the whole ball of wax."

Sharon made a face. "Oh."

They drove on in silence for a moment. Jake stopped at a traffic signal.

Finally he continued. "The odd thing was, her cancer started to regress. The lump seemed to shrink, and I couldn't feel the lymph nodes anymore." He shook his head. "I could hardly believe it myself. I thought that either God was miraculously healing her or—"

"Or what?"

"Or maybe there was more going on at the Wellness Facility than Sarah knew about." He checked for Sharon's response.

"What makes you say that?"

"Maybe it was just my lack of belief that any of the therapy could really make a difference." He let out an angry snort. "I mean, I was pretty upset that my wife was fleeing from the very therapies I'd built my life around studying. But it was more than that, I guess. Subtle things started happening. Her urine turned blue. She said it was the kelp juice, but I could remember somewhere that some chemotherapy drugs did the same thing. Later, toward the end, her hair started falling out. This even distressed Sarah." His eyes turned misty. "She had the most beautiful auburn hair."

Sharon took it all in. Jake remained silent for a few minutes. She could tell he was remembering.

◆　◆　◆

"I assure you, Dr. Hampton, it is merely a natural phenomenon. Sarah's hair will grow back when her body has completely cleansed itself of the cancer." Susan Rolan was becoming exasperated.

"I only want to talk to the pharmacist or whoever mixes up this green powder," Jake responded. "I just want to know what's in this stuff."

Sarah shot him a look that said, *Enough!* She put her hand over her lower abdomen, which was now visibly swollen with her pregnancy. It was her fourth visit to the facility, and her health had started to decline.

Jake changed gears. "What about the vomiting?"

The nurse said with obvious irritation, "We've told you. The body is attempting to rid itself of toxins. It's a natural part of the process." She looked at Sarah. "Plus she's pregnant. Maybe it's related to that. Ever heard of morning sickness?" She glared at Jake.

Just then the night nurse coordinator arrived. "Is there a problem here?"

Jake sighed. "I only want some straight answers about my concerns for Sarah's therapy. I just want to know exactly what she's getting."

The coordinator shook her head. "It wouldn't matter, Dr. Hampton. If there's one thing we have realized here at Ocean Sands, it's that all components of a person's care are important. It all works together—the physical, the emotional, the spiritual. The patient's attitude is critical to the success of the therapy. It's all tied in together," she explained. "It matters little what the exact components of her therapies are, Dr. Hampton. If you continue to bring negative energy here, nothing will have a lasting, positive effect."

Jake persisted. "If it doesn't matter, let me speak to the person who makes this." He held up a canister.

The coordinator ignored Jake's request. "Sarah told us that you would be a hard sell. We know you've been questioning our methods from the very beginning. I had hoped that our early success would have convinced you, but not even that has been able to penetrate your concrete mind-set."

The surgeon stiffened. Sarah wilted into the padded wicker chair in her room. She didn't seem to have the strength to argue. "What are you suggesting?" Jake asked tentatively.

"That you stay away, Dr. Hampton. Let us try to help your wife without your constant interference and doubts. If you continue to raise questions in Sarah's mind, the therapies are doomed."

"Stay away?" Jake raised his voice. "She's my wife!"

"And she's our responsibility!" The coordinator stood only five and a half feet tall, but she had the emotional constitution of an angry pit bull.

"It's my right to visit her."

"And it's our right to forbid your visits on the grounds that they are detracting from our patient's well-being."

Jake's face went crimson.

A large security officer arrived. "Problems?"

"Help Dr. Hampton find his way out please."

Jake looked at Sarah. Slouched in the chair, she seemed helpless. She threw her arms up and remained speechless, exasperated by the commotion.

The guard reached for Jake.

"Don't touch me!" Jake turned to go. "I'll pick you up Friday, Sarah." Jake realized the futility of staying any longer. The large guard was only too willing to make that clear. "I'll see myself out," he said, looking at the guard.

Jake headed down the hall with a huff. The security guard followed from a distance, keeping the angry surgeon within eyesight at all times.

◆　◆　◆

"Jake?" The voice was soft and feminine.

He snapped out of his thoughts and looked over at Sharon.

"Isn't Green Valley up route 68?"

He nodded appropriately.

"We just passed it."

Jake cringed. "Oops." He pulled into the next driveway and turned around. "Guess I was a little spaced off there." He laughed nervously.

Sharon laughed too. That made Jake feel better. In fact, he was amazed at just how comfortable he was feeling with her already.

"Jake?"

He looked at her again. The light was reflecting off her brown hair, creating a natural shine. "What?"

"I don't understand about the night Sarah died. Why don't you remember?"

"Oh. I was getting to that." He paused and took a deep breath. "Well, you see, the more I saw, especially toward the end, the more convinced I was that things weren't so straightforward at Ocean Sands. We were paying big bucks for her therapy. The insurance company wouldn't pay for it at all, so, because I was financing the whole thing, and because I thought we had a right to know, I started investigating . . . asking questions mostly. Well, this evidently made the director pretty upset, because eventually they just refused to let me come see Sarah any longer. They said I carried too much negative healing energy because I questioned the therapy. When her health declined again, I blamed it on ineffective therapy. They blamed me for not believing."

Sharon raised her eyebrows. "They actually wouldn't let you visit your own wife?"

Jake nodded.

"Pretty weird if you ask me."

"You've got that right."

"What did you do?"

"I stayed away, mostly. I didn't want to make things too difficult for Sarah. She wanted so desperately for it to work. Then, toward the end, when I realized that I might not have much time with her anymore, I began to sneak in."

"You snuck in?"

Jake smiled. "Right." He looked at Sharon. "Don't I look like the law-breaker type?"

Sharon laughed.

"You should see this place. It's on a little peninsula surrounded by water on three sides. The side with the land connection has a high wall and an unmarked entrance with surveillance cameras and an electronic gate—the whole works."

"How did you get in?"

"I waited until the lowest tide possible. Then I'd wade and hop through the salty puddles left by the receding tide on the southernmost border. Once, when the tide wasn't right, I paid a guy with a catamaran to drop me right on the shore. I thought for sure someone would catch me that night." He shook his head. "But they didn't because I would stay out of the light and crouch down and sneak along a high row of bushes until I was under Sarah's balcony."

"Balcony? I thought we were talking about a hospital."

"We are. But you have to understand how these alternative health facilities are run. People pay for it themselves, most of them anyway. They are really more like resorts than anything else." He smiled. "I'm serious."

He looked at Sharon, who shook her head incredulously. "Anyway, I'd climb the latticework outside her balcony and enter her room from the ocean-side sliding door."

"Unbelievable."

"Believe it. So anyway, on the night Sarah died, they say they found me lying on a rock beneath her balcony. I must have slipped or something."

"But you'd done it before, right?"

"A half-dozen times, at least." He squinted at a road sign. "The police report and the media blitz suggested that I'd killed my pregnant wife and then jumped off the balcony in an apparent suicide attempt." He shook his head. "That really makes no sense to me. Number one, I'm not suicidal, and number two, it's really not that big of a jump."

"Why would they make something like that up?"

"I don't know. Maybe it has something to do with the guys at Ocean Sands. I think they're the ones who found me and forwarded that theory. It makes sense to me that if they were trying to disguise the way my wife really died, it might be to their advantage for the police to think I did it."

"I'm not sure I follow."

"Look, Sarah was going to die of her disease. I know that. But she wasn't that close to death. There's no doubt in my mind that she died of unnatural causes. So if I didn't do it or help her do it, who did?" He looked at Sharon and shrugged.

"Ocean Sands? Somebody at the hospital?"

"Maybe."

"Why?"

"Perhaps it didn't look so good to have their prize patient die of cancer. Maybe it was more convenient to have everyone think she died of something else."

"That's a bit far-fetched, don't you think?"

"Maybe. But maybe that whole place is a bit far-fetched. They claim some pretty amazing things on their pamphlets . . . Cure rates over 90 percent for certain types of cancer, for example."

"How can they say that?"

"Very limited follow-up, for one thing. Most of the people are declared cured after the first few treatments. Then if the cancer ever comes back, it's because the patient failed to follow their strict nutritional guidelines or something."

"What's the motivation?"

"Money. Cold, hard cash," Jake explained. "We were paying over $4,000 a week for in-patient care. At one point I counted over 100 in-patients, all getting therapy for one ill or another . . . Everything from chronic fatigue syndrome to systemic fungal infections. It's big. It's huge." He looked at Sharon. "And I think I stepped on its toes."

"So why did the story about you stick?"

"Because I couldn't refute it. Don't you see? Without my memory, I look pretty stupid saying anything against their claim that I jumped from the balcony in a fit of apparent anguish over snuffing out my suffering wife."

Sarah nodded and remained silent. Jake drove on and turned at a sign that said, "Green Valley, 14 miles."

◆ ◆ ◆

Kyle obviously hadn't heard what happened to Todd Gifford or he would have never agreed to go into the old jailhouse alone. The assignment wasn't that tough: go in alone, travel to the second floor, find a window, signal the guys below.

Todd ushered him to the open window leading to the basement. Kyle looked unsure. "Look, Kyle, if you want to hang out with us, you gotta join the club. I did it. Now you've got to do it. And you have to have witnesses. That's why we're here."

Kyle bit his lower lip to keep it from quivering.

Slowly he shimmied through the window. "Man, it stinks in here!"

"Go down the hall to the right. I think you'll find some stairs back there." Todd's memory of the building was fuzzy at best.

Lenny looked at Todd. "I don't know about this," he whispered. "What if he doesn't come back out?"

Todd cast a look at Lenny that clearly said, *Shut up!* He looked at Kyle. "Go ahead! We'll be watching."

Kyle stepped timidly into the hallway and out of view. His footsteps were so light, he barely made a sound.

Lenny whined, "What will we do if he stays in there? We can't just go in and get him."

Todd shrugged. "I thought about that. We'll call 9-1-1 and hang up."

"They trace those calls!"

"Not from these!" Todd pulled out a folded portable cellular phone from his jacket.

"Wow! Where'd you get that?"

"It's my brother's. I took it from his car." Todd smiled. "I thought we might need it."

That made Lenny feel a little better. At least Todd wasn't going to let Kyle die without trying to get some help. The two walked over to the front of the building and looked at the row of windows on the second floor. "See anything yet?"

"No." Lenny looked at his watch. "It's only been three minutes."

They waited two minutes longer.

"Think we should call 9-1-1 yet?"

"Don't be stupid, Lenny. He's probably just looking for a way to get up there."

◆ ◆ ◆

Inside, Kyle crept along the dark corridor. Once he got to the center of the building, it was hard to see. He kept his hand in contact with the wall so he wouldn't get lost. Finally, at the end of the hall, he found a metal door.

"Ugghh!" He strained to open it. Pushing with all his might, he made just enough room to squeeze in. The door slammed shut behind him with a thud that reverberated throughout the empty hallway.

◆ ◆ ◆

Outside, the slam was muffled but audible. "Did ya hear that? Someone's shootin'!" Lenny looked at the cellular phone. "Give me that!"

"No way. That wasn't gunfire!"

◆ ◆ ◆

Kyle immediately tried the door. The doorknob didn't budge, but the door latch had been removed. He knew that if he could somehow get the door back open, he could return the same way he'd come. He crept up the stairs. He could see some light coming through a window on the door leading to the second floor. That door was easier to open, and he slipped into the hallway. Now to find a window and give the signal.

Footsteps! Kyle froze and listened. Instinctively he backed into the shadows next to the wall. "Todd! Lenny! That's not funny! Come out where I can see you!"

◆ ◆ ◆

"I can hear him screaming! Call 9-1-1!"

"Shut up, Lenny! We're not calling 9-1-1 yet!"

◆ ◆ ◆

Inside, no one replied to Kyle's pleas. He held his breath. He thought his heart would jump out of his chest. The stench nauseated him. He took another step. Ahead was a row of cells. When he crept forward, he was sure he heard a noise again.

He wanted to cry. He needed to vomit. "Stop! You're scaring me!"

◆ ◆ ◆

"Todd, did you hear that?"

"Shut up, Lenny. Of course I heard. He's just scared." Todd snorted to show his opinion of his friend's fear. "He's chicken, just like you."

"He's in trouble!"

◆ ◆ ◆

Kyle inched forward, staying in the shadows. He steadied his breathing. He had come this far, and he wouldn't back out now. His foot stumbled on a rock. He picked it up. Must have been thrown in from the outside, he thought. Slowly he edged ahead. Soon he stood adjacent to the first room. It had a window all right—right up against the ceiling. The window was designed for light, not for gazing out of. This place wasn't made for comfort.

Great, Kyle thought. *How am I ever going to signal the guys when I can't even reach the windows?* He walked freely into the cell, since the doors had all been removed. *Maybe if I stand on the commode, I can grab the bars over the window and climb up.*

As he walked toward the commode, the pungent smell nearly over-powered him. He looked at the yellow water in the small toilet. *Someone's been in here!*

Just then he heard a noise again. This time louder—and closer.

Something brushed against his foot.

"Ahhhh!" Kyle screamed as he jumped back against the wall. His cry echoed loudly throughout the deserted hallways.

◆ ◆ ◆

"Give me the phone! He sounds like he's dying in there!"

Todd held the phone tight. "Shut up!"

A second scream followed on the heels of the first. Then there was a loud *thunk*.

Todd looked at Lenny. "I'm calling! I'm calling!"

◆ ◆ ◆

The rock ricocheted off the metal bar with a loud *pop*. Everything seemed louder because of the empty surroundings. He had missed! Kyle strained to see. A rat the size of a small cat had run right across his foot and into the hall. Kyle's rock had clearly scared it, probably as badly as it had scared Kyle. Whatever had been in its mouth had dropped in a damp heap on the floor.

This time Kyle spoke out loud to himself. "I'm getting out of here!"

He started for the exit when the object on the floor caught his eye. The rat had dropped a blue candy wrapper.

There, in white letters, still legible in spite of the gnawing, was one word: *Zero*.

Kyle started to scream.

◆ ◆ ◆

"9-1-1 emergency."

"Someone needs help in the old Taylorville jailhouse. We can hear screaming. It sounds like someone is dying in there!"

The 9-1-1 operator could tell the caller was a child. "Where are you calling from?"

"The jail! Just get someone over here." Todd could hear Kyle screaming in the background.

"What is your name? Stay on the line. I'll have somebody coming to help real soon." The operator's voice was steady and calming.

Todd looked at the phone. He hesitated, then pushed the Off button. "Let's get out of here!"

CHAPTER
15

Todd and Lenny scrambled for their bikes. They wanted to be long gone by the time the police arrived. They had just crossed the railroad tracks when two police cruisers with lights flashing arrived at the scene. The officers didn't notice the two boys scurrying off on their bicycles.

◆ ◆ ◆

Inside the jailhouse, Kyle stood frozen in a small cell, clutching the Zero bar wrapper. Eventually he stopped screaming, collected his wits, and started for an exit. At first he headed for the stairwell he came up. Then, hearing footsteps, he retreated down the long, dark hallway toward the building's far end. At the end of the hall he came to a heavy metal door. This one was hopelessly frozen in place. It didn't really seem to be locked, but it was just too heavy, even for a large eleven-year-old. He started back for the other exit when he heard the stairwell door creak. He held his breath and jumped into the nearest cell. This one had a mattress in addition to a few old wooden boxes.

Kyle cowered in a corner, crouched behind one of the wooden crates. The footsteps were getting closer. In a few more seconds Kyle could see a flashlight beam searching the hallway, sweeping first left, then right, entering every room. Should he run? Where could he go?

The light beam caught him off-guard. It shone brightly in his eyes. He squinted and put his hand over his face.

"It's just a kid," Deputy Don Rawlings reported on his radio. "We won't need any backup."

"Come out here, boy!" Deputy Steve Branson called to Kyle. "What are you doing here?"

Kyle stepped out from behind the crate. He was just glad it was the police. "I was just looking around," he mumbled. He decided not to mention Lenny and Todd, in case they weren't outside. He didn't want to get them in any trouble.

"Look at this place," Don muttered. "Looks like this little guy's been hidin' out here!"

Steve laughed. "Sure smells like it."

Don started looking around the room while Steve talked to Kyle. "What's your name?"

"Kyle," he said, looking down. "Kyle Hampton."

"Hampton?" Steve looked at his partner. "Dr. Hampton's son?"

Kyle nodded.

"Your dad's the one who just operated on the mayor?"

"I guess so."

Don picked up an old scrap of paper from the floor beneath the bed. Apparently it had been dropped and ended up under the bed. It was a photograph of Sarah Hampton. "What are you doing here, Kyle?" he asked. Then he showed him the photograph, a shot taken from the *Grantsville Gazette*. "Do you know this woman?"

Kyle nodded again, this time wide-eyed. "It's my mom."

"You've got quite a camp here, son," Steve said with concern. "But this place is off-limits. Could be dangerous."

"Today's the first time I've come here."

The deputies looked around the room—the only one with a mattress, wooden crates, and a few old food cans and candy wrappers. Don looked down at the photo of the boy's mother. It was obvious that someone who knew Sarah Hampton had been using the room. "Right, son, and I'm the president."

Kyle raised his voice. "It's true."

Steve looked at Kyle's fist, still clenched around the candy wrapper. "What've you got there?"

Kyle slowly unwrapped his fingers from around the Zero bar wrapper. Steve's gaze went from that wrapper to several identical ones thrown into the corner. "You've never been here before?"

Kyle shook his head.

Just then something else caught Don's eye. A glint of metal next to the front wall reflected his flashlight. He picked it up. It was an unused round for a .38. He put the bullet in his pocket but didn't say anything. He would record his finding in a formal police report.

Steve looked at Kyle and at his partner. "Let's get out of here. I'm not sure I can stand this sewer much longer." He wrinkled his nose.

Don nodded and took Kyle by the arm. "Let's go, son."

◆ ◆ ◆

At the edge of the woods, Frank peered out, watching everything. First the boys, now Kyle coming out of the jailhouse with the police. "They're looking for me," he mumbled. He shook his head. "Jake, Jake, Jake," he whispered, "you send your boy over to do your spy work, eh?"

He watched as Kyle got in the back of the police cruiser. "You called to show them my home, didn't you, Kyle?"

The police car pulled out as Frank looked on. *Great*, he thought. *Now Jake has the girl across the street watching me, and his son has called the police to investigate my little hideaway.* He wasn't sure where to go. He looked around. It was getting cold. *I'll stay in the woods until dark*, he thought as he pulled some leaves up over his legs. *Then I'll move.*

He shook his head. "Jake, Jake," he whispered, "I'm going to have to do something about you soon."

◆ ◆ ◆

Jake knocked on the hospital door gently.

"Come in." The voice was Linda's.

Jake and Sharon entered. Linda was sitting up in the bed. Matt was in one chair, and Sandra Stone, Matt's mother, was holding Mark Aaron in a second.

Jake looked at the baby, who was sleeping. He kept his voice low. "Hi." He looked at Matt and Linda. "I've brought along a friend." He held his arm out toward Sharon. "This is Sharon Isaacs. Sharon, this is Linda and Matt."

"Hi, Sharon," Linda smiled. "And this is Sandra Stone, Matt's mother, and of course Mark Aaron."

"He's so cute." Sharon looked over Sandra's shoulder.

Matt and Jake shook hands. "Good to see you, Jake."

Jake nodded. It was good to be among friends.

After they talked a few minutes longer, Jake steered the conversation back to Mark. "So how's he doing? He looks good. Are they sure he'll need surgery?"

"Dr. Morra came by again this morning. She's the pediatric cardiologist. It looks like we have a week to decide."

Linda frowned. "I could tell something was wrong this morning, almost like he found it hard to get his breath when he cried."

"Have you thought any more about Dr. Simons?"

Matt groaned. "We've done little else but think about this whole problem, Jake."

Jake and Sharon nodded.

Linda added. "We just want what is the very best for our baby."

"What does Dr. Morra recommend?" Sharon asked.

Matt shrugged. "That's what started this whole dilemma. She thinks Dr. Simons is the man for the job."

Jake realized Sharon was in the dark. "It's a long story, Sharon. Back in residency, Dr. Simons was a professor of ours." He paused. "Then he started using live, late second trimester aborted babies for transplant research."

Matt continued, "And I found out about it and blew the whistle."

"Eventually Simons lost his tenured faculty position at the university over it. Now he shows up at the same hospital where Matt works to start a heart program for children."

"Oooh. A pretty remarkable set of circumstances, to say the least."

Matt shrugged. "I think it might be divinely directed. Why else would I be constantly thrown together with this man?"

Jake shook his head. "I'm not sure." He waited a moment, then added, "Have you considered the opposite?"

Matt took on a puzzled expression but remained silent.

Jake continued, "That maybe it's our spiritual enemy's design. I mean, he tried to ruin your career before and it didn't work. Maybe this is strike two?"

Linda looked concerned.

Sandra rocked the baby gently. "I'm still praying for a miracle."

Jake waited a few moments, then asked about Simons. "How does Simons feel about all this? Is he angry at you? Or has he left the past behind him?"

"I don't really know. It has only been in the last few weeks that I've seen him again. He acts cold toward me, but then again, he was never very personable. That's just the way he is."

"I know he's always been hard for me to read," Jake added. "Have you considered just talking to him to see if he has any feelings about it?"

Linda answered, "We really wanted to have our feelings sorted out first."

"Sure," Sharon responded. "That's understandable."

◆ ◆ ◆

Don Rawlings and Steve Branson were completing their shift.

"Did I show you this?" Don retrieved the bullet from his shirt pocket and handed it to Steve.

"It's a .38."

"I have an uneasy feeling about this kid. He's trouble."

"Wise beyond his years, I'm afraid."

"Probably just a product of his environment," Don added. "His father fought off a murder rap. His mom's gone. Now he's just fighting to make his own way. Just an eleven-year-old with pent-up frustrations and no outlet."

"Could be trouble," Steve agreed. "Do you think we ought to get Protective Services involved?"

"Not yet. So far all we really have is a kid trespassing in an old jail."

"But with his father's reputation . . . It doesn't look like the kid has a role model at all."

"Just some jerk who takes the law in his own hands and knocks off his wife."

"And gets away with it."

"We'll have to watch the kid real close." Don closed a file folder. "Did you find out who was supposed to be watching him?"

"I called the lady he told us about. It's a neighbor, a Mrs. Gifford. She said her boys told her that Kyle insisted on going to the jail. He was bragging about how he wasn't scared to go in there. They heard him scream and put in the 9-1-1 call."

"He was probably just screaming to scare the other boys. He didn't figure on them calling the police." He chuckled. "Does the sitter know where the father is?"

"She told me he's in Green County visiting a friend. At the Bridgewater University Hospital. She gave me a number he left."

"Let's call this surgeon and give him a little update." Don slapped his partner on the shoulder.

◆　◆　◆

Frank found lying outside exhilarating. Sure, he knew he had enemies. He knew they were after him, and they might be closing in. But at least the fog had cleared. Cutting back on the medications had sure helped that, he mused. He wondered how many years he had missed, under the cloud of false security that the medicines had caused. It was one thing to have enemies, and another to have them and not be aware of them. *That's what taking the medicines did to me*, Frank remembered. *It didn't keep my enemies away. It just kept me from recognizing them.*

Maybe that's why Dr. D recommended cutting back. The last time we talked, he spoke of taking them away altogether. What was it he said? "The time to clarify your mission has come." He smiled. It was good having someone believe in him again. He would accomplish his purpose. His doctor believed in him.

He felt in his pocket for his Haldol. He was still taking a small dose. Dr. D wouldn't let him quit altogether. He said these things must be done in the proper time. He would leave that up to his doctor. He knew best.

He thought back to the time when the fog began. It was a long time ago, long before his recovery.

◆　◆　◆

"Is he still in seclusion?" Dr. Eagle, the psychiatric attending, looked at Grimsted's chart.

"Ever since he broke my hand," Dave Foley responded.

"Have you upped the medications?"

"Tripled them," Jim Maley, the intern, answered.

"What's he like now?"

"He walks around the perimeter of his room in a silent stare," Maley stated.

"Any more violence?"

"He hasn't really been tested," Foley responded. "He's only been in the padded room."

"For three weeks?"

Foley checked the records. "We wanted to be careful. He tried to kill me with a piece of glass."

"He did bomb a health clinic, too, let's remember," the intern added.

"Let's start getting him out," Eagle instructed. "Even outside in the fenced yard. The fresh air will do him good. Just make sure a few of those linebacker attendants are nearby."

"Don't worry. I'll make sure we keep this one adequately medicated," Foley replied, rubbing the cast on his hand. "I don't want to take any chances."

"Let's have a look at him."

"In here?" Foley looked concerned.

"Let's go down to his room." The psychiatrist stood. "Is he in a room with a two-way mirror?"

"Not after he broke the mirror in his room. We haven't even given him eating utensils."

Maley, the intern, chuckled. "I can just see Frank eating his Jello."

Dr. Eagle failed to see the humor. "Let's go. I want to talk to him." He led the group down the hall. In moments he was knocking on Frank's door. "Frank? It's Dr. Eagle. Can we talk?"

He unlocked the door and pushed it open. Frank was sitting in the corner.

"Jim and Dave are here too. Is that OK?"

Frank nodded and stared straight ahead.

"Are you hearing any voices, Frank? Voices telling you to do bad things?"

Frank shook his head. "No voices."

"Do you want to hurt anyone? Do you want to hurt yourself?"

"No."

"Is anyone trying to hurt you, Frank? Does anyone want to hurt you?"

Frank looked at the trio of doctors for the first time and squinted. After a moment he gave his brief answer—"No" and returned to staring blankly at the wall.

"What about Sarah, Frank? Has anyone been trying to hurt her?"

He continued to look at the wall. "No."

The psychiatrists conferred with a silent look and a shrug.

"Would you like to go outside?"

Frank hesitated and looked at the floor. "Maybe later. I feel better in here."

"Would you like to go back to a regular room?"

"Maybe later."

"Can we do anything for you? Get anything for you?"

Frank looked at a smear of chocolate pudding on the floor. "Can you get me some spoons?"

Dr. Eagle smiled. "Sure, Frank, sure." He walked over and put his hand on Frank's shoulder.

Frank withdrew from his touch.

"Everything's going to be OK, Frank. You're going to be OK."

◆　◆　◆

Frank remembered the words even now as his mind reeled with paranoia. He waited until dark, then slipped into the jailhouse through the window. There were a few items he needed to store more carefully, just in case the police returned for a complete search.

◆　◆　◆

Sharon smiled as she cradled the infant in her arms. It felt, well, natural. She looked at Jake, then back at Linda, who was smiling too.

"When did Pastor Kreider say he was coming by?" Linda looked at her watch.

Matt responded. "Should be anytime now."

Linda looked at Sharon and her son. "Our pastor from Green Valley Christian Fellowship is coming by to pray for Mark."

Matt looked at his watch too. "We'd like you to stay if you can—"

A nurse entered, cutting short Matt's words. "Dr. Hampton?"

Jake looked surprised. He looked at Sharon and wrinkled his brow. "That's me."

"I have a telephone call for you at the nurses' station."

Jake followed her out and took the phone from the ward clerk. "Hello."

"Dr. Hampton?"

"Yes."

"Officer Don Rawlings here, Taylorville Police. We're holding your son—"

CHAPTER
16

IN spite of heavier traffic, the trip back to Taylorville was quicker than the trip to Green Valley. Jake was quiet, lost in thought, whispering a prayer. Sharon was thinking too, and praying for Kyle and Jake and the new friends she had made that day. The Stones were warm people. Although she had known them for only a few hours, she understood them as only a fellow member of the family of God could.

Jake opted to drop Sharon off before going to the station. He wanted Kyle to be comfortable with a family-only confrontation. At Sharon's he said good-bye. He had enjoyed her company. She smiled and assured him that she was thinking of him and praying for him.

Once at the station, Jake signed a form, and Kyle was released. The walk to the car was quiet. Inside, Jake saw the start of a tear.

"Want to tell me about it?"

"They've got it all wrong, Dad." Kyle looked at his father and pleaded, "I didn't go in there by my own choice."

"What happened?"

"The older boys told me I had to do it if I wanted to be in their club."

Jake shook his head. "The police already talked to Mrs. Gifford. She says you were the one with the idea—"

"It's not true! They're lying!" Kyle tried to hold back a sob.

Jake looked at his son. "Kyle," he said calmly, "trust has always been a big part of our relationship. You know you can tell me anything, and I'll believe you."

"I went in there on a dare, but I got scared. I started screaming, and they called the police. They must have run off 'cause they were nowhere to be found once the police came."

Jake thought for a moment. "Kyle, the police say it looked like you had made a camp in one of the cells. They said you had obviously eaten there before and that you had used the bathroom there."

"The police are lying!"

"Maybe they are just uninformed."

"Somebody had been there before, but not me. It was my first time."

"But, Kyle, they showed me a picture of Mom. Why would anyone else bring that into a jail cell?"

"I don't know." Kyle was silent for a moment. "You believe me, don't you, Dad?"

Jake made eye contact with his son, then returned his attention to the road. "If you say you've never been there before, then I believe you."

Kyle dug deep into his jeans pocket. "Dad, I found this in there." He handed him the candy wrapper.

"Another Zero bar!" Jake shook his head. "Something is sure weird about this. First I find them in the Trooper, then in the mailbox, and now you find them in the jail."

"Don't forget the picture of Mom! Maybe she's still trying to signal us!"

"Kyle, these aren't from Mom. After you die, you don't leave candy wrappers lying around. Dead people don't make messes."

Kyle laughed at that. "I still think maybe she's trying to tell us something. I saw something like this on *Unsolved Mysteries*."

"Kyle!"

The boy smirked.

"But I'm beginning to think you may be right about the message thing. Maybe someone *is* trying to tell us something."

"If it's not Mom, then who?"

Jake shrugged. "I don't know." He thought for a moment. "Someone who knew something about your mom. That might explain the picture."

"Why would someone want to live in a deserted jail?"

"I don't know, Kyle. What was it like in there?"

"Dark," he responded, remembering his scary adventure. "Dark and smelly . . . like a sewer or something."

"What about this cell that was fixed up?"

"Fixed up isn't exactly what I'd call it, Dad." Kyle rolled his eyes. "It had a dirty old mattress on an old metal bed and a few wooden boxes on the floor. There were old cans and some candy wrappers. That's about all, I think." He stared at his father. "Maybe we should go in there together and check it out."

"No." Jake looked at his son. "They're probably watching the place now. That's the last thing I need to be caught doing. I can see the headlines now: 'Former Murder Suspect Caught Violating Trespass Law. He Wants to Be in Jail.'" He chuckled. So did Kyle. "Yeah, that's all we need."

Kyle laughed and blew his nose. "What's for supper?"

"I haven't even thought about it."

"Can we eat out?"

Jake tried to think of something at home. His mind came up as empty as their refrigerator. "Sure. Where do you want to go?"

"McDonald's."

Where else?

◆ ◆ ◆

"Check this out, Steve," Don Rawlings reported. "I called the principal of the elementary school. Even though the Hampton kid is new, they've already got a fat file on him. Seems he's been seeing a counselor over there. Said they even made a referral out to a doctor. The principal wasn't sure, because the counselor was out, but said he thought he had some attention disorder or something."

"Great. Now we got a kid with a criminal father, and on top of it the boy's some sort of mental case. We're gonna have to watch him, Don."

"The deck is starting to stack against this kid pretty early. Bad role model at home, no mother, psychiatric illness . . . It starts with stuff like this—bragging to the older boys, acting up for attention—who knows where it ends?" He thought for a moment. "And who knows why the kid had a bullet out there? Maybe he's even got a gun."

"Wouldn't surprise me." Steve shook his head. "What gets me is the way these punks can lie through their teeth. Even when we confronted him with the evidence of two other witnesses, he still claimed it wasn't his idea to go into the jail."

"The kid isn't so smart. I just hope he realizes it in time."

"Really. Let's hope some things start falling into place for him or we're going to have a real problem on our hands in Taylorville."

Don nodded. "I think we already do."

◆ ◆ ◆

Jake wasn't the only one with an empty refrigerator. Sharon opened the fridge door and sighed. She picked through a few Tupperware containers of leftovers and peered into a moldy container of low-fat cottage cheese. "Yeech!" She tossed the container into the trash and looked in the cupboard. Tomato soup and a can of mixed fruit sat lonely beside the spices. Not exactly king's fare. She opted for a trip to the Taylorville Foodmart.

On her return to Apartment C, she dropped the groceries on the landing outside her door with a clatter. Inside his apartment Frank stirred. He immediately went to full alert. Slowly he crept to the door. He hadn't had time to replace the barricade yet. *Maybe that's why the enemy is attacking now*, he speculated.

He looked through the peephole. "It's only my neighbor," he whispered to himself. He thought for a moment and remembered she was a friend of Jake's. He decided to watch her carefully. She would likely be collecting data for Hampton.

Sharon put the key in the door and turned it. The door opened, but she couldn't get her key out. She huffed and pulled again. She pulled the groceries inside, bracing the door open with her foot. She jiggled the key again, but it wouldn't budge. She groaned again and looked at her watch. The office was already closed. She looked across at the door opposite hers. From inside that apartment, it appeared that she was staring right at Frank.

Frank pulled his face away from the keyhole. *She can see me! She knows I'm watching her! They're out to get me, just like they got my Sarah!* His mind was racing as a crisp knock sounded on his door.

Frank began to panic. What could he do? He pressed his head against the peephole again. *She doesn't seem to be armed. Maybe I could pull her inside and overpower her.* A knock came again, interrupting Frank's paranoia.

"Who's there?" Frank tried to sound stern.

"I'm your neighbor. I just need some help getting my key out of my doorknob."

Was it a trick? No, Frank decided. He had watched the whole thing. She seemed legitimate enough. Maybe this once.

Frank edged the door open but kept the chain-lock intact. He pressed his face up to the crack. "Step away from the door."

Sharon looked at him curiously. "Why—"

"Please."

Sharon stepped back. As Frank opened his door, she caught a quick glimpse of the kitchen beyond. A table on its side, chairs pulled aside, and . . . a pistol? Yes, she saw a pistol on the floor beside a sleeping bag.

Sharon pointed to her door. "It's stuck." She tried to smile. "I don't believe we've met." She held out her hand to the man who wore a green army jacket. "I'm Sharon Isaacs, your new neighbor. You must be Frank Grimsted."

"You know who I am all right."

The statement caught her off-guard. "I read your name on the mail slot," she explained. He held her hand limply for a moment, then turned to the doorknob.

"Mine used to do this."

He wiggled the key, held it to the far left, and pulled. "Here," he said, handing it back to her. "Try spitting on it before you put it in."

Sharon tried not to wince outwardly. "Thanks."

In a moment both people disappeared into their apartments. Neither realized how much the other wanted to get away, and neither saw the other move inside his or her apartment so quickly.

◆ ◆ ◆

By the time Jake laid his head on his pillow, he was exhausted. Maybe it was the conversations with Sharon, maybe it was work pressures, maybe it was the situation with Kyle, but for whatever reason, his subconscious remained active, and his dreams were colorful and disturbing.

◆ ◆ ◆

Jake could see by his watch that he didn't have much time until the tide would come in too far to allow him to escape by way of the beach. He would have to make quick work and get back to his car. He ducked and ran along the low wall and then along a hedgerow that came up to within a few yards of Sarah's hospital room. He climbed the lattice and hoisted himself over the balcony railing. He tried the door. It was unlocked just like she'd promised.

Sarah had fought a good fight, but now every breath brought new pain. Her eyes met with Jake's as he came through the open balcony sliding door. She had been crying again.

"You came."

"Of course." He smiled and gripped her hand.

"I wasn't sure I'd see you again."

"I told you I'd come."

"I'm hurting, Jake. I can't take it anymore."

Jake stroked her salty cheek. "Don't worry."

"Will you help me?" She bit her lower lip until she trembled, then could not hold back her sobs. "Please, Jake! I want to die."

"The baby isn't ready." He made the argument, but he knew he would help her anyway.

"I'll never make it until the baby's viable, Jake. You can see that."

Jake stared at her for a moment. "I love you."

"It's been good being with you." Sarah's glistening eyes met Jake's again. This time he cried with her. "Did you bring the medicine?"

Jake nodded.

"I'm ready, Jake. Send me home." She closed her eyes.

Jake pulled out a syringe of clear fluid. He looked quickly at Sarah's arms but found no suitable veins. She was too dehydrated. He pulled down her sweatpants and felt for her femoral pulse. He pierced the appropriate spot on her thigh and advanced the needle until he aspirated blood. Then he emptied the syringe into the bloodstream. But suddenly the syringe was a scalpel. He looked down at the blood pouring from Sarah's groin. The femoral artery pumped a pulsating fountain into the room.

The sheets, his clothes . . . everything he touched turned red. He looked up just as he heard a noise on the balcony.

Someone was coming! Hospital security guards swarmed the room. "Stop him!"

"Murderer!" The accusations became louder and louder. The voices reverberated around the hospital bed and chased him. Large, dark words hung like smoke in the room. "Hypocrite!"

Jake suddenly became aware of the baby. The baby was kicking. The baby was crying. "Daddy!"

Violent kicks . . . rapid, pounding heart sounds . . . then silence.

The guards chased Jake around the room, then onto the balcony. Jake prepared to climb down when a large guard grabbed him around the waist. He shook Jake like a limp doll, then threw him off the balcony.

In the dream it took a long time to hit the ground as he plummeted in slow motion. In the background he could hear them doing CPR on Sarah.

"One and two and three and four and . . ."

In his hand the syringe, now filled with blood, erupted in another red fountain, a witness to the world of Jake's ugly accomplishment. He watched in horror as it emptied its scarlet contents onto his clothing. The syringe was alive, pumping vast quantities of Sarah's blood into the air.

Jake screamed, "She wanted to die! She wanted to die!"

Then his head smacked the rocks below and interrupted his scream.

◆ ◆ ◆

Jake awoke with a start, his head wet with perspiration. He tried to calm his racing heart. It was only a dream, wasn't it? He wiped his forehead and stared at the ceiling. He opened his clenched hand, half-expecting to see the syringe, but finding only the fingernail imprints in his palm. His hand was empty.

Jake sighed and sat up.

He didn't feel much like sleeping anymore.

◆ ◆ ◆

Kyle tossed on his bed, his legs moving as his mind whirled.

Darkness. Smelly darkness. *Something is rotting in here.*

Images of metal bars and concrete floors filled his mind.

A large metal door slammed. He wasn't alone.

There were rats. Lots of rats. Rats carrying messages from his mother.

"Kyle!" He recognized his mother's voice.

"I'm here, Mom."

"Kyle!"

"I'm here!"

"Kyle, answer me!"

Frustration built as he realized he wasn't getting through. Somehow he could hear her, but she was shut off from him. He ran to find the source of the voice. "Mom! Mom!"

He tripped over a rock, and the rats closed in. "Ahhh!"

He could hear Lenny and Todd laughing. "Kyle's chicken!"

A rat bit deep into his toe. He struggled free, only to see that his toe now resembled a candy bar. White chocolate oozed from the wound.

"Kyle!"

He ran to a cell, one with a small window letting in a ray of light. He saw the photograph now. It was his mother. She was calling to him. He lifted the newspaper clipping, watching with horror as his mother called his name again. "Kyle!"

He looked up to see the police. Images of the patrol car, the police station, and McDonald's filtered by. He could hear the police talking.

"The kid doesn't have a chance. Rotten father. No mother. This kid's got to be watched."

Kyle ran from the police.

"He's nothing but trouble."

A rat chased him, dragging along a Zero bar. Kyle turned on the rat, consumed with the new idea that he had to catch that rat. He had to get the tip of his toe back.

The smell became overwhelming.

Kyle shook his head and opened his eyes. His covers were twisted in a tight knot. He felt afraid.

He slipped out of bed and went into his father's room.

"Kyle? What are you doing up?"

"Bad dreams."

Jake nodded. "Me too." Kyle snuggled in next to his father. "Want to pray?"

Kyle nodded.

Jake prayed and chased their fears away again.

CHAPTER
17

THE following day, on the second page of the *Taylorville Times*, an article was tucked away in the far column. Jake made a cursory inspection of the paper but missed the article:

PIN OAK SOCIETY VOWS FIGHT
FOR PRO-DEATH LEGISLATION

Steve Smith, director of the local chapter of the Pin Oak Society, promised to step up their lobbying activity to assist the passage of the right-to-death legislation that will be debated later this month. Following the lead of several other states, including Oregon and California, the bill seeks to decriminalize physician-assisted suicide and gives patients more autonomy in deciding when to choose death as an appropriate treatment option. The society is conducting a fund drive to help finance several local chapter events to help broaden awareness of the society's agenda. Included in the upcoming planned events is an awards banquet honoring those who have fought so valiantly in the fight to win patients the right to choose death when and where they deem appropriate . . .

The same day, Dr. Willie was sorting through the office mail. A letter with the return address of the Pin Oak Society caught his eye. It was addressed to Dr. Hampton, but he opened it anyway.

Dear Dr. Hampton:

We are pleased to inform you that you have been selected as a nominee for an award at our upcoming banquet to honor those who have been influential in the fight for a new right-to-death bill in our state legislature. Your particular case came to our attention through the coverage of your wife's death. Please accept our sincere condolences.

Would you be willing to participate in our dinner as our guest? Please use the inclosed RSVP card for your convenience.

Thank you.

Sincerely,
Steve Smith

Dr. Willie smiled. *Maybe this is just what Jake needs. A nice community award . . . a show of support for all he's been through . . . Maybe it will help him accept the past for what it was . . . and maybe it will convince him to stay on in our comfortable community.*

He thought for a moment while turning over the small RSVP card in his hand. *Jake will never accept an award like this,* Willie mused. *But maybe if I fill the card out for him, I can convince him to go. Or maybe I'll just surprise him and take him to the dinner myself.*

He checked an affirmative response and shoved the card in a return envelope. *Won't Jake be surprised when he finds out the community is honoring him instead of criticizing him?*

This is just what he needs. A thin smile crept over his face. "Just what he needs," he muttered aloud.

◆ ◆ ◆

Michael Simons was amazingly straightforward. So was Matt Stone. The combination proved electric.

Simons stood in a dimly lit room with the video recorder playing. On the screen, the images of Mark Aaron Stone's cardiac angiogram ran on, the black and white shadows revealing the underlying pathology with marked clarity. "Here is the septal defect," Simons said mechanically as he pointed to the screen. "You can appreciate it even better in this oblique view." He fast-forwarded the tape. "Blood is flowing across the defect."

Matt nodded with understanding. Linda simply nodded.

"The child needs an operation." Simons's demeanor, which had never been warm, softened. "It could be risky. The child may have a stroke, cardiac rhythm problems, any myriad of serious complications . . ." His voice trailed off.

"What choice do we have?" Linda's voice was noticeably strained.

"An operation is the child's only chance of survival." They knew Simons was speaking the truth.

Matt and Linda sat silently for a moment. There were other issues, so far unspoken, that needed to be verbalized. Matt sat forward in his chair. "How do you feel about operating on my child?"

Simons looked at Matt and squinted. He remained silent.

Matt continued, "In my residency—"

"You tried to ruin my career," Simons interrupted, his voice remarkably calm.

Matt stiffened and exhaled cautiously before speaking. "I only felt it important to reveal what I felt was unethical in the treatment of unborn babies, Dr. Simons. I did not intend on ruining your surgical career, only to expose the transplant research."

"The effect was the same—"

"But my intention was different," Matt injected, raising his voice. "Besides, I felt it was you who sought to end my career."

Simons raised his eyebrows but did not issue a disclaimer.

Matt continued, "You should understand that I am separating how I feel about your surgical skills and how I view your stand on ethical issues." He paused. "I think my feelings about your surgical skills should be quite obvious, since I am bringing my only son to you for help."

Simons contemplated that for a moment.

"You know, Stone, it's interesting to me that the very research you disagreed with could have helped your son right now." He looked at Matt. "A twisted bit of irony perhaps."

Matt remained silent for a moment longer before refocusing his question. Linda silently rocked the infant in her arms. "So does any of this affect your feelings about operating on our child?"

"The truth of the matter remains—I am the world's expert on this problem." He spoke with a practiced, academic air. "It would seem unethical for me to withhold my surgical skill from this patient just because I've collided with his father in the past."

Matt stood. "Thanks." He reached out his hand. This time Simons took it.

"I know it took a lot to ask me for help. I'm not sure I would have done the same." Simons's voice sounded sincere. "I'll have my nurse set up the first available surgery date."

Linda stood, still holding the baby. "We'll let you know, Dr. Simons. We still need to process this further."

With that, Linda turned and walked away, clutching her baby to her chest. Matt issued a quick "Good-bye" and bounded out to catch up with Linda.

In the hallway Matt hastened his pace and touched his wife's elbow. "What was that all about?"

"Gut reaction, I guess," she stated with a shrug. "He gives me the creeps." She shook her head. "I don't know, Matt. There's just something about him. I don't know if I could put Mark in his hands and feel right about it."

◆ ◆ ◆

Back in his office, Simons shuddered. Would Stone actually allow him to operate on little Mark?

He paced on the plush carpeting. Could he resist the temptation for revenge? He shook off a second chill.

An evil presence gnawed at his heart, whispering plans of deceit and destruction. Simons stiffened. *Murder.*

Did he sense the message correctly? A mistake maybe, but . . . murder? He shook his head. He didn't want to think in those terms again.

He sat down at his desk, a dark cloud of heaviness pushing him to listen . . . to obey.

Murder! This is your chance to avenge the destruction of your academic career! Was that any less of a loss? You were destined for greatness. Stone took that all away. In essence, that was a death too.

He shook his head. His mind filled with oppressive contemplations.

Simons sank deeper, the bitterness he'd harbored for so long opening the way for increased satanic strongholds. Whether he knew it or not, a fight was on for possession of his soul.

He sat silently, his head lowered to his desk, until his secretary called him. "Dr. Simons? Your next patient is here."

◆ ◆ ◆

Frank's later years in the state hospital were characterized by the absence of color . . . or black and white for that matter. Nothing stood out. Everything was gray to Frank, who lived his life under a haze of anti-psychotic medications.

It's not to say that nothing changed.

Plenty changed. Just not Frank. He went from day to day with a durable sameness, speaking little, walking the same path, at the same speed, with the same blank expression that made his caregivers wonder if there was really anyone home in Frank's body at all.

The nurses turned over about every six months. Few could take the pathetic patients and constant challenges that presented themselves on an hourly basis longer than that. The chief residents changed every four months. The interns turned over monthly. The attendings traded coverage for a month at a time, preferring the more lucrative university patient population to the state's parade of chronic hospital-dwellers.

Frank's chart turned into two volumes, then four, then a dozen as the new interns wrote out their longhand summaries of their new patients. Layer upon layer, page upon page was piled atop Frank's violent history. His chart was thinned and thinned again until finally no one really knew why he was there at all.

No one remembered the bombing. No one knew of his violent outbursts against the staff. No one knew of his traumatic electric shock therapy.

Day by day Frank passed the front desk and turned around at the front door. He rarely went outside. He would turn down the main corridor, his head tilted slightly to the left as he shuffled to the end of the hall and went up the stairs. As he walked, he held his hands close to his side, never swinging them to balance his eccentric gait. It gave him the appearance of gliding along in an unnatural, eerie sort of way. On the second floor he would exit the stairwell and turn left again. Down the hall, up the stairs, then down the hall again—a pattern repeated on every floor, from bottom to top, then top to bottom. Over and over and over.

"Fifty-two, fifty-three, fifty-four," he muttered as he counted the steps in the stairwell. When he exited the stairs, he would stop counting, only to start again when he reached the stairwell at the end of the next floor.

There were 130 steps to the top floor. One hundred and eighteen steps down the hall. Two hundred and forty-eight to the fence through the front door. Every day the same. Every year the same. Everything was gray in the everyday sameness of Frank's hospital stay.

◆ ◆ ◆

Kyle looked out the window. He knew his dad didn't like the videotape he'd just taken out of the cabinet. It would make him mad. It would make him remember, Kyle thought. But the coast was clear. His grandmother was napping, so Kyle had the living room and the TV all to himself.

He slipped the tape into the VCR and pressed Play. The blue screen appeared. The word *Play* was displayed, followed by white fuzz. Then Kyle saw his mother again.

Sarah was walking along the ocean. She was wearing a sweat outfit with "Ocean Sands Wellness Facility" embroidered over the pocket. Under that, her name was clearly printed, and beneath that was written "Cancer Survivor." The wind kicked up her auburn hair. She was smiling at the camera. She began by saying. "Hi. I'm a cancer survivor."

The camera panned quickly to a group of children throwing a beach ball. The ball flew toward Sarah, who caught it and heaved it high into the air. Children's squeals and her laughter filled the scene. The camera zoomed out and took an angle right under the ball. The ball floated, as if suspended by the children's laughter, then fell toward the camera lens. Just when the ball completely filled the screen, the scene changed to Sarah sitting in a wicker chair in one of the hospital rooms. The camera angle made it obvious Sarah was pregnant. "When I was diagnosed with breast cancer, I thought my happy world had come to an end. Because of my pregnancy, I was afraid of taking harmful chemotherapy or radiation. I didn't want to harm my baby . . ."

The camera panned to an air shot of the compound. Patients were seen swimming in a crystal-clear pool. Others were sipping cool drinks with their feet dangling in the water. A male voice continued after Sarah's voice faded. "Sarah, a surgeon's wife, had the best conventional medical care available to her. Yet she chose the completely natural program at Ocean Sands Wellness Facility. Our treatment specializes in restoring the body's own natural ability to fight cancer."

Sarah again was seen center-stage. "I'm making my recovery at Ocean Sands. I've seen amazing results, without harmful chemotherapy. My body is stronger. My immune system is fighting the cancer. Do yourself a favor. Don't delay. Call today. I'm glad I did."

Music filled the background and softened. A voice-over urged, "Call 1-800-4-CANCER for your free information booklet on how Ocean Sands Wellness Facility can meet your health-care needs."

Kyle pressed Stop and Rewind. He repeated the process three times. As they had never purchased a video camera, it was the only videotape of his mother that he had.

During the fourth viewing, Jake hurried through the front door. Kyle snapped off the set and looked at his father. "Dad!" His cheeks flushed.

Jake had seen enough to know what he was watching. "Where did you get that tape, Kyle?"

"Grandma. She lets me watch it." He smiled and wrinkled his nose. "It's the only tape I have, Dad." He looked at the floor. "Is it OK?"

Jake softened. As much as he hated that tape, he couldn't deny his son the only video images of his mother he had. "I guess so." He tousled his son's hair and walked into the kitchen. "Where's Grandma?"

"Sleeping."

Jake checked his watch. "Want to go home? We can leave Grandma a note."

Kyle shrugged. "Sure." He walked to the kitchen where his father was scribbling a note. "Why don't you like the tape of Mom?"

Jake looked at his son and sighed. "It's not that I don't like seeing your mom. I loved her—you know that. It's just . . . Well, it's just that I don't like seeing her advertising for that hospital. I didn't like that place. They don't treat people the way I was trained, Kyle. They don't allow the medicines that I use to help people. They think my methods are wrong." He paused. "And I think their methods are wrong. I guess I just don't like seeing Mommy try and talk others into the same mistake."

"Why did you let her go?"

Jake bit his lip. "Mommy was an adult. Adults make up their own minds. I hated to see her go. She knew I didn't like it, but she was too afraid that the treatments Daddy gives would hurt the baby she was carrying. Do you understand?"

Kyle nodded.

"Mommy did what she thought was right. I tried to convince her to get some other treatment, but she refused, Kyle. In the end I just let her go. I didn't think it would help, but I didn't think it would hurt either." He sighed. "Then she agreed to make this ad for them . . . and other doctors in Grantsville got kind of upset."

Kyle nodded again. "I know." He headed for the door. "Let's go. I'm hungry."

Jake put the note to his mother in the center of the kitchen table. "I'm with you, son."

◆ ◆ ◆

Dr. Michael Simons walked around his new house with a heavy sense of dread. A fight was on within himself, and the battle was leaving him emotionally drained. The years of resentment had etched like corrosive acid upon his soul. Now that he stood on the edge of revenge, the thought of fulfilling the hatred made him quiver. With excitement? No, it was more than that. There was power being offered to him, a destiny that he had felt before. He sensed he could triumph over any obstacle that would stand in his way. Hadn't that been part of the promise he'd sought?

So why this dread? Why did he feel almost helpless beneath an oppressive darkness? Why couldn't he rejoice now that the chance to right the injustices done against him had finally come so completely? Just days ago he would have given anything to see Matt Stone coming to him for help—Stone in a vulnerable position, seeking favor from him. So why did it seem so empty now? Where was the sweetness in the revenge he'd dreamed of?

He paced the length of his great room, from the massive stone fireplace on one end to a row of kitchen bar stools at a counter at the other. As he paced, the questions loomed. Why, now that he had the chance to punish Stone, did it seem to lack the luster he'd imagined?

He cursed Matt Stone under his breath. He despised the apparent rightness of Stone's motivations. Had he merely stood up for what he believed? Was it possible that Stone really wasn't trying to destroy Simons's career, just as he'd claimed earlier?

He thought of Matt coming with his only son, humbling himself to ask for favor from him even though he had gone after Stone's career with a clear intent to destroy him. *Could it be that Stone is willing to forgive and let the past be forgotten?*

He pounded his fist into his hand. *But I'm not ready to forget!* he told himself. *Now's my chance to even the score. Destiny has brought us together again, Stone,* he mused, *and I won't be the object of your ridicule a second time.*

Simons poured himself a drink and collapsed into a leather recliner. Quietly dark forces tried to seal his decision. Who could fault him if a tragic mistake caused the infant Stone to suffer or die?

For years the cardiothoracic surgeon had opened himself to the dark strongholds who were trying to finalize their grip upon him now. For the first time, however, the forces had encountered some resistance. Why now, after years of comfortable dominance, were they encountering adversity?

Simons tried to silence his mind, tried to close his eyes to rest. The words that Matt had spoken to him echoed in his ears: "I think my feelings about your surgical skills should be quite obvious, since I am bringing my only son to you for help." Simons shook his head. "My only son" echoed in his mind. *My only son. My only son. My only son.*

The surgeon pinched his eyelids, as if the absence of sight could quiet his repetitive thoughts. Slowly another memory of a story heard long ago, when Michael was a child, clamored for recognition.

Around him a fight continued.

An angelic force pried loose a memory of Another who sent his only Son into the hands of evil men.

Simons opened his eyes and tilted his head, as if he sensed another voice fighting for attention. He squinted and rubbed his forehead. He mouthed the words, "sent his only begotten Son."

He shook his head. The verse, now only a light flicker of memory from childhood, shot across his consciousness.

Dark forces countered. Unheard, except in Simons's thoughts, they screamed, "His only Son was sent to die! Stone too is bringing his only son to *die*."

Simons lifted his drink and imbibed deeply to diminish the clarity of the Holy Spirit's prompting. *For God so loved the world* . . .

"Get revenge!" a spirit hissed. "Maim the baby. No one will know. No one will fault you."

Simons's gut churned. He nodded in surrender.

It was a matter of destiny.

◆ ◆ ◆

"Amen." Matt concluded their prayers as he slowly stroked his sleeping son's head.

"Amen," Linda echoed. They had finished every day in this manner since the baby was born, praying earnestly for healing and guidance.

Matt looked at his wife. "How are you feeling?"

Linda held her finger to her mouth and motioned toward the door. She didn't want to wake the baby. Once out in the hall, she began to answer as she walked to the living room. "I just don't get a real peace about Dr. Simons. Maybe it's just me, maybe it's a message from the Holy Spirit, but I just don't feel right about putting our baby into his hands."

Matt nodded. "I know what you mean." He slouched down onto the old couch. "I guess we should talk to Dr. Morra about other surgeons. Maybe she'll have some additional recommendations."

"Won't Simons be mad at you if you take your child somewhere else?"

Matt shrugged. "I hadn't thought of that." He paused. "Maybe he will, but so what? What can he do to me? I'm on equal ground with him at Crestview. It's not like it was back in residency."

Linda sighed. "Right. What could he do?"

◆ ◆ ◆

Once Kyle was in bed, Jake sat down with his yellow legal pad to sort out his thoughts. The videotape of Sarah was enough to bring back a flood of unpleasant memories . . .

◆ ◆ ◆

Jake sat opposite Richard Dearborn, M.D., senior partner of the Grantsville Surgical Associates. "You're going to have to rein her in, Jake. We can't have her spreading this kind of foolishness around Grantsville."

Jake let out a huff of protest. He didn't take kindly to this kind of paternalistic conversation.

Richard continued, "We had another three phone calls from patients just this morning asking for referrals to the Ocean Sands Wellness Facility." He shook his head. "Enough is enough."

"Look, Richard, I don't like this any more than you do, but honestly, Sarah didn't know they were going to report that she was the wife of a surgeon. She didn't even know the ad would air on local TV. She thought it would just be part of a promotional video they use at the facility."

"Well, it's not!"

Jake rolled his eyes. "What do you want me to do?"

"Call the facility. Tell them they can't run the ads."

"I tried that." He sighed. "They say Sarah's permission is all they need. And they've got that."

"Then get her to change her mind!"

"Right, Richard! Like I can do that! She's had a mind of her own the whole time. This wasn't my idea, I assure you. I'm as embarrassed about it as you are."

"I don't care about embarrassment. I care about losing patients to this health gimmick racket. It's going to have to stop one way or another, Jake." He stood up and paced the small office. "Look, your associates have talked about this. You're going to have to do something to silence your wife or I'm afraid we'll be left with no choice but to distance ourselves from you. We can't have the good name of this practice being tarnished like this any longer."

"Just what are you saying, Richard?" Jake glared at his senior partner. "What do you mean, 'silence' her?"

Richard returned the glare. "Just that. Make her stop giving glowing testimonials about these idiots."

"Or else what?"

Richard shrugged. "We associates hope there will be no 'or else,' Jake. We don't want to push you out." He paused. "But we can't afford to keep losing patients while your wife is convincing the naive to forsake the good care we've been offering and seek help from these nutritional gurus."

"It's her business, Richard. It has little to do with me."

"She's your wife. You should be able to control her."

Jake rolled his eyes again. "You don't know Sarah. I hated to see her refuse good therapy. I hated to see her run to these alternative healers, but—"

"But?"

"I had no choice. I protested, but it didn't do any good. She had her mind made up. When she couldn't have conventional therapy, I think she must have felt guilty doing nothing. This gave her something to do." Jake shrugged.

"I'm sorry, Jake. Either silence her or else."

Jake dropped his head, then stood and walked slowly from the room. There was nothing more to say.

CHAPTER
18

F RANK Grimsted was back on the job. After three days of seclusion in his apartment, nothing had shown up in the papers, and the police hadn't come for him. He thought back to his last trip to the jail. *The kid must not have seen me*, he concluded. *And Jake seems to know where I am, so why not go to work? I mustn't let him know I'm on to his surveillance.*

Frank flipped burgers thirty-seven and thirty-eight, both quarter pounders. He liked to hear them sizzle. Somehow concentrating on the sound seemed to quiet his mind.

From the corner of his eye he caught a glimpse of her standing at the counter. *She's acting like she doesn't see me, but I know she does*, he thought. He watched her for a few moments, his mind racing. *I should send her a sign . . . a sign that I am also watching her . . . to let her know that I am on to her and Dr. Hampton's little secrets. Maybe I can put something in her sandwich.* Frank managed another quick glance. She sure was pretty to watch.

Sharon ordered a chef's salad and a Diet Coke.

Frank cursed under his breath. The salads were made in advance. No way to signal her there.

Sharon sat in the corner and ate her food in silence. Once, when she saw a student she recognized, she talked for a few minutes before going on with her dinner.

When she stood to go, Frank slipped from behind the counter. "I'm going on break."

He hesitated for a few moments until Sharon left. Then he stepped outside and leaned against the building. As Sharon got into her Honda Accord, Frank watched with apparent detachment. He memorized her plate number and observed her short drive to a parking place across the street at their apartment building. He watched carefully to see that she didn't lock the car.

"Perfect," he muttered. "It's nice to live in such a safe town, isn't it, Sharon?"

◆ ◆ ◆

Two weeks after Richard's warning, Sarah made a turn for the worse. She was back home, on maintenance-only therapy. She still drank her nutritional drinks, but she wasn't required to continue the high-colonic irrigations every day.

Sarah walked to the kitchen counter. She hadn't felt well all day, almost as if she were coming down with the flu. As she reached to hold her aching back, she noticed a tremor in her right hand.

"You OK?" Jake asked as he walked in from the backyard.

"I don't feel so well. I think it's just influenza or something. Kyle said he didn't feel well either. Maybe something's going around."

Jake squinted with concern. "Why don't you let me take care of dinner? You should lie down for a while."

Sarah nodded listlessly and headed for the couch.

Jake checked on Kyle in the backyard, then returned to the kitchen to fix dinner. He opened some frozen french fries and scattered them on a cookie sheet. He then started a search for a can opener to open a can of southern-barbecued beef.

"Sarah, where's the can opener?"

The only answer he received was a *thud* from the living room.

"Sarah?"

More thrashing noises.

Jake ran to investigate. There he saw Sarah flailing wildly on the floor, arms and legs jerking with a horrible irregularity. Her breathing was shallow and fast. By the time Jake reached her, the seizure had lessened. He tilted her head. Her airway was open. "Sarah?"

She didn't respond. "Sarah?"

Kyle walked in, banging the rear screen door. "What's for supper?"

"Kyle!" Jake shouted. "Call 9-1-1! Mom's had a seizure."

Kyle ran in carrying the portable phone. He pressed 9-1-1 and handed the phone to Jake.

"9-1-1 emergency. How may I help you?"

"I need a rescue squad at 101 Meadowbrook Lane. My wife has had a seizure."

"Is she breathing, sir?"

"Yes, she's breathing. She's just post-ictal." Jake used a medical term to describe the coma that follows a seizure. "I'm a doctor. I just need some help getting my wife to the hospital."

"OK, sir. Help's on the way."

"Thanks. I want a paramedic unit if I can get one. My wife needs oxygen."

"On the way, sir. What is your name?"

"Jake Hampton."

"OK, Dr. Hampton. A unit should be there shortly."

"Thanks. I'll be waiting. Good-bye." Jake hung up the phone.

Sarah's eyes were open and glassy, her stare distant and unfocused. She breathed through clenched teeth, foaming and spitting with every labored breath.

"Sarah?" Jake stroked her auburn hair. "Sarah, I'm here. You're at home. Sarah. Sarah."

She remained unresponsive and motionless. Jake looked at his wife. For the first time in his life that he could remember, he felt totally helpless. There wasn't a thing he could do to help her. He continued staring into her glassy eyes, hoping for some sign that she recognized him. He stroked her hair, not knowing what else to do.

"Do something, Dad." Jake realized Kyle was crying.

Jake looked at his son. "She'll be OK, son. She'll be OK."

"Mommy! Mommy!" Kyle cried.

Jake gripped his son around the shoulders. "It's gonna be OK." Jake checked a sob and squeezed his eyes so he wouldn't cry. "She's going to be OK. I promise."

Ten minutes later a paramedic squad hoisted Sarah into a waiting rescue vehicle for transport to Grantsville General Hospital.

Jake watched as they loaded his unresponsive wife into the van, knowing for the first time that he was losing his love—if not now, soon. The fact that her time was short had finally begun to hit home. He hadn't wanted to believe it before. In fact, because her cancer seemed to have regressed with treatment, he had wanted to believe a miracle had happened. Now, however, for the first time the cold reality of death's approach seemed inevitable.

Jake shook off a chill and turned back to the house to get Kyle.

◆ ◆ ◆

Sixty miles away, while Sarah was being transported to the hospital, a wide-eyed Frank Grimsted was staring at the TV screen. He sat transfixed, riveted to the electronic image on the box in front of him.

A beach ball. A beautiful sandy surf. Laughing children. And Sarah Hampton!

"Sarah!" he whispered. "Sarah, it's you." He watched the ad to the end and copied the phone number, writing it on his palm. "1-800-4-CANCER."

His heart raced. How long had it been? Frank tried to remember. Sometime before the bombing. He had seen her last right before . . .

He looked back at the screen. A used car salesman was screaming about value and was lighting a birthday cake. Frank shook his head. With his eyes closed, he tried to remember the ad. She looked exactly as he'd remembered.

He got up and began to pace. Thirty steps to the front of his apartment, turn, and come back thirty steps, turn and go to the kitchen wall, seventeen steps. Back and forth, always aware of how many steps he had made. "It's a sign," he said aloud to himself. "A sign that I'm to be with her again."

Thirty steps to the front of the apartment, a glance through the venetian blind at the McDonald's across the street, turn, and back thirty steps again. Frank closed his eyes, the image of Sarah's profile burning into his mind. *She's pregnant . . . just like before.* Frank smiled. *It's all a dream come true. I bet it's our baby. The one she tried to kill.*

Frank turned, stepped seventeen times over to the kitchen wall, and turned around again, his delusions flowing. Another thought persisted. *She's signaling me.* Her words seemed to stick out from the constant gray background of Frank's consciousness. "Don't delay. Call today. I'm glad I did."

Frank smiled. "She wants me to call," he said to himself. "She's finally answering me after all these years."

Thirty paces back to the front of the room. "Nothing will stand in our way this time. Destiny has appointed this."

Thirty paces back and turn toward the kitchen.

Frank's wrist alarm went off, signaling an end to his delusions and issuing the routine call to empty his bladder. *You can't be too careful when you're on medication*, he assured himself as he headed for the bathroom.

◆　◆　◆

Sharon went from plant to plant, watering, encouraging, snipping a few leaves here, adding a fertilizer stick there. She was in her own world. She was in charge, and she felt right at home. The phone rang, interrupting her daily evening routine.

"Hello."

"Hi, Sharon. It's Jake."

"Hi. I've been thinking about you." She paused. "How'd it go with Kyle the other evening?"

"He's OK." He thought for a moment, then added, "Really. He's all right. Some older boys pulled quite a trick on him, and he ended up getting stung pretty bad. He'll get over it. He's been through worse."

Sharon nodded, even though Jake couldn't see her. Jake went on, "I really called to thank you. I had a great trip to Green Valley." He stuttered, "I—I just got so wrapped up in Kyle's situation, I'm afraid I didn't even express that to you."

"No problem. I think I can understand." Sharon poured another ounce of water into a pot holding a large jade plant. "Kyle's a special boy." She paused again. "I think he's pretty lucky to have a father that cares. I see plenty who don't."

Jake smiled. "I'd like to see you again, if it's OK." He coiled the phone line around his finger nervously. "Would you care to be our guest for dinner some night?"

"Do you cook as well as your mother?"

The comment took Jake by surprise, but then he laughed, remembering Sharon's visit with his mom. "No."

Sharon laughed too. "I'll come anyway."

"Friday?"

"If you let me bring dessert. I make a terrific 'Death by Chocolate.'"

"That sounds horrible."

"Trust me—it's wonderful."

"All right. If I burn dinner, at least we'll have something to eat for dessert."

Sharon laughed again. "What time?"

"How about 6:30? Willie's going to take calls. I should be home by then. Can I pick you up?"

"Why don't I drive myself over? That way you can work on dinner. I don't mind."

"OK. I'm on Willow Drive. Third house on the left. You'll see my Isuzu out front."

Sharon smiled.

So did Jake.

◆ ◆ ◆

Linda knew almost instinctively that something wasn't right. She awoke abruptly from sleep and listened for a moment to baby Mark's rapid breathing. *Something's wrong!* She nearly jumped from the bed. Quickly she lifted the small infant into her arms. Even in the room's dim light she could tell his color was dark, but his forehead glistened. His breathing was shallow and rapid.

"Matt!"

Matt aroused easily.

"He's having trouble breathing."

"He needs oxygen." Matt thought about 9-1-1, then remembered their closeness to Crestview Women's and Children's Health Center. "Let's get him over to the E.R."

Matt called Dr. Morra while Linda threw a few items into the diaper bag. "Can you meet us at Crestview?"

"I'm not on staff there, Matt." She paused, sensing the anxiety in his strained voice. "But I'll come. Maybe I can offer some advice off the record."

"Thanks," Matt offered. "We're on our way."

Click.

Matt, Linda, and the baby made the trip in two minutes. In another minute after that, Linda carried her limp infant into the emergency room.

The nurses recognized Dr. Stone.

"It's my son! He needs oxygen!"

A swarm of nurses and respiratory therapists went to work. An E.R. physician, Dr. Ed Talbot, listened with a stethoscope. "Let's get STAT blood gases, an IV, and a portable chest film. Get him undressed, and turn on the warmer lights."

A nurse put a small tourniquet on the baby's upper arm and plunged an IV needle into a tiny vein. Mark Aaron didn't respond.

Dr. Talbot looked at Matt. "He's in heart failure, Matt. What's going on?"

"He was born with a large V.S.D. We've been anticipating his need for surgery in a few weeks."

"Looks like he's starting to decompensate. Maybe I'd better call Dr. Simons."

"No!" Linda spoke up for the first time. She had been standing wide-eyed in the corner of the room.

Dr. Talbot looked surprised.

Matt looked at Linda, then back at the E.R. physician. "We've already called Dr. Morra, his cardiologist."

Dr. Talbot didn't ask for details. "Fine. Let's see what she thinks."

"Shoot!" An X-ray technician shouted the warning for those close to the baby's stretcher to hear. One nurse, clad in a lead jacket, stood by the bed.

The film was retrieved from beneath the baby, and a respiratory therapist palpated for a brachial pulse. Gently she inserted a needle into the artery to obtain a sample to check the oxygen and carbon dioxide pressures.

Matt and Linda looked on. Mark's little body had pinked up a little since an oxygen mask had been strapped to his face. Slowly his heart rate slowed from 200 to 150.

A few long minutes later, Lucille Morra quietly approached.

"Dr. Morra, thanks for coming." Linda accepted a motherly hug.

"Hi, Linda, Matt." She looked around. "Where's the baby?"

Matt pointed at a curtain that had been drawn around the baby's bed. "In there."

Dr. Morra unwound her stethoscope and slipped behind the curtain. Matt followed.

Linda gripped his arm as she walked beside him.

Lucille Morra looked up. "He's got rales." She used a medical term describing the sound the lungs make when the heart is failing. "He'll need some Digoxin and Lasix."

"Can we transfer him to the university? We'd feel better knowing you were caring for him," said Linda.

"Moving him in this condition could be dangerous. He doesn't need me. What he needs is surgery—sooner than we thought, I'm afraid."

Linda looked with alarm at Matt.

"When?" Matt asked the obvious.

"Let's get him stabilized first. I would hope we could proceed with the morning's first light."

"Matt!" Linda's voice carried a hint of alarm. "We haven't seen any other surgeons yet!"

Matt looked at Linda's glistening eyes, then at Dr. Morra.

Dr. Morra stiffened. "Look, you've seen Dr. Simons, haven't you?" Her eyes seemed to glare at them.

Matt and Linda nodded silently.

"Then, in my opinion, you've seen the best. Let me call him." She folded her hands over her chest and looked at the baby. "You don't really have any other choice. To delay in order to find another capable surgeon could be a lethal mistake."

Matt and Linda clung to each other helplessly. Linda cried. Matt nodded. He spoke resolutely. "We don't really have any other choice."

Linda bit her lip. "What else can we do?"

Dr. Morra shook her head. "Surgery can save him. Let me call Dr. Simons."

Matt made up his mind. "Call him."

Linda sobbed.

Lucille Morra walked to the nurses' station.

Matt held his wife in the middle of the busy emergency department, just outside the trauma bay where their only son lay fighting for his life. The background noise began to fade as the gravity of real life began to sink in.

"Let's have the Lasix," Dr. Talbot called out.

"Oxygen saturation, 82 percent," a respiratory therapist called, waving the results of the blood gas analysis.

"Bring the crash cart nearby," the head nurse called.

The intercom cracked. "I have Dr. Simons on line 2."

Matt hoped *this* wasn't a lethal mistake.

◆ ◆ ◆

Jake stared at the ceiling. It was no use. Sleep was elusive. His mind was too full. First he'd think about Kyle and his recent run-in with the local police; then he'd think about Sarah, then about Sharon and the dinner, then about his job, wondering if he'd ever really be respected in this small town.

Finally he slid from the warmth of his covers and onto the floor, where he spent the next few minutes pouring out his heart, with all its anxieties, to the Lord. Once his heart was lighter, he flipped on the light and looked at the legal pad on his nightstand. There was still so much to write, so much to remember . . .

◆ ◆ ◆

Jake stood with the oncologist, Brian Barton, in the waiting room outside the Grantsville General Hospital emergency room. Dr. Barton sighed heavily. He knew the story. He'd known Jake and Sarah since they first came to Grantsville to practice. He'd shared many patients with Jake over the years, just never his wife.

"She's coming around some now, Jake. The next step is to figure out what caused the seizure. I guess you know we're worried about brain metastasis from the breast cancer."

Jake nodded. "Sure."

"Could it be anything else? Has she been on any medication?"

"She won't take anything, Brian. I've argued with her about this until I'm blue in the face. I've just had to step back and let her do what she wants."

Brian nodded. "I've seen her ad for Ocean Sands. Any idea what kind of treatment she's getting there?"

Jake sighed. "Mostly just nutritional stuff . . . kelp juice, coffee enemas, olive oil . . . that kind of thing."

"I've seen it before. Some of their patients come in here with terrible electrolyte imbalances from prolonged cleansing water fasts." The oncologist shook his head. "Pretty sad, really." He looked up at Jake. "No other drugs that you know about?"

"Not unless they're doing it covertly," he responded. "And to tell you the truth, I've suspected that a time or two since she had an apparent regression of the cancer."

"I wouldn't think that would be too likely. I think those guys aren't smart enough to be real doctors."

Jake huffed and kept his opinions to himself. "So what's next?"

"CT scan of the head to rule out metastatic brain cancer. If that's clean, I'll do a spinal tap to see if she might have an unsuspected meningitis."

"OK." Jake looked around the waiting room. He wasn't used to being on this side of things. "I think I'll go wait in the doctors' lounge," he added. "This room kind of gives me the creeps."

"I understand. I'll catch up with you after the X-ray."

Dr. Barton headed off to the chart rack, and Jake walked slowly to the doctors' lounge.

Thirty minutes later, Barton was back with a solemn expression on his face. Jake stood to meet him.

"I'm sorry, Jake," he said, extending his hand. "The cancer has spread to Sarah's brain."

Jake slumped into a soft chair. "Oh, God, help us."

Brian Barton looked down at his old friend. He didn't know what to say. "At least we know we won't have to do a drug screen."

Jake nodded numbly. "So what's next?"

"She'll need steroids to help shrink any swelling associated with the tumor. That shouldn't hurt the baby. It may even help it mature a little faster."

"That's it?"

"We can consider radiation therapy, with an abdominal shield."

"I'm sure she won't go for it any other way." Jake heaved a heavy sigh. "Is she awake?"

"She's coming around. She responded to her name." Brian stepped back. "I think you should see her. She's been moved to a room on first south."

Jake stared at the wall. Dr. Barton excused himself.

The surgeon held his head in his hands and began to weep.

◆ ◆ ◆

This time there wasn't any mention of past differences between Matt Stone and Michael Simons. Those battles were part of extraneous history, hopefully adding nothing to the current situation at hand.

Simons studied the baby intently. "He's decompensating." He folded his hands across his chest. "I'll have the nurses prepare the paperwork. I'll operate in the morning if his lungs have cleared of the fluid."

Linda bit her lower lip. "What of the risk?"

Simons answered with a question. "Will he live if we don't operate?" He looked at Linda, who for a brief moment sensed something vulnerable, something human, about the cardiothoracic surgeon. "No," Simons stated, answering his own question. "He will die if we do nothing. All other risk is secondary."

Matt squeezed Linda's shoulder. "Of course it's risky. What Dr. Simons is pointing out is that we don't really have a choice."

Simons nodded. "Exactly. Your choice is to do nothing, and that option is certain to be lethal, or to operate and have a chance at life."

"Or death," Linda added.

"Or death," Simons echoed.

With that, Simons excused himself and walked to the O.R. to make sure the team would be ready in the morning.

Matt and Linda quickly turned their attention to another necessary item: the job of assembling appropriate prayer coverage for little Mark. The doctors and nurses weren't the only ones hoping that everything would be in place in the morning.

CHAPTER
19

IRONICALLY, Sarah's brain metastasis, as horrible as it was, provided just the leverage Jake needed to force Ocean Sands Wellness Facility to withdraw Sarah's ads and save his job in Grantsville. Jake well remembered the ploy. Apparently money was something that interested the facility enough to make them pay attention to Jake's threats.

◆ ◆ ◆

"There," Jake muttered to himself, proofreading his letter. Asking nicely hadn't helped. He hoped this letter would. It was addressed to Medical Director, Ocean Sands Wellness Facility, an elusive man he still hadn't met.

Dear Sir:
    Be advised that a patient of yours, Mrs. Sarah Hampton, who has been treated by you for breast carcinoma, has now developed brain metastasis.
    You are hereby requested to remove the false television advertisements that depict Mrs. Hampton as whole and healthy after treatment at your facility. The continued use of these ads in spite of my previous requests for their discontinuation has now reached a point of blatant and willful deception. Should you continue with the ads any longer, I will seek legal action against you and will bring

to public knowledge the true state of health of your patient, so everyone can see the outcome of your treatment.

I have enclosed a copy of her cranial CT scan that documents clearly the metastatic breast cancer.

I am forwarding a copy of this letter to my attorney, Mr. Welby Beckler.

Sincerely,

Jake Hampton, M.D.

Jake folded the letter and stuffed it into an envelope. Evidently the fire in his eyes was hard to misinterpret because Sarah, lying on the couch, called to him. "Jake," she said, her voice weak, "I never dreamed it would hurt you."

Jake came to her side and sat down beside her on the floor. "I know, baby, I know."

"I felt so good. How can everything have changed so fast?"

Jake shook his head. He really didn't know.

"I want everything to be OK between us," she said slowly, her eyes moist with emotion again. "I know I haven't done what you wanted."

"I'm sorry too. I haven't been very gracious." Jake bit his lip. He reached to touch Sarah's quivering hand.

Her eyes reflected her understanding.

Jake whispered, "Are you hurting?"

"There's pain . . . in my back mostly," she reported. "It seems to be increasing since I got out of the hospital." She grunted and paused. "It's nothing I can't stand at this point."

"Can I get—"

Sarah touched her finger to Jake's lips. "Not yet. I'm OK without pain meds so far."

The two sat quietly holding hands, an understanding growing between them that the strains of their relationship needed to be put to rest. In those few silent moments they let forgiveness rule again. No one needed to tell them that time was running out.

"Can I get you anything else?"

Sarah shook her head. "Just stay with me."

Jake nodded. "I'm here." He wrapped his arms around her and wiped her tears with his sleeve. "I love you."

She nodded. Her lower lip quivered. After a few moments, she spoke again. "Jake?"

He responded by raising his eyebrows.

"What will we name the baby?"

Jake continued staring at his wife. "If we have a girl," he responded, "I'm going to name her Sarah."

"Jake—"

This time Jake silenced her with his finger pressed to her lips. "I've thought about it a lot. It's what I want." His expression said, *Don't argue*.

Sarah nodded. "What if we have a boy?"

Jake shrugged. "You decide. I ran out of boy names after Kyle."

She smiled and remained quiet.

Silence became the medium for their deeper communication. Eventually she verbalized her previously unspoken fear. "Do you think I'll make it until the baby can be born?"

Certainly Jake had the same fear. The child would not be viable for at least another eight weeks. Without treatment, a horrible race was certain to take place—the baby versus the cancer. Jake couldn't articulate his real anxiety. His expression would betray him.

"Of course," he whispered. "Of course."

◆ ◆ ◆

At 6:30 in the morning, exactly the time when Mark Aaron Stone was transported from the I.C.U. to the operating room, a small band of believers formed a circle of prayer. Matt, Linda, Matt's mother, Sandra, along with Mark Kreider, the pastor of their local church, and his wife Martha bowed their heads to intercede.

In the O.R., a team of anesthesiologists set up the monitors and started the appropriate IVs. Mark's body, now under a deep drug-induced paralysis, lay completely exposed under a bank of operating lights and a warmer. A cardiothoracic bypass pump technician readied her machine. Nurses scurried to document times, along with the accurate instrument, sponge, and needle counts. Forty minutes after Mark's arrival in the room, an assistant began a sterile betadine prep, scrubbing the skin gently from his chin to his toes. An intervenous antibiotic was dripped in. Anesthetic gases were given via a small tube placed into the baby's trachea.

By all appearances, except for the rhythmic rise and fall of the patient's chest and the continuous blipping of the overhead cardiac monitor, the body appeared lifeless in the middle of a room of cold technology. Four separate tables had been meticulously prepared with row upon row of instruments, each set up for easy access, ready for the surgeon's request.

Outside the room, standing at a bank of deep porcelain sinks, Dr. Michael Simons began a ten-minute wash-up. He was clothed in green scrubs and wore black-framed glasses equipped with protuberant telescope lenses that would magnify the operative field three and a half times. His face was covered by a surgical mask, his hair by a disposable blue paper hat tied in the back. His assistants stood beside him but did not speak. Simons preferred it this way. He spent the moments before an operation in mental solitude, going over each step of the procedure in his mind, so each step could be accomplished in a smooth, practiced flow.

Simons's mind reeled with a darkly-hatched plan of attack. Somehow, some way Matt Stone would be made to remember this day. He would be made to suffer just as Simons had, languishing these past years in obscurity, away from the popular eye of the academic community.

The lethal intervention would have to be done subtly, with precise timing, so as not to alert his team's suspicions. Simons moved with quiet resolve. Today he would be vindicated. Today he would punish his enemy.

He entered the room, water dripping from his elbows. The nurse, already in full sterile dress, handed him a sterile drying towel. Simons bent at the waist, careful not to touch the sterile towel to his unsterile scrubtop. He then donned a sterile gown and gloves and took his place on the patient's right. He looked at the clock. 7:15.

"Knife," he uttered mechanically.

Overhead, unseen, an angelic warrior unsheathed his sword.

"Scissors." Simons gently spread the tissues above and below the infant's breastbone. Next, he deftly divided the bone with a heavy scissors.

"Pickups . . . scissors . . . stitch," he demanded. Silk sutures were fastened to the cut edge of the pericardium, the sac enclosing the heart within the chest.

Another unseen visitor clawed at Simons's cranium. A third whispered in his ear while carefully watching the angelic warrior who stood with his sword high in the air, his eyes unmoving from the operative field.

◆ ◆ ◆

Outside in the waiting room Mark Kreider felt uneasy. "I need some fresh air."

Matt nodded. The pastor stood and walked into the hallway away from the O.R. and into the hospital lobby beyond.

◆ ◆ ◆

Kyle stood alone at the bus stop. The other elementary students were on Mrs. Kratzby's front porch, and Lenny and Todd were standing by the curb. Kyle stood by the mailbox and opened his reading book.

Lenny approached. "Hi, Kyle."

Kyle grunted and stared at his book.

Lenny grabbed his arm. "Look, Kyle, you can't avoid us forever." Kyle pulled away. "I want to know what you saw in the jail."

Kyle faced the older boy, who was now joined by Todd. "Why did you tell the police it was my idea to go in there?"

"H-h-hey, m-man—" Lenny stuttered.

Todd interrupted with a lie. "We wanted to give you the credit for being brave enough. That's all."

Kyle looked down and tried to process the new information. "Oh."

Lenny still wanted to know what was in the jail. "What did you see in there?"

"Rats."

"Is that why you screamed?"

Kyle thought back to the smelly jailhouse. "Yes."

Lenny looked at Todd and snickered. "So you were attacked by . . . rats?"

"Shut up, Lenny. I'm not afraid of little rodents," Todd countered.

"They were huge," Kyle offered.

"What else?" Lenny leaned closer. "Anything else in there?"

"It looked like someone was camping in there. In one of the rooms there was an old mattress and some boxes." Kyle wrinkled his nose. "Somebody's been using the bathroom in there."

Lenny looked at Todd. "I told you someone lives in there. What if it is a criminal gang?"

"I told you, you watch too much TV. There are no gangs around here."

"It's perfect, don't you see? A criminal hiding in a jail? No one would think to look for them there." Lenny put his hands on his hips.

"So *you* go in there." Todd put his hands on his hips to imitate his friend.

Lenny snorted.

"Your bus is here." Todd motioned with his head to Kyle. "See ya."

Kyle jumped on the bus and took a seat by himself in the back. What were the guys talking about? A criminal gang?

He stared out of the window and intentionally fogged the cold glass with his breath. He thought back to the dark jailhouse. He thought about the picture of his mother. Was it a sign or a trick? Did Lenny and Todd plant it in there for him to find?

He wrote his name with his finger on the foggy window. *No*, he reasoned. *That's too much for Todd to figure out.* They didn't even know his mom. That left him with only one other option—that his mom was trying to signal him somehow. Unless Lenny was right and it was a gang hideout. *But why would they have a picture of Mom?* He shook his head. He couldn't seem to keep his mind from spinning. Did he remember to take his medicine that morning? He wasn't sure. Nothing was making any sense. Maybe he should pray. Maybe he should ask for a sign from his mom. He thought for a moment longer. He wasn't sure his dad would approve. He could keep it a secret—just ask and not tell anyone.

He closed his eyes and put together a prayer. In a minute he opened his eyes again. To his eleven-year-old understanding, it seemed a logical way to sort things out.

He wasn't sure if what he was about to do would work, but he knew he needed to figure things out somehow.

Mom, if you're out there, let me know.

◆ ◆ ◆

Sharon jogged up the steps and inserted her key into the doorknob. She opened the door and this time, before pulling it out, turned it hard to the left. The key slipped easily from the lock. *Mr. Grimsted may not be as dumb as he looks*, she realized, looking at the key in her hand.

She quickly went in, showered, and prepared for school. She didn't need to be there until her first appointment at 8:30. As she readied herself, her thoughts turned to Jake and his invitation for dinner that night. She thought back to other relationships that she had abandoned for fear of being hurt, for fear of failure or the feeling that everything had to be perfect before letting someone really know her.

She looked at herself in the mirror. Could she allow herself to open up to Jake? Or would her old anxieties sour another meaningful relationship?

As she dried her hair, she remembered the circumstances that had led her to protect her heart so completely. She had been jilted a time or two, but nothing really hurt her as much as seeing the love of her parents run cold after thirty-one years together. The day they divorced, her own secure world unraveled. That same day, she called her fiancé and broke their engagement. If her rock-steady parents couldn't handle the long-term commitment, she feared she couldn't either.

That was ten years ago. Her boyfriend had long since married someone else, leaving Sharon to add a few more protective layers around her shielded emotional core.

She wondered if she would react to Jake the same way she had to other friends who had attempted to get close. No, she thought, *I have resolved to open myself to all that God has for me . . . including relationships.*

She wasn't ready to throw all caution to the wind by any means, but she had systematically prayed through her problems with a pastoral counselor back in California before moving to Taylorville. She wanted to be sure she wasn't just running again. She had come to a restful understanding of God's unconditional love, love given without return demands. She had started to understand that successful relationships require self-acceptance built on allowing oneself to be a channel of God's unconditional love.

She hadn't expected a test of her resolve so soon. She wasn't sure she was ready.

She shook her head. "Stop putting so much pressure on yourself," she verbalized. "Start trusting, and stop worrying," she added with resolve. She nodded her head in response to her own advice and smiled.

Maybe it would be a good day after all.

◆ ◆ ◆

Outside the O.R. at Crestview Hospital, Pastor Mark Kreider sensed a heavy burden to pray. It was an unusual burden. He had prayed for many others who underwent surgery, but this was different. This felt like war.

He walked back into the waiting room, where the small band of believers had gathered in a corner. "I'm not sure what is going on," he said quietly, "but I feel a need to pray." He motioned for the group to join him. "Let's intercede for little Mark again."

◆ ◆ ◆

Inside the O.R., Mark's heart was still, intentionally frozen between beats by the high potassium levels and the temperature. The bypass pump whirred softly. Simons deftly placed each stitch around a patch closing the hole between the small cardiac chambers.

Every time the angel warrior relaxed his sword, the dark creature clinging to Simons's back began to whisper. And every time the demon whispered, the angel lifted his sword again.

Each whisper manifested itself as a new thought in Simons's consciousness. But each time the surgeon was tempted to follow the sinister suggestion, the thought mysteriously vanished, leaving Simons's fingers following a practiced pattern, unable to deviate, unable to harm.

He looked at his assistant with disdain. *This idiot is totally oblivious to the struggle going on,* Simon mused.

He tried to focus on the situation at hand. He would need to act soon or any move to harm the child would be too obvious.

After another ten minutes, Simons closed the heart. "Begin rewarming," he instructed his pump technician. He fidgeted with the hemostat in his hand. "Let me know when you have 33 degrees."

A dread grew within him. *Kill the baby! Do it now!*

Simons looked up. Apparently he was the only one to hear the command.

At 33 degrees, Simons restarted the heart. "Internal paddles, fifteen joules."

"Fifteen joules, ready."

"Discharge."

Unseen swords flashed. The dark visitors reeled away from the table as an invisible covering protected the baby.

The little heart obeyed the shock promptly and settled into a regular rhythm. Simons shook his head. He wasn't sure he understood. Why hadn't he worked his vengeance?

"Excellent work, Dr. Simons," his assistant commented with true admiration. "I don't think we ever did it this fast where I trained."

He is blinded by my skill, the surgeon asserted. *I don't seem capable of making a simple mistake—not even intentionally!*

Simons looked at the clock and shook his head again. Now he knew he didn't understand. A dark voice screamed from within, *You're a failure! You are wasting your best opportunity to crush your enemy!*

He closed the pericardium and looked at his assistant. "You close the sternum and the skin. I'm going to talk to the parents."

Simons walked from the room, rubbing the sides of his head. A gnawing sensation in his upper abdomen intensified. He had failed! He shook his head in wonder. He had planned a lethal error, but when he got to that point he couldn't respond as intended. He had performed the operation correctly—in fact, better than ever before. Slowly he trudged up the central O.R. corridor, every step hampered by the demonic weight that sought to oppress him. The forces he had yielded to so often now turned on him in disgust.

Though he had anticipated elation at a job well done, he instead felt humiliation at his own inability to exact the revenge he had planned. In the changing room, he pounded his fist into his hand. He leaned his head on his locker and sighed. He took a slow, deep breath and tried to focus. What had gone wrong? Why did he seem impotent to perform the very act he was sure would provide freedom from his soul's bitterness?

A wave of nausea drifted over him. *What is wrong with me?*

He steadied himself for a moment, then walked into the bathroom. He stood there washing his hands for a long time, the cold water providing an excuse to stare at himself in the mirror. "Remember to be true to yourself, Michael," he whispered. "Remember what he did to you."

His expression tightened as he formed a new resolution. *The baby's not out of the woods yet*, he thought with a smile. *Perhaps it will look better for me if the surgery goes well and the nurses make a mistake in the I.C.U.*

He dried his face and walked out to meet the Stones.

In the waiting room, Simons remained sober. He reached for Matt's hand. "It's good news. The operation has been a success."

"Thank God," Pastor Kreider responded.

Simons flinched.

"Thank you, Dr. Simons. Thank you." Matt smiled, then turned and hugged Linda.

Simons interrupted their celebration. "He's not out of the woods by any means, Matt. The operation has been a technical success, but the ball game isn't over. There are still a myriad of problems that could assail him at any time."

Linda nodded through tears of relief. "Everything's going to be all right. I just know it."

Her positive attitude irked Simons. "Didn't you hear what I said?" He paused for a moment, unable to share in their joy. "Anything can happen. Anything!"

With that, Simons turned and walked out of the room. His step was light. His resolution for revenge had been revitalized.

CHAPTER
20

FRANK pushed the calendar back into the drawer. This month he would celebrate his third year of freedom. That he had gotten out at all amazed even him. Evidently he was in the state hospital so long that no one remembered the court mandate anymore. His discharge occurred on a winter day following the forced closure of the state facility. While other patients considered violent or unsuitable for outpatient treatment were transferred out of state, Frank was discharged into the care of his local physician.

Frank easily remembered that day. He was excited . . . excited and scared. He had written to his brother two weeks before, when the closure was announced. When he received no reply, he decided he would just strike out on his own. He had a small bank account, money collected by doing yardwork around the hospital. He would go back to Taylorville, the only place he knew—the place where he and Sarah had known a little of life's happiness. He would return and start over.

An orderly gave him a lift to the bus station. All of his possessions were stored in a large brown suitcase, except for the cardboard shoe box he clutched under his arm. In it were his memories—the articles about a lost love, his unfulfilled fantasies. He wouldn't trust those things to his suitcase. He would hold the box instead, clutching it much like a baby squeezes a blanket for the invisible security it carries.

Back at the hospital, buried deep within the boxes bound for the incinerator, was Frank's initial patient record, the careful recordings of a bright mind twisted by paranoia and violence, the marks of his compulsive personality traits and his schizophrenic and affective disorders. No one remembered the bombing. No one remembered his early violent temper.

No one but Frank. And now he was free.

◆ ◆ ◆

Frank's memories were interrupted by a door-slam. Sharon was leaving. He listened for a moment until he heard the steps on the stairs, followed by the outside door's squeak. Then he swiftly moved down the stairs and into the shadows made by the bushes at the front of the apartment house. He watched her get into her car.

He followed slowly on foot. If she stayed in town, if his hunch was correct, he thought he could find her. He quickly cut across the road and across the back lot of McDonald's, then stood beside a small fence hiding the trash cans. He could see her turn left onto Main Street. He squinted to see if she would slow down . . . Yes. Just as he expected, she turned left again onto Grove Avenue. *She must be heading for Willow Drive.*

He took off again at his usual slow exaggerated pace, gripping his green army coat around him as he walked. There was no need to hurry. He had a strong feeling he knew just where to find her. Fifteen minutes later he was rewarded by seeing Sharon's Honda Accord in the driveway beside Jake's Isuzu.

It was dark and cold. Frank huddled for a few minutes behind a large shrubbery hedge before slipping quietly into Sharon's Honda.

◆ ◆ ◆

Inside, Sharon began assisting with final meal preparations. Kyle sat on the floor of the living room playing a video game on the TV. Sharon and Jake traded smiles and stories about their day.

The phone interrupted them momentarily. Sharon listened to the one-sided conversation.

"Hello. Well, hi! I've been thinking about you . . . Yes . . . Oh no." Jake became quiet for several minutes before interjecting, "Wow . . . Uh-huh . . . That's great . . . How long will he have to stay? . . . Uh-huh . . . I understand . . . OK . . . Thanks for calling . . . OK . . . Bye."

Sharon looked at him without speaking. She was curious but didn't want to pry. Jake volunteered, "That was Matt. Mark had emergency surgery this morning."

"Oh, no!"

Jake nodded. "He's doing OK, Matt said." Jake shook his head. "Dr. Simons did the surgery."

"Simons?" Sharon wrinkled her brow with concern.

"Yes. Evidently the baby had deteriorated so quickly, they didn't have a chance to seek another opinion." Jake shook his head incredulously. "Matt said he talked to them afterwards. He said Simons didn't seem happy at all that things had gone well. It was almost as if he was mad or something."

"Maybe old grudges die hard."

Jake nodded. "Anyway, it's over and the baby's OK."

He pulled a steaming pizza from the oven. "Kyle . . . dinner!"

"Mmmm. That looks good." Sharon seemed surprised.

Kyle loped into the room. "Hi, Ms. Isaacs."

"You can call me Sharon here, Kyle."

Kyle looked down. "Thanks."

After dinner Kyle returned to his game, and Jake began filling Sharon in on Kyle's little visit to the jail.

After a full explanation, Jake shook his head. "What I can't figure out is the connection between all of these Zero bar wrappers and the picture of Sarah that the deputy found in the jail cell."

"Why does there need to be a connection?"

"Circumstances, I guess. It's just weird. Her favorite candy wrapper in my car, my mailbox, then in a jail cell?"

"What does Kyle think about it?"

Jake laughed. "He thinks his mom is trying to contact him." He rolled his eyes. "Kind of like a message from beyond or something."

"Maybe it's Kyle that's doing the message sending around here."

Jake looked at her and squinted.

Sharon explained. "Come on, Jake, think about it. Not too many people would know about Sarah's favorite candy, right? And certainly not too many people would have access to an old newspaper photograph of his mother." She paused, trying to sense Jake's response to what she was inferring. "Maybe Kyle's making up this story in order to send *you* a message. Maybe he even wants to send you a message from Sarah."

"What?" Jake definitely wasn't following. "Why not just tell me himself?"

"Maybe he thinks you'll be more likely to listen if it comes from Sarah. You know, maybe he thinks dead people have insight into the future or something—maybe a kind of supernatural message."

"And just what kind of message would Kyle be sending me?"

"Is he happy here?" Sharon shrugged. "Maybe he wants to move back to Grantsville."

Jake shook his head. "This isn't making much sense. Why would Kyle do something like this?"

"Maybe it makes sense to an eleven-year-old."

"I don't know. I guess it is pretty unlikely to think that someone else would know about Sharon's love for Zero bars or have access to her picture."

"Exactly."

Jake took a dish towel off the counter and began rubbing a wet pizza pan. "But why would he pretend to not know anything about it?"

Sharon shrugged again. "Maybe it's all part of his elaborate little message." She stared at him in silence for a moment. "Maybe you should try listening to your son's unspoken messages. What's he trying to tell you?"

"Now you're really starting to sound like a school counselor. Unspoken messages!" Jake stuck his chest out in an exaggerated fashion and smiled. "We men have more direct ways of communicating." He exhaled slowly, allowing his chest to return to its normal contour, then returned to a serious comment. "Besides, I'm not sure Kyle is sophisticated enough to figure all this out. Sending subtle messages has never been his forté before."

Sharon smiled. "Criticism accepted," she said smugly. "But I am a trained counselor, you know."

"Pretty scary thought, actually," Jake teased.

"Very funny." Sharon laughed.

The two walked into the living room, where Kyle was still playing Nintendo. "Homework done, sport?"

Kyle looked up and kept playing. "Not yet."

"Time to get to it."

Kyle looked up again and decided not to press the issue in front of

Sharon. He liked her. "OK," he responded, turning off the set. He disappeared up the stairs in a flash.

Jake looked at Sharon. He returned to their previous conversation. "OK, counselor, what do you suggest I do next?"

"I'd go with the direct approach. Talk to Kyle. See what he has to say. Maybe he'll come clean."

Jake defended his son again. "Assuming he's not already clean," he responded.

Sharon stayed quiet for a moment. "If it's not Kyle, who is it?" She paused. "Who else in Taylorville knew your wife loved Zero bars?"

Jake shrugged. "Maybe it's purely coincidental. Maybe no one knew she liked Zero bars. Maybe it's just the neighborhood boys. Todd Gifford lives next door. He could have easily planted the wrapper in my car and in my mailbox, and he was at the jail on the day Kyle was caught."

Sharon nodded. "Fair enough. If your talk with Kyle goes nowhere, talk to suspect number two." She paused again. "That is, if all of this bothers you enough to spend time figuring it out."

"Well," Jake mused, "it might be valuable if for no other reason than to convince Kyle that his mother isn't sending him messages from beyond the grave."

Jake excused himself and left the room. When he returned a minute later, his arms were full of firewood. "I thought this might be a nice touch. I haven't had a fire in this fireplace yet."

He crumpled some old newspaper and readied a few small pieces of kindling. He opened the flue and lit a match. In a few minutes he had a roaring fire. "There."

"I love a fire," Sharon added.

Jake sat down on the couch. "I think I owe you an apology."

Sharon looked at him curiously.

Jake continued, "We've been together a few times now, and all I've done is talk about what I'm going through." He looked down. "I don't know much about you." He looked up. "Will you tell me why you came to Taylorville?"

"Don't apologize, Jake. I've been fascinated by your story. Mine's pretty boring next to yours." She fidgeted with her fingers. "I told you I came out east to be close to my father." She paused. "That's partly right." She shrugged. "I guess I wanted a new start myself."

Jake nodded.

Sharon went on, "My parents divorced when I was twenty-five. It kind of exploded my little perfect world—kind of shook up everything I believed in. I always thought they were so solid, that we were such a perfect family. Well, when they split, I wasn't sure where my anchor was. I guess I was just holding on to them, even though I was an adult." Her eyes met Jake's. "I broke an engagement, and then I couldn't seem to make myself commit to any relationship for the longest time. Finally, I came to a new understanding of a true solid foundation. I found my strength in knowing that God loved me no matter what. I found out I was keeping people out because I thought they would reject me the same way I was rejecting myself. I had set my perfectionistic standards so high for myself, I could never live up them. I guess I just had the feeling that others would feel the same way."

"I understand."

"It's taken me a while to sort it out. Anyway, this job came up, and I wanted a fresh start. And it is closer to my dad," she added with a smile. "So I took it and moved from sunny Southern California to Taylorville."

Jake shook his head. "What a switch."

He stirred the fire. The two sat for another hour talking, laughing, finding common ground in their struggles with perfectionism, and joking about the Zero bar mystery.

They said good-bye, and Jake stood on the porch until she was safely in her Honda Accord. Sharon sped off, leaving a smiling Jake Hampton and a freezing Frank Grimsted, who still lurked in the bushes beyond the driveway.

When she arrived home a few minutes later, she grabbed her purse and noticed a scrap of paper on the seat beside her. As she reached for it, she opened the car door, turning on the dome light. A chill seized her as the light fell upon the crinkled paper. There on the seat beside her was a Zero bar wrapper.

◆　◆　◆

Night in the neonatal intensive care unit is just like any other time. Invasive monitoring requirements respect no one, especially the nursing staff. When Dr. Simons entered to see his post-operative patient, he was pleased to see the nurses busy with the routine business of a shift-change report. The nurses huddled in the central nurses' station, mechanically passing on the details of ins and outs in less than glorious description. Their voices droned monotonously as he paused, happy to see that Mark Stone had been temporarily abandoned due to the necessity of handing over the management baton. "He had thirty out in urine this shift, twenty out of the gastrostomy tube," a feminine voice reported. "Did he get Lasix with the blood transfusion?" "Two bowel movements in the last hour, both mostly water and mucus."

Simons smiled at their attention to detail. "Secretion secretaries," he muttered as he turned his attention to his little patient, placed in the incubator farthest from the nursing station at his special request.

He quickly assessed all of the lines, finding an available injection port dangling free several inches above the infant's central venous catheter. He looked back at the nurses' station. Everyone's attention seemed riveted elsewhere. Normally upset when he went unnoticed, Simons smiled at his relative invisibility during shift-change.

He pulled a clear syringe from his pocket, holding the intravenous port steady so he could plunge the needle through the rubber membrane.

"Dr. Simons . . ." A bleary-eyed Matt Stone stood up from his concealed location behind a nearby scrub sink. "How's he look?"

Simons froze, then stealthily pocketed the syringe. "Oh," he said, jerking his head around in response to Matt's voice. "I didn't know you were here."

"I couldn't leave him."

Simons frowned. "He's in good hands. You should get some rest."

Matt looked back without replying.

Simons cleared his throat. "He looks fine," he added, looking back toward his little patient.

"Thanks again," Matt responded. "Thanks so much."

The cardiovascular surgeon huffed, busied himself by checking the small bandage over his patient's sternum, and walked to the unit's exit. Outwardly calm but inwardly steaming, he gripped the syringe with his knuckles blanching.

CHAPTER
21

PERHAPS one of the hardest days for Jake Hampton, in his recent memory, was the day that Sarah returned to Ocean Sands Wellness Facility. They had convinced her of the necessity of completing a treatment course, saying that no treatment could be credited with a failure unless the entire course of therapy was rendered and the patient had been compliant with all of the treatment phases. Cancer often waxes and wanes within the course of treatment. Sure, she had a minor setback, they conceded, but small setbacks on the road to complete remission were not uncommon.

Sarah swallowed it hook, line, and sinker. Maybe it was her own denial. Maybe it was her unfading hope that she could be healed. Maybe she felt God was obligated to heal her since she had acted on a righteous refusal to harm her unborn child. Maybe it was the strange, almost brainwashing power that the clinic held over its patients. Regardless of the reason, Sarah felt she must return in order to complete the last phase of her therapy. She had to do *something*, she insisted, and this was all she knew to do.

Jake was disheartened, to say the least. Sarah had consented to a minimum of conventional therapy directed at controlling her seizures. Having no therapy at all might permit more seizures, she figured, and each seizure carried a risk of oxygen deprivation to the baby. Score one for conventional medical reasoning.

Jake had been thrilled to see their relationship finally entering a stage of peace—peace with each other and a quiet resolve to face the future, no matter what it held. The long arguments over Sarah's treatment were said and done and put behind them. Now when Sarah brought up going back to the facility one last time, Jake bit his tongue.

Sarah closed the suitcase. This time she hadn't asked Jake to drive her. Maybe she understood that would be too hard on him, almost asking him to condone the therapy she knew he disagreed with. This time she would be picked up by the hospital's private limo. After all, she was the hospital's newest shining media star.

"Can I come to see you?" Jake looked at his wife, wanting desperately to cling to the good feelings they had between them at last.

"I'd like that." She paused. "I suppose you'll have to sneak in again."

"Right." Jake nodded. "I'm such a negative force," he added.

"That's what they say," Sarah added with a shrug. She kissed him. "But I don't believe it. Please come anytime." Jake put his arms around her and squeezed. Sarah winced.

Jake pulled away. "Are you OK?"

"It's just my back." She rubbed her spine. "Maybe it's just the baby."

Jake feared otherwise. Any woman with breast cancer that has spread to the brain and has back pain probably has bone metastasis too.

Outside, a stretch limo arrived. Jake called to Kyle. "Kyle, your mom's leaving!"

Kyle met them at the door. He hugged his mother quickly until the limo distracted him. "Wow, Mom! Did you see this?"

Sarah limped toward the car. Jake watched, trying not to frown.

The driver opened the door for Sarah and placed her luggage in the trunk. Kyle jumped in too.

"It has a TV!" Kyle's eyes were wide. "Look at this! A refrigerator!"

Kyle bounced on the seats.

Jake and Sarah kissed.

"OK, sport, let's go. Mommy needs to leave."

"Look, a phone!"

"OK, Kyle, time to get out."

Kyle hugged his mom one more time. "Bye, Mom." He looked at the car again. "Have fun."

Sarah managed a weak smile.

"Bye, Kyle. I love you."

They were the last words she would ever speak to her son.

◆ ◆ ◆

Meanwhile, back in Taylorville, Frank Grimsted opened his shoe box and spread the contents out on the kitchen table. Compulsively, he sorted and resorted the material, placing items about Sarah in one stack, old articles about the bombing in another, and articles about Jake Hampton in a third. Now he started a fourth stack—information he'd received from Ocean Sands Wellness Facility. He wanted to know all he could about the facility that had brought Sarah back into his life.

He had never given up on her certainly, but this new ad had confirmed their destiny together. And to think that she was pregnant again. It was as if they could start right where they left off before Frank had to go to the hospital. They would have a second chance!

Frank thought back to his last visit with his physician. *Hadn't he seemed surprised, even pleased, at the news of my Sarah? This only confirms to me the rightness of my current feelings about her*, he thought. *Why else would he ask me to keep him posted on every detail? Why else would he give me information about how to reach her at Ocean Sands? Why else would he warn me not to mention my destiny to others who might want to interfere? Why else would he warn me about Dr. Hampton, who would certainly not look too kindly on me seeing Sarah again?*

Yes, he realized, straightening the edge of the stack of papers in front of him, *I have been given a rare gift—my Sarah has returned.*

He checked his watch and readied himself for work. His manager was a definite stickler about being on time. Frank put on his McDonald's shirt and a pair of blue pants.

While he was at work, he would plan his first trip to Ocean Sands.

◆ ◆ ◆

That night, on a veranda overlooking the ocean, Dr. D managed a thin smile. The cards he held weren't worth squat, but he knew his opponents well. He could bluff with the best of them. He tossed two red chips on the table.

Len Griffin offered a steely eye. "I'll call." He threw in an identical bid.

Steve Gomez hesitated, then matched with two chips.

Lane Timmons folded and threw his hands in the air. "I just can't get anything tonight."

"You can't get it together any night," Len offered.

"I need two cards," Steve announced.

"Two for me as well," said Len.

"I'll take one." D smiled again.

Steve cursed, then sat back and looked at the ocean. "I'm hungry. It's been a long time since lunch."

"There are some pretzels on the table inside the door," D responded. Steve got up. "Bring the whole bag."

Steve returned with his mouth full, carrying a bag of Pennsylvania Dutch style pretzels.

"What's wrong?" Lane asked. "Isn't Barbie feeding you?"

"Funny, Lane, I don't remember your wife being such a great cook," Steve snorted. "I had to go to Taylorville to meet with a new client." He shook his head. "You'd think they'd have something other than a McDonald's there by now."

D laughed.

"Too sophisticated for you?" Lane grunted.

Steve threw in one more chip. "I'm in." He looked at his opponents, trying to guess their response. "And get this—the guy behind the counter looks at me and says, 'That's the forty-second burger I've cooked today.' What a weirdo!"

D laughed again. "That's just old Frank. He's harmless." He thought for a moment. "As long as he takes his medication," he added.

D threw in a chip.

"I'm folding." Len threw down his cards.

"What've you got?" Steve asked.

D opened his hand.

Steve looked at him and revealed his own hand, three threes. "You're a fool, old man." He slid the chips into his corner.

D took a handful of pretzels and threw one of them in his mouth. "That's the fourteenth pretzel I've eaten," he added smiling.

"You're as crazy as that guy at McDonald's," Steve countered.

D raised his eyebrows and lowered his voice. "You'll never believe this.

Old Frank is obsessed with one of my patients here. He saw one of our ads. He thinks it's destiny for them to be together." He laughed.

"You know this guy?"

D smiled again. "I do a little of everything in my private practice you know. It's the variety that keeps me from staying down here all the time." He paused. "This guy is one barrel of psychiatric pathology, I've got to say. He's like a bullet. The only thing that keeps him from firing off is his medication. I tried to wean him a time or two, but he became so paranoid, I thought he'd kill someone, so I put him back on."

Steve shoved another pretzel in his mouth. "Weird. Deal the cards."

"Remind me not to eat in Taylorville," Len responded.

"Really. Never know what they might be serving up." Lane laughed diabolically.

"Come on, guys," D responded. "The guy's OK. I shouldn't have said anything."

"Right," Len snapped. "Just keep the cap on his meds so he doesn't flip out."

D nodded and became quiet for a few moments as he processed the advice. After a minute, he lifted his head in attention. "I'm in," he said, flipping a single chip onto the table.

The foursome played on into the night, until the chill forced them inside. With that, his guests excused themselves and Dr. D lumbered into his office. He picked up his mail, noticing a letter from J. Hampton, M.D. on the top. He paused and read the letter. *Hmmm*, D thought. *That's odd. I could have sworn his wife came back up here for treatment today, and yet he still writes these threatening letters. They must have some great relationship, these two.*

He studied the letter again for a moment. *This isn't good. If this is true, she's likely to die of her breast cancer soon. Maybe we'd better pull the ads. If she dies and he goes public with the story, that could really hurt us.*

We'll have to treat those two carefully, D strategized. *I can't have things getting out of hand, can I? Maybe we'll have to alter Sarah's treatment again, to assure Dr. Hampton of a positive response.*

◆ ◆ ◆

On Saturday morning, true to his normal routine, Jake got up early, dropped off Kyle at his grandmother's, and opened the office for walk-ins.

It was a concept that Taylorville wasn't used to. Dr. Willie didn't really go for it, but if it would help Jake attract a few patients and keep him around, he was all for it. Jake had tried it for three weeks now and had almost grown to like the concept. That time sector wasn't terribly busy, but at least it gave him time to catch up on his reading and clean off his desk between patients.

On this particular morning, Jake saw several businessmen that wanted moles removed. They just didn't have time to get checked out during the week. They liked the weekend hours, and they liked the "walk in anytime" convenience. Jake smiled and did the minor procedures in the office.

Later in the morning he even saw a friend of Kyle's who had cut his finger with a pocket knife. All in all, he didn't see anything too dramatic, but the morning paid for itself and kept Jake's mind off Sarah.

At noon he closed up shop, pleased at the morning's schedule, telling himself that next week he would advertise in the paper about his new hours.

As odd as it seemed, he enjoyed the Saturday hours. It was one time when he was sure to have the office to himself. He usually ran the morning clinic with just one assistant. Dr. Willie was certain never to show up.

As Jake stepped out of the office's back door, Frank Grimsted stepped into the shadows behind a panel truck parked in the next lot. He checked his watch. *That's good, Jake,* he observed. *You're falling into a very predictable schedule. I like this Saturday morning routine—you all alone in the office without any other physicians in the way. Maybe it will be the perfect time for us . . . or a time to give you a little surprise when you are by yourself.*

Frank made a notation of the time in a small notebook and shoved it under his coat. Then he trudged along past the office complex, pretending not to notice Jake's Isuzu as it pulled out behind him.

It's not good to be so predictable, Jake. Someday you may get surprised.

◆　◆　◆

Once Jake was in the Trooper, his phone chirped. It almost scared him. No one ever called him on his car phone. He picked it up, wondering who it might be. "Hello?"

"Jake, it's Sharon. I tried your office. The recorder was on." She sounded stressed.

"Sharon? What's up?" Jake was startled to hear from her in his car.

"It's Kyle. I think he may have been up to a little more than just homework last night. I found a Zero bar wrapper in my car."

"Hmm. So now it's happened to you too." Jake thought for a moment. "Maybe it's just the neighborhood kids again. Maybe they always put their trash in the cars along the street for a joke."

"I don't know, Jake." She paused. "I don't know why it bothered me. It felt weird knowing that someone was doing something to me, knowing I wouldn't know who did it. It was almost spooky."

"Don't let it bug you."

"I think you should talk to Kyle."

"OK, I'll talk to him. I'm on my way to pick him up right now." Sharon paused. Jake made a left turn.

"Jake?"

"Yes."

"Thanks for last night. I had a nice time."

"Do I cook as well as my mother?"

"I said I had a nice time. I don't want to discuss it further." She laughed.

"I am getting better," Jake protested. "By the way, it was nice, wasn't it?" Jake turned into his mother's driveway. "Well, I'm at my mom's. I'll let you know how it goes with Kyle."

"Bye, Jake."

"See ya." He put down the phone and walked to the house. Kyle was eating lunch. His mother was sipping tea.

"Hi, Mom. Hi, Kyle." He tousled his son's hair.

"Hi, Jake."

He sat, had a cup of tea with his mother, and made small talk. He decided not to raise the issue of the candy wrapper until he was alone with Kyle. His mother would only worry.

On their way home, Jake approached the subject with a question. "Kyle, do you know anything about something left in Sharon's car last night?" He decided to stay vague to see how much Kyle knew.

"What are you talking about, Dad?"

"Do you know what she found in her car last night?"

It hit Kyle like a lightning bolt. His prayer for a sign had been answered! Kyle brightened. "It was a Zero bar wrapper!" To Kyle this was more of a guessing game than an inquisition.

"How do you know that?"

"I just knew it!" He slapped his leg. "Dad, it's Mom! I know it now. She's trying to give us a sign!"

Jake thought back to his conversation with Sharon. *Maybe she's right*, he speculated. *How else would Kyle have known?*

Jake decided to follow it through. "What do you think she is saying?"

Kyle stared straight ahead. "I don't know. Maybe that she's OK or something. Maybe that she likes to eat Zero bars in heaven?"

A typical eleven-year-old explanation, Jake thought with a chuckle. If Kyle was sophisticated enough to fabricate messages from beyond the grave, it would seem like he would have something to say besides, "I'm eating Zero bars in heaven." Jake laughed again. He looked at Kyle. He didn't want to offend him.

Kyle laughed too.

They drove on for a moment. Then Jake spoke again. "OK, just this once, for my peace of mind, tell me you didn't know anything about that candy wrapper. You didn't put it there, did you?"

"Dad!" Kyle shouted. "It's a sign!"

"How'd you know what was there?"

Kyle was silent for a moment. Then he shrugged sheepishly. "I prayed for a sign. When you suggested something was in her car after last night, I just knew, that's all." He looked at his dad. "It was an answer to prayer."

Oh boy, Jake pondered. *How am I ever going to convince him of something else?* He thought for a moment longer. *Maybe I don't need to right now. Sooner or later all of this will make sense.*

He turned onto Willow Drive. He was starting to hope for sooner rather than later.

◆ ◆ ◆

Sharon didn't take such a relaxed posture. After hearing about Kyle's denial, she began wondering if someone else out there was intentionally targeting Jake and his friends with this little game. She didn't like the idea. The one thing she had looked forward to in little Taylorville was getting away from big-city problems like crime.

Paper candy wrappers are no big deal, she told herself. *But what if Kyle is right in a way? Not that it's a message from beyond the grave, but a warning from someone else? Could someone be playing tricks on Jake? Is it just a bunch of kids?*

Yes, she assured herself, *it's probably just some kid's idea of a practical joke. It's better than stealing cars, which is what they'd be doing back in Southern California.*

She went through the morning cleaning her apartment, watering her plants, and doing the grocery shopping for the week. Once the groceries were put away, she checked the mail.

That's when she found a second Zero wrapper. It was smoothed out so it would fit through her mail slot and had obviously been put in today after the other mail came, perhaps when she was at the supermarket.

She quickly went upstairs and locked the door. She turned the dead bolt and fastened the chain-lock.

◆ ◆ ◆

Across the hall, Frank watched through the peephole. He could hear the dead bolt being slid into place and the jangle of the chain. "You're afraid, aren't you, Sharon?" he whispered. "You should know by now that if you're threatening me, I will be watching." *Maybe you were a part of this whole plot, you and Jake*, he theorized. *Come to think of it, you moved to town just after Dr. Hampton did, didn't you? Coincidence? I doubt it. You and Jake probably had it all planned. You and Jake needed Sarah out of the way, didn't you?* He twisted his face in horror. *You just wanted to be with Jake, didn't you?*

I saw her in the ad. She was healthy. She was beautiful. She was pregnant again, he remembered. *Ready to pick up with me right where we left off. She wasn't close to death as Hampton claimed. He killed her. I saw him.*

Frank smiled at his own ability to see through their little plan. He was smart, all right, and now that he was taking less medicine, he could see his enemies so much clearer.

◆ ◆ ◆

Sharon didn't know what to make of this new development. It kind of blew the neighborhood kid theory. She just didn't live close enough to Jake's neighborhood. But who would do this?

Kyle? Could it be that he is blatantly lying to his father about this? He's the only one who knows where I live, she reasoned. *But if it's Kyle, why would he insist it's a sign from his mother? What message would Sarah be giving me?*

She collapsed on her bed, trying to make sense of the mystery's newest twist. *Is Kyle really this smart . . . and this devious?* She tried following her theory about Kyle through. *If it is Kyle, and he is trying to simulate messages from Sarah, why would she be signaling Jake and me at the same time? Is he trying to imply that we are to be together? A bit of celestial matchmaking perhaps?* She smiled at that thought but blew it off as unlikely. *A bit too complex for Kyle,* she concluded.

So who else could it be? The other kids that lived around Jake certainly wouldn't have recognized her car, would they? Unless they've seen it at school. *But how would they know where I lived? Could they have looked at my car registration in the glove box?* She shook her head.

Jake? He certainly knows where I live, but why would he be doing something so juvenile? Besides, why would he hide wrappers in his own mailbox and in his own car? *No,* she figured, *Jake's out. Besides, other than a few moments when he went out for firewood, I was with him the entire evening when the wrapper showed up in my car.*

Well, she thought, *it was on top of the other mail, so it's unlikely it was put there until after the mail delivery. That means it was placed there while I was at the grocery store. How long was I gone? Thirty minutes? Was someone watching to know that I would be gone? Did they care? I wouldn't have seen them even if I was home.*

Maybe I'll call Jake. I'll see if he knows where Kyle is.

She picked up the phone and dialed. She already had Jake's number safely in her memory.

"Hello." The voice was Jake's.

"Jake, it's me again. Where's Kyle?"

"He's at a friend's. It's OK—I can talk. I'm alone."

"No, it's not that. I just needed to know where he's been." She sighed. "There was a Zero wrapper in my mailbox. Someone just put it there while I was out shopping."

"In your mailbox?" Jake queried with raised voice.

"It had to have happened in the last forty-five minutes or so." She paused. "Has he been gone long?"

"About an hour. He left on his bike."

"Hmmm."

"What do you mean, 'Hmmm'?" Jake reacted.

"I don't know. I'm just trying make sense of this whole thing. Maybe it's nothing, or maybe there's some sort of twisted little message." Sharon shrugged. "I guess I figured that Kyle is one of the few people who had access to my car last night and who knows where I live."

"But Kyle says he didn't do it. I told you that." Jake sounded defensive.

"I just thought I'd ask."

"Sharon, I believe him. He's never lied to me before."

"Who else then, Jake? This has me wondering."

Jake thought for a moment. "I'm not sure. I guess it could still be some kids playin' pranks."

"How would they know where I live? Explain that!"

Jake shook his head. "I can't." He paused for a moment. "This thing's really gotten to you, hasn't it?"

Sharon rolled her eyes and sighed. "I guess so. When I got my mail, I ran right upstairs and locked the door. It kind of spooked me. I'm not sure why."

"There has to be some logical explanation. We'll figure it out."

There was silence for a moment or two longer. "Jake?"

"Yes?"

"Do you think I should tell the police?"

Jake chuckled. "Tell them what? That someone put a candy wrapper in your mailbox?"

Sharon protested, "Jake, I'm serious. Not just that, but the whole thing. What if some weirdo out there is following us around?"

"Leaving a trail of candy bar wrappers?"

"It does sound a little stupid, but . . . but what if something else happens? Shouldn't we tell them up front that someone's been doing these things?"

"I don't know, Sarah. I think maybe you're taking all of this a bit too seriously. It's probably just some kid's idea of a joke."

"It bothers me, Jake."

Jake softened. "I suppose it wouldn't hurt to call them."

Sharon paused for a moment longer. "If this turns out to be Kyle and I get him in trouble, I'd feel awful."

"Don't worry about that. It's not him," Jake said, hoping to reassure both of them. "But if it is him, he deserves to get reported."

"OK. I'll talk to you later. See you in church?"

"I don't know. I'm on call, so you never know."

"OK, well, I'll let you know what's happening. Bye."

"Bye, Sharon."

CHAPTER
22

DON Rawlings took down the information on a notepad.

"Could you spell your last name for me?"

"I-s-a-a-c-s."

"What is your relationship to Dr. Hampton?"

"I'm a friend." Sharon paused. "Well, actually I met him through his son, Kyle. I work as a counselor at the elementary school. I became acquainted with them at school."

"And now someone is putting Zero bar wrappers in your mailboxes and your vehicles?"

Sharon sighed. "I know it sounds pretty stupid, but, yes, that about sums it up."

Deputy Rawlings shook his head. He propped his feet up on the desk, looked at his partner, Steve Branson, and rolled his eyes. "And you think someone is trying to send you a message?"

"A message, a warning—I don't know. Maybe it's just some kids playing a prank. I just thought I should tell someone in case this sort of thing keeps happening."

Don remembered back to his night in the old jailhouse. "I don't mean to sound disrespectful, ma'am, but the perpetrator may be right under your nose. When I picked up this boy, Kyle Hampton, the other afternoon he had the very same wrapper in his hand." He paused. "Just think about it, miss. The boy may be trying to spook his father, maybe to get back at him for some punishment, I don't know. Maybe the kid's even mad at him for what happened to his mother. The media made the dad out to be the one responsible for her death, you know. Anyway, maybe he's mad. Maybe it's just his way of getting him back." He paused again, smiling at his own insight. "And now he has to deal with you, another authority figure, telling him what to do. Maybe he just transferred some anger over onto you and thought he'd play the game with you as well."

"I don't know. Kyle denies it."

"Ma'am, no disrespect intended, but come on! This kid's been through a heck of a lot lately." The deputy began rhythmically listing Kyle's problems. "He lost his mom. His father may have killed her. He has to move to a new town. He has trouble concentrating in school and has to see a counselor. He gets picked up by the town police for trespassing in an old jailhouse where he had obviously been spending some time. I'm not sure I'd put a lot of stock in what this kid is telling you. He's a troubled child." He paused. "Just think about it, ma'am. The answer is right under your nose."

Sharon hated to admit it, but the things he said did sound reasonable. "Is that all you need, Officer?"

"That's all, unless you have some other information. I'll make a report of it, OK?"

"Thank you."

Rawlings hung up. He looked at his partner.

Steve responded to his look. "What's up?"

"Remember the Hampton kid we picked up?"

Steve nodded.

"I think he's playin' little tricks on the adults in his life." He snickered. "It sounds as if he really has this counselor lady shaken up."

"What's going on?"

"Nothing much really. She just called to report that someone has been putting empty Zero candy bar wrappers in her car and mailbox. The same goes for the kid's father. She thinks someone might be out there following them around."

Steve laughed. "Right. The candy bar stalker!"

"Ha. Ha. That's great. He'll probably leave chocolate fingerprints!" Don Rawlings roared.

"Come on, funny man. Let's hit the street."

"Yeah, and keep our eyes open for those wrappers." He snickered again and followed his partner to the cruiser outside.

◆ ◆ ◆

Sarah's final weeks at the Ocean Sands Wellness Facility were characterized by periods of increased physical pain and depression. She was losing, and losing fast. She recounted the details to Jake during his visits. Later Jake would remember them, spilling the pain onto his yellow legal pad in search for the spark that would bring his memory back again.

Sarah awoke one morning and struggled to open her eyes. Her head ached nearly all the time now, especially early in the morning, typical for those with brain tumors. Once she was up and about, the pain would ease, only to return if she was supine for a few hours, allowing the brain swelling to return.

She rubbed her eyes. She needed to vomit again. The room slowly came into focus. She pushed herself up into the upright position, struggling to orient herself. A small clock on the bedside table read 6 A.M. *Good*, she reasoned. *It's at least an hour before I have another cleansing treatment*. She stood, an action that sent excruciating pain into her back, hips, and legs. She struggled into her private bathroom and dry-heaved over the commode. She then turned and sat down.

In a minute she struggled to make the return trip. *Funny*, she thought, *the blue urine has returned. Must be the kelp juice*. She rubbed her arm where a bandage covered a recent IV site. They had restarted the IV hydration therapy as soon as she returned. It was designed, they reported, to help flush her kidneys of toxins. One thing she did know was that it caused her to make the painful trip to the bathroom over and over and over.

She looked at the bed and the chair and opted for the wicker chair. It was a horrid set of choices in front of her—lie down and let her head pound, or sit up and accept the stabbing in her back and legs.

When Susan Rolan entered an hour later, Sarah was attempting to read her Bible.

"It's good to see you sitting up. I can see you are getting stronger every day."

Sarah didn't feel much up to the positive jazz. As far as she could tell, there wasn't much positive about what she was going through. In fact, she was sure she didn't want to be any closer to hell than she already was. Not wanting to discuss it, she forced a smile.

"Have you been practicing the meditation techniques for pain control?"

"I've been trying to focus my thoughts on my favorite Bible verses."

Susan smiled and let it drop.

Sarah shifted her weight in her chair. Just that movement alone was enough to bring her to a sweat. She winced.

Susan took her blood pressure and pulse. "We do have an acupuncturist here on Fridays. Perhaps we can book you a session."

Sarah raised her eyebrows. The idea of sticking needles into her pain-racked body didn't appeal to her.

"He's excellent, really. I've seen some people have amazing results."

"I don't know, I—"

"It's completely safe," the nurse interrupted. "No side effects for the baby." She smiled. "You think about it. If you want to try it, let me know tomorrow, so I can have you scheduled." Susan walked into the bathroom and hung up a large plastic container with the day's first enema. "I've prepared your first morning cleansing." She walked to the door, then looked back over her shoulder. "By the way, the acupuncture treatment isn't covered in the basic hospital plan, so if you'd like me to check with your insurance carrier to see if it's OK, I can." She paused. "In case it's not covered, we charge $250 per session." With that, she was out the door.

Sarah looked up at the setup in the bathroom and groaned. "God, help me!"

◆ ◆ ◆

Kyle sat on the curb in front of the 7-Eleven store on Main Street in Taylorville between Todd and Lenny. Todd's mother had reluctantly let the trio go in spite of the cold weather, just to get the noisy crew out of the house for some fresh air.

Todd munched on potato chips. Lenny sipped a Slurpee. Kyle was carefully unwrapping a Zero bar. He liked to eat them. Somehow it made him feel closer to his mom.

Todd looked at Lenny and rolled his eyes. "You must be crazy. It's freezing out here, and you go and buy a Slurpee."

"I like them," Lenny responded as he cradled the cup in his gloves.

Todd coughed. "I like ice cream too, but I don't eat it when it's freezing."

"It's never too cold for a Slurpee," Lenny said through chattering teeth. "Besides, real men don't care about the cold."

"To you, Frosty the Snowman's a real man."

"Shut up, Todd."

"You shut up."

The boys stopped arguing as a patrol car pulled up.

Todd elbowed Kyle. "Look, they're coming for you."

Kyle didn't speak. He tried to swallow some of his candy bar, but his mouth seemed suddenly dry.

Officer Rawlings got out, leaving his partner in the car. He walked past the boys and into the store. In a minute he was back, carrying two steaming cups of coffee.

Kyle nervously folded his candy wrapper and looked up.

"Afternoon, boys." He handed a cup of coffee to Steve Branson who had stepped in front of the patrol car.

"Cold day for a Slurpee, son," Steve commented.

Lenny wrinkled his nose and shrugged his shoulders. "I like 'em."

Rawlings looked down at Kyle. "What about you, Kyle?" He thought using his name would impress the boy. "What are you eating?"

Kyle unfolded the candy wrapper and remained silent.

The deputies looked at the wrapper and at each other.

Coincidence? The officers doubted it.

"One of my favorites," Rawlings offered. He sipped at his coffee. They walked back to their car.

"Make sure you find the trash can with your paper," Steve urged.

The two officers slipped into their car and waved as they drove away.

◆ ◆ ◆

George Latner, M.D. approached the nursing station on five north where Dr. Simons sat quietly, writing a progress note. "Hi, Michael."

"Hey, George. Late night?"

"The routine. Couple of cases of appendicitis to keep the midnight oil burning."

"Fortunately for me, most of my cases are still daylight."

"Lucky you," George muttered as he sat down with a stack of charts. He began writing his first progress note and then looked up. "What we need here is another general pediatric surgeon, not another subspecialist."

"From the looks of your charts there, I'd say you're right." Simons chuckled.

"Not that we're not pleased to have you on board. We do appreciate the depth of services we are able to offer now that you're here." George paused. "And by the way, I'm hearing good things about you down in the O.R. Way to go on that Stone kid. I'm sure glad that worked out, since Matt's on staff here."

Simons mumbled a thank-you. *If it weren't for the father's constant bedside vigil, you wouldn't be saying this!* Simons bit his lip and kept silent.

George leaned back on his chair. "I guess it's kind of neat—he helped you, and you helped him."

Simons tilted his head to the left, a question on his face. "What do you mean, 'He helped you'?"

"Come on. You can't believe you would've gotten this job without us talking to Stone, do you?" He lowered his voice. They were alone at the desk except for the ward secretary. "We knew there had been some trouble in your past. We needed to talk to someone who had been there . . . someone who had seen you operate." Latner paused. "I guess I understand how Matt could put his child in your hands, knowing how he felt about your technical skills. His recommendation letter reads like something out of *Who's Who in Surgery.*"

"Recommendation letter? Matt Stone recommended me for this job?"

George shook his head in disbelief. "Yes, Michael, he recommended you." His tone was simplistic and condescending. "Do you think we'd hire you without talking to someone who'd worked closely with you in the past?"

Simons was silent for a moment before muttering, "I guess not."

George finished his chart work, scribbling quick notes on each chart in his stack. He patted Simons on the shoulder as he left.

The cardiothoracic surgeon continued the intricate diagram he was drawing on a patient's chart. The drawing was in two colors, red and blue, to show the pathway of oxygenated and unoxygenated blood.

Simons slowly shook his head. *So I didn't get this job in spite of Stone . . .*

I got it because *of Stone?* He hung his head for a moment, letting his thoughts penetrate his understanding. *George acted as if it should have been obvious.* He looked up and sighed. *Has my bitterness blinded me?* He clenched his teeth. *No! Regardless of Stone's present performance, there is still the matter of an old debt to settle! And yet . . .*

He finished the drawing on the chart and signed his name at the bottom. His signature was clearly legible, unlike most physicians'. The periods following the "M" and the "D" after his name were crisp and exactly on the line.

He stood to leave, noting the time on his watch. *Could it be that I misjudged Stone?* He walked slowly to the exit doors of five north, his head low, his mind full. *Maybe it's time Stone and I had another talk.*

◆ ◆ ◆

Two floors down, in the neonatal I.C.U., Mark Aaron Stone struggled against his restraints. To let him move his arms and legs too much would risk dislodging his arterial line and his IVs. His cardiac monitor overhead blipped a regular rhythm. His ventilator lay unconnected and silent beside his incubator. He had been breathing on his own since the morning after surgery. A pressure transducer led from a minute catheter inserted in his right femoral artery, transmitting a waveform to the dancing pressure recording just below his E.K.G. stripe on the overhead screen. His body was exposed except for his head, which was covered by a plexiglass enclosure from the neck up, making his head look like it was in a bubble, with corrugated oxygen tubing leading from the top. It all gave him a surreal appearance, much like something out of a sci fi movie.

There he was, the little astronaut, seemingly suspended in a maze of tubes and monitoring wires. His eyes were bright and responsive to his mother, who leaned over his foggy oxygen bubble.

"Hi, little precious," she whispered. "Mommy is here." She leaned closer, between the web of IV tubing. "I love you, honey."

A young nurse stood nearby. "He's doing so well that Dr. Simons will probably de-line him tomorrow. He pulled his mediastinal tubes this morning. After today, you should be able to hold him again."

Linda smiled. "When do I get to feed him?"

"We'll be starting him out on a balanced electrolyte solution in a bottle today. If he tolerates that, we can let you try tomorrow."

"Tomorrow." Linda nodded, leaning back over her son. "You hear that, punkin? Mommy will feed you tomorrow. You'll like that, won't you? Yes, you will."

The nurse smiled and recorded Mark's heart-rate, blood pressure, and arterial saturation for the top of the hour. She then carefully measured his output for the last hour. Everything was meticulously tabulated on a complex bedside form filled with columns and boxes.

Of course, the nurse wasn't the only sentry at the infant's bedside that day. Overhead and unseen, a bright soldier stood vigilantly on guard. His assignment had been ordered from on high, then extended by the continuous prayers of the Green Valley Christian Fellowship.

"Really, Mrs. Stone. Visiting hours are over," the nurse reported softly. "Some of the other parents are getting jealous over all the time we let you spend back here."

Linda squinted and wrinkled her forehead. "Well, I suppose there are a few things I need to do elsewhere."

"He'll be fine," the nurse reported. "Dr. Simons will probably be by in an hour."

"OK," Linda replied. She turned to her baby. "Bye, bye, Mark. Mommy will be back. Mommy loves you." She turned away, her eyes moist with tears. Oh, how she longed to hold him in her arms again! Linda lifted her head to the nurse. "Thanks. I'll be back at 2."

The nurse nodded. Linda sniffed and headed for the door. The angel stood at attention as Mark Aaron closed his eyes and slept.

◆ ◆ ◆

In Taylorville, Dr. Willie took off his paper gown and sterile gloves and walked over to the bassinet. There a male infant whom he had just delivered by C-section squawked madly. "Whoa there, little feller." The white-haired physician chuckled. "You're gonna blow my ears out," he said, trying to time the placement of his stethoscope on the infant's chest with the gasps between the baby's cries. He quickly listened to the chest, counted the fingers and toes, examined the hips, and made sure the anus was unobstructed. He looked back at the mother, who was resting comfortably with the aid of her epidural anesthetic. "He looks great, Mom," Willie called. "This one's gonna be a preacher."

The child squawked again.

"See what I mean?" Dr. Willie laughed. The mother beamed.

The scrub nurse pointed at the sterile C-section instruments. "OK if I break this table down?" They always asked permission before contaminating a sterile field.

"OK with me, Ruth. Nice job." He looked around the room and thanked his help. "Thanks, Connie. Thanks, Jan. Thanks, Regis."

With that, he was out the door. In a moment he was in the locker room. Jake Hampton was changing his clothes, preparing for a laparoscopic cholecystectomy on a patient he'd admitted the day before.

"How's it going, Jake? Busy weekend?"

"It's picking up. Saturday morning I saw eight walk-ins over at the office. And yesterday I admitted a hot gallbladder to do today."

Willie chuckled. "That new-fangled laparoscopic stuff amazes me."

"What amazes me is how you old guys get to do so much. It's not every day you see a guy do a C-section, then walk over and play pediatrician to the baby he just delivered, then go to the office and do a little general medicine." He shook his head. "I'm just glad to focus on one area."

"And I'm glad to have you." Willie struggled with his bow tie. "I never was much good at tying these things."

The two were silent for a moment. Then Willie looked up. "How are things going otherwise, Jake? We haven't really spoken much since the article in the paper—"

"Talk about misrepresentation!" Jake interrupted. "He might as well have added a picture of me in a striped prison uniform." Jake shook his head. "It sure doesn't do much for community confidence in their newest surgeon."

"Taylorville isn't as backward as you might think, Jake. There are a lot of progressive thinkers here. Some would easily support more patient autonomy in choices about death. Why, I'll bet I sign five or ten new patient natural death papers a week over in the office. No one wants to be told when to die, Jake. When it comes down to it, we're all control-hungry. We want to control birth, life, and death, even down to the timing. People are growing to understand it as a right."

Jake shook his head. As nice as it all sounded, he wasn't sure Willie understood him at all. He sounded as if he assumed Jake had assisted his wife's death and wanted to let Jake know he understood and that it was OK. Since he had a patient waiting, he didn't have time to discuss it. All he managed was a mumbled, "I don't know."

Jake took a step toward the O.R. and stopped. There was something else that was bugging him that he wanted to discuss with Willie anyway. "Willie, something's been bothering me, and I keep forgetting to ask." He looked up to see Willie's response. "Do you remember anything about any chemotherapy drugs that cause blue urine?"

Willie raised his head suddenly and screwed his mouth into a frown. "Why do you ask?"

Jake shook his head. "Just something that came up when Sarah was alive. I've been going over her final days, searching for some answers again. It was kind of strange, actually. While she was getting the treatments down at Ocean Sands, her urine turned blue." He shrugged. "I started wondering if they were giving her more than they were admitting to." He shrugged again. "Just a hunch." He looked at Willie.

The older physician slowly shook his head. "No, I don't recall anything like that, Jake." He looked at his younger colleague and squinted. "This thing's really got you, hasn't it? Can't you just let it go?"

Jake shook his head silently.

Dr. Willie nodded. "I've got to run." He turned to go. "See you at the office."

CHAPTER
23

APPROXIMATELY a month before Sarah's death, Frank Grimsted intensified his search. Sarah was calling for him. She needed him. She wanted him to be close when the baby was born. He could hear her voice regularly now.

Slowly he picked up the phone. He had the number memorized. It certainly wasn't hard. Carefully he dialed, 1-800-4-CANCER.

"Hello. Thank you for calling the Ocean Sands Wellness Facility. All our receptionists are occupied at this moment. If you know the extension you wish to dial, please enter the number now. If you would like a patient directory, please push 1 now. If you are a patient and have a concern about your bill, please press 2 now. If you are a potential patient looking for information, please stay on the line and one of our receptionists will take your call as soon as possible."

Frank stayed on the line and listened to the recording.

"At Ocean Sands Wellness Facility you can enjoy year-round swimming in our oxygenated rejuvenation pool. Come and try our new four- and seven-night Step into Fitness vacations. Enjoy the sun while you undergo extensive health and nutrition seminars taught by our leading experts. Are you bothered by chronic pain? Come for our newest clinic, specially staffed by expert acupuncture artists who can help you cope with one of medicine's biggest challenges. And why not check out our immune boost therapy for the treatment of the A.I.D.S. virus or cancer? Through a series of detoxifications, you can reenlist your body's own army of defense against these harsh enemies of good health. Sample our refreshing and healthy array of tropical fruit—"

A female voice interrupted the tape. "Ocean Sands Wellness Facility, Sandy speaking. How may I help you?"

Frank looked at the *Family Medical Encyclopedia* open in front of him. "Yes, I'm calling to see if I can tour your facility."

"Are you a potential patient, or is it a friend or family member?"

"I-It's me," Frank stuttered. "My doctor says I'm suffering from chronic fatigue syndrome. He doesn't seem to offer me much except for waiting it out." He paused. "I'm a busy man. I can't just wait around." He halted again nervously. "Do you know if you can help me?"

"Of course we can, Mr. uh—"

"Grims—" Frank halted again and decided to use a fake name. "Mr. Grim."

"We specialize in picking up treatment where conventional medical therapy has failed. Chronic fatigue syndrome is one of our specialties."

"Can I come for a tour?" Frank paused.

"We offer tour packages that include a lecture about our philosophy, a sample health meal, and overnight accommodations for out-of-town guests. Will you be needing a room overnight?"

"No, thank you."

"Will you be alone? Or should we expect someone else?"

"No, uh—I will be alone. My wife, Sarah, will not be coming."

The receptionist nodded. "Our tours start promptly at 10 every morning Monday through Thursday. We do not give tours on Fridays except for selected private tours for our most faithful supporters." She paused. "What day will you be arriving, Mr. Grim?"

Frank looked at the work schedule that he had written on his calendar. "How about the fifteenth?"

"That will be fine. I'll reserve a spot for you. Thank you for calling, Mr. Grim."

Frank hung up the phone. That was easy enough. *Now my Sarah's only a bus ride away.* He circled the fifteenth with a red marker. He tilted his head, as if hearing something in the wind.

"Yes, I'm coming, darling. I'm coming to see you and our baby."

That day Frank called the number eight more times. Each time he carefully listened to the information given on the phone recordings. Each time when a receptionist answered, he hung up. Each time he took notes so he could ask intelligent questions about Ocean Sands's special programs. Each time he hung up, he smiled. It sounded like a wonderful place, and if they were caring for his Sarah, he was all for it.

◆ ◆ ◆

Willie straightened his tie. "Have you seen my W.D. cuff links?"

His wife, Dee, huffed, and called from the bathroom, "They're on the dresser. I set them out for you."

"How about my vest?"

Dee shook her head. "It's hanging on the ironing board. I had to press it." She looked at her husband. He actually looked quite striking with his white hair and deep red tie. "Honestly, Willie, do you have this much trouble finding things at the office? If I didn't know better—"

He interrupted her with a kiss. "If I didn't know better, I'd probably lose my wife too." He laughed.

She slapped him on the shoulder playfully. "Let me go, old man. I've got to put on my face."

"You look great to me." He stole another kiss before letting her go.

She looked at her watch. "If you're not careful, we're going to be late."

Willie smiled. "It's good to be fashionably late on formal occasions. Besides, the guys at the country club would drop over if I actually showed up on time."

Deloris rolled her eyes. "I'll be old before my time, living with you."

Willie found his cuff links and vest. He smoothed it out while looking in the mirror. "Do you remember what's scheduled for Friday night?"

Dee peered out from the bathroom doorway. "The Pin Oak Society dinner?"

"Yes."

"I do hope you've invited Jake by now."

Willie slapped his thigh and looked up sheepishly. He caught the end of his wife's glare.

"I'll ask him, I'll ask him," he protested. "I just get so caught up in work that I forget."

"Have you even told him what it's about?"

Willie implied the answer with his silence.

Dee went on, "I sure hope you know what you're doing."

"Come on, honey, we've talked all about this. Jake needs to feel some community support. This award may be just the thing."

"But it sounds to me like he hasn't quite owned up to assisting his wife's death. Are you sure you should have told the Pin Oak Society he'd accept their award?"

"Dee, the only one he hasn't admitted it to is himself. What he did was perfectly righteous in the eyes of the Society. 'A time to be born . . . a time to die'—that's even in the Bible. Everyone has the right to decide when, where, and how, without the influence of the law." He paused and looked his wife in the eye. "Was I wrong to bring him here when his own medical community was ostracizing him?"

Dee softened and silently shook her head.

"Am I wrong now to try and silently convince him to come into the open about his past and become the leader for our cause? Am I wrong to want him to feel the acceptance that a community award is capable of delivering?"

"No." Dee put her hands on Willie's shoulders. "You've always been on the side of the downtrodden, haven't you?" She patted him gently. "You seem to believe in others when nobody else will, until they wake up and start believing in themselves."

Willie smiled. "You'll see. It will work out just the way I've planned." He checked himself out in the full-length mirror. *Yes, just the way I've planned.*

◆ ◆ ◆

Sharon grabbed the phone on the first ring. She was hoping it would be Jake.

"Hello."

"Ms. Isaacs?"

"Yes."

"Deputy Don Rawlings calling. I just wanted to give you some follow-up on our conversation yesterday."

"OK." Sharon wondered what he was going to say.

"My partner and I went out on patrol shortly after I talked to you. I circled around your complex and through the McDonald's lot looking for kids out for trouble. We then went on over to the 7-Eleven store. That's where we found Kyle, along with a couple of older neighborhood boys."

"Did he admit to putting the wrapper in the mailbox?"

"Didn't have to, ma'am. He had a folded Zero bar wrapper right in his hand."

"Oh, boy." Sharon sighed.

Officer Rawlings stayed quiet.

"Thanks for the call, Mr. Rawlings."

"Just doing my job." He paused. "Look, ma'am, I'm sorry if this is hard for your friend, Mr. Hampton. Do you want me to call him? I thought I'd call you since you made the report."

"No, that will be OK. I'll call him. I'm sure he'd rather hear it from me."

"OK, Ms. Isaacs. Call again if you need us. Anytime."

"Thanks."

Sharon hung up the phone and sighed. She wanted to believe Kyle was innocent, but now this! *He had the same kind of candy wrapper on him just moments after someone put one in my mailbox.* She thought back over the deputy's words from their earlier conversations.

She dropped into a large overstuffed chair. *Oh, Kyle! You've had it pretty rough, haven't you?*

◆ ◆ ◆

Jake looked at the assistant across the operating table from him. The patient was anesthetized, his abdomen prepped with betadine and bordered by sterile blue towels. Jake looked at the anesthesiologist. "May we begin?"

The anesthesiologist nodded.

"Scalpel."

The nurse handed Jake a fresh number ten scalpel blade. He glided the knife over the patient's upper abdomen, the flesh parting easily with gentle pressure from the razor-sharp blade.

The patient, a thirty-three-year-old male executive, had strained his shoulder six weeks ago. Now, in the wake of daily anti-inflammatory drug use, he had developed an ulcer. Six hours before, he had come to the emergency room complaining of severe abdominal pain. An X-ray revealed "free-air"—gas that leaked outside the confines of the intestinal tract, only to be trapped within the abdomen—"free" because it was outside the stomach.

As soon as Jake saw the X-ray, he began preparing the patient for emergency surgery. Antibiotics were given, an IV was placed in his fore-arm, his abdomen was shaved. Discussions took place, and an operative permit was signed. Since it was afterhours, Jake summoned an operative team and an anesthesiologist.

Now the operation was underway. A search for the leaking organ had begun.

Jake opened the abdomen from just below the sternum to a spot just above the patient's belly button. He opened the upper abdomen, know-ing that under these circumstances the likelihood of a duodenal ulcer was high. If he had suspected diverticulitis of the colon, he would have opened the lower abdomen.

The surgeon deftly opened the fascia, the tough whitish fiber layer sur-rounding the abdominal muscles. He then carefully incised the peritoneum, the inner layer of the abdomen, between two clamps, lifting the peritoneum safely away from the abdominal organs. Jake was greeted immediately by a large amount of thin yellow fluid, followed by evidence of the patient's last meal. Jake washed out the abdomen with sterile normal saline and located the hole, caused by a peptic ulcer. The ulcer was in the duodenum, the first part of the small intestine, leading out of the stomach.

Jake patched the hole with silk sutures and a tongue of the patient's omentum, the fatty layer attached to the stomach. After thoroughly irri-gating the abdomen, Jake began to close the fascia again.

Jake smiled. In spite of all of life's trials, the operating theater had always been a wonderful refuge for him. He could never be interrupted. No problem, big or small, seemed great enough to distract him from the operation at hand. Even though surgery contained occasional great pres-sures of its own, the problems were limited by time and the four walls bor-dering the sterile environment. Here the problems demanded an instant answer. It was a pressure Jake almost enjoyed. Here he couldn't be touched by the outside world. Here he was the captain of the ship. Here he was in control.

"Closin' music," Jake requested. The nurse promptly responded and turned on Jake's C.D. player. The sounds of Steven Curtis Chapman filled the air.

◆ ◆ ◆

Sharon dialed Jake's number.

The phone was picked up on the third ring. The voice was cheerful and female. "Hello."

The feminine voice startled Sharon. "Uh, oh, I must have the wrong number. I was trying to reach Jake Hampton."

"You've reached the Hamptons'." She paused. "I'm a baby-sitter."

A baby-sitter. Of course. Sharon sighed and smiled. "Jake is gone then?"

"Yes, to the hospital for an emergency."

"Could you just tell him that Sharon called?" She looked at her watch. Seven o'clock. "If he gets home and it's not too late, you can have him call." She paused. "He has my number."

Laurie Simpson smiled. "Sure." She wrote down, "Sharon called."

◆ ◆ ◆

Frank stepped gingerly over the concrete floor. *This place is too cold to stay here much longer,* he reasoned, *unless I can get a better heater.*

He fumbled with his matches to light an old kerosene heater. It eventually coughed, then roared to life. It was one of the few things he had inherited from his father when he died the year before. The protective screen was dented at the top, the automatic starter was broken, and the vent at the bottom had rusted in two spots where the paint had peeled. But it worked, and if Frank put his mattress on the floor right next to it, he could stay fairly comfortable most of the night.

He had thought about trying to seal up the broken window, but that would mean eliminating his only source of light, so he decided against it. He could have moved to another cell, but this one carried the most memories for him. It had been his room once, and he felt most comfortable here. *Anywhere is safer than living where Jake and his friends can get me,* he conjectured.

Frank sat alone on the mattress and sighed. It was dark now, and although it was only seven o'clock, he decided to try to sleep. Once the sun went down, Frank went down too, unless he worked the closing shift at McDonald's.

He pulled the mattress closer to the heater, which smelled of old kerosene. He was careful not to let the mattress touch the unit, knowing the danger of fire. He snuggled into an army surplus sleeping bag on top of the mattress and closed his eyes.

Tonight he would begin to plan his revenge. Tonight he would dream of defending himself against the evil that killed his Sarah and robbed him of his happiness—the evil that took the life of his unborn child. The voices were calling again, warning him to strike first, warning him not to wait for his enemies to work their baneful schemes.

Frank laughed out loud, his hollow voice echoing through the concrete structure around him. His confidence rose with his voice, but not without an audible warning from within. "Don't be too excited, Frank," he spoke softly to himself, mimicking the style of his old hospital counselors. "Remember the bombing, Frank. You left too many witnesses last time, Frank—too many trails that led them straight to you."

He laughed again, this time guttural and mocking. "I won't make the same mistake this time," he answered himself. "This time I'm listening to you."

The kerosene heater hissed.

Frank lay motionless and dreamed of destiny. He dreamed of greatness. He dreamed of revenge.

◆ ◆ ◆

It was 9:30 before Jake called Sharon back. First he had to take Laurie Simpson home and then get Kyle to bed.

"Hello."

"Hi, Sharon." Jake knew she would recognize his voice. "I got your message."

"Hi, Jake," Sharon responded with a sigh. "I just thought we should talk some more about this candy wrapper stuff." She paused and shifted gears. "I missed you in church. I thought maybe I'd talk to you then."

"It just got crazy over at the hospital. I couldn't break free."

"It must be picking up for you, huh?"

"When Willie's away, Taylorville just doesn't have many choices. They either see me for their surgical problems or head on up to Jones City. Most of them want to stay in town."

"It seems he's away a lot," Sharon responded. "Where does he go?"

Jake thought for a moment. "I don't really know. I think he's just enjoying having someone cover for him for a change."

Sharon waited a few seconds, then spoke again. "I was really calling about Kyle."

Jake didn't speak.

"I went ahead and talked to the police, just to let them know something was going on." She swallowed. "Well, as it turns out, they went right out on patrol around my place, and they found Kyle over at the 7-Eleven with his friends, not too far from here."

"That doesn't mean—"

"They said Kyle had a folded Zero wrapper in his hand, Jake." Sharon sighed again.

So did Jake.

"Look, Jake, I'm not trying to make trouble—I just thought you ought to know."

"You sound as if you've made up your mind . . . that Kyle is responsible."

"I didn't exactly say that. It's just that, well, after talking to the police, that made more sense than anything else I could think of." She paused. "He's gone through so much. Losing his mom, moving, the adjustments at school . . . Well, maybe he's just acting out against everything . . . Maybe it's his way of asking for help . . . Maybe he wants to be caught."

Jake shook his head. "I'm not sure."

Sharon lowered her voice. "Maybe you're too close to this thing, Jake," she said softly. "Maybe you're a little biased? You are his father."

"But, Sharon, he's never lied like this before," Jake protested.

"He's never lost his mom, never had to move and make new friends, never had to see a doctor and start medication, and was certainly never picked up by the police before either."

Jake heaved another sigh. "I guess I haven't really been thinking much about all the stress he's been under."

"You need to now, Jake."

"It's so much easier to get caught up in my own little struggles. Maybe I'm missing the cries for help coming from my own son."

Sharon nodded.

Jake shrugged. "I'm not sure what to do next."

"I've been thinking about this. Maybe I should talk to him at school. He seemed to open up to me before. Maybe school would be a better place for me to confront him. I won't accuse him of lying . . . I can just talk to him about what happened with my car and my mail."

"Maybe that's best. He certainly tells me the same thing every time." He paused for a moment. "Yes, maybe that's a good plan. He might feel comfortable talking to you." He nodded. "I know I do," he added.

Sharon smiled. "Thanks, Jake," she responded. "I still think Kyle's a lucky little man. It's not often you find a caring man at the helm to guide you through life's tough times."

Jake sluffed it off. "It's what any father would do." He was silent for a moment, then added. "So did I miss anything at church?"

"Didn't you ask your mom?"

"No. She always says the same thing anyway." He imitated his mom. "'You missed a stirring message.'" He chuckled. "She never seems to remember the Scripture passage, though."

Sharon defended her. "Come on, Jake. She must be almost eighty."

"In fact, she's eighty exactly. I'm surprised she hasn't told you."

Sharon pondered that for a moment. "So that must make you . . ."

"Considerably less than forty."

"I can always ask your mother."

"You wouldn't do that, would you? It's too devious. Too behind-the-back. The Sharon Isaacs I know is much more upfront . . . direct—"

"Abrasive?"

"No."

"Forward?"

"Hmmm, maybe, but not obnoxious." He put his hand to his chin. "Just straightforward, a cut-through-the-baloney style. Everything in the open. No shadows." He smiled and thought of their first meeting. "Remember when we first met?"

"Yes . . ." Her voice carried a note of uncertainty.

"I remember thinking about your style then. I remember thinking that you'd make a good surgeon."

"Right! I can see me now, knee-deep in blood and guts. No thank you!"

Jake shrugged. "I'm just telling you what I thought."

"You still haven't told me how old you are. You really don't want me asking poor Phyllis Hampton?"

"You haven't told me how old you are either."

"Thirty-five," she responded quickly. "And holding," she added with a laugh.

"And I'm thirty-eight."

"Perfect," Sharon responded too quickly, then bit her lip.

Jake smiled. "I guess you won't have to ask Mom after all."

"That's OK. She filled me in on all the other details when I ate lunch with her."

Jake rolled his eyes. "Right!"

His beeper sounded, and Sharon heard it. "You need to go?"

He checked the number and breathed a sigh of relief. "It's a safe number. Just the third-floor nursing station." The E.R. number wasn't considered "safe" because it usually meant a trip back to the hospital. "I guess I'd better answer them."

Sharon paused. "OK. Night, Jake."

"Good night, Sharon. I'll see you soon. Let me know how it goes with Kyle."

CHAPTER
24

IT was a black night without a moon last spring when Jake made his first covert visit to Sarah at Ocean Sands. Visiting hours were over at 8 P.M., and the lobby was well watched. Even if visiting hours had been unlimited, Jake had been specifically ordered not to come. The administration had had enough of Jake's questions and his skeptical moods. "Ocean Sands stands for positive health and wellness, not doubts and negativity," the nursing coordinator had stated flatly. "You are welcome to provide her a ride home when her therapy is over. Otherwise, since you do not agree with our care-plans, please do us the courtesy of staying away."

Jake had thought about trying to come in the front door anyway and making a stink but had second thoughts when he saw a local police car parked next to the front entrance. He opted for plan B—the beach entry. He drove his Isuzu slowly past the complex and over a small bridge. He was now off the peninsula upon which the wellness facility was built. He found a secluded area just beyond the bridge and pulled off into the sand. Thanks to the four-wheel drive, he was confident of getting out again. He locked the Trooper and set out on foot toward the beach. If his thoughts were correct, the tide should be low enough for him to keep his shoes on while crossing the canal. It was difficult to see without the moon, but there was little in the way of plant growth anyway. So he just followed the noise of the waves and made slow, steady progress.

Once on the harder sand next to the ocean, he made better time. He could see the lights of the hospital in front of him as the terrain fell away toward the canal. Once at the canal's edge, he could see that the low tide had helped him, though large puddles still littered the sandy bottom. He slowed down even more to avoid soaking his feet. Once on the other side of the canal, the short grass of the hospital ground provided sure footing. Jake paused, standing beside a large palm. He was sure the trees weren't native, but they seemed to be thriving in the mild coastal climate. He squinted at the lights streaming from the hospital windows. Slowly he counted. One . . . two . . . three . . . four. *There*, he thought. *She's the fourth door from the end on the second floor.*

He could see her balcony. *Yes, there's her coat hanging on the chair, just as I requested.* It wouldn't look good to climb into the wrong room. Jake stayed next to a large hedge until he was only a short distance from Sarah's room. There he crouched and waited until her light went off. *That's my signal.* After checking quickly for other people, he sprinted to the wall below her room. He scaled the lattice brickwork without much difficulty. Soon he was standing on the balcony, slightly winded and a bit more exhilarated than he would have imagined.

He peered through the glass sliding door and could see Sarah lying in her bed. He could see that she was alone. He tapped gently on the pane and slid the door open.

"Sarah," he whispered.

"Jake!" Sarah shook her head. "I can't believe you really did this!" She smiled.

Jake kissed her forehead. "I'll do whatever I have to do to see you." He kissed her again, this time on her lips.

"I'm glad you've come," she said. She pointed to the clock on the wall. "The night nurse will check me at 11."

"So we have one hour."

Jake pulled up a wicker chair and sat down. He grasped her hand and held it, cradling it gently, as if it would break if he squeezed too strongly. "I've missed you. How've you been getting along?"

"Good and bad. My back is the worst. It aches almost constantly. Walking is almost out of the question. The pain shoots into my legs like a knife when I try to stand."

"Do they have a wheelchair you can use to get around?"

"Only at mealtime," she responded slowly. "They are better equipped for the patients who aren't so sick." She shifted her weight and winced.

Jake looked concerned and flinched when she winced.

"I'm eating most of my meals right here, such as they are."

"What about the pain? Can they give you anything for it?"

"No medicine, if that's what you mean. I have been receiving acupuncture therapies that have helped some."

"Acupuncture?" Jake started to roll his eyes but stopped himself. He knew that whatever was done now, comfort was the name of the game. As long as she was happy, he was happy, he told himself. There was no use straining the relationship again.

"Yes. They have a specialist who comes in. He usually brings his equipment up to my room."

"Kyle really misses you. Every day at supper, he talks about you. And the only thing he'll eat for dessert is a Zero bar."

"A Zero bar!" Her eyes lit up. "I'd kill for one of them right now."

"I can bring you some."

"Jake! They'd have a fit if they thought I was eating something that wasn't on the approved list." She shook her head to protest. "They are very serious about this detoxification stuff."

"You're the boss. But I'll do anything you want."

"I need to use the bathroom." She signaled with her hand. Jake pulled back his chair. Watching her move was pure torture.

Slowly, she swung her legs over the side of the bed. Once she was standing, she shuffled like an old woman until she was facing the commode. Then, in a series of shuffle steps, she turned around. Fortunately, there was a metal bar mounted to the wall beside the commode. Slowly, she lowered her sweatpants and sat down.

Jake watched all of this with increasing horror. Sarah was sweating profusely, just from a ten-foot stroll to the bathroom.

Jake assisted her to a standing position and flushed the toilet. He saw the color of her urine as he reflexively flushed the blue evidence away. He wanted to grab something, anything, to collect a quick sample but sighed in frustration at seeing nothing at hand. He had tried to get Sarah to save him some at home, but she had refused to cooperate with his suspicious desire to get a urine drug screen. Jake looked down at the water and shook his head. What difference would it make now anyway?

The trip back was equally as agonizing for both Sarah and Jake. Once she was safely back in bed, she broke down completely. She cried and clung to Jake. "I d-didn't want you to have to see m-me like this," she whispered haltingly. Jake held her and felt her sobs coming in rhythmic, pain-releasing spasms. "I want to die, Jake," she whispered. "I'm not sure I can take it anymore." She sobbed intensely for another minute. Finally she stopped heaving and held to Jake in silence.

Jake felt like his heart had been ripped from his chest. Never before had he loved someone so much. Never before did he have to watch someone he loved so deeply suffer so intensely. He felt empty, foolish for letting his wife be in this place of pain, so inadequate to relieve her agony and her cries.

Soon Jake's cheeks were wet. He pushed her gently away and looked into her eyes. "Please come home. I can get you medicine for pain relief. You won't have to suffer."

"I have to stay. I promised myself I would try."

"Why? For what benefit?" Jake shook his head. "Look at you!"

Sarah's hand lifted to her breast. "I can tell the tumor is getting smaller again, just since I returned."

Jake sighed. "But at what cost?"

"I must try, Jake."

He started to protest again but stopped himself with a silent inner rebuke. "At least let me bring you some pain medication. An oral narcotic would do wonders for your pain, and it won't affect the baby."

Sarah's tears were starting again. "The p-pain is what is killing me."

"Let me bring some medicine."

Sarah bit her lip. She wouldn't say it, but she nodded her consent.

He placed his arms around her gently and held her without speaking. He felt so helpless to ease her suffering. Nothing in his long training had ever prepared him to deal with this.

After another half hour, Jake kissed his wife tenderly again and said good-bye.

He slipped onto the balcony and stared at the ocean. He prayed he would see her alive again. Then he stopped and wondered if his prayer was selfish. *Why should she live if all she does is suffer? Is my desire for Sarah to live contrary to what she really wants . . . to what would really make her happy?*

Jake shook his head. He could process his heavy thoughts later. For now he had a tide to beat. Unless he wanted to wade across the canal, he would have to hurry.

◆ ◆ ◆

Jake looked up from his yellow legal pad. Remembering his evening with Sarah, especially his thoughts on the balcony, disturbed him deeply.

He shuddered and put down his pen. Quietly he prayed, "I don't know, Lord. Maybe this is all a mistake. Maybe some things are better left buried. Maybe Matt is wrong. Maybe I should let the past go and stop seeking to remember."

His next thoughts he didn't express aloud. *Maybe there are things I'd rather not remember.*

◆ ◆ ◆

The following morning, Frank rose with the sun. His cell was cold, and he needed to eat and change for work. He crept out of his sleeping bag and reached for his shoes. He had slept in his clothes for warmth. He turned the kerosene heater down but not off, thinking it might make the room a little warmer for his return that evening. He donned his green coat and stumbled to the door, kicking his mattress into contact with the heater.

Maybe I'd be warmer with some blankets, he told himself as he picked up his sleeping bag to take it back to his apartment. He had to hurry, so he headed straight for the basement exit. He hated leaving when the sun was up. He paused at the window and looked out at the frost. He pushed his sleeping bag through the open window, then hoisted himself through and ran quickly to the nearest shrubs. He waited there for a moment longer, then adopted his best I'm-just-out-for-a-stroll look and sauntered toward the railroad.

Behind him, his mattress was already beginning to overheat.

◆ ◆ ◆

Linda Stone held Mark Aaron gently in her arms as the baby slept. His mother smiled. Matt looked on and beamed.

Matt took out a stethoscope and placed it on the infant's chest.

Linda frowned and whispered, "Can't you stop playing doctor when it's your own son?"

"Playing doctor?" Matt pouted. "I don't play doctor." He put his stethoscope away. "Doctors don't play doctor."

"You know what I mean."

"I was just curious."

Linda smiled. "Well?"

"Well what?"

Linda's voice was quiet. "Well, what did you hear?"

"Oh, so look who else is curious," Matt responded. He remained silent for a moment to increase the suspense. "It sounds normal to me."

Linda continued rocking her baby. "I knew you'd say that."

"How'd you know?"

She suppressed a smile. "Doctor Morra was by earlier. She said the same thing."

"Excellent," Matt replied, sitting on a padded armchair next to Linda's rocker. "This calls for a celebration."

Linda raised her eyebrows. "Just what do you have in mind?"

"The vending machine in the waiting room has Twinkies." Matt said it without a smile. He was Mr. Serious.

Linda glared at him, and Matt smiled sheepishly. "I was only kidding."

"You'd have bought them if I went for it."

Matt shrugged. "Can't blame me for trying."

Linda smiled. She put up with but never understood her surgeon-husband's junk food penchant.

"Did Simons come by yet today?"

"The nurse said he was by while I was at breakfast."

"Did he mention any plans for discharge?"

"'After a few more days,' is all he said. He's not making any firm promises yet."

"I've hardly even seen the man since we talked to him right after surgery. It almost seems like he's so busy, he doesn't have time to talk. And when I did talk to him the other night, he seemed edgy." Matt paused and wrinkled his nose. "Maybe even fearful."

"Or else he just doesn't want to talk, Matt."

"Maybe. But I never saw him miss a day talking to the parents back at the university. It was his day in the sun. All the parents thought he was God's right-hand man."

"Maybe that's why he rounds before we come in." Linda's eyes caught Matt's. "He knows not to expect that from us."

"He may think he knows how we feel. I, for one, couldn't be happier. Our backs were against the wall—"

"And we had no other choice," Linda interrupted.

"But—let me finish—but it couldn't have worked out any better. I talked to the nursing team about it. They were all singing his praises after this one." He paused. "No, my guess is he's just been soaking up the compliments elsewhere. Maybe he doesn't feel like he needs to hear them from us."

"Then again, maybe the past is still getting in the way, Matt," Linda responded quietly. "Maybe he really thinks we only chose him because we didn't have any other choice."

Matt shrugged. "That is kind of true, Linda, but I think it must have been God's way of getting done what he wanted done. Our plan would have been a bit different."

"Maybe we should send him a thank-you card or something."

"Good idea. Not too many folks do that sort of thing anymore." Matt nodded. "It would stand out. Let's do it."

Linda nodded and looked down at the baby again. She smiled and closed her eyes. Regardless of the past, everything felt right with the world at that moment. Everything seemed fine with her baby, and that was all she wanted to know.

◆ ◆ ◆

Down the hall, Dr. Simons handed Mark's chart to a staff nurse and sighed. "Don't his parents ever leave the bedside?"

"Not since he's been moved out from the N.I.C.U. Our policy allows for unlimited parental visitation." She smiled. "It sure is nice to see loving parents so involved."

"Nice is not what I had in mind," Simons muttered under his breath. Louder, he said, "Perhaps we should think about changing the policy for my open-heart patients. Their care is so intricate." He paused and lifted his head. "Parents may interfere with the patient's proper management. Yes . . ." He nodded. "We must revisit this issue very soon."

The nurse tightened her upper lip and held her response. Quietly she observed the haughty cardiothoracic surgeon as he walked away. Finally, when he was far enough away not to overhear, she lifted her nose in the air and looked at a coworker. "Perhaps we should revisit this issue," she mocked with playful arrogance. She rolled her eyes.

◆ ◆ ◆

Jake was finishing morning rounds when Willie caught up with him just outside the main elevators. "Jake . . ." Willie appeared winded.

"Hi, Willie. Don't worry. I'm on my way to the office."

Willie looked at his watch. "Don't worry about that. I've been meaning to ask you something. Dee's been after me for two weeks to tell you about this, and I keep forgetting."

Jake looked at him curiously.

"We'd like you to be our guest at a special dinner over at the country club. It will be mostly locals. A few upstanding people will be recognized. There might be a speech or two. It's a real warm community event. An annual thing—not much really."

"People will be recognized? Is this an awards ceremony?"

"Not exactly." Willie didn't want to give his little surprise away entirely. "But I'm sure any new doctors in town would be warmly welcomed." He winked. "I'm sure quite a few of our staff here will be represented." He paused. "Have you seen the new country club?"

"No, I—"

"Bring a date." Willie smiled. "My wife said she talked with your mother and . . . well, you could bring that nice schoolteacher you've been seeing."

"Willie, I—"

"It's this Friday night." He gave Jake a stern look. "Please don't say no. I know I've not given you much notice, but Dee will kill me if I forget another day, and—"

"Slow down, Willie. I'll go. I'll go," he interrupted with a chuckle, shaking his head. He rolled his eyes.

Willie grasped his arm. "I knew you'd come through for me." He turned to go. "Look, I'll be holding the beeper Friday night anyway, so you have no excuses."

"I'll go, Willie," he assured him a second time.

Willie walked away as quickly as he came, calling over his shoulder, "I'll meet you in the country club lobby at 7 P.M."

Jake nodded and sighed. He called out after him, "She's not a school-teacher!" but it didn't appear that Willie heard.

Jake shook his head and headed for the exit, muttering under his breath something about a small town, secrets, and his own mother.

◆ ◆ ◆

Sharon avoided sitting at her desk while she talked to students. It just got in the way, and the students seemed to clam up. Even though her office was small, she had arranged two chairs and a lamp over a small throw-rug beside a bookcase; it actually seemed quite homey. For other encounters she took students on walks. For yet others, she sat in the cafeteria and talked over sodas. For still others, she chose the gym floor. She was known to throw a few hoops just to stay on the same level as the kids. In California she even once chatted with the captain of the cross-country team over a five-mile, hilly workout.

For Kyle, she chose her office. He had been there before and seemed comfortable. Hopefully he would be so again.

"Do you know why I wanted to see you, Kyle?"

Kyle smiled. "You want to date my dad. You want my permission, right?" Kyle beamed like he had the right answer. "I saw the same thing on TV once," he said nodding. "This man had a son named Eddie and—"

"That's not it, Kyle."

The boy looked down. "It's not?" He cringed.

Sharon spoke softly. She wanted to start on a positive note. "Your teachers have noticed a lot of improvement in your work. How do you think things are going?"

Kyle wrinkled his forehead. "OK, I guess. I think the medicine is working."

"Your father told me about all of the to-do lists. I think that's a great idea."

"Lists help me keep on track."

Sharon nodded. "I don't think the medicine and the lists should get all the credit."

"Why not?"

"I've been praying for you as well."

Kyle looked down, suddenly shy. "Me too, Ms. Isaacs," he responded softly.

Sharon paused. "There is something else I wanted to mention, Kyle. I wanted to talk to you about the candy wrappers."

Kyle stiffened.

Sharon had thought through her approach and had decided a direct one was most appropriate. "I spoke to a police officer who says he saw you right after someone put their trash in my mailbox. You weren't far from my apartment, Kyle. He says you had a Zero bar wrapper in your hand."

Kyle looked alarmed but didn't speak.

Sharon continued, "Kyle, it's important to tell the truth. I'm not here to punish you. I'm here to help you. If you tell me the truth, you won't get in trouble. I promise. I'm here to help you work out this problem." She looked down on the red-headed boy in front of her. "Kyle, if you think your mother has a message for me, I want to hear it straight from you, not indirectly through some candy bar wrappers."

Kyle continued looking down. "I didn't do it. It wasn't me."

Sharon reached out and touched his hand. "Kyle, I—"

He raised his voice a notch and repeated, "I didn't do it!"

Sharon tried hard to watch her body language. She took her hand off Kyle and leaned away from him in her chair. "Why would a policeman say he found you with evidence?"

"I like to eat candy bars! It was my mom's favorite kind!" He looked up and glared at Sharon. "They're my favorite kind now!"

Sharon paused for a moment and tried to approach it differently. "Do you really think your mother is trying to send us a sign?"

Kyle looked down again. "I'm not sure."

"Fair enough. It's OK not to know." She thought for a moment. "If she was, what do you think she would want to tell us?"

Kyle brightened. "That she's all right. That she's in heaven."

Sharon's brow furrowed. "But why with a Zero bar wrapper?"

"They were her favorite. I sent one to her while she was in the hospital. Now she sends back the wrappers. That makes sense to me."

Sharon nodded. She didn't feel like she was getting anywhere. If she persisted in accusing him, she might isolate him completely. "If it isn't your mother, who else could it be?"

Kyle thought for a moment. "Whoever is living in the old jailhouse."

The answer made sense. Sharon hadn't really thought about it before.

Kyle looked up at her, his eyes pleading. "You do believe me, don't you?"

Sharon studied him for a moment. "I want to, Kyle. I want to."

"It's the truth. I swear it!"

"Kyle, swearing won't make me believe you any more. A simple yes or no will do with me."

He lifted his head and looked at her, hoping she would believe him. "I didn't do it."

"OK, Kyle. You can go back to your class now."

Kyle got up and walked to the door. "Bye, Miss Isaacs."

"Good-bye, Kyle."

◆ ◆ ◆

By the time school was over, Kyle had thought through his conversation with Sharon at least ten times. *It sounds as if she doesn't believe me*, he moped silently while heading for his locker. *And it sounds as if she doesn't think my mom is sending messages either.* He threw his books on the locker floor and slammed the door. *But if it's not my mom, then maybe someone over at the jailhouse is trying to tell us something.* He shook his head. None of this was making much sense. He found his bus and took a seat behind the driver.

"Hi, Mr. Dillenbeck."

"Hi, Kyle. Why so glum, pal?"

Kyle frowned. "Ever had someone blame something on you that you didn't do?"

"Afraid so." Bill Dillenbeck chuckled. "Once my dad blamed me for breaking a window in the garage. My brother did it."

"What did you do?"

"I went to my brother and tried to talk him into coming clean."

"Did he do it?"

"No."

"What happened?"

"I got switched." Mr. Dillenbeck chuckled again.

"I bet it wasn't so funny then," Kyle commented sadly.

"How about you? You get blamed for something, Kyle?"

Kyle nodded.

Mr. Dillenbeck started the bus.

"What will you do about it?"

"Maybe I should do what you did. Find the person who did it."

Mr. Dillenbeck pulled out from the curb and smiled.

In a few minutes, Kyle got off the bus muttering, "I guess I should just go down to the old jailhouse and set things straight."

Mr. Dillenbeck heard the remark and turned his head to respond, but Kyle was already running for his house. *Hmmm*, he thought. *I wonder what he means.*

◆ ◆ ◆

Frank heard the fire engines at four o'clock. Anytime there was any excitement in Taylorville, the news would eventually spread to McDonald's, so he made a mental note to keep his ears open to see what was happening.

Sure enough, come 5:30, two of the volunteer firemen came in for a little supper. Gladys, the manager, knew the younger of the two and asked him about it.

"Tim, what's going on?"

"Nothing much too exciting. A little fire down at the old jailhouse . . . just an old mattress burning. That's about it. If that place was made out of anything less than bars and concrete, we'd have had a real mess on our hands."

Frank edged his way into position behind the sandwich bin so he could hear better.

"What started it?"

"I talked to the deputy. He's pretty sure some town kids are responsible. He says he caught one of them in there the other day."

Frank glared. *Those boys burned my mattress!*

He leaned closer, but all he heard was Tim's order. Frank silently fumed. *I thought I scared those boys pretty good the other day. I guess they've come back looking for trouble. I'll show them.* He nodded silently. *An eye for an eye, that's what my father used to say.* He chuckled slowly. *An eye for an eye . . . and a fire for a fire. I'll show those boys not to mess with me.*

◆ ◆ ◆

Three blocks away at police headquarters, Don Rawlings looked at Steve Branson and hung up the phone. "Boy, sometimes it pays to work in a small town. It can sure cut down on the investigative work, I'll tell ya."

Steve squinted. "What's up?"

"That was Mr. Dillenbeck. He works as a bus driver for Taylorville Elementary. You know him. His daughter played the trumpet solo at last year's—"

"Yeah, yeah, I know who he is," Steve interrupted. "Why's he calling?"

"He heard about the fire down at the old jailhouse. He thought he'd better call and let someone know that he heard one of his kids talking on the bus today about going down to the jailhouse to, quote, 'set things straight.'"

"I guess they set things straight, all right." Steve laughed. "More like set fire, you mean!"

"Wait a minute. I haven't told you the best part." He paused for suspense. "Who do you think he was talking about?"

Steve shrugged.

"Our little candy bar stalker."

"The Hampton kid again?"

"Exactly."

"That kid," Steve said shaking his head, "is nothing but trouble lately."

"Looks like I'll have to make another trip to talk to Dr. Hampton."

Steve nodded. "Let's go."

CHAPTER
25

"LOOK, Officer, if my son says he didn't do it, he didn't do it," Jake repeated with a sense of exasperation.

Don Rawlings stood straight. "Let me see if I have your story straight, son. You say you came home from school and stopped at home just long enough to get your bike and then went straight to the Simpsons' place?"

"That's what he said, isn't it? Laurie Simpson helps watch Kyle after school," Jake responded for him. "Why don't you call Laurie and ask her what time Kyle got there?"

"The jailhouse is on the way. Starting the fire could have only taken a few minutes."

"Look, you don't have any witnesses. Why are you so confident that Kyle was over there?"

"Kyle's bus driver says he heard Kyle state that he should go over to the jailhouse."

Kyle looked on with alarm and said nothing. Jake looked at Kyle. Kyle only returned his stare with eyes that pleaded, *Don't you believe me?*

"Did you say that, Kyle . . . that you were going to the jailhouse?" Jake's eyes didn't move from his son.

"Yes," Kyle admitted despondently. "But I didn't go! Honest!"

Don Rawlings grew impatient. "Look, I've got reports to file. I'll call Laurie Simpson just to be complete. I won't be back today, but I'll be watching." The officer gave Kyle a stern look and turned toward the door.

Once he was gone, Jake looked at Kyle again.

"Tell me what's going on."

"I told you, I didn't do it!"

"What's all this about you saying you were going but didn't go? What about that?"

"I talked to Miss Isaacs today. She got me thinkin'. If it's not Mom trying to give us messages with the Zero bar wrappers, who is?" Kyle shrugged. "That's what she asked me. So I started thinking that it might be whoever was eating Zero bars over in the jailhouse, that's all."

"And you told this to your bus driver?"

"Not exactly. Mr. Dillenbeck said he was accused of doing somethin' once that he didn't do. He went to the person who really did it." Kyle paused. "So I thought maybe if I was accused of putting wrappers in Miss Isaacs's mailbox, I should find out who did, that's all." He looked up at his dad sheepishly. "So I said that I should go to the jailhouse to set the record straight." He threw up his hands. "I guess he thought I started the fire."

"Kyle, Kyle," his dad repeated, shaking his head, "how do we get into such fixes?"

"You believe me then?"

Jake smiled and tousled his son's red hair. "Sure, I believe you." He looked at Kyle. "But I will not have you going near that jailhouse again. If you get caught back there, there's no telling what Officer Rawlings and his friends will do."

Kyle nodded.

"Do you understand? I forbid you to go close to that old jail!"

"I understand." He shrugged. "It stunk in there anyway. I didn't really want to go back, except to see if someone lived there who ate Zero bars."

"Why don't you just leave the mysteries to the police? I think we've been under enough scrutiny for a change."

Kyle nodded and changed the subject. "What's for dinner?"

◆ ◆ ◆

On the day that Frank Grimsted, alias Mr. Grim, visited Ocean Sands Wellness Facility, Sarah Hampton was in no condition for guests. Frank arrived forty-five minutes early for his scheduled tour, thanks to the bus schedule. He looked amazingly good for Frank and wore a pair of khaki pants with a dark blue blazer over a white shirt and tie. He was freshly changed and freshly showered. He was ready to meet his love at long last.

While he was waiting for the tour, he stopped at the registration desk and inquired about Sarah.

"What room is Sarah Hampton in?"

A well-tanned woman of about twenty smiled and quickly tapped a computer keyboard. "Room 232. Second floor."

She's here! I just knew it. Trying not to show his surprise or joy, he responded casually. "Thanks."

He contemplated running right up and surprising her, then decided against it, thinking it might be fun to run into her spontaneously during the tour. He had fantasized over and over about seeing her lounging by the pool or sipping a cool drink down by the ocean. He dreamed about every detail of their reunion . . . her surprise, her affectionate greeting, the way they would walk off together with the surf dancing at their feet. *Yes,* he figured, *everything is going according to plan.* He couldn't believe how much his life was turning around again.

He sat down in the lobby and concealed his face behind a natural foods magazine, so as not to be identified if Sarah frolicked through the lobby.

He waited patiently until the tour began, reading over a short list of questions about chronic fatigue syndrome that he had copied from his health encyclopedia. He wanted to appear intelligent. He wanted to be the type of patient they would accept into their program.

"The ten o'clock tour is beginning in the lobby," a mechanical voice announced over an intercom. Frank stood and joined four others who were visiting from other states. A cheerful woman in a nurse's uniform smiled pleasantly. She looked at her clipboard.

"I show that we should have five on the tour this morning. May I match your names with your faces?" She read over her list. "Mr. and Mrs. Fields?"

An elderly couple lit up. "She's calling for us, Frank."

Frank Grimsted looked up with alarm, then realized Mrs. Fields was talking to her husband, Frank. *Settle down,* he scolded himself silently. *Don't blow your cover.*

"Deb Pearson?"

A young woman with braces smiled and nodded her head.

"Randy Fletcher?"

A Santa Claus look-alike chuckled, "That's me."

"And you must be Mr. Grim." She looked at Frank. "Funny, I don't have a first name. We're pretty informal here. Could I have your name for our records?"

Frank cleared his throat. "Theodore Grim. My friends call me Ted. It's short for Theodore."

The tour guide smiled sweetly and recorded his name. With that, she held her hand up toward a side door. "Let's begin our time in here with a video presentation of our facility."

Frank smiled. He loved movies.

◆　◆　◆

On the floor above, Sarah slowly eased to the standing position. She needed to get to the bathroom. The nurse had been by a few minutes earlier to prepare a two-liter soap suds enema for colonic irrigation. Unfortunately, she hadn't pinched the clip holding the fluid in the administration set tightly enough, allowing a slow drizzle onto the bathroom floor.

Sarah looked up as she neared the bathroom and noticed the fluid on the floor. "Shucks," she verbalized as she moved into the bathroom to tighten the clip. She was fine until she stepped onto the floor, then slipped on the glass-like surface. She landed on her bottom with a sickening thud.

The impact partially collapsed her third lumbar vertebrae, already weakened from a bony metastatic tumor deposit.

The fall sent sharp pain into both legs as she screamed in agony. She collected her wits for a moment and attempted to stand to reach the enema bag. It was no use. She slumped back to the wet floor, which was being slowly flooded with cold suds. A tormenting throb settled in her lower back. She couldn't stand. She couldn't crawl. She couldn't shut off the dripping water.

Sarah rested her forehead in her hands and cried.

◆　◆　◆

"OK," the tour guide said, snapping on the lights. "Unless you have any specific questions about the video, let's head out on the grounds for a look around."

Frank followed obediently. He flinched every time the excitable Mrs. Fields called her husband's name.

"Frank! Just look at the flowers!"

Ted Grim turned his head.

"Frank! Have you ever seen such blue water?"

"No, I—" Ted blushed and stopped talking.

"Frank, I believe you're breathing better just being next to the ocean!"

Ted cleared his throat nervously and shook his head.

◆ ◆ ◆

Sarah was cold and wet by the time Susan Rolan came in to check on her progress. She looked up as soon as she heard the door open.

"Ms. Hampton! What's going on?"

"The floor was wet, and I slipped. Can you help me get up? I can't do it on my own."

Susan pinched off the clip leading from the enema bag, now empty, and cursed. "Dr. D's not going to like this," she muttered. She looked down at Sarah. "I'll get some help."

She practically ran to get some assistance, leaving the door wide open.

In a few minutes she returned with two young orderlies. The three of them managed to get Sarah back into bed.

Sarah winced. "My back!"

Susan looked at her in horror. "Tell me you can still move your toes."

Sarah responded by wiggling her big toes.

Susan looked relieved. She looked back at Sarah's face. "We need to get you into some dry clothes."

They struggled to change her sweats, with each little movement sending a new wave of pain into Sarah's back and legs.

"I'm going to have to call Dr. D." She frowned. "I'm sure he'll want X-rays."

"I need something for the pain."

She looked at the orderly. "When is Dr. Chin supposed to get here?"

"He's not scheduled today."

Sarah's eyes widened. Something had to be done for the pain.

"I'll be back," Susan promised. "I need to talk to the director first."

◆ ◆ ◆

The tour group finished looking at the kitchen facilities and sat down for a sampler lunch.

Frank looked at the colorful centerpiece of fruit.

"This looks great." Frank started reaching for a banana, then stopped himself when Mrs. Fields called her husband's name again.

"Here is a sample lunch menu. It highlights our detoxification and immune amplification program. We have a separate diet for those with arthritis," the tour guide said, smiling. "Before we eat, we encourage everyone to take a fiber supplement to enhance the intestinal scrubbing effect of the roughage."

She handed a glass of water and a psillium fiber packet to Ted Grim. "Mix it quickly and consume it right away, before it solidifies." Frank obediently gagged down the liquid as the others looked on.

"Good, Mr. Grim. If you would enter our detoxification program, you'd soon be as clean inside as you are out!"

Joyous bliss, Frank thought sarcastically. *How does Sarah put up with this?*

Next they were served an assortment of fruit and vegetable juices, all prepared fresh by the kitchen staff.

The group seemed partial to the fruit drinks and shuddered a bit when it came time for the kelp and wheat supplements.

Frank looked at his watch nervously and craned his neck to see through the windows. He hoped to see Sarah on her way to the pool or perhaps on her way to the cafeteria for a light lunch.

◆ ◆ ◆

"He wants an X-ray," Susan reported.

Sarah nodded. "That doesn't hurt, does it?"

"It's painless," Susan responded. "And they will shield the baby from the radiation."

Two orderlies wheeled in a stretcher.

"Can't you do the X-ray in my room with a portable unit? They do that all the time where my husband practices."

"This isn't where your husband practices," Susan snapped. "Besides, we don't have a regular X-ray unit, much less a portable one."

"You don't?" Sarah's voice conveyed alarm. "Where are we going?"

"Beach Memorial emergency room."

"I can't travel! Not now." Sarah looked afraid.

"I'm sorry, Mrs. Hampton. We need to X-ray the back. We have no other choice!"

Carefully, they loaded her onto a padded stretcher. The orderlies were in charge of the transport. Susan stayed behind to clean up the room as the two men wheeled her down the hall to the elevator.

Susan mopped the bathroom floor and put away the enema set-up. She made the bed and was just smoothing out the last of the bed wrinkles as Frank Grimsted slipped in behind her to surprise Sarah.

Silently he swept in and abruptly encircled her with his arms. "Don't be afraid, Sarah," he spoke. "I've come for—"

Susan spun around. "Eeek!" She glared at him. "What do you want?" she demanded.

Frank stumbled backwards. "I—I—" His mouth dropped open. "I thought this was Sarah's room."

"It is Sarah Hampton's room," she responded, eyeing him suspiciously. "And you are?"

"Fr— . . . uh, Ted, uh, Ted Grim," he stuttered, not wanting to give away his surprise except to Sarah. "She must be down at the pool or at the ocean. I'll look for her there."

"No!" Susan caught herself and softened her tone. "Mrs. Hampton is not taking visitors today."

Frank looked at her curiously.

Nurse Rolan shrugged nonchalantly. "Director's orders. She needs additional rest to augment her therapy. She won't be seeing anyone."

Frank cursed inwardly. "I can return later this week . . . maybe tomorrow," he added soberly.

Susan thought about Dr. D's words. "Close her off to visitation. We can't have it getting out that she fell while under our care!"

"No," the nurse responded firmly. "She won't be taking visitors anymore. She needs time for rest. It's a part of her total wellness program," she added, hoping to sound authoritative.

Frank nodded. *I wonder if there's any other way to get into this place.* He quickly scouted the room, walking to the sliding doors. He acted like he'd lost interest in talking about seeing Sarah. Instead, he opened the door and stepped out onto the balcony. "Nice place."

"Yes, it's a wonderful place. Very relaxing, Mr. Grim. Now if you'll kindly excuse yourself, I need to complete my preparations."

Frank nodded and counted the outside doors leading to Sarah's room and the windows leading up to it so he could identify it from the outside. He slipped back into Sarah's room. Susan watched him suspiciously. His eye met hers. "Please don't mention my name to Sarah. I'm an old friend. I wanted my visit to be a surprise."

Susan shrugged. "Of course."

"I'll see myself out." Frank walked to Sarah's door and then looked back at Susan. "Will Sarah be here much longer?"

"A few weeks." Susan thought about the fall. She needed to make a report and wanted this inquisitive visitor to leave so she could get to it. "But that's up to the doctor." She forced her lips into a tight smile and reminded him, "And there will be no visitors for Ms. Hampton."

This time Frank shrugged. "Of course."

◆ ◆ ◆

Late in the evening, after the police investigation had concluded for the day, Jake Hampton called to invite Sharon to the Friday night dinner with the Dansfords.

"I don't know, Jake, I'm not really much for fancy social gatherings."

"Oh, come on, Sharon, it'll be fun. Willie described it like some community appreciation dinner or something. They recognize community contributions or whatever. He hinted they might even show me some thanks, as a new doctor in town . . . probably for operating on the mayor."

Sharon sounded less than enthusiastic.

Jake added, "Besides, Willie suggested that I ask you." Jake smiled.

"Willie suggested it? What does he know about me?"

"Only what my mother must have told Willie's wife, Dee."

"Small town, huh?"

Jake laughed. "My thoughts exactly."

"Well, OK, as long as I'm being recommended." Sharon giggled.

"OK. I'll be by at 6:45 on Friday."

Sharon remembered her conversation with Kyle earlier that day. "Do you think I ought to get Kyle's permission?"

Jake's face showed surprise. "What?"

"Oh, he was so cute this morning. When I called him into my office and asked him why he thought I wanted to talk to him, that's exactly what he said. 'You want to ask my permission to date my dad.'" Sharon laughed. "He said he saw it on TV once."

"Maybe you should."

Sharon frowned. "Maybe you should ask him for me."

"I'll see what I can do."

"I'll see you on Friday." Sharon softly laid the receiver in its cradle and smiled.

◆   ◆   ◆

Living in a small town carried some advantages for Frank. He knew just about everyone from his job at McDonald's. That's also why he was convinced he would be recognized by Todd from his visit to the jailhouse. It was also how he knew exactly who Todd Gifford was and where he lived. Todd lived next to the Hamptons with his lot bordering theirs on the edge of the cul-de-sac on Willow Drive.

Frank waited until dark. He wouldn't wait another day. His revenge would be executed in a timely fashion to make a sharp statement: *Mess with me at your own risk!*

Quietly, he moved into the shadow of the hedge bordering the Hamptons' lot. From the corner of the Hampton home, he could see Todd's window. He moved silently into the backyard until he crouched beside an old tire swing. In his hand a can of kerosene grew heavier by the minute. Ahead of him, his target loomed: Todd's treehouse.

Positioned in an old oak tree, the treehouse was visible from the street, which is how Frank first noticed it during one of his days spent watching the Hampton house. The treehouse was accessible via planks that were nailed to the trunk of the massive tree or by a rope suspended through a hole in the bottom of the treehouse.

Frank looked the situation over and opted for the wooden planks. To climb the rope and carry the fuel seemed too cumbersome. He glanced back at the Gifford home. All was dark. He grasped the wooden planks and lifted his feet to the first board. He then balanced for a moment and tried to hold the kerosene with one hand and the trunk with the other. He tried to move his hand to the next higher board but lost his balance and stepped back off the planks onto the ground with a huff.

He looked nervously back toward the house. This wouldn't do. He cursed silently and studied the situation again. He eyed the rope and then, in a flash of insight, tied the rope to the kerosene can. He easily manipulated the wooden planks until he was in the treehouse, then pulled up the kerosene can with the rope. He smiled as another idea hit him. *This rope will make a nice wick! My escape won't be as dangerous if I don't light the fire until I'm on the ground again.*

Carefully, he doused the floor and walls with the fuel. Then he coiled the rope and poured the remaining fuel over it. He lowered the rope to the ground, then climbed back down the wooden plank ladder.

After checking both the Gifford and Hampton houses for lights, Frank lit the rope and watched the flames climb up the rope into the tree-fort.

"Bye, bye," he chuckled, seeing the flames quickly engulf the wooden platform. "Bye, bye."

Frank scrambled through the backyard, crossed the street, and cut diagonally across the front yard of the house across the street from the Hamptons. There he stumbled on a decorative yard rock, sending him and his empty kerosene can into an uncontrolled sprawl. The can skidded noisily across the driveway. Frank jumped up and retrieved it, then continued his retreat through the backyard and onto the street beyond. In five minutes he was walking along the railroad, with his pace slow and his breathing labored.

◆ ◆ ◆

Kyle awoke with a start as rats converged on him from all directions. *Only a dream!* He rubbed his eyes and sat up. He looked at the clock. 2:30. As he looked at the wall beyond the clock, he noticed a dim shadow dancing across the room. *Is there a light on in the backyard?* He looked toward the window and noticed an eerie glow. Slowly he stood and walked to the window. Flames engulfed the oak tree behind Todd's house!

"Dad!" He shrieked. "Fire!"

He ran to his father's room, yelling, "Fire!"

Jake opened his eyes. He could hear Kyle yelling. He shook his head and sat up. His son burst through the door and grabbed the phone on Jake's nightstand. "Dad! Todd's tree-fort is on fire!" Kyle punched 9-1-1.

Jake walked bleary-eyed to Kyle's bedroom, which faced the backyard. Kyle stayed in his father's room.

"9-1-1 emergency. How may I assist you?"

"There's a fire in a tree on Willow Drive!"

"In a tree?"

"Yes. It looks like a treehouse is burning."

"Is there anyone in the treehouse?"

"I don't think so. We need a fire truck!"

"I'm dispatching a truck right now. Can you tell me your name and where you are calling from?"

"Kyle Hampton. I'm calling from my dad's bedroom."

"Where do you live, Kyle?"

"124 Willow."

"Where exactly is the fire?"

"I don't know the address, but it's in a tree behind the house at the end of the cul-de-sac!"

The dispatcher typed the approximate address onto the computer screen in front of her.

Kyle hesitated a moment, then added, "I've got to call the Giffords! It's their tree!" With that, he hung up the phone.

Jake ran back in and pulled on some blue jeans and a sweatshirt. He grabbed the phone book. "Better let me call the Giffords."

Quickly he called their neighbors. A sleepy-sounding Blake Gifford answered the phone.

In a few minutes Mr. and Mrs. Gifford, Todd, his little sister Amy, and Jake and Kyle Hampton all stood in the Giffords' backyard. In another minute, the wail of sirens punched through the dark night.

A limb of the oak tree fell like a flaming torch to the ground, spreading the fire to a bed of pine-needle mulch below. Mrs. Gifford screamed. "Blake, it's going to burn the house!"

Mr. Gifford turned on a water hose and extinguished the small ground fire. The tree, however, burned with flames reaching higher and higher into the night sky.

Firemen quickly dragged a hose from the closest fire hydrant. Soon a heavy white spray fought back the blaze, and after a ten-minute fight, the battle was over.

With the oak tree smoldering, the firemen were joined by deputies Don Rawlings and Steve Branson. Don walked up to the small crowd and began the questioning.

"The dispatcher reported that Kyle Hampton made the 9-1-1 call. Is that correct?"

Kyle beamed. He was confident he had done the right thing for once. He was especially anxious to appear like a hero to the same officer who had found him in the jailhouse.

Jake gripped his son's shoulder. "That's right," he replied.

Officer Rawlings looked at Kyle. "What's your story, son? What were you doing up at such an hour?"

"I just woke up, that's all." He didn't want to tell them he had been scared by a dream. "Then I saw the flames in the tree from my bedroom window."

Rawlings nodded.

Kyle continued excitedly. "I woke my dad up and called 9-1-1!"

The policeman looked up at Jake. "Was Kyle dressed when he came in your room?"

Jake wasn't sure why the officer asked that. "He was in his pajamas." He thought for a moment and tried to remember. "Weren't you, Kyle?"

"Sure."

"Did you happen to see anyone around when you looked out the window?"

"No. Just the fire." Kyle shifted his weight from foot to foot.

"What are you getting at, Officer?"

"Just trying to gather information, Mr. Hampton. Obviously, fires of this nature don't just happen. They are started willfully, or accidentally, by people." He sighed and looked at his watch.

The firemen gathered up their equipment and talked among themselves. It was very unusual for Taylorville to have two fire calls in one week, much less in one day.

Don needed more information but decided to talk later, in the light of day. He nodded to the Giffords and to Jake. "I'll be seeing you later to complete my report."

CHAPTER
26

B<small>Y</small> 4:30 the excitement had died down, and Jake plopped into bed for the second time in a troubled night. Maybe it was the fire, or maybe it was the way Don Rawlings implied that Kyle might have been involved in starting it, but once Jake fell back asleep, nightmares tormented his already agitated state of mind.

He was back in Sarah's room. She was deathly pale, with her forehead moist with sweat, a terrible look of agony on her face. "Don't make me suffer on and on," she whispered.

"But the baby . . ." Jake protested. "The baby isn't ready."

"I . . . can't . . . make . . . it . . . until . . . then," she added, with gasping, halting breaths. "Did . . . you . . . bring . . . it?"

"Honey, don't make me—"

"Don't let me suffer!" Sarah winced as she spoke as forcefully as her weakened condition would allow. "Did you bring—"

Jake put his finger to her lips and interrupted her speech.

She began to weep. With every sob her pain intensified, bringing on more tears and more excruciating anguish.

Jake encircled her shoulders gently with his arms. He helped her lie back once her sobs subsided.

"Help me, Jake. H-h-help me."

Jake sat holding her hand for a long time, stroking her skin, flinching every time her body stiffened in response to another wave of torment.

Suddenly her hand turned cold. Something was amiss. He squeezed her hand but received no response. He looked at her hand, which was cool and unmoving. He looked at her face, but a sheet now covered her. "Sarah?"

He pulled the sheet from her face, which was now frozen in a twisted plastic scowl.

"Sarah?" A dark feeling of horror enveloped him.

"What is happening?" Jake screamed. "You can't die. The baby will die! The baby!"

Suddenly fear gripped him. A hidden knowledge sickened him. He looked away from his hand. He didn't want to see what he was holding.

Every cell in his body seemed to focus on his right hand. He held a firm tubular object. Somehow he knew what had happened. He didn't want to see. He couldn't look. He shook his head, but something controlled him. Something forced him to see.

He dropped his eyes. In his hand he held an empty syringe.

Cold sweat poured from his forehead as Jake abruptly sat up in bed.

"Oh, God . . ." he whispered. His recall was returning. Somehow he knew the syringe was more than a dream. The syringe was a memory.

Slowly his turmoil spilled out in large, warm tears. "Oh, God . . ." He held his head. Somehow he knew it was true.

The syringe was real.

◆ ◆ ◆

The following morning, Don Rawlings stroked his thick black hair and sipped his coffee. He looked up as Steve Branson walked in. "What did you find out?"

"Get this—I called the school to see if the Hampton kid has been toeing the line over there . . . to see if there were any other hints of irregular behavior, right?"

Don nodded. "So?"

"So they tell me he's been acting pretty normally." He squinted. "But when I pressed them about it, they did admit that his record reflected that he'd been pulled from class yesterday to talk to the counselor again. It's that Isaacs woman who called you."

"Oh, I get it. The kid gets angry at the woman and takes it out by starting fires."

"Maybe. They wouldn't give me the details of the reason for the meeting, but they did confirm that she mainly deals with behavior-related problems."

"Bingo." Don tapped his pencil.

"And get this—I looked back over our reports from the day we picked him up at the old jailhouse, and I discovered that the boy whose treehouse was torched was the one who made the 9-1-1 call. He admitted it after we talked to his mother, who was supposed to be taking care of Kyle that day."

"He was probably just trying to get them back for ratting on him."

Steve nodded. "Did the Fire Department come up with anything?"

Don nodded and patted a stack of white paper. "They're 90 percent sure it was a kerosene fire."

"Just like at the old jailhouse." Steve shook his head. "What's it going to take for this kid to come clean? Do you think we should bring the kid in? After all, we do have an adult witness who claims he heard the boy saying he was going to the jailhouse before the first fire was started."

Don thought for a moment. "No, I don't think so. Unless a judge sends me down there, I'm afraid we're going to have to catch him redhanded at something."

"It wouldn't hurt to give him a stern warning."

Don chuckled. "Maybe I should talk to him again."

◆ ◆ ◆

Jake sipped his coffee with a prayer on his lips. "God, help me to know the truth. Help me to face the truth."

He had slipped from bed early in the morning, driven by his nightmares and propelled by the feeling that he was on the edge of remembering. Now, with Kyle at school and his first case not scheduled until 11 A.M., he sat with pen in hand, seeking to finish his story.

◆ ◆ ◆

It was late evening when Jake had finally broken away from his duties in Grantsville to head for Ocean Sands. When he arrived on the beach an hour later, his worst fears were realized—the canal to the south of the Wellness Facility's property appeared full. He thought about wading across but changed his mind when he remembered the medicine in his pocket that he'd brought for Sarah. He couldn't risk getting it wet. He was tempted to curse his misfortune when he noted a young man pushing a catamaran into the surf a few hundred yards away. He ran toward the man and arrived just as the sailor was standing in water up to his knees.

"Can you give me a lift up the beach?" Jake yelled so he would be heard above the surf.

The man, who appeared about twenty, looked at Jake curiously.

Jake went on to explain, "I need to get to the Wellness Facility, but the tide is too high. I can't cross the canal until low tide." He pointed to the hospital lights. "It's only a few hundred yards up the shore."

"I need to get the catamaran over to the sound. It's already dark." The young man looked up. "Sorry." He turned to the surf again.

"I'll pay you!" Jake yelled. "Please."

The young man sighed and pushed the boat toward Jake. "Get on."

Jake scrambled into a seated position. "Thanks."

In a few minutes the man deposited Jake on the shoreline and left twenty dollars richer.

Jake walked toward the hospital shaking his head. "I wish I'd had a ten," he muttered to himself.

Poorer, but glad to be on the hospital grounds, Jake slipped into the shadows at the edge of the large hedgerow. He counted windows and looked for Sarah's coat hanging on a balcony chair, the signal that it was safe to approach.

He strained to see in the dim light. No coat. Jake sighed and looked at his watch. 9:30. *The nurses aren't in her room now, are they?* Jake wondered. He decided to wait and leaned up against one of the large palms that grew about thirty feet from her balcony. If he stayed close to the tree and didn't move, he wouldn't be seen by a casual observer. Jake strained to see into Sarah's room. *It's no use*, he thought. *I can't see through the curtains.* All he could tell was that the lights were on. Their little plan called for her to switch the lights off, another signal that it was safe to approach.

Jake shook his head. *I can't believe I've been reduced to this! A grown man, a professional, stooping to sneaking around just because I'm afraid of some big hospital security goons.* He checked his watch again and waited. After

ten minutes, which seemed like an hour, Jake slowly approached the balcony, thinking he could back off if he heard anyone talking.

The room seemed silent. Jake climbed and hoisted himself over the
balcony railing. Slowly he slid open the balcony door.

The room was still and quiet except for Sarah's breathing.

"Sarah?" Jake whispered.

Sarah aroused easily and looked at Jake. One look was enough to start
her tears again.

"Sarah . . . What's the matter, honey?" Jake rushed to her side and sat
beside her on the bed.

"Jake, today's been awful." She spoke between sobs. "I slipped and fell
in the bathroom. My back hurt so much, I couldn't even get up again."

Sarah recounted the whole story and told how she needed to be taken
to Beach Memorial just to get an X-ray.

"They say I have a small wedge compression fracture of my first lumbar vertebrae. It's a stable fracture, according to the E.R. doctor I saw."

Jake had listened with as much patience as his surgical personality
could muster. "They call this place a hospital, yet they don't even have
the staff to help you get around? They let you fall, and then they don't
even have an X-ray unit here to make the diagnosis?" Jake stood up and
began to pace. He was livid. "The director is going to hear from me about
this!"

Sarah looked at him, her expression a composite of pain and fear.
"Don't do anything you'll regret, honey. They're trying to help me,
remember."

"I can't take this anymore, Sarah. You've got to come home with me.
Just look at you. Can you even walk?"

"Jake," she insisted, reaching for his hand, "I've got to stay. Look." She
pulled back her gown. "Feel." She placed his hand upon her breast. "See?
It's getting smaller!"

Jake pulled his hand away. "But, Sarah, what about your back? You
don't fracture a normal backbone with a little fall in the bathroom." He
looked at her, knowing he had to be honest enough to convince her to
come home. "I'm afraid the cancer has spread to the bones in your back.
You've got to come home where we can get you full-time help . . . not this
resort health food!"

Sarah winced with pain. Jake sat back down again. He continued, "Look, honey, I just want what is best for you . . . and the baby," he added.

Sarah shook her head. She remained stubbornly committed to following the plan through, regardless of the cost. "Jake, it seems to be working."

"It seems to be killing you," he responded emphatically.

"It's the only hope I've got."

Jake shook his head and bit his tongue. Seeking to preserve peace, he changed the subject. "I've brought you some pain meds." He reached into his pocket. "I've got Darvocet, Tylox, and a few Vicodins. I got them from the office sample supply."

"Put them in the bottom drawer, under my sweats."

Jake obeyed. "Why the secrecy?"

"When I mentioned that the doctor at Beach Memorial had given me some pain tablets, the nursing coordinator demanded that I surrender them until Dr. D approves."

"Why, that—"

"Jake," Sarah interrupted, squeezing his hand, "it's just like at your hospital. You don't let your patients take the medicines they bring in from home, do you?"

"Yeah, but this isn't—"

"They're just doing their job."

Jake shook his head and remained silent. He didn't like this place, but he didn't want to be at war with Sarah either.

Jake sighed and changed the subject again. After a few minutes of small talk, he smiled. "I almost forgot," he said, reaching for his windbreaker now hanging from the wicker chair. He reached in the pocket and pulled out a Zero bar. "Kyle sent you a present. He bought it with his own money."

Sarah cried again, reaching for the present. "A Zero bar!"

Jake handed it to her and then sat quietly by her side for a few more minutes. He wanted to savor this moment when she seemed happy again. He knew from experience that he wouldn't have much more time with her.

Sarah sat silently, too, clutching her candy bar like it was a delicate offering. Finally she looked up. "Tell Kyle I loved it."

Jake nodded.

"You'll tell him I love him, won't you?"

"Yes."

Jake held her quietly for a long time. Together they listened to the surf, which was audible through the open sliding door.

"I want you to know I love you, Jake," Sarah whispered softly. "I've known you were the one for me since our first date."

"In college?"

"Sure." She squeezed his arm. "Get my purse."

He picked it up from the nightstand and looked at her with curiosity.

She opened to a group of wallet photos and folded it over until she found just the one she wanted. "There," she said, pointing at a yellowing photograph.

Jake leaned in and looked at the picture, taken on a ski trip during his junior year of college. He was wearing a blue ski cap that covered his ears but not his long sideburns.

"I loved you then," she said, turning the page.

"Even with those sideburns?" Jake made a choking sound.

"And I love you now," she said, pointing at a new family photograph that was six months old.

"And I love you."

◆　◆　◆

Jake laid down his pen and searched the kitchen for a Kleenex. He had remembered all he wanted for now. *Maybe I can get back to this tonight,* he hoped. He blew his nose and looked at his watch. He needed to make some hospital rounds anyway. *I can try to remember more later.*

◆　◆　◆

On that same night, while Jake visited Sarah, Dr. D made an urgent trip to Ocean Sands, forsaking his other obligations. He needed to see the X-rays of Sarah's lumbar spine.

He hurriedly opened the X-ray jacket and held a film up to a naked light bulb. He didn't even have an X-ray viewbox at the facility, but removing the lampshade from his desk lamp provided all the light he needed to read the ominous findings on Sarah's films.

D cursed. The film wasn't hard to interpret. Several lytic areas of the lumbar vertebrae stood out as clear evidence that Sarah's breast cancer had spread to the bones. The fracture, an anterior wedge compression break, had been caused by the cancer eating away at the vertebral body, weakening it to the point of collapse.

"Now what am I going to do?" D spoke to no one in the room but himself. "Here is my celebrated patient, advertised to all who would listen . . . with cancer that is eating her alive."

If her husband doesn't sue us over this, I'll be lucky, he realized, rubbing his neck. *And if he makes a public point of her case like we did, it could weaken our credibility and spoil our profit . . . and that's the bottom line.*

He looked at the X-ray again. *But how can I stop him from bringing her case to the public eye? Certainly she will die of her cancer soon . . . and that's only likely to stir up Dr. Hampton's anger even more.* He stood and paced, opening his door and stepping onto the veranda. He stared at the ocean and breathed deeply of the salty air.

He walked back inside and poured himself a drink. *If Sarah Hampton dies of breast cancer, Dr. Hampton's likely to tell the world.* He shook the ice in his glass nervously. *Somehow, some way, I have to prevent Sarah from dying of cancer . . . but how? Her death appears inevitable.*

Isn't there any way to shift the blame away from our treatment program? D shook his head and took a gulp of his drink, then poured another. *Maybe this will help*, he thought. *Or maybe at least it will help me not to care.*

◆　◆　◆

At Taylorville Elementary School, Kyle had been pulled from class to have a talk with Officers Rawlings and Branson. This time, because they were on school grounds, an adult representing the school needed to be present, and the principal had appointed Sharon Isaacs. "You know him. Perhaps he'll talk in front of you," he'd said as he informed Sharon of the meeting. The police liked the idea. They knew Sharon suspected Kyle of playing a little prank on her and had even reported it to them. She certainly wouldn't mind if they put a little fear of God into the little guy, would she?

Kyle sat across from the two officers in Sharon's little office.

"You really shouldn't question him without his father's presence, or at least his permission," Sharon protested. Her comments caught the officers cold.

"We're only here to ask Kyle a few questions," Don Rawlings replied, glaring at Sharon. He softened and looked at Kyle. "That's all right, isn't it, son?"

Kyle shrugged.

"What were you doing up at 2:30 in the morning, Kyle?"

"I was just up, that's all."

"People are sleeping at 2:30, Kyle. What were you doing?"

Kyle groaned. "I had a bad dream, OK?" Kyle looked at the floor. "I woke up because of a nightmare."

Rawlings thought he had him trapped. "What was the dream that woke you up?"

"I dreamed that I was being attacked by rats." He looked around nervously. "Like over in the jailhouse."

"You know a lot about that place, don't you, Kyle?"

"Not really. I was only there once."

"Isn't it true that you were mad at Todd Gifford about calling us that day you went to the jailhouse?"

"Yes, I was mad," Kyle responded. "But we made up."

"Isn't it true, Kyle, that you thought you could get even by setting his treehouse on fire?"

Kyle looked at Sharon and then back at the officers. "No!"

Sharon stood up. "Kyle, you don't have to answer these questions. He is entitled to a lawyer, isn't he? You can't just ask him questions like he's committed some crime or something."

"He doesn't have to cooperate, but we will find out the truth," Steve Branson added. "Besides, we're not arresting him. We just wanted to question him," he stated flatly. "We thought he might be able to lead us to whoever started the fire."

"You're here to accuse him . . . to scare him into admitting something to you, but you heard him. He says he didn't do it!"

"Come on, Ms. Isaacs. Just let us ask a few more questions!"

"Only if his father or an attorney is present! This interview is over." Sharon opened the door for the officers.

"Miss, you're getting in the way of our investigation. We have the right—"

"He has the right to an attorney!" Sharon stood her ground.

The deputies huffed and stood. They knew she was right, but they had wanted to put a little fear into Kyle anyway, in hopes of straightening out his antisocial behavior patterns.

"Gentlemen," Sharon added, holding her hand up to the exit, "you may leave now."

Don barged past his larger partner. "You'll see, ma'am. You'll see."

Steve nodded sternly and marched out to catch up with his fellow officer.

Sharon exhaled sharply and looked at Kyle. "I can't believe those guys!" She sat back down. "You'd better get back to class, Kyle."

He nodded. "Are you going to tell Dad about this?"

"I think I should."

Kyle nodded his assent and smiled. "Thanks. You were great."

Sharon nodded and smiled. "You better run. I'll see you after school."

Kyle jumped out of his seat and looked back from the doorway. "Thanks again."

◆ ◆ ◆

By 9 that night, Officers Rawlings and Branson decided not to question Kyle any further. They had to admit that they had more suspicions than hard evidence, and they didn't want to talk to a judge, at least not yet. Sharon had filled in Jake, who had shown more than a little concern over the matter. Next door, tree surgeons had worked through the afternoon and reduced the Giffords' oak tree to a large stump and enough firewood for the rest of this winter and the next.

Now, with Kyle in bed and Jake's beeper in the Off position for the evening, Jake sat across the kitchen table from Sharon sipping a cup of decaffeinated tea.

"I still can't believe how unfair the police were to my son," Jake commented. He shook his head. "I know Kyle has had it rough lately. Losing his mom, the move . . . Everything has been so stressful, but this is only adding to it, in my opinion. I believe my son, and if he says he didn't do something, I'd say he didn't do it."

"You know, I'll admit that for a while I thought Kyle might just be acting out, trying to tell us something, but now I don't think so. He's not the type of kid to go this far."

"He didn't start the fires, Sharon." Jake shook his head. "Something else is up, and the authorities are pinning it on the easiest suspect." He looked up. "The evidence is circumstantial." He paused again. "I'll admit too that Kyle seems to have a superficial motive, but he has never been this way before. Kyle has never been vindictive or violent."

Sharon nodded. She studied Jake for a moment, then responded, "I don't think I've ever seen you so angry as when I told you about the police visit to the school."

Jake smiled sheepishly. "I guess you still have some things to learn about me." He sighed. "I can be pretty intense."

"You'd never have made it this far in life if you weren't."

Jake thought back a few months. "If you think I was angry now, you should have seen me right after Sarah's death."

Sharon furrowed her brow. "Want to tell me about it?"

Jake sighed again. "I was just so frustrated. Sarah was gone, and I suspected the Wellness Facility had something to do with it." He paused and shook his head. "I really had it out with the medical director of the facility, a doctor they all just call 'Dr. D.' I brought up my suspicions to him on the phone one day. He was livid." Jake hung his head. "He warned me not to mess with him or his facility if I knew what was good for me. He said he would sue me for interfering with his work, that he would see that I would never practice medicine again." He paused. "It's weird. I never even met the guy face to face, but I could tell he was extremely vengeful." Jake shivered. "I was afraid of him."

"What did you do?"

"I pursued it for a while and even had my attorney write a letter, warning them of a possible suit, citing her death and their negligence concerning Sarah breaking her back while under their care. But after that, the whole thing exploded. The media became intensely interested in me again. Somehow they found out I was present when my wife died. They even knew that I had brought her some pain medicines. The only way they could have known that was if Dr. D told them. No one else knew." He shrugged. "Regardless, the more I snooped into what really happened to Sarah, the more interested the media and the police became in my case. Eventually the prosecuting attorney's office decided they had enough to try and pin a double murder rap on my shoulders. It was horrible. My part-ners were forced to distance themselves from me."

"What happened?"

"Eventually the whole thing fell through. I stopped looking into Sarah's treatment, and then suddenly a grand jury thought there wasn't enough evidence to take me to trial. Everything blew over. Although I couldn't prove it, I think Dr. D pulled as many strings as he could to make my life miserable with the media and the local authorities. Finally I just decided to start over, and when I stopped trying to find out what was going on at Ocean Sands, the media left me alone."

"Just like that?"

"Just like that."

"And what happened to this Dr. D?"

"He still works at the Wellness Facility, I guess. I haven't heard from him since I stopped trying to find out exactly what he had to do with Sarah." He shuddered. "He's an evil man, Sharon."

She stayed quiet for a moment, then responded, "Then you came here."

"Right. Dr. Willie came to my rescue. He offered me a job just when everything was falling apart." He looked Sharon in the eyes. "I jumped at the chance for a new beginning."

Sharon played with her tea bag. "I'm glad you did."

"Me too." Jake walked over to the teapot on the stove and refilled his cup. "So now you know I have a temper."

"You seem to control it well, Jake. Most people would have exploded long ago." Sharon smiled softly. She paused for a moment and studied Jake's profile. "So all the while you suspected Ocean Sands and Dr. D had something to do with Sarah's death, but you won't let yourself off the hook. You can't seem to believe you didn't have something to do with it."

Jake nodded without speaking.

"I see a double standard here."

Jake looked at her and tilted his head. "Double standard?"

"Sure. Your son, whom you love, is suspected of wrongdoing. There is plenty of circumstantial evidence against him, and yet you, in your heart, refuse to believe it. You love him. He isn't guilty. End of story." She caught Jake's eye. "But you have circumstantial evidence linking you to Sarah's death, and you can't seem to let a minute go by without condemning yourself for what you may or may not have done."

Jake dropped his head and stared at his hands. For a minute he didn't speak. "I have nightmares about it," he said slowly. "Last night I remembered something in a dream . . . something that ignited a buried memory," he added. "I was holding an empty syringe in my hand. I'm not sure what it means. I just know it had something to do with Sarah."

"A syringe? Jake, you work with syringes all the time. How do you know the syringe has something to do with her?"

"It was just a feeling . . . something odd. I just knew it was more than a dream. It was a memory, for sure."

"A memory of a syringe?"

"In my dream I held her hand. I sat by her bed as she suffered." His voice quickened. "Suddenly she changed. Her hand was cold. I knew she was dead. I looked . . . and in my hand was an empty syringe."

"It was only a dream, Jake."

Jake nodded and looked at Sharon. "Right." He hadn't convinced himself.

Sharon stirred her tea. "You know, I've been thinking about all this stuff . . . the fires, the candy wrappers . . . Do you think all of this stuff could be related?"

"Related?"

"Yeah, you know, Kyle found a Zero bar wrapper in the jail, where there was a picture of Sarah and where the mattress fire occurred. Maybe all of these things are connected somehow."

Jake scratched his chin. "You may be on to something," he responded thoughtfully. "I guess I've just been too frustrated by each event to imagine a connection. What do you think?"

"I'm not sure. It just seems funny that all these things should start happening at the same time. What do you suggest we do next?"

"I know what I do when I need answers," he responded.

Sharon's eyes met Jake's. "Me too." Their unspoken communication was understood.

Jake reached out across the table and took Sharon's hand. It was the first time he'd done so. She squeezed his hand firmly.

"Dear God," Jake began, "we want to know your wisdom. We need to know your way . . ."

CHAPTER
27

AFTER Jake brought the pain medication, Sarah's life became only slightly more tolerable. The pain pills did take the edge off her agony, however, and allowed her to accomplish the minimal ambulation from her bed to her bathroom. She usually took the medicine with her meals, which were now delivered to her room because of her difficulty in getting to the dining hall. Besides, unknown to Sarah, Dr. D did not want her to be seen in public anymore. He certainly didn't want anyone else finding out how sick she really was.

Her medicines, she found out, worked best if she took them on a schedule—one with her kelp juice in the morning, a second tablet just before a coffee enema at ten, one with her fruit juices at lunch, and two tablets before attempting to sleep.

Sarah pushed back the tray of liquids. For three days now she had been on a fruit juice fast, a way of further cleansing her body of toxic buildup that might be feeding the cancer. In addition to the juices, she had been required to breathe supplemental oxygen, given through a small nasal cannula. This, she was told, would heighten her body's oxygen level and would in turn create a toxic environment for the cancer cells.

Sarah swallowed a Tylox with her grapefruit juice. She quickly shoved the bottle under her pillow when her nurse, Susan Rolan, appeared in the doorway.

"Done with lunch?"

"All done."

Susan picked up the tray. "Better put your oxygen back on." Sarah had taken it off to eat.

She adjusted the flow rate on a portable oxygen tank.

"Can the orderly wheel me out by the ocean today?"

"I'm afraid not."

"Why not?"

"Dr. D wants you on oxygen at all times. For that you'll need to be in your room."

Sarah sighed. Ocean Sands was a lot more fun when she was healthy enough to be out of her room.

"Maybe you could wheel my oxygen tank over by the sliding door. I could at least sit out on the balcony that way."

Susan studied her patient. Sarah looked weak and pale. Dr. D wouldn't like the other patients looking up and seeing her this way. The nurse bit her lower lip nervously. "I'll have to ask for permission."

Sarah rolled her eyes and fluffed her pillow, knocking her Tylox bottle to the floor with a clatter. Sarah looked up nervously. Susan's eyes went to the floor.

Susan picked up the bottle. "What is this?"

"It's pain medication," Sarah admitted reluctantly.

"You know you can't have this here!" She gripped the bottle tightly. "Only approved therapies are acceptable."

Sarah's eyes widened. "Please," she pleaded. "Don't take the medicine away. It's all that's making my life bearable."

"You must cooperate with the regimen."

"Please!" Sarah looked fearful. "I want to cooperate. I think this stuff is working, but my back . . . The pain is excruciating. You've got to know that the pain of a broken back isn't going to go away with a little green tea." She paused. "Please!"

"I-I'm sorry," Susan softened. "But the rules are plain." She looked at the bottle in her hand. "Maybe I can get the acupuncturist to come today."

"Don't bother."

"Look," Susan responded, "I'll ask Dr. D. Maybe he will approve it. I know he uses regular medicines in his family practice. Maybe he'll make an exception in your case."

Sarah sighed. "I hope so."

Susan nodded and retreated to the hallway. She walked straight for the director's office.

"Is Dr. D in?"

"Sure, Susan," Dr. D's receptionist replied. "Hold on a minute." She pressed the intercom button. "Dr D?"

Dr. D picked up his private line. "What's up, Alice?"

"Susan Rolan is here to talk to you."

"Send her in."

Susan stepped into the director's office. Her expression showed anxiety.

"What's on your mind, Susan?"

She held out the pills. "Dr. D, I found these in Sarah Hampton's room."

He took the bottle and rolled the container around in his fingers. "Tylox," he muttered. "That's a pretty strong oral narcotic."

Susan squinted. "She's really pretty pitiful. She's always complaining of pain. When she seemed better this week, I thought maybe we were making headway." She looked at the pills. "Do you want me to destroy them?"

Dr. D didn't answer. "Where did she get them?"

Susan shrugged. "I didn't ask."

"Maybe her doctor husband got them to her somehow."

"Perhaps." Susan nodded. "So what would you like me to do?"

"Save the pills," Dr. D responded thoughtfully. "She's breaking the rules. She isn't going along with our treatment regimen. We can't be responsible if she isn't compliant, can we?"

"She does everything I ask," Susan responded. "It's only some pain pills."

"Save the pills, Susan. Don't give them back. If she doesn't do well, we must have evidence of her noncompliance."

"She's going downhill, Dr. D. We're going to have to face it. We'd better get her home if she's going to have any time with her son."

Dr. D looked at her sharply. "She won't die of breast cancer here, I can assure you."

"Have you seen her? She can't even walk without help."

The director sighed. "Keep her out of sight. I won't have her seen by the other patients. It's not good for their attitudes."

Susan shifted from one foot to the other. "Can I let her have her pills? She almost cried when I took them. She's a desperate woman, Dr. D."

"She needs to take our therapies. Schedule her for some whirlpool treatments."

"It's pure agony just to move her to the bathroom. How can we do that?"

"You'll figure it out."

"Dr. D, she's dying!"

"Not of breast cancer. Not in my hospital! If she dies, it will be because she took these poisons!" The director held up the oral narcotics.

"How can you be so sure—"

Dr. D shot a lacerating glare in her direction. His expression clearly dictated, *No more questions!*

Susan sighed and left the room.

Dr. D pondered the medicine bottle in his hand and quietly hid them in his desk drawer. *These will come in handy*, he mused. *They might be just what I need.*

◆ ◆ ◆

By the time Friday rolled around again, Jake felt he could use a break. He came home from work, took Kyle to his grandmother's, and returned to prepare for the evening. He showered and put on a charcoal suit with a white shirt and a dark silk tie. He looked forward to seeing Sharon. It would be their first formal outing together in Taylorville.

He picked Sharon up at 6:45. She was waiting, and Frank was watching.

Sharon opened the door in response to Jake's knock. She was wearing a knee-length dark blue dress with a single string, pearl-appearing necklace. Her hair was up in a french braid.

"Hi."

"Well, hi," Jake responded. "You look great."

Sharon smiled. "Thanks."

◆ ◆ ◆

Frank looked through the peephole. "This just confirms it," he muttered. "You two must have planned Sarah's death just so you could be together."

He rubbed the pistol in his hand and watched until the couple disappeared down the steps.

Then he walked to the front window, muttering about vengeance and destiny.

◆ ◆ ◆

Jake drove the Trooper through Taylorville on the way to the country club.

"Who all will be at this dinner?" Sharon looked out of the window.

"I'm not sure. It sounded like community leaders, a few of the doctors, that sort of crowd."

Sharon nodded and lifted her nose in the air. "How do I look?"

"Perfectly snobbish," Jake teased.

"Sure you don't want to just skip this and grab a pizza?"

"Right!" Jake slowed down to turn onto Country Club Road. "I promised Willie. He wouldn't forgive me if I stood him up." He looked at Sharon. "You can put up with this for one evening."

Sharon feigned a weak smile. "Sure."

Jake found a parking place and opened Sharon's door. Once inside in the lobby, Willie and his wife, Dee, greeted them. Willie smiled and shook Jake's hand. On Willie's lapel was a small golden oak leaf. "I knew you'd make it."

"Hi, Willie. I'd like you to meet Sharon Isaacs."

Willie took her hand warmly. "So glad to meet you."

Dee held up her hand and smiled nervously. "Nice to see you again, Jake."

The foursome was stopped in the hall by the Pin Oak Society's Steve Smith and a photographer for the *Taylorville Times*.

"Dr. Hampton? Steve Smith here," he said, holding out his hand. "Thanks so much for responding to my letter. We're glad you're here."

Jake smiled and shook his hand. Silently he searched his memory. *What letter? What response? Am I supposed to know you?*

Steve looked at the photographer. "Bob, could you get a picture of the two couples together? Jake is one of our award recipients, and Dr. Willie has been a long-time supporter. This is Dr. Willie's wife, Dee."

"Sure," he said and held up his hand. "Why don't we have you stand over here by the fireplace?" He motioned to Willie, Dee, Jake, and Sharon. The four obeyed.

"That looks good. Smile. Good. Dr. Dee, could you move in a touch?"

Dr. Willie flinched. "It's Dr. Willie. This is my wife, Dee."

"I'm sorry. Here, let me get everyone's name on record for the caption." They each gave their name and the proper spelling. The photographer took a few additional shots and retreated into the ballroom.

Sharon grabbed Jake's arm for security and walked with him into the dining area. The spacious room was adorned for the winter holiday season. A large, fully decorated Christmas tree stood in the corner. A podium sat prominently at the front of a central aisle that divided the tables into two sections.

Jake recognized two pediatricians, one radiologist, an orthopedic surgeon, and the mayor. Everyone had a small decorative gold leaf lapel pin.

Jake squinted as another man in a gray suit passed. "Do you see all of these lapel pins?" Jake whispered.

Sharon nodded. "It's probably some country club membership thing," Sharon responded. "See the leaf on the podium?"

"Yes." Jake moved quietly over to a nearby table and picked up a program. The title at the top screamed at him: *Pin Oak Society Awards Banquet*. His eyes widened. He pushed the program in front of Sharon. "Look at this!" he uttered in a strained whisper. "The Pin Oak Society!"

Sharon looked at him, sensing his alarm. "I don't understand."

"Sharon," he whispered, his face flushing, "this is a pro-assisted suicide society. It's a political organization pushing for the Death with Dignity Act."

"Oh boy." Sharon shook her head. "Didn't you know?"

"Of course not," Jake whispered. He stood still for a moment and then slapped his head. "Of course," he said quietly. "Steve Smith. I knew that name from somewhere. He's the local director of this organization. They've been in the news lately, rallying for support in the state legislature."

"What letter was he referring to?"

"Beats me," Jake said, shaking his head. "I never replied to any letter."

"What are we going to do?"

Jake scanned the program. There, under award recipients, he saw his name. "Great," he whispered. "I'm getting an award." He sighed and looked at Sharon. "I can't receive this. It will look like I support what they believe in." He paused. "It's almost like admitting that I helped Sarah die."

"Let's get out of here before it gets going."

"What'll I say? I have to talk to Dr. Willie." Sweat beaded Jake's forehead.

Willie was chatting with three gray-haired women a few yards away. Just as Jake made a step toward him, a heavy hand clapped his shoulder. "Jake . . ."

He spun around. "Oh, hi, Mayor."

Bob Rivers smiled. Jake noticed his lapel pin right away. "Good to see you." He looked at Sharon.

Jake made the introductions. "Mr. Rivers, I'd like you to meet a good friend of mine, Sharon Isaacs." He looked at Sharon. "I'm sure you recognize Taylorville's mayor, Bob Rivers."

"Jake fixed me right up, he did," the mayor responded winking at Sharon. He held her hand gently for a moment. "So nice to meet you."

Jake watched out of the corner of his eye as Willie and Deloris took a seat at a nearby table. Suddenly the room seemed to be filled with people finding seats. Willie motioned for Jake and Sharon.

The mayor looked back at Jake. "Willie told me you'd fit right in around this place." He looked around. "Guess I'd better find my seat." He winked, this time at Jake. "Congratulations, doc."

Sharon tugged Jake's arm. "Jake!" she whispered. "Everyone's sitting down."

Jake pushed his lips to her ear. "We've got to get out of here."

Willie motioned for them again.

Jake looked at Sharon. "I've got to tell Willie."

"Everybody take a seat please," Steve Smith requested from the podium. "Before we eat, the Reverend Bill Fornsburg II will give an invocation."

Jake and Sharon took their seats. Jake whispered, "I can't interrupt the prayer."

The reverend opened a piece of paper and began to read a flowery oracle full of thee's, thou's, and other piety.

"Amen."

Jake leaned over to Willie as Steve Smith began an introduction. "I'm sorry, Willie. I really can't stay."

Willie and Dee looked shocked.

"This is all very pleasant, and it was so nice to be invited, but it's . . . well . . ." Jake stumbled. "I just can't accept any awards." His eyes met with Willie's. "I didn't know this was the Pin Oak Society dinner. I don't agree with their philosophy, that's all."

"Jake, I thought you—"

"Please stay," Deloris interrupted her husband.

Jake looked at Sharon and back at the Dansfords. "I just can't. Tell them whatever you want. I can't just stand there and take their award. It wouldn't be right." Jake stood with Sharon gripping his arm. "I'll see you in the morning."

With that, they quickly departed without speaking another word.

Deloris looked at Willie and scowled. "I thought you talked to him about this!"

"I did," Willie sulked. "I guess I just didn't mention the Pin Oak part."

"Great, just great! Now you've offended him," she snapped quietly. "The only guy to consider this practice in years, and you try and flood him with your philosophy."

"Hey, I'm not the one that is issuing the awards around here," he responded. "I thought it might do Jake some good to feel a little community support. We all know how hard the media was on him. I wanted him to know there were people around that understand."

Dee softened. "I know, dear," she said, patting his hand. "I know. You've tried so hard to help this young surgeon," she added. "I know you mean well."

Willie frowned. "He'll be OK. I'll apologize to him later."

Dee nodded and smiled.

Willie smiled, too. The prime rib looked good. He would stand in and take the award for Jake. The evening wouldn't be a total loss.

◆ ◆ ◆

Jake screeched the tires as he pulled out onto Country Club Road. Sharon looked at him. "Easy, Jake."

He slowed down. He hadn't spoken since their rapid exit from the banquet. "Sorry." He shook his head. "I just can't believe that. Why would Willie invite me to a Pin Oak Society dinner without knowing how I feel about them?"

"It looks to me like he thought he knew how you feel."

"That's the trouble. Everyone seems to have me figured out," he protested, "except me!" He glared in Sharon's direction. "And why would the Pin Oak Society want to give me an award?"

"Mr. Smith seemed to indicate that you'd replied to a letter."

Jake shook his head. "The only letter I remember from them was a letter asking me to speak at one of their functions. They said something to the effect that the story of my struggle with Sarah and her assisted death would be beneficial to their supporters."

"Either they've been reading old newspapers or someone else is pushing you forward from behind the scenes."

Jake downshifted the Trooper as his face showed unbelief. "Willie?"

Sharon shrugged. "I think he meant well. He must be into this Pin Oak thing. Maybe he is just being friendly . . . showing his support."

"I guess so." Jake sighed. "He's been about the only support I've had in this town," Jake responded, looking over at Sharon, "until you came along."

Sharon laughed. "Some support I am. I wanted to get pizza."

Jake smiled. "It's not too late." He did a U-turn and headed for the only place with Italian food in town, Tony's Little Italy.

"Can we do takeout?" Sharon looked at her dress. "I think we'd stand out at Tony's."

"Sure. Why don't we call ahead?" He pointed at the car phone. "We can drive around for a few minutes until the pizza is ready."

Fifteen minutes later they were on their way to Jake's with a hot pepperoni, sausage, and mushroom pizza. Once they were in Jake's kitchen, he looked at Sharon and then at the pizza box in his hand. "Something's not right here," he said with a smile. "It's just not right to eat pizza out of a box dressed like this." He walked to the pantry, brought out his only white tablecloth, and spread it out on the table. Then he looked at Sharon and asked, "May I show you to your table?" He held up his arm.

"You may." Jake pulled the chair out for her and placed the pizza in the middle of the table. He then found a single Christmas candle and put it in the center of the table. He quickly put out two plates and lit the candle, then lowered the room lights.

"There," he said. "That's better. What may I get you to drink?" he asked, opening the refrigerator door. "Water, Diet Pepsi, or milk?"

"Diet Pepsi please."

"A woman after my own heart." Jake poured the drinks and sat down.

After a prayer, they enjoyed the pizza together. Every few minutes Jake just shook his head.

Sharon watched him. "Just forget about it, Jake. Eventually all of this will pass. In a few months no one will remember the Pin Oak Society dinner, and no one will care whether you were there or not."

"You're reading my mind."

"You were shaking your head. You were either thinking about the dinner or you are allergic to mushrooms. I just took my chances." Sharon smiled.

Jake laughed, nearly choking on his pizza, and dropped a piece of pepperoni on his white shirt.

That even made Sharon laugh. She pointed at the stain on his shirt. "I like it. You look good in red."

Jake plucked the pepperoni from his shirt and smiled. "Thanks." He dabbed at the spot with a napkin. "I knew better than to eat something out of a box in a suit."

"It's only pepperoni. It will come out."

"I hate doing laundry," Jake mumbled. It was the task that he and Kyle had struggled with the most since Sarah became ill.

After the pizza, Sharon looked at the stain again. "Here, I'll help you," she said. "Show me where your laundry room is."

Jake smiled sheepishly. "I don't think you really want to see it."

"Sure, I do. I'll just pre-soak your shirt in a little stain remover." She looked at Jake. "I'm serious. I don't hate laundry like you do. Just go change your shirt and let me help you."

Jake shrugged and headed for his bedroom. "I'll be right back."

He changed into a casual shirt and a pair of jeans. He led Sharon to a small room that housed the washer and dryer. There were at least six piles of clothes, some sorted, some in random distribution. Three large plastic baskets sat in the center, and a laundry hamper overflowed beside a large dryer. To the side, on the floor, another box held a few clothes items, and overhead an economy box of laundry detergent sat conspicuously unopened.

"Good grief!" Sharon sighed. "Don't you ever wash your clothes?"

"Like I said, I hate doing laundry," Jake responded with a shrug.

"How do you get by?" Sharon asked, shaking her head.

"Kyle and I own a lot of underwear," he teased sheepishly. "It keeps us from having to wash clothes as often."

Sharon began picking through the piles, sorting them into whites and colors. "Do you have any spot remover?"

"I think so." Jake disappeared and returned with a spray can.

"Where'd you find that?"

"Under the sink in the bathroom."

"Nice place for it," Sharon said sarcastically. "Here," she offered, handing Jake an armful of whites. "Put these in there," she instructed, pointing at the washer. "There's no time like the present."

Jake obeyed. Sharon looked at him and laughed. "Does your mother know about this room?"

"It's a military secret," Jake said with a smile. "You're the first to be let in on it."

"Ugh," she responded. "What a privilege!" She grabbed an old box from the floor in the corner. She pulled out a pair of jeans with a dark stain on the thigh. "What is this?"

Jake stiffened. "Jeans," he said, taking them in his hand. He promptly folded them and shoved them back in the box.

Sharon eyed him without speaking.

He explained, "I was wearing them the night Sarah died." He shrugged.

Sharon picked them up again. "You moved them, but you didn't even bother to clean them?"

"I moved a lot of dirty laundry with me when I came to Taylorville." He paused. "I know I need to wash them, but the blood is hard to get out. Maybe I should throw them away."

Sharon held the pants at arms length and frowned. "This is blood?"

Jake nodded.

"I don't remember you telling me you were cut. I thought you hit your head."

"I did." He studied the pants for a moment. "I haven't really put much thought into it." He paused again. "I don't remember having a cut." He rubbed his leg where the stain was located.

"Ever wonder if it's not yours?"

"Not mine?"

Sharon put the pants down. She felt funny holding them. "Could it be Sarah's?"

Jake shook his head. "She wasn't bleeding." He hung his head momentarily. "She died from an overdose."

Sharon looked at him for a moment. Uncomfortable, she decided to change the subject. "Where's your shirt? I want to work on that pizza smudge."

He picked up the shirt and handed it to Sharon. At the same time, he pushed his stained jeans off to the side with his foot. He didn't want to think about them either.

Sharon sprayed the stain and threw the shirt in with the load of whites. She poured in some detergent and started the washer. "There. That ought to do it."

Jake nodded and followed her into the living room. He wished every stain was as easy to deal with.

CHAPTER
28

THE following morning, Jake rose early and forced his son from his bunk bed for breakfast. "Come on, Kyle. I have clinic duty this morning. I need to take you to Grandma's."

"It's Saturday! I get to sleep in."

"Not today, Kyle. I've started a Saturday clinic to help get my business going." He pulled some clothes from the drawer and placed them on the bed. "Here. You can wear these," he said, walking to the doorway.

Kyle groaned. His dad had left the light on. He must mean business. He put on the clothes, then grabbed a small black notebook and shoved it into his jeans pocket. *This might come in handy today*, he thought. *I've got a mystery to solve.*

He walked into the kitchen where his dad was pouring milk over two bowls of cereal. "Can I take my bike to Grandma's?"

Jake shot a glance toward the window. "I suppose. But take your hat. It's chilly out."

Kyle sat and ate his cereal in silence, with the only background noise provided by the crunchy breakfast fare.

"Can I read the comics?"

"I didn't bring in the paper yet." Jake checked his watch. "No time this morning. I've got to be at the office in fifteen minutes. Bring your bike around to the Trooper. I'll put it in for you."

Kyle pushed away his bowl. "OK."

Jake gulped down the rest of his lukewarm coffee. "Let's go."

◆ ◆ ◆

Sharon Isaacs felt compelled to deal with the abundant pizza calories she'd consumed the night before. She didn't feel like swimming, and her stationary bike seemed too boring, so she opted for a jog. After putting on her sweats, she mumbled something about the benefits of sunny Southern California and hit the streets for a run.

After five miles she savored her victory over her calories and slowed to a walk in front of her apartment. She picked up the paper that was lying on the landing outside her door. She untied her key from her shoelaces and unlocked her door. The key came out without a catch.

As she fixed a warm cup of tea, she opened the paper. On the front page of the second section she saw a prominent photograph of Jake, the Dansfords, and herself staring back at her. The caption referred to the adjoining article:

> Dr. Jake Hampton, Sharon Isaacs, Dr. Willie Dansford, and Deloris Dansford enjoy the festivities during the Pin Oak Society Awards Banquet. Dr. Hampton received an award in appreciation for furthering the cause of the Society's fight for passage of right to death legislation being considered in the state legislature.

"Oh boy," Sharon muttered out loud. "This is all Jake needs."

I wonder if Jake has seen this yet. She knew Jake had to open the office for Saturday morning walk-ins. *He probably saw this before he went to work.*

She sat at the table and sighed. *I'd better pray.*

◆ ◆ ◆

Jake unloaded Kyle's bike and waved to his mother. "I'll see you at noon," he shouted. "I have to run."

Phyllis nodded at Jake and welcomed Kyle with a hug. "Have you had breakfast yet?"

"Yeah, but I could always eat again. What are you havin'?"

Phyllis's voice faded as Jake jumped into the Isuzu. In another five minutes he pulled into his office parking lot.

From his position behind a lamppost in the next lot, Frank Grimsted scribbled the time on a small notebook. *Excellent, Jake. You're right on time. And you're always the first one. It's nice for you to be alone like this every week.*

Jake entered the building by the back door, the same way he did every week. In a few moments the lights were on. Ten minutes later, just before nine o'clock, his nurse arrived, carrying a cup of steaming coffee.

Frank entered another notation in his book. *Ten minutes, Jake. That's all I need.* He smiled. *It's not so good for you to be so predictable.*

◆ ◆ ◆

Michael Simons also ran a Saturday morning clinic at Crestview Women and Children's Health Center. On Saturdays, because the radiology studies were limited, Simons saw mostly post-ops. He preferred doing pre-op and new patient workups during regular hours.

He picked up a chart and went into exam room A, where Matt, Linda, and Mark Aaron Stone were waiting.

The ever-professional, always-efficient Dr. Simons omitted any greeting. "How's this little one?" He reached out and put his index finger in the baby's palm. Mark responded with a squeeze.

Linda and Matt looked on.

"How's he eating?"

"Like a little horse," Linda responded. "According to your scales, he's put on another ten ounces since discharge."

"That's great." Dr. Simons motioned toward the exam table. "Can you place him over here so I can see his incision?"

"Sure." Linda put the baby down.

Simons pulled up his little shirt and looked at the scar. He gently placed his fingers on both sides of the incision and palpated while the baby took a breath. He then took out his stethoscope and listened. "Everything seems fine." He nodded in the parents' direction.

"Thanks."

Dr. Simons shuffled his feet. "Matt . . ." he said, his voice strained. He halted. "I—I had no idea you recommended me for this job." He shook his head. "Dr. Latner told me about it just last week. He says they put a lot of stock in your recommendation."

Matt nodded. "It looks like it's good I did," he responded, looking at his son.

"Exactly." Simons shuffled his feet again and cleared his throat. He thought about saying more but couldn't bring himself to do it. *The past will never change*, he forced himself to remember. *Stone tried to ruin me. Nothing he does now can change that. Perhaps his baby has escaped, but my bitterness will live on.*

"Well," Simons added, "the baby has a cardiac patch, so if he ever gets any procedures, he needs to take antibiotics first." He checked a box in the chart that said, "Discussed antibiotic prophylaxis."

Matt looked at Linda. "For dental work . . . that kind of thing."

"Exactly. You can pick up a prescription from my office anytime you need it."

"Thanks," Linda responded.

"Well, if you don't have any questions, I guess that's about it." Simons stepped to the door.

"Here," Linda responded, holding up a little note. "It's just our appreciation in writing."

Simons received the note with a curious look on his face. "Thank you."

"Oh, Dr. Simons," Matt said, "I talked to Jake Hampton the other day. He told me to tell you hello."

The cardiothoracic surgeon remembered Jake as a resident. "How is Jake? I heard about his wife," he added soberly.

"He's doing OK. After his wife died, he took a job down in Taylorville with a local doc down there."

Simons wrinkled his forehead. "Dr. Dansford?"

Matt squinted. "I think that's right. Seems like maybe Jake called him Willie."

"That's him." Simons shook his head and kept his thoughts to himself. *Willie Dansford hired Jake Hampton?*

"You know him?"

Simons nodded. "Uh, there aren't too many doctors in Taylorville." He paused and opened the door. He looked back at Matt, who was helping bundle up his son. He felt a second urge to apologize and again successfully rejected it. Michael Simons, M.D. wouldn't humble himself for anyone.

Two weeks later when the Stones received their son's surgeon's bill, the statement had been stamped, "Professional courtesy. No payment due."

◆ ◆ ◆

Months earlier, in the weeks following Sarah's death, Dr. D sat in his office and smiled. It was hard to keep his mind from wandering while his patient, Frank Grimsted, sat on the couch and mumbled about his paranoid delusions. It had been an unbelievable set of coincidences, D thought with a smile, with Jake Hampton showing up and taking care of things just at the right time . . . at least by all appearances and by the media's latest report. Who would believe it? He tried to prevent the smirk from spreading across his face.

And now Frank Grimsted, a true believer in destiny, personalized every news item related to the event. Sarah Hampton was his Sarah. Her baby was his baby. Her death was a murder plot aimed at destroying his personal happiness. Jake Hampton, a suspect in assisting his wife's apparent suicide, was the perpetrator of an evil plan to eliminate Sarah, her baby, and, if Frank understood things correctly, Frank himself.

"Have you been taking your medicines, Frank?" D spoke calmly. "You know you always feel afraid when you haven't been taking your medicines."

"I take them just the way you say. Honest I do."

"OK, Frank. I'm sure you do." Dr. D paused. "Why do you think Dr. Hampton is out to get you?"

"It's just a feeling. He killed my Sarah. I've told you that, right?"

"Yes, Frank." D sighed. "You've not been thinking of harming yourself, have you, Frank?"

Frank shook his head. "No."

"What about doing harm to others?"

Frank sat still and stared at the wall.

"Frank?"

"I just want to protect myself."

"You're not thinking of revenge, are you, Frank?"

Frank remained silent.

Dr. D lowered his voice. "You know you have a tendency to be afraid when you're under stress, Frank." He carefully avoided the p word. Frank hated it when he called him "paranoid."

"I know." Frank fidgeted in his seat. "If he ever comes close to me, I'll know it's more than that." He stared straight ahead. "I'll know he's coming after me."

"Then what, Frank?"

"I'll have to defend myself."

"He lives a long way from you, Frank. Do you ever see him?"

Frank shook his head.

D scribbled a prescription and handed it to Frank. "I'm adjusting your medication. Let's see you again in a month."

Frank stood and went to the door of the exam room.

D went to his office and sat down. There a thought began to form. *Jake Hampton's been an albatross around my neck . . . and now Frank hates him too*. He stroked his chin. *Now, how can I get Jake Hampton close to Frank?*

◆ ◆ ◆

Frank returned from the parking lot beside Jake's office holding a cup of coffee from 7-Eleven in one hand and holding his notebook beneath the flap of his green army jacket with the other. Once he entered the outside doorway of his apartment, he relaxed a little, though he eyed his mailbox suspiciously on his way up the stairs. It had been a few days since he'd checked his mail. He'd have to do it later today.

He picked up his paper, opened his door, and headed for the kitchen to make a sandwich. He didn't have to work this weekend, which meant he'd have to make something at home. He searched his cupboards and finally settled on a box of crackers and some tomato soup. Once his soup was hot, he sat down with the paper to read the day's headlines. He scanned the front page, then turned to find the comics.

When he saw the front page of the second section, his eyes widened. He focused on the picture of Jake Hampton, then scanned the article, nodding his head as he read.

"Jake, now you're flaunting this evil deed of yours to the world." He shook his head, showing his disapproval. Then, for a moment, he froze, looking at the picture again.

He thought back to the bombing, to how he felt then, like he had fulfilled a high calling for revenge. *Yes,* he thought, *I will have to stand up for justice again. Jake, you shouldn't have let everybody know.*

He gathered his coat around him. He would need to go back to the jailhouse tonight for some supplies. It looked like Jake might be running out of time.

◆ ◆ ◆

Kyle spent most of the morning watching cartoons and playing with his Gameboy. Finally, when his grandmother suggested that he go read, he retreated to his father's old bedroom and sat at the small wooden desk. His mind had been busy anyway. He hadn't really been thinking about the TV shows. He was trying to come to grips with his own thoughts about the fires and the mysterious candy wrappers.

For one thing, he was tired of being accused of doing things he hadn't been involved in. If the police didn't believe him, and if they were successful in convincing Sharon and his father, who could he turn to?

He pulled out the little black appointment scheduler his father had given to him. On the cover was the name of a drug he couldn't pronounce. He didn't want to schedule anything. He just wanted a secret place where he could record clues. If the police couldn't figure out the mystery, maybe he would have to look into it himself.

He opened to an unused page and wrote, "CLUES" at the top. Beneath that he wrote, "1. Zero wrappers in jail, our mailbox, Sharon's mailbox, and in the cars." He thought for a while and then wrote, "2. Jail fire. 3. Treehouse fire."

He turned the page and tried to think of everyone who could have put the candy wrappers in the jail, mailboxes, and cars. He wrote down Lenny's name, Todd's name, and a question mark. He knew the other guys had been to the jail before. Could they have put the candy wrappers there?

The thought of the candy wrappers distracted him momentarily. He dreamed about candy, eating, going to the 7-Eleven, his bike, riding in the cold, dressing warmly, going sledding in the winter . . . He shook his head and quietly chided himself. "Pay attention. Keep your mind on your task."

He turned back to the first page, remembering an additional clue. He wrote, "4. Mom's picture." He shook his head. Lenny and Todd wouldn't have known his mother or have a photo of her.

He looked at his list of suspects. The only person around who would have pictures of his mom were his father and grandmother. He decided not to write their names down. It didn't seem right to put them on a list of suspects.

He circled the question mark on his page. "It must be someone else," he muttered to himself. "Someone who likes to eat Zero bars."

He turned the page and put "SUSPECK" at the top of the page. Beneath this, he wrote the characteristics he could think of: "1. Eats Zero bars. 2. Lives at the jail? 3. Knows Dad and Sharon. 4. Knows Mom?"

On the next page, he wrote "PLAN." He stopped when he heard his dad's Trooper. Quickly he scribbled, "1. Talk to suspecks. 2. Find out who buys Zero bars."

He shoved the black book into his jeans pocket and hurried down the stairs to meet his dad.

◆ ◆ ◆

When Jake walked in the door, he was greeted by his mother, who had a serious expression on her face.

"Hi, Mom. What's up?"

"Sharon just called."

Jake flinched. "Did she tell you about the laundry room? Don't worry about it, Mom. I'm going right home to do another load—"

"She didn't call about your laundry, Jake." Phyllis rolled her eyes. "Have you seen the paper this morning?"

"No," he responded, his curiosity rising. "Why?"

His mother sighed. "Look at this," she said, plopping the paper open on the kitchen table.

Kyle burst into the room. "Hi, Dad."

Jake looked up soberly. "Hi, Kyle." He rubbed his red bangs absent-mindedly while scanning the article. "Oh boy." He sighed. "They act like I've come out of the closet about this physician-assisted suicide theory surrounding Sarah's death." He shook his head. "This is all I need."

"It's just a small-town paper, Jake. Nobody really reads it."

"Only my patients. Only the people of Taylorville. Only the people who I hoped would never find out about this junk," he huffed. "I wanted to leave all of this controversy back in Grantsville."

Kyle looked at the picture. "Hey, neat, Dad. You made the paper!" He pointed his finger. "And here's Dr. Willie and Sharon." He looked at her a moment longer. "She looks a lot different than when she's at school." He sighed. "Wow."

Jake looked back at the photograph. It was a nice picture of Sharon.

"Maybe you can write a letter to the editor. Tell the folks how you really feel about physician-assisted suicide."

"Mom, it would look like I'm afraid of being accused again."

"Aren't you?"

Jake looked down. "Maybe," he sulked. "Maybe I just want to know the truth myself before everyone else tells me what to believe."

His tone of voice told Phyllis to change the subject.

"Want some lunch?"

Jake shook his head. "I'm not too hungry anymore."

"Come on, Dad. Can we eat here? All we have at home is baloney," Kyle whined.

He looked at his mother and back at his son. "You can have something, son."

"How about a grilled cheese?" Phyllis offered.

"Oh boy." Kyle sat down at the table and looked at the picture again. "Do you think Sharon's pretty?"

Jake looked up. "Do you?"

"I asked you first."

"Yes. I think she's pretty."

"Me, too."

Phyllis started cutting long slices of cheddar cheese. "Sure you don't want a sandwich, Jake?"

Jake looked back at Sharon's picture and smiled. "Oh, OK, I'll eat. No use in letting a stupid newspaper's misinformation ruin my appetite," he said, trying to convince himself it was so.

Phyllis laid a buttered cheese sandwich in a large black skillet. "By the way, I think she's pretty too, if anyone's askin'."

CHAPTER
29

ON Monday morning Willie stuck his head in the office, where Jake was sorting through charts. When Jake saw the old physician, he sighed. "Ever think that there would be this much paperwork in medicine?"

"Enough to swim in, my boy . . . and getting worse every year." Willie chuckled. "Mind if I come in?"

Jake shook his head. "Be my guest."

"Look, Jake, I won't take much of your time." He hung his head. "I've been presumptive. I should have been upfront with you about the Pin Oak Society dinner. I thought you'd be honored." He paused. "Maybe I've just misjudged the whole situation. I know you haven't really told me much about it." He looked back at Jake. "I guess I just took what I read in the paper at face value. It never bothered me, Jake. I thought you could fit in real well here, regardless of what happened in your past. Enough of us here think physician-assisted suicide is appropriate mercy, I just thought—"

"Willie," Jake interrupted, "I know you meant well, but I'm not ready for that philosophy. I doubt I'll ever be."

"But what about your wife?"

"I'm not sure I helped her die, Willie." He shook his head. "I know I looked guilty. I was there. I certainly feel guilty about it, but—"

"But what, Jake? Why can't you just admit it? My idea in bringing you out to the dinner was to help you see that it's not something to feel guilty about."

Jake shook his head again. "I'm not ready to admit anything, Willie."

"How do you think she died then?" Willie probed.

"The autopsy showed a narcotic overdose. I think she was intention-ally overdosed by her caregivers at Ocean Sands. I think they couldn't accept that their therapy was a failure, that their prize patient was going to die in their hands, so they made it look like something else. That way if I claimed the therapy didn't work, they would say she didn't even die of breast cancer."

"You've thought about this a lot, haven't you?"

"Every day since she died," Jake muttered. "If I didn't kill her, some-one else did, I'm convinced of that." Jake pounded his fist in his hand. "If I could only remember a little more about the night she died."

"You need to let it go, Jake. Forget it ever happened." Willie fidgeted nervously.

"I can't." He paused and looked at Willie. "I won't. I'll find out what happened to her, I promise you that."

Willie backed away. "The past is history, Jake. Forget it."

Jake shook his head.

"Don't hurt yourself, Jake," Willie added, looking at him for a moment before turning away. "Anyway, I came in here to apologize. I'm sorry about Friday night."

"Forget about the dinner. I'll be OK."

Willie shook Jake's extended hand. "Thanks."

◆ ◆ ◆

Frank worked the morning shift at McDonald's. He made thirty Egg McMuffins and fourteen pancake plates. He had orders for only thirteen, but that would never do for Frank. His paranoia and superstitious charac-teristics ran hand in hand; so when he had orders for thirteen of some-thing, he always made, and usually ate, a fourteenth.

He was glad to be off by noon so he could check his mail. No one else would be around to see him that way. Yesterday every time he decided it would be safe, he heard noises in Sharon's apartment.

He stepped into the foyer and glanced up the stairs. Listening atten-tively and hearing nothing, he groped behind the stairwell until he found the broom handle with his mail key. Now that he was sure Jake had located him, he couldn't be too careful. He stood with the broom handle held at arm's length and inserted the key after several tries. He shielded his face by looking away and covering it with his free hand.

Sharon Isaacs opened the outside door just as Frank covered his face. She wasn't sure if he was hurt or perhaps trying to pry open someone else's mailbox.

"Mr. Grimsted?"

Frank lurched. "Stay back!" he screamed as he turned the key. Nothing happened. No explosion. His mailbox had not been wired. He looked up sheepishly and saw Sharon. "Oh, hi," he muttered. *I can't believe it's her!*

"Are you OK?"

Frank looked down. "S-sure. This mailbox is always so hard to get open," he complained. "Even more temperamental than my lock upstairs."

Sharon wanted to check her own mail, but after seeing Frank she decided against it. She continued up the stairs to her apartment to retrieve the student file she'd left behind. She eyed Frank with suspicion and pity for a moment, then retreated into her apartment. She closed the door and turned the dead bolt. She whispered a phrase to herself that she had picked up from her students: "Weird with a beard." She pressed her eye against the peephole to watch a moment longer.

Meanwhile, Frank grabbed his mail—two bills and a survival outfitters catalog—and hid his broomstick back under the stairs. He climbed the stairs to his apartment, staring at Sharon's door, with his face taking on an expression of surprise, anger, and fear. He paused on the landing in front of her door and put his ear to her door.

Inside, Sharon got a close-up view of Frank's left ear. She recoiled from the peephole.

Hearing nothing, Frank opened his own door and slipped inside.

Sharon looked through the peephole again. Frank's ear was gone. "Weird with a beard," she whispered again. She shook her head. *What was he doing down there? And why is he listening at my door?*

Inside his apartment, Frank slumped onto a grease-spotted couch and cursed his misfortune. Or was it? Sharon hadn't seemed reluctant to walk close to the mailbox. She must have known it wasn't wired to explode. *And since she saw me, she'll know I'm on to their schemes. Certainly Jake won't try a mail-bomb if they know I'm watching.*

◆ ◆ ◆

At the final school bell, Kyle ran to his bicycle. He had just enough time to detour to the local grocery store before going to the sitter's. He put on his backpack and unlocked his ten-speed. In a flash he was peddling toward the Taylorville Foodmart. If anyone would know who ate what in this town, Mr. Dithers would certainly be the best person to ask. Kyle turned down Main Street and ducked in behind his father's office. He didn't want to pass by the front, in case his dad happened to be looking out the window.

Behind the office, through the next parking lot, and right on Grayson Street he flew. In a few minutes he was locking his bike in the rack beside the Foodmart. His cheeks were cold. Fortunately it hadn't snowed in Taylorville yet, or he wouldn't have been able to conduct his investigation. Once inside, he looked for Mr. Dithers. Everyone knew him by the large red apron he wore with the embroidered name "Clayton Dithers" in bold white letters, just under "Taylorville Foodmart."

Mr. Dithers prided himself on being able to answer any question about food that anyone could possibly ask. He knew what cut of meat to buy, how to cook it, and what side dish to serve it with. He also knew who bought what and who drank what in the small town of Taylorville.

Kyle found the store proprietor stocking shelves on aisle 3, Cereal Row. Kyle approached timidly. "Mr. Dithers?"

The white-haired man stood five feet, five inches tall, not quite tall enough for the two hundred pounds he carried. Mr. Dithers smiled. "What can I do for you, son?"

"I'm doing an investigation." He tried to look serious and mature. He held up his pen, ready to write his response in his little black notebook. "Would you know who buys a lot of Zero bars in this town?"

"Zero bars?"

"Yes, sir."

"What kind of question is that for a little boy?"

Kyle fidgeted with his pen. "Someone has been littering." Kyle squinted his eyes. "Leaving Zero bar wrappers in odd places." He paused. "I'm trying to figure out who eats 'em."

Mr. Dithers scratched his thinning white hair. "I can't say how I would know that, son."

"I figured if anyone would know something like this, you'd be the one," Kyle said slowly. He frowned. "Thanks anyway." Kyle hung his head.

Mr. Dithers studied the lad for a moment. "Tell you what, son. I'll keep my eyes open for you. You stop back by later and I'll tell you what I've come up with."

Kyle lifted his head. "Really?"

"I'll see what I can do. All I can do is watch."

"Good deal," Kyle responded as he scampered to his bike. He glanced at his watch. If he hurried, the Simpsons wouldn't even notice he was running late.

◆ ◆ ◆

Jake took off his pants and grabbed a pair of green scrubs from the rack in the doctor's lounge. His last patient had been an add-on, a fifteen-year-old boy with a bottle cap stuck in his esophagus. He had been showing off to his friends, demonstrating how he could take the bottle cap off with his teeth, when the mishap occurred. The boy came in quite agitated and unable to swallow. A quick X-ray over in the office showed the bottle cap lodged in the cervical esophagus. Jake scheduled him for emergency rigid esophagoscopy and extraction of the foreign body.

Now he sat on the wooden bench in front of his locker and rubbed his bare thigh. His mind went back to his conversation with Sharon over the bloodstain on his jeans. He inspected his leg. *Hmmm*, he reasoned, *there's no sign of a scar here or anything. Seems to have healed up without much sign of injury.*

The intercom interrupted his thoughts. "Dr. Hampton, you're wanted in O.R. 4. Dr. Hampton, O.R. 4."

Jake pulled on his scrub bottoms and tucked in the green scrub top. Time for work! He donned a pair of paper shoe-covers, a paper hat, and a mask with a clear eye shield and exited the lounge into the restricted operating room arena.

◆ ◆ ◆

Frank used his own grocery cart for shopping. He kept it chained to the bike rack behind his apartment. He'd gotten it for free when the Taylorville

Foodmart got new ones two years before. Mr. Dithers had given them away to any of his customers who walked and didn't drive to his store.

He collected what he needed, mostly canned items that wouldn't spoil fast, and things that required limited preparations just in case he could safely go back to the jail again. He'd only been there twice since the fire— once to check the damage and once to get explosives . . . just in case Jake decided to strike.

He loaded up on pork and beans and tuna and the small canned Vienna sausages. There were six sausages in the small cans and seventeen in the large. Frank had counted them himself, and he repeated the ritual every time he opened a new container. He threw in a frozen pizza and some orange juice, the kind in a cardboard carton, so he wouldn't have to mix it. He never bought the fresh vegetables. Since they weren't sealed in a package, they were potential tools by which his enemies could poison him. And he would certainly never buy the fresh baked goods. One of the bakers had gone to high school with him; besides, he couldn't trust something without a wrapper.

Frank glanced into the bakery. His old high-school classmate wasn't there. Even if he was, Frank didn't think his classmate had ever recognized him. In fact, it was Frank's invisibility that made life in Taylorville so appealing. At first he thought people would remember the bombing and not like him coming back to town. They might try to kill him, he thought. But the longer he stayed, the more he realized that people didn't know about the bombing or just didn't care, since it happened so long ago and in another town.

Frank studied the milk and found one that was close to expiration date. No one would expect him to pick that one. Certainly it wouldn't be laced.

His final selection was a large bag of Zero bars. He placed them prominently on top of his frozen pizza and headed for the checkout counter.

Mr. Dithers observed quietly from the end of the aisle. He smiled and made a mental note. *Hmmm,* he thought. *Maybe I've found the litter bug.*

◆ ◆ ◆

Kyle closed his little black book and shoved it into his jeans pocket. He yelled for his father. "Dad, can I go over to Todd's?"

"Did you study your spelling words?" Jake called up the stairwell to his son.

"Yeah. I'm all done."

"How do you spell Mississippi?"

"It's not one of my spelling words."

"Come on. Humor me."

"M-I-S-S-I-S-S-I-P-P-I." Kyle jumped down one step as he yelled each letter.

Jake rolled his eyes. "OK." He smiled. "Have fun."

Kyle grabbed his coat and bounded out the back door. He cut across the Giffords' backyard, moving past a large stack of firewood. He knocked on the back door.

Mrs. Gifford answered. "Hi, Kyle."

"Is Todd in?"

"Come on in. He's in the basement playing with Lenny."

"Thanks, Mrs. Gifford." Kyle walked down the steps whispering to himself, "M-I-S-S-I-S-S-I-P-P-I," one letter for each step.

"Hi, Kyle."

"Hi, guys."

The two older boys were playing a video baseball game. Kyle sat down to watch. He wanted to ask them about the jailhouse and the Zero wrappers but still wasn't sure they didn't have anything to do with it. He sat and watched the game until Lenny lost in overtime.

"Did they figure out who started the fire in your tree yet?" Kyle asked.

"No," Todd responded.

Kyle looked down. "The police seem to think I did it, but I didn't do it! I promise."

"Why do they think you did it?" Lenny asked.

"Because of the fire in the old Taylorville jailhouse. Ever since I got caught in there, they seem to think I had camped in there and that the fire was my fault . . . like I was using a kerosene heater to keep warm or something. Then when they said your tree was started on fire with kerosene, they just blamed me for everything."

"Wow. Were you arrested?"

"No. Nothing like that. But I figure if I'm gonna clear my name, I'm going to have to figure it out myself. They don't seem to see any reason to look beyond me."

"Bummer." Todd pitched a baseball in the air and caught it with his hand.

"What do you think happened? Have you guys ever been in the jail?"

Lenny glanced at Todd and stayed quiet. "Why?" Todd asked.

"I bet whoever set your tree on fire was the same person who set the jail on fire."

Todd leaned forward. "How so?"

"Just think about it—two fires on the same day, both started with kerosene. Maybe whoever was in the old jailhouse started the fire."

"Why would they do that?"

"If the police thought some kids started the jailhouse fire, maybe whoever lives there thinks so too. Maybe the fire in the tree was some kind of revenge."

"I don't know."

"I've been thinking about this a lot. I just need some proof."

"How do you know someone has been staying in the jail?" Lenny asked.

"There was a mattress and some old food containers there," Kyle responded.

"Plus someone used the bathroom in there. It smells terrible," Todd added.

"So you have been in there?" Kyle looked at him and narrowed his eyes.

"Once."

Kyle waited. Lenny didn't say anything. He didn't want to make Todd mad.

Finally Todd spoke up. "I went in there, but something happened. I hit my head or something. The last thing I remember I was walking down that dark, stinky hall. Then I woke up outside the jail near the railroad tracks with a splitting headache and a bump on the back of my head."

"Somebody hit you!" Kyle shouted.

Todd looked at him sharply. "Keep your voice down. My parents wouldn't want to know I went in there."

Lenny nodded his head. "I think some criminal gang must be hiding out there. It's a perfect hideout."

"Right. I think you watch too much TV," Todd responded.

"Then who else?" Kyle added with his voice barely audible. "And get this—my dad and Ms. Isaacs have been finding Zero bar wrappers in their cars and in their mailboxes."

Lenny looked at him curiously. "What does that have to do with this?"

"I'm not sure, but when I went into the jailhouse, I found a Zero bar wrapper." He shrugged. "I just thought it might mean something. Maybe whoever lives in the jailhouse eats Zero bars and likes to start fires."

"I don't see a connection."

"We need to go to the jailhouse and check it out," Kyle said.

"I'm not going near that place," Lenny asserted strongly.

Todd rubbed his head. "I don't like the idea," he said, rubbing the back of his head. "What if someone does live in there?" He paused for a moment. "But then again, I would like to get back at whoever burned down my treehouse."

"You should go," Kyle encouraged. "You're the oldest."

"Why don't you go? It's your idea. It's your name we're trying to clear here."

Kyle sighed. "My dad won't let me. He told me specifically not to go there. If the police catch me there, they'll be sure I was the one who was hanging out there."

Todd looked at him sternly. "Sometimes you gotta do what you gotta do, pal. It may be the only way to clear your reputation."

Kyle sighed again. He was afraid his friend was right.

◆ ◆ ◆

Dr. D poured himself a shot of straight Kentucky bourbon. He sipped at the golden liquid and sighed. *Apparently Jake can't let dead dogs rest,* he surmised. *It's a shame really. He just has to keep searchin'.*

D rubbed his hand through his white hair and sighed. It wasn't that he didn't like Jake. But controlling him hadn't turned into an easy task. He looked over at the news clipping his wife had given him. *Jake looks so unsuspecting in this newspaper photograph. So young . . . and so naive. Too bad it has to end this way.*

D picked up the phone and dialed the Taylorville pharmacy. After two rings, Bill Henson, Taylorville's pharmacist, picked up.

"Taylorville pharmacy. Bill speaking."

"Hi, Bill. Dr. D here. It's time for Frank Grimsted to come in for his medications again."

"Routine renewal, sir?"

"Not this time, Bill. I'm taking him off."

"Off? Ol' Frank has been on that stuff for a long time. He—"

"Just tell him he wasn't approved for any more refills," D interrupted. "I want him to come see me. I want to try something new out on Frank. It's time for reevaluation."

Bill shook his head. "OK. Whatever you say. No refills. I'll tell him to contact your office."

"You do that. Thanks."

"Good night, sir."

"Good night, Bill."

D put the phone in its cradle. *That should end my worries.* D smiled. *And I never had to dirty my hands at all. Who would have ever believed it? No one can ever suspect me. Not after all the good I did for Sarah . . . and after all I've done for Jake.*

D smiled and sipped at his bourbon. *With all the talking Frank does about destiny, he's almost convinced me of it.*

CHAPTER
30

KYLE got up early the next morning and was dressed and setting the table for breakfast by the time Jake called.

"Down here, Dad," Kyle yelled back. "What do you want for breakfast?"

Jake walked in. "What's the occasion?"

"I wanted a little extra time this morning so I could ride my bike to school again."

"It's pretty cold out there, Kyle."

"It's OK, Dad. I wear my ski mask."

Jake shrugged. "As long as you're on time." He turned on the coffeemaker. "Mr. Dillenbeck didn't throw you off the bus or anything, did he?"

Kyle threw up his hands. "Why does everyone think I do bad things?" He let loose with an angry snort and slammed his cereal box on the table. "The police think I start fires, Ms. Isaacs thinks I put candy wrappers in her mailbox, and now you ask if I've been thrown off the bus!"

Kyle sat down and poured his cereal and milk in a sulk. Jake stayed quiet. He hadn't seen Kyle this upset about things for a long while.

"Look, son, I'm sorry. I shouldn't have suspected anything. I guess I was just thinking what it would take to get me on a bicycle in 30-degree weather."

Kyle nodded his response and chewed his Captain Crunch cereal. Soon he was drifting off in a cartoon world with pirates and stormy seas. Captain Crunch would save the day . . .

Jake poured himself a bowl of cereal. "Did the kids at school say anything about my picture in the paper?"

Kyle's imaginary distraction disappeared. "Huh?"

Jake smiled. "Did your friends say anything about my picture in the paper? The picture implies that I agree with this organization, the Pin Oak Society. It's not true. I don't agree with them at all."

"Kind of like me, huh?"

Jake hadn't seen the connection before. "What do you mean?"

"It doesn't feel good to have someone saying something about you that isn't true."

"Oooh," Jake responded with a nod. He crunched his cereal. "I guess you're right."

They ate in silence for a moment. Jake got up to get coffee. "Want some coffee?"

"Sure." Kyle fixed a cup half full of milk and added two tablespoons of sugar, then put in a small amount of coffee. "Dad?"

His father looked up.

"What are you going to do to make people believe the right thing about you?"

Jake shook his head. "I don't know. I thought about writing a letter to the editor, but I'm not sure. Probably I'll just let it blow over. People will see after I've been here awhile what I'm all about." He shrugged. "Maybe I'll just keep doing what I've been doing. Eventually it will blow over."

Kyle rolled his eyes behind his father's back. In Kyle's eyes, that didn't seem too likely. The boy sat and drank his "coffee." Jake set his medicine in front of him. Kyle opened the bottle and swallowed one pill. "Some of the kids did see the picture."

"Oh?"

"They teased me about you and Ms. Isaacs."

"Did that bother you?"

Kyle tilted his head. "Not really." He took his bowl to the sink. "She's pretty cool."

Jake smiled. "Maybe *I* should try wearing sweats to work."

Kyle looked at his father and shook his head. "I don't think so."

"I mean, if it works for Sharon . . ."

"Dad!"

Jake laughed and looked at his watch. "Watch the time. If you're rid-ing this morning, better hit the trail by quarter till."

"OK."

Kyle disappeared to brush his teeth and prepare his backpack. After he loaded his books, he pulled his little black book out of its hiding place under his mattress and shoved it into his pants pocket. In it he had care-fully recorded the findings of his conversation with Lenny and Todd and had crossed off their names from his suspect list. It just didn't seem like they knew enough about the fires and the wrappers to be guilty. Besides, Lenny was too afraid to go near the jail, and it seemed unlikely that Todd would torch his own treehouse.

Before he left his room, he looked at a checklist beside the door. "Make bed," he muttered. "Did that. Put homework in backpack. Did that. Get lunch money. Did that. Take medicine. Did that." He smiled and headed for the stairs.

Kyle bounded down the stairs with his backpack, shouting, "Been there! Done that!"

Jake just looked at the blur of his son and shook his head.

Kyle donned his coat, gloves, and a ski mask. From the outside, it was impossible to tell who he was. Kyle preferred it that way. *Undercover work is best done in secret*, he figured as he opened the door to leave. "Bye, Dad."

"Bye, Kyle. See you after school."

The door slammed, and the masked detective slipped away.

◆　◆　◆

Later that morning Jake saw a work-in, a Mrs. Boris Underwood, who had called the office just that morning, demanding a visit.

She listed her chief complaint as "Cancer." Nothing more. No specifics. Just "Cancer."

Jake's nurse came out of the room first and rolled her eyes. "She won't give me any information. She's acting very strange."

"What's she here for?"

The nurse looked at the form. "Cancer." She shrugged. "She just insists on talking to you. I didn't get anywhere with her."

Jake held up his hands. "I'll see what I can do."

The surgeon went into the exam room and held out his hand. "Hello, Ms. Underwood. I'm Dr. Hampton. What can I do for you today?"

"Oh, doctor, I hope you'll help me."

Jake sat down on a stool beside the exam table. "What is it that is bothering you?"

"I'm dying of cancer." The elderly woman fidgeted with her blouse.

"Hmmm. What type of cancer do you have?"

"It's in my bowels. It's in my lungs. I think it's in my back too." She hung her head, her eyes moist.

"I'm sorry." Jake looked at the form. The space beside "Referring Physician" was blank. "Who is your family doctor? Who referred you to see a surgeon?"

"I don't have a doctor," she responded quickly. "That's why I've come to see you. Won't you help me?"

"I'll be glad to try and help you," he reassured her. She seemed quite upset. "However, I'll need some other information first." He opened her chart so he could make some notes. "How was the diagnosis of cancer first made?"

"I have had such bad gas," she said, gripping her ample abdomen. "And I stay so bloated." She rubbed the fat over her waist. "I'm not normally this big."

"Have you had any tests that showed the cancer?" Jake asked, squinting his eyes.

"I stay so constipated," she reported, choosing to ignore Jake's question. "I can't move my bowels unless I take something." She sat perched on the edge of the exam table looking perfectly normal. "I'm afraid the end is close."

"Have you had any X-rays or blood tests?"

"I've had to resort to doubling my fiber intake, mixed with prune juice and mineral oil," she reported like a martyr. "I'm sufferin' terrible," she choked.

"Who made the diagnosis of cancer?"

"My sister just died of cancer last week," she added, dabbing her cheeks with a stained handkerchief.

Jake started to get the picture. "Are you on any medications?"

She held a plastic grocery bag out at arm's length. "Here."

He sorted through a hefty assortment of cold preparations, laxatives, and over-the-counter pain relievers. When he had them all out on the table, he counted them.

"You take all of these?"

"Most every day. I'm dying, you understand," she added with a sniff.

Jake pushed back from the table, rolling his stool against the wall so he could lean back. "Just what is it you expect from me?"

"Relief from my suffering," she reported with a sob and a wink.

"I'm not sure I understand. At first glance, you don't appear to be dying."

"Oh!" she shrieked, grabbing her abdomen with both hands. "The pain just seizes me!"

Jake pondered his new patient for a moment. "It seems to me we should start with an exam and some tests, to see if you indeed have cancer."

"Oh, doctor, that's unnecessary," she responded. "And too expensive." She twisted her pocketbook handle into a knot. "I saw your picture in the paper. I've been reading about the Pin Oak Society. I thought maybe you could help me end my suffering with dignity."

"Ma'am, we don't even have a firm diagnos—"

"Don't worry about me spreading any of this around. I know what the law is. I respect the confidentiality of the doctor/patient relationship," she interrupted, her head now held high. "You just write the prescriptions, and when my suffering gets unbearable, I'll have them filled."

"Ms. Underwood, I'm not even sure what's wrong with you yet. And even if I knew, maybe your symptoms aren't life-threatening—"

"I was with my sister night and day for six months. I know what suffering is all about. I'm not going to go through what she did!"

"Even if you had a life-threatening disease, there are better ways of relieving your suffering than just ending it all."

Ms. Underwood had heard enough. She slipped from the table, gripping her abdomen. "The newspaper has it all wrong about you!"

"As a matter of fact, they do," Jake added. "I would be glad to help you sort out your physical ailments."

"I've gotten all the information I need," the patient added with a huff. "Maybe Dr. Willie will help me." She opened the exit door with a moan. "Somebody's gotta do something for a dying woman," she snorted, loud enough to be heard in the waiting room.

Jake flinched. With that, the patient was gone. He didn't even have a chance to say good-bye.

"Good grief," he whispered. "Taylorville," he added, shaking his head. *Maybe Kyle is right. Maybe I should do something about these misconceptions.*

◆ ◆ ◆

After school Kyle repeated his quick bicycle run to talk to Mr. Dithers at the Taylorville Foodmart. He didn't want to appear too anxious, so he made it appear that he was just stopping in to buy something. He looked around for something he could afford, keeping one eye out for Mr. Dithers. After counting his change and looking at the candy aisle, he shook his head and selected a beef jerky in the meat department. That's when he saw Mr. Dithers.

"Hi, son."

"Oh, hi, Mr. Dithers." Kyle hesitated. "Any luck on the Zero bar wrapper case?"

"As a matter of fact . . ." the grocer responded slowly while Kyle held his breath. "I have had some luck."

"Who is it?" Kyle had raised his voice in excitement.

Mr. Dithers lowered his voice. "Now mind you, I'm not saying this person discarded his Zero bar wrappers inappropriately. All I'm saying is that this person bought a large bag of Zero bars." He put his large palm on Kyle's shoulder. "This doesn't mean you've found your man."

"OK."

"Have you ever seen a fella loping around town in a green army jacket? Kind of a loner, I think. Some folks make fun of him."

Kyle thought hard. "I think so."

Mr. Dithers lowered his voice again. "He comes in here all the time. I think he works over at the McDonald's. His name is on his jacket pocket. Grimsted or Grimsteed—something like that," he added.

Kyle opened his little black book and wrote down the name. He pointed at the name. "Like this?"

"I think so. Might have two e's though."

"Thanks, Mr. Dithers," Kyle responded, stuffing the notebook back in his pocket. Kyle turned and ran for the exit.

Mr. Dithers called out from behind him, "Don't you want to pay for the beef jerky?"

Kyle cringed. He'd almost run out without paying!

He sheepishly returned to the checkout counter. "Oops," he said. "Almost forgot." *The police would have really been after me then*, he worried. He looked back at Mr. Dithers, who smiled. "Thanks."

◆ ◆ ◆

At 7:30 P.M. Mrs. O'Donnell exited the rear door of Jake's office with a load of cleaning supplies in her hand. As was her observed practice, she put the articles in her trunk and started the car to warm the engine. Then she went back inside to finish up and turn out the lights.

A dark figure slipped from behind the dumpster and got into the driver's seat of the old Buick. He searched through the key ring where it hung in the ignition. This was taking longer than he wanted, but he finally found what he was looking for: the office key.

The last light went off in the office. There was no time to remove the key. Frank would have to take the car and take his chances! Hastily he jammed the car in reverse as the back door to the office swung open. He pressed the accelerator. The old car lurched backwards, barely missing the metal dumpster. Mrs. O'Donnell screamed. "Hey!" She began running toward the car. "Come back here!"

Frank slammed the car into drive and swerved to miss the madly waving woman. Mrs. O'Donnell began pounding the passenger window as Frank picked up speed. "Come back here, you thief!"

Frank floored the accelerator, rocketing the car into the street. He turned right on Main Street, veering wildly over the yellow line. Then he smashed the brakes and turned left on Grayson. Mrs. O'Donnell stood helplessly in the middle of the parking lot. The office was locked. In a state the store owner described as pure panic, she ran to the 7-Eleven store down the street.

Meanwhile, Frank slowed the car so as not to attract attention. He didn't want her vehicle, just her office key. He knew Mrs. O'Donnell. She had lived in Taylorville all her life. He turned right on Simms and left again on Brighton Drive. There he finally found out where to turn on the headlamps. He pulled into Mrs. O'Donnell's driveway. She lived alone. He should be safe here for a little while. Hastily, he pulled her keys from the ignition, then sorted through the keys until he found the one he wanted. There!

He jumped from the car, then leaned back in and put the keys back in the ignition. He was wearing gloves. He wasn't worried about leaving fingerprints. *She probably won't even miss this,* he told himself as he pocketed the key. *Besides, she won't need it until she's ready to clean next week, and by then there won't even be an—*

His thought was interrupted by a siren wailing in the distance. Frank slammed the car door and ran through the backyard, knocking over a cement birdbath in his haste. A neighborhood dog barked. Frank never looked back. After a block, he backed into the shadows of a large tree and ripped off his ski mask and sweatshirt. Beneath it, he wore a striped sweater, which he also stripped off. Then he carefully replaced the items in reverse order, so that the sweater would be showing. He kept the ski mask off and put on a Taylorville Knights baseball cap. He quietly moved along the street in the shadows, cutting diagonally across the backs of the frozen Taylorville yards until he was back on Main Street again. In another five minutes, his breathing had returned to normal and he was resting in his apartment.

Back at Jake Hampton's office, Mrs. O'Donnell was met by the police. She had run into the 7-Eleven screaming that her car had been stolen. The clerk made the 9-1-1 call. Mrs. O'Donnell exited as quickly as she came, yelling that she would meet the police back at the office.

Steve Branson and Don Rawlings handled the call and attempted to console the irate woman.

"He stole my car!" she yelled.

"We understand that, Mrs. O'Donnell. Did you get a look at him?"

"I pounded on the window! He looked right at me." She burst into a tearful wail.

"Can you give us a description?"

"No," Mrs. O'Donnell sobbed. "He was wearing a m-m-mask!"

"A mask?"

"Yes. A knitted mask, like you would wear outside in the winter."

"Did you see what else he was wearing?"

"No. It was dark in my car."

After a few more minutes looking around the parking lot and further questioning Mrs. O'Donnell, the officers drove her home.

"My car!" she screamed. "That's my car!" she yelled, pointing at the Buick in the driveway.

"The car that was stolen?" Officer Rawlings shook his head.

"Somebody brought it home!"

The officers stepped from the car, leaving Mrs. O'Donnell safe in the backseat.

"Hey! There's no handle in here!" She pounded the window. "Let me out!"

Don Rawlings signaled for Steve to go to the other side. They approached the car cautiously. It appeared empty. A quick inspection confirmed that no one was still inside. Don reached in and retrieved the keys. "Nice of him to bring it home."

Steve rolled his eyes. "If it was ever gone."

"Don't you believe her?"

"I don't know. She seems to have lost a screw somewhere," he said in exasperation. "Just listen to her."

Don turned his ear to the patrol car where Mrs. O'Donnell continued pounding on the door. Don shrugged.

Steve looked at him sharply. "Stranger things have happened."

"Could be some kids just playin' a prank, I suppose."

They walked to the patrol car and opened the rear door.

"Here are your keys, Mrs. O'Donnell. The thief left them in the ignition."

"Oh my. I was starting to feel a bit claustrophobic in there." She ran to the car and looked around. She accepted her keys and clutched them closely, as if someone might grab them again at any moment. She opened the trunk. "Everything's here."

The officers shrugged. Mrs. O'Donnell hugged them. "Thank you for the ride."

After seeing her to her door, the officers excused themselves. "If you think of anything else, just give the station a call in the morning."

◆ ◆ ◆

Kyle pulled his little black book out from under the mattress. He would need to start a new page to record his findings. This time he wrote, "Grimsteed." Underneath, he wrote the information that he'd obtained from Mr. Dithers. "1. Works at McDonald's. 2. Wears a green coat." He thought for a while longer and then put down his pen. He slipped downstairs and saw his father apparently napping in his easy chair. He tiptoed behind him into the kitchen to get the phone book. He thumbed through the pages until he got to the G's, then ran his finger down the page.

"There," he whispered. "F. Grimsted." Only one e. "Hmmm. Apt. D, Abington Apartments." Kyle scratched his head. *That's where Ms. Isaacs lives, I think . . . right across from McDonald's.* He opened his book and copied the address and phone number. Then he quietly closed the book and tiptoed upstairs.

There he started a new page. Time for a brainstorm. What should he do now? It wasn't like he could just call him. It's not likely anyone would admit to hanging out in a jail or trashing people's mailboxes. *Maybe I should call him and pretend I'm doing a survey. But what would I ask? "Have you ever started a fire in a tree?"* No! Kyle scolded himself mentally. *That's not gonna work. Maybe I should tell the police.* No, *they'd just think I was trying to take the heat off of me.*

He sat for a minute. *I'm just going to have to catch him in the act,* he concluded. *Maybe I could watch the old jailhouse?* Kyle shook his head. His dad wouldn't like that at all. He had made it pretty clear that he couldn't go back there. He felt his stomach knot up. What should he do?

He thought back to Todd's advice. *Sometimes you gotta do what you gotta do.* He nodded his head resolutely. No one else seemed too interested in clearing his name. So if anyone figured this out, it would have to be him. So far every adult he'd been around, outside of his father, acted like the case was closed.

"Well, it's not closed, not yet," Kyle whispered to himself. "I'm going to figure this guy out," he said, putting his finger on the name he'd written in the book: "F. Grimsted." He thought back to his original theory about his mom sending messages. He squinted. *Is that what this guy is doing? Sending messages? What message? And why to my dad and Sharon? And what was this guy doing in the jail with a picture of my mom?*

Kyle tried to calm his racing brain. *It could be that I'm running ahead of myself. I'm not even sure this guy is the guilty one. Maybe he just got a sudden craving for Zero bars.* He sighed and patted his stomach. *I know I do.*

Kyle closed his book after writing, "Watch F. Grimsted." *If someone is going to figure this out, it will have to be me,* he reasoned again.

He slipped the book under the mattress again.

Maybe I can talk my dad into taking me to McDonald's tomorrow, he hoped.

He changed into his pajamas, then opened a box he kept by his bed. In it, his father had allowed him to store things that helped him remember his mother. The video of her at Ocean Sands was on top. Beneath it, an assortment of pictures from family vacations, a poem Sarah had written when Kyle was a baby, and her old Taylorville High yearbook. He opened the old book to a black-and-white photograph on page 30. "Sarah Fields." He put his finger on her name just as his father walked in.

He looked at the photograph with him. "She sure was cute."

"Yeah," Kyle responded. "Did you like her back in high school?"

"I didn't know her then, Kyle. My family moved to Taylorville right after Mommy graduated."

"Oh."

"But if I'd have known her, I'm sure I would have fallen for her at first sight." He pointed to her picture. "Just look at that smile."

Kyle grinned.

"You have it, too." He brushed his son's bangs. "Her smile, I mean."

Kyle studied the picture for a moment longer. His grin melted into seriousness. "Why couldn't I visit her before she died?"

Jake shook his head. "I didn't know she would die so suddenly. The hospital didn't even want me to visit her. I had to sneak in myself. I didn't think I could possibly get you in."

Kyle nodded. He'd heard it before.

"I'm sorry, Kyle."

Kyle nodded again. He folded the cover of the old yearbook and put it into his memory box.

Neither of the two looked at the photographs on the opposite page. There, nestled among the G's on the opposite page, was a name with a heart drawn around it: "Frank Grimsted."

"Ready for bed?"

"Almost. I need to brush my teeth."

Jake kissed his son's forehead. "I love you."

"I love you too, Dad."

CHAPTER
31

B<small>Y</small> breakfast time, Kyle experienced another detective brainstorm. He couldn't ask the police about F. Grimsted, but maybe his dad could. They might listen to an adult.

"Dad?"

Jake looked up from his Captain Crunch.

"I think I might know who put the Zero bar wrappers in the mailbox."

Jake looked at him and squinted. He thought at first that Kyle was getting ready to confess.

"It might be a guy named Grimsted."

That wasn't a name that Jake recognized. He wasn't a part of Sarah's life when she knew Frank, and when she told Jake her story, she only used the name "Frank."

"What makes you think that?"

"I asked Mr. Dithers down at the grocery store."

Jake looked puzzled. "How would he know?"

"I just asked him who buys Zero bars in Taylorville. That's all." He shrugged. "He told me a guy named Grimsted does."

"A lot of people buy Zero bars, Kyle. It doesn't mean he's the one."

Kyle sighed. "By the bag?"

"Maybe," Jake responded, handing Kyle his medicine bottle.

"Don't you think we should tell the police to watch him?" Kyle folded his arms across his chest. "I think it's him."

"We don't have any evidence, Kyle. Just because the guy buys a few candy bars—"

"Dad!" Kyle raised his voice.

"Kyle!" He mimicked his son's tone of voice. "I'm not calling the police to have them watch this guy just because he bought some candy bars. That's still legal in the United States if I'm not mistaken."

Kyle groaned and rolled his eyes. His thoughts had been correct. If anyone was going to solve this mystery, it would have to be him.

Kyle sulked in silence. Jake let him stew and returned to his cereal.

Kyle moved the cereal box and pretended to look at the puzzle printed on the back. In his mind, however, he began planning his next move.

◆　◆　◆

Later that day Jake and Sharon met for a lunchtime rendezvous at Tony's Little Italy. Sharon ordered a Caesar salad. Jake ordered two slices of sausage pizza.

"I'm staying away from the pepperoni," he explained with a smile. "It's too hard to launder out those stains."

"Since when would you care?" she retorted. "I thought you were the man with a hundred shirts."

"Underwear maybe, but not shirts."

Sharon laughed.

They sipped their diet sodas for a few minutes, and Sharon talked about the kids at school. Once Tony brought out the food, Jake brought up his conversation with Kyle.

"Kyle is turning into quite the little detective."

Sharon tilted her head. "What do you mean?"

"He went to the grocery store and talked to Mr. Dithers about who buys Zero bars."

"Ooooh." Sharon nodded her head and munched her salad for a moment. "Pretty smart, really."

"Takes after me."

Jake was hoping for a response. Sharon let it fall.

"What did he find out?"

"Kyle claims some guy named Grimsted bought a bag of Zero bars. It's got him convin—"

"Grimsted!" Sharon put down her fork. She leaned closer to Jake and whispered, "Grimsted?"

Jake pulled back. "Yes." He looked at her with a puzzled expression. "So what?"

"There's a guy by that name who lives just across from me," she responded. "Talk about weird!"

Jake listened with interest as Sharon described the several encounters she'd had with him. She shook her head. "He gives me the willies. I've seen him in McDonald's a time or two." She curled her lip into a distasteful snarl. "I won't even go in there anymore. I always get this feeling he's back there watching me." She shuddered. "And when he stuck his ear to my door . . . it gives me the creeps thinking he was trying to hear me."

"Do you think it's the same Grimsted?"

"How many of them do you think there could be?" Sharon looked at the pay phone in the corner. "Just a sec." She got up and thumbed through the phone book. When she got back to the table, she nodded her head. "Just as I thought . . . only one Grimsted." She looked back at her salad. Talking about Frank had made her lose her appetite. "Hungry?"

Jake stabbed a clump of salad. "Thanks."

He chewed and thought for a moment. "I'm not sure that being weird or buying Zero bars makes him our man."

"Jake!" It took an effort for Sharon to talk with her voice hushed. "This guy is watching me, listening at my door, looking at me in McDonald's, putting stuff in my mailbox." She reached over and touched his hand. "You've got to tell the police."

"Tell them what? That some guy who opens his mailbox with a broomstick buys Zero bars and is therefore the person who has been putting the candy wrappers in our mailboxes?"

Sharon sighed. "I guess it does sound pretty stupid, but . . ." She trailed off.

Jake looked up. "But what?"

"Well, it's just that the last time, I was the one who reported the candy wrapper to the police, and I ended up feeling pretty stupid."

"So you want me to do it, so I'll be the one looking foolish?" Jake looked at her with a serious but playful expression.

Sharon bit her lower lip and looked up. She wrinkled her nose. "Yes," she replied timidly. "Do it for me, please?"

"Sharon!"

"Please, Jake. This is starting to scare me. What if he's trying to tell me something? I don't like being alone over there too much anyway. Now, knowing this . . ."

Jake rolled his eyes and sighed. He shook his head. "I'm not sure why I'm about to agree to do this."

"You are?" Sharon smiled sweetly. She looked at her watch. "That's what I like about you, Jake." They stood up, and he helped her with her coat.

"What? That I'm a pushover?"

"No," she said, turning and facing him. "That inside that tough surgeon exterior, you're a sensitive guy." She stood on her tiptoes and kissed his cheek softly. "Thanks."

Jake smiled. "I guess this means I have to go through with the call."

Sharon nodded. "I've got to get back to the school. Let me know how it goes."

Jake picked up the bill and settled with Tony.

As he walked out, he shook his head. *What wouldn't you do for her, Jake?* he asked himself.

◆ ◆ ◆

Michael Simons hung up the phone. No answer at Jake Hampton's house. Ever since he'd talked to Matt Stone about Jake, he had a hunch there was some information that Jake didn't know and should know—and the sooner the better. He was quite certain that Jake had walked into a dark pit unknowingly, and he wanted to warn him if he could.

Simons looked at his watch and sighed. The paging operator had said Jake's pager wasn't on, and Jake wasn't at home or the office. It wasn't like he could just leave a message. *Oh, well,* he sighed, *I hope Jake knows what he's doing.*

He thought for a moment while he stared at the phone. Why was he doing this anyway? It really wasn't his business. *Right,* he thought, *but Jake was a resident of mine, and I have some obligation as a former professor to guide him along the way. Strange that I don't feel that kind of loyalty to Matt Stone. I guess I would if he hadn't been so disloyal to me.*

He strode down the hospital hallway at a surgeon's clip and made a mental note to try to get through to Jake later.

◆ ◆ ◆

Kyle made what was becoming a regular bicycle run down Main Street right after school was dismissed. His plan: Go to McDonald's to see if he could identify his suspect, then make it to the Simpsons' before it was apparent that he had been anywhere.

He pushed his bike into the rack and skipped into the restaurant. Kyle walked slowly to the counter. No one else was there. The supper crowd wouldn't start for another hour.

"May I help you?" asked a teenaged girl with braces.

Kyle strained to look behind the counter.

"Have you made up your mind?" the girl prompted again.

"Oh, I'll have a regular order of fries," Kyle responded. "That's it."

"Would you like a sundae with that?" The girl was wearing a big button with a sundae pictured on it. Beneath the sundae, it said, "We ask or it's free."

"No, just the fries."

As she went to the deep fryer, Kyle saw a man in the back peer around a stack of McDonaldland cookies. He jerked his head back quickly, but not before Kyle had a chance to read his name tag: "Frank."

Hmmm. I wonder if that's F. Grimsted. Kyle nodded and kept staring into the back of the restaurant. *I think that's the guy I've seen around in the green coat, all right.*

Kyle took his fries and paid with exact change. "Thanks."

Frank glanced again in Kyle's direction. Kyle returned his gaze without flinching, certain he had found his man.

Kyle turned and walked out, jumped on his bike, and stuffed a handful of fries in his mouth.

Behind him, Frank's grip on reality eroded. Since running out of medication a few days before, nearly everyone was out to get him. He wasn't even sure about his coworkers anymore.

That was Kyle! I've seen him in here with his father before. Certainly Jake is stooping to no ends . . . He's using my neighbor, his son . . . And he's flaunting Sarah's death in the newspaper too! Frank's mind raced. His eyes shifted nervously. He started breathing faster and faster.

"Frank! What's wrong?" The pleasant young female from behind the counter looked at him. "Are you feeling OK?"

Frank backed away with his hands in the air. "Stay away!"

"Frank?"

"Get away!" Frank picked up a large pancake turner and raised it in the air. "That guy!" Frank mumbled. "He's out to get me," he said softly. He looked wild.

"Frank?"

He threw the utensil to the side with a clatter and rushed for the door and out into the street.

He would never return to McDonald's again.

◆ ◆ ◆

"Look, Dr. Hampton," Don Rawlings explained, "I do appreciate your concern, but we can't investigate someone just for buying Zero bars."

Jake sighed and felt foolish. He was hearing the same arguments he gave to Sharon earlier in the day.

"Remember, we have the same evidence about your son. He buys the same candy bars, and by your own admission it doesn't imply his guilt about anything."

"All I wanted to do was report a suspicion. Maybe just keep your eyes open in case something else happens."

"Our eyes are open, Dr. Hampton. Thank you for calling."

Jake realized the conversation was over. "Thanks."

"Bye."

Jake put down the receiver and sighed. *It might be best not to share this with Kyle,* he realized. *He seemed so excited about this lead.*

Rawlings chuckled after hanging up the phone. He rolled his eyes and explained the situation to Steve Branson.

"Sounds to me like he's trying to take suspicion away from his son."

"Yeah," Steve responded. "Can't say as I blame him."

Don shrugged. "I could run a computer check on this Grimsted guy . . . see if he's worth watching."

"Our computer files are only up for the last five years so far."

"I know, but that ought to be enough," he responded. "Even if this guy did throw out a few candy wrappers, the presence of the Zero bar wrapper in the jail doesn't mean he lived there or started the tree fire."

"I agree, that's a pretty big jump in logic." Steve looked at his partner. "I'll tell you what. I'll check out my number one source for people information in Taylorville while you check your computer."

"Dr. Willie?"

"Bingo. He knows everyone in this town. I'll see if he's heard of a guy named Grimsted and if he's any trouble."

Steve picked up the phone and dialed.

After two rings, a pleasant female voice answered. "Doctor Dansford's and Hampton's office. How may I help you?"

"Maggie? This is Steve Branson with the Taylorville Police. Is Dr. Willie available for a few questions?"

"Sure, Steve, but he's with a patient. Do you mind waiting a few minutes?"

"I'll wait." He sat for a few minutes, reading a thick *Police Digest*.

"Hello."

"Dr. Willie, Steve Branson here."

"Hi, Steve. What can I do for you?"

"I'm looking for some information on a guy by the name of Grimsted."

Willie flinched and stayed quiet.

"I don't have a first name, but I know he's a male about thirty-five or so."

"Hmmm. I've seen so many people." He paused. "What is it you need to know?" he probed as he fidgeted with his pen.

"Just the basics. Someone has complained about some littering." He paused, then added, "And there's a slight chance this guy was involved in starting a fire the other night. Any chance you know a patient by that name?"

"Off the record, as usual, right?"

"Sure, Dr. Willie. Just like usual."

"I do recall seeing a man by that name, a Frank Grimsted, a time or two." He paused again. "But offhand, I certainly don't recall anything odd about him . . . certainly not the sort of thing that would lead me to believe he'd be involved in any wrongdoing."

"OK. Just thought I'd ask. It's more of a favor than any official suspicion of criminal behavior anyway. Thanks for your time."

"Sure. Bye."

Steve hung up the phone and looked back at Don Rawlings, who was busy at the computer. "Any luck?"

"Taylorville only has one Grimsted, a Mr. Frank Grimsted. He's clean as a whistle as far as I can see. Nothing on our computerized records. He doesn't even have a driver's license. I suppose I could call the guys up in Grantsville to do a background check. Their system is on-line and can get older records."

"I wouldn't bother. Dr. Willie says this guy is OK. His records go back longer than this guy's been around."

Don nodded. "Anyway, we've done more than we needed to." He leaned back. "I still think the kid is guilty as charged."

"Yeah," Steve added. "I guess it's just a little hard for his old man to accept."

"Let's get a bite to eat."

"Pizza?"

"It's either that or McDonald's."

"Pizza," Steve responded.

Don shook his head and mumbled about the size and limited opportunities of Taylorville.

◆ ◆ ◆

Michael Simons let Jake's home phone ring ten times. Finally he sighed and hung up. "Sorry, Jake, I've got a plane to catch. Maybe I'll be able to reach you in a day or two," he whispered to himself. He grabbed his briefcase and checked his tickets. Everything was set. He looked at his watch. He didn't have time to try again.

His mind spun with frustration. *Jake*, he thought, *you're on your own. I sure hope you know what you're doing in Taylorville.* He stopped when he got to the door, barely able to suppress the desire to try Jake again at the hospital. The grandfather clock in the hallway chimed, reminding him of his deadline. He shook his head and wondered, *Just what are you up to this time, D?*

◆ ◆ ◆

Dr. Willie sat back down at his desk and moaned. The stack of charts on his desk was growing. He pulled the first one from the stack. It belonged to an F. Grimsted.

On the front of the chart was a yellow sticky note: "Please initial prescription medication change."

CHAPTER
32

FRIDAY evening Frank watched everyone leaving the building all Taylorville called "Dr. Willie's Office." He stood in the shadows of the trash dumpster with his tools until everyone was gone. Then he made his move.

Stealthily, he moved to the back door. In a moment's time he was in, thanks to Mrs. O'Donnell's key.

He worked for thirty minutes, first removing the small shield over the hallway light switch just inside the back door. He concealed a wire that ran to his dynamite supply, which he placed in a medical supply box he'd retrieved from the dumpster earlier in the evening.

When he was through, the box could be seen in a dim light to be unwanted medical trash, sitting close to the door, ready for discard. But turn on the light to get a better look and *boom!*

Frank smiled at his creation and carefully checked the wiring. He then replaced the light switch shield and slipped out the back door. His blasting training back at the quarry had not been forgotten.

He paused with the door open and inhaled the clear, cold air. He felt powerful . . . in control again . . . his mind unclouded and in full understanding of his destiny. He knew his enemies, and he would overcome. Frank was going to be free.

Jake would be the first to come for his clinic on Saturday morning. Jake was predictable—always the same, always arriving before anyone else.

"It's not good to be so predictable, Jake," Frank whispered with a sneer. "You thought you'd gotten away with it. You even thought you could flaunt it." He thought of Jake opening the door in the morning and chuckled softly. "Now judgment will begin." He moved slowly into the shadows and walked down a side street.

"Your life for Sarah's," he muttered. "And Sharon's for the baby's."

◆ ◆ ◆

By Friday evening, Kyle's frustration had grown. No one liked his ideas. No one wanted to help. His father didn't want to talk to the police about Grimsted, and Lenny and Todd refused to go to the old jailhouse to see if they could find any answers there.

Since going to McDonald's and seeing the man named Frank, Kyle had spent many hours contemplating the meaning of the man's relationship with Zero bars, the jail, and his mother. Carefully he wrote his speculations down in his little black book. The picture of his mother in the jailhouse made him think Frank must have been a friend. And since it had been a long time since his mother lived in Taylorville, he must have been an old friend from her days here. The Zero bar wrappers could only mean that he liked the same kind of candy his mother did. Maybe it even meant they both liked them together, or that this guy Frank ate them for the same reason Kyle did, because they reminded him of Sarah. It all made perfect sense to Kyle's eleven-year-old mind. What didn't make sense is why the wrapper and the picture were found in the jail; and even if the fire there had been an accident, it still didn't explain the fire in Todd's treehouse.

Over and over Kyle studied the facts. More and more he became convinced that he would need to speak to Frank Grimsted face to face. He knew the police wouldn't help him. They were the ones who thought Kyle was the guilty party. If his father and the other guys wouldn't help him, he would just have to do it himself.

He was supposed to be staying at the Giffords' until his father came home, but Lenny and Todd wouldn't go out with him, so he begged Todd not to tell and left by himself on his bike, racing for the Abington Apartments. If he timed it right, he could locate Grimsted's apartment and check out the possibilities of spying on Frank there, then race home before his father arrived and before Mrs. Gifford asked Todd where he was.

With the wind in his face and the cold so bitter it made his ears sting, Kyle raced on to find some answers. Kyle wanted to clear his name if it was the last thing he did.

◆ ◆ ◆

Frank ditched his supplies in the dumpster behind the 7-Eleven, then gathered his tattered green army coat around him and scuffed his feet toward his apartment. He felt exhilarated, powerful. As he breathed deeply of the cold air, he shivered. He wanted to sleep in the jailhouse tonight. Since stopping the medicines, the voices were returning, and he knew that if he stayed in the jail, he would hear them more clearly. But voices or no voices, it was getting terribly cold, and he would need some extra blankets to keep warm. So he moved steadily down the street, gripping his coat tightly and planning the night ahead. First, home to his apartment, then out to the jailhouse for the night.

◆ ◆ ◆

Jake listened to Sharon's report of her day. It had been a busy one, and frustrations at Taylorville Elementary seemed to be mounting.

"At least it's Friday," Jake added, balancing the phone against his ear and looking across the intensive care unit nursing station. "You won't have to deal with it again until Monday."

"Yeah. I'm glad for the weekend," she sighed. "How do things look for you?"

"I'm taking calls. Willie says he's disappearing again."

"Just where does he go on all these weekends?"

"I'm not sure. I guess he just feels like getting away. I suppose he's been cooped up here for a long time."

"You're on tonight too?"

"Afraid so."

"So what are you doing for dinner?"

"I thought I'd just scrounge up something with Kyle. Maybe grab a burger at McDon—"

"Don't say it!" she interrupted. "That boy is going to be one big eleven-year-old ball of cholesterol." She paused. "Why don't you let me fix something?"

"Sharon, you don't have—"

"Don't argue. I want to. Besides, you don't have time to cook—you're on call. And Kyle deserves better than McDonald's."

"OK." He smiled. "I know when I'm beat." He looked at his watch. "I should be done here in a minute or two. I just have to finish up one consult. If this beeper cooperates, I should be home in a half hour. I need to stop by the neighbors' and pick up Kyle. Then I'll be in."

"Why don't I just go over now? I can get Kyle from the neighbors' and start supper. You come on when you can. If you're late, I can go ahead and feed Kyle."

Jake shook his head. "You're a gem."

"It's a deal then?"

"Sure. I'll see you soon."

"OK. Bye."

"Bye."

◆ ◆ ◆

Kyle drove his bicycle slowly by the Abington Apartments. From the parking lot, he could see into a half dozen lighted apartments. He squinted at a window. He could only see a few people within the apartments, and no one looked like the man who worked in McDonald's. He stopped his bike and pulled the little book from his coat pocket. He looked where he had written, "Apt. D, Abington Apartments." He parked his bike and opened the door that led into the building where Sharon lived. *I need to check the mailboxes,* he figured.

Kyle leaned close to the mailboxes to read the names. He saw S. Isaacs under the C and F. Grimsted under the D.

Just then Frank came in. His eyes met Kyle's with equal surprise and suspicion. "What are you doing here?" Frank demanded.

"Just looking at the mailboxes."

"Did your father send you?"

Kyle's expression showed true confusion. "No. He doesn't know I'm here."

Frank twisted his mouth and studied the boy for a moment. "Are you alone?"

Kyle nodded.

"Why are you looking at the mailboxes?"

"I wanted to see where you lived," Kyle answered honestly. "You knew my mother, didn't you?"

The question seemed like a genuine one. Frank looked at him for a moment. *Maybe your father hasn't told you too much about me,* he thought.

"Yes." Frank spoke slowly. "We were very close."

"I'm Kyle Hampton," the boy stated nervously.

"I know."

"I thought you might be able to help me."

Frank looked down at him without speaking.

"Do you like to eat Zero bars?" Kyle asked, compulsively trying to find a way to see if Mr. Grimsted was actually the person he wanted.

"Yes." He paused. "They were your mother's favorite."

Kyle's excitement mounted. *It's got to be him!* he reasoned. "Mine too."

Frank squinted. "Has your father ever mentioned me?"

Kyle shook his head. "No."

"How did you find me?"

"I asked the grocer who likes Zero bars," Kyle stated proudly.

"Your father never talked about me?"

Kyle shook his head again. "You were friends with my mom?"

"Yes." Frank pondered the situation for a moment. "There are some things you need to know."

He turned and walked up the stairs. "Come with me."

"I can't believe I found you," Kyle chattered nervously, following Frank up the steps. *Wait until I tell Dad that I've solved the mystery.*

Frank struggled to open the door and held it for Kyle.

Kyle disappeared into the apartment, the door slammed, and Frank turned the dead bolt. *You've got a lot to learn, Kyle.*

◆ ◆ ◆

Across the hall, Sharon shut off the stereo and grabbed her coat. *Fixing supper for the Hamptons beats talking to my plants any day,* she told herself happily. She smiled and headed out the door, bounding down the steps and into the night air. She didn't notice Kyle's bicycle parked at the edge of the building. She was too busy thinking ahead about dinner.

◆ ◆ ◆

"You can sit over there," Frank began.

Kyle obeyed.

Frank walked to the kitchen and came back carrying two candy bars. "Here. You can have a snack." He handed him a Zero bar.

"Thanks." Kyle's voice trailed off. "But my father says I shouldn't eat right before dinner."

Frank looked at the boy with plastic compassion. "There's a lot of stuff your father has told you that isn't necessarily right." He took a noisy bite of his own Zero bar.

Kyle squirmed and fingered the candy bar. *Maybe a few bites wouldn't hurt.*

◆ ◆ ◆

A few minutes later Sharon knocked on the Giffords' door. "Mrs. Gifford? I'm Sharon Isaacs, a friend of Jake's. I'm here for Kyle."

"Hello, Sharon. Jake called to let me know you'd be by." She motioned for Sharon to come in. She turned away and yelled, "Todd, send Kyle up!" She turned back to Sharon. "They've been so quiet, I've hardly heard a peep out of them. Must be playing a game."

"Does he have to go now? Can't he just walk home in a few minutes?" Todd's voice boomed.

Mrs. Gifford looked at Sharon. "It's OK by me. They're playing so nice for a change."

"Well," Sharon responded, "I guess that will be OK. I haven't got supper ready. Just send him over in a few minutes." She smiled and stepped back out on the front steps. "Thanks."

◆ ◆ ◆

Frank let the boy enjoy his candy bar before interrupting him.

"Just put the wrapper on the table."

Kyle nodded and looked up. "So it was you who put the wrappers in dad's Trooper."

Frank nodded.

"Why?"

"I wanted him to know I was watching."

Kyle didn't understand but felt excited to know that he was finally getting some answers.

"There are some things your father hasn't told you." He looked at him curiously. "He didn't tell you about me?"

"No." Kyle squirmed.

"Why do you think you came to Taylorville?"

"For my dad's work," he responded quickly. "He's a doctor."

Frank shook his head and explored the gap in his front teeth with his tongue. "He told you the reason he wants you to believe," he stated slowly. He looked up at Kyle and spoke with a serious look on his face. "Some of this is going to be hard for you to take."

Kyle was starting to feel uncomfortable. He found it hard to sit still.

◆ ◆ ◆

Sharon picked up the phone. "Hampton residence."

The voice was male and serious. "May I please speak to Dr. Hampton?"

"He's not here right now, but I expect him any moment. Can I give him a message?"

Michael Simons shook his head and looked at his watch. His frustration at not reaching Jake mounted. This was the first time he'd been able to call in a few days. At least he had reached his home. "I'd really rather speak to him personally." He paused. "My name is Michael Simons. Jake will know me. There is something extremely important that I need to tell him."

"He should be back in a few minutes, Mr. Simons."

Simons looked at his watch again. He was standing in the Atlanta airport. "I'm really pressed for time, unfortunately. I guess I'll try again later."

Sharon shrugged. "I'll tell him you called."

"Thanks."

Sharon hung up the phone.

"Who was that?" Jake had snuck in behind her.

"Oh!" Sharon spun around. "Jake! You scared me."

He looked sheepish. "Sorry. I came in the back way." He looked around. "Where's Kyle?"

"Still at the neighbors'. Mrs. Gifford said he could stay a few more minutes longer since they were playing so nice. I figured I'd call him when dinner was ready."

Jake nodded and sorted through the mail.

"That was some guy . . . Michael Simons."

"Michael Simons?"

"Sounded pretty serious. He said he had something extremely important to tell you."

"I wonder what he wanted. He's a cardiothoracic surgeon. He's the one who operated on Matt's baby."

"Oooh." Sharon nodded.

"I'm surprised he didn't identify himself as 'doctor.' He's really into prestige."

"The way he sounded, I'm sure he'll call back."

"I hope there hasn't been trouble with Matt."

"Certainly Matt would call himself."

Jake nodded. "What's for dinner?"

◆ ◆ ◆

"Your father killed your mother," Frank stated mechanically.

Kyle shook his head. "That's only what some people said. It's not true."

"I know it, Kyle." He paused. "I've got proof."

Kyle shifted. "I think I'd better go home."

Frank looked at him sternly. "I didn't say you could go."

Kyle's stomach churned. He returned Frank's leering gaze. "What kind of proof?"

"I was there . . . I saw him."

The boy's eyes widened.

Frank nodded. "There's more. Your mother and I were lovers."

Kyle shook his head. "No."

"Yes, Kyle, it's true. I went to see her the night she died. Unfortunately, I arrived too late. Your father was still standing over her . . ." His voice trailed off. He walked to a desk drawer, then returned carrying a small object. "With this in his hand."

He opened his palm.

"A shot?"

"A syringe, Kyle. It's for injecting medicine."

"I don't believe you!" Kyle stood up. "I want to go home now."

"Sit down!" Frank grabbed the boy's arm, pinching it tightly. "You need to hear this! Your life might be in danger too!" He shoved Kyle back onto the couch.

"Ow!"

Frank scowled and began to pace. "Why do you think your dad brought you to Taylorville?" He stared into space. "I'm one of the few who know what really happened." He began silently counting his steps as he walked from the kitchen to the front den and back. "He needs to silence me. He came here to make sure I don't talk."

"He came here to work with Dr. Willie!" Kyle protested.

Frank turned away for a moment, pacing toward the kitchen. Kyle placed his hand over the syringe and closed it.

"That's what he tells you, Kyle."

"Let me go home!" Kyle screamed, shoving his hands into his pockets.

Frank softened. "Don't be afraid, Kyle. I might be your only hope." He stopped pacing for a moment. "Your father is an extremely jealous man. Your mother loved me. Jake has come for revenge against me."

"That's not true!"

Frank pondered for a moment. He walked over to his desk again, this time returning with an old high-school yearbook. He opened it to the picture of Sarah Fields—the same one Kyle had stored away in his bedroom. "Look at this, Kyle. It should be pretty obvious how your mother felt about me."

"How did you get Mom's book?"

"It's not hers," he responded. "It's mine. I was in her class. Just look."

◆ ◆ ◆

Sharon set the salad bowl on the table, next to a steaming plate of spaghetti. "Call Kyle. I'm just about ready."

"Boy, it smells great. You're sure I had all this stuff around?" He picked up the phone.

"Hello . . . Giffords'."

"Hello. This is Jake. Can you send Kyle on over?"

"Sure thing."

"Thanks. Bye."

Mrs. Gifford hung up the phone. "Kyle! Your dad called."

There was no response. She walked to the stairs. Everything was quiet. "Kyle?"

◆ ◆ ◆

"Sharon's in on it, too, Kyle," Frank added. "She's been watching me."

"Ms. Isaacs?"

"She and your dad have been scheming." He pulled out the latest addition from his shoe box, the newspaper photograph of Jake, Sharon, and the Dansfords. "See, Kyle, your father is starting to admit what he did." He slapped the paper. "That's what these people believe . . . that you can kill if you want to."

"But my dad doesn't believe that!"

Kyle looked down at the yearbook again. He started crying. "You're lying to me." His finger traced the words beneath his mother's picture: *To my one and only love, Frank.* "You wrote these words to trick me."

"I know it's hard to believe, Kyle." Frank reached out and touched the boy's shoulder. He paused for a moment. *Jake really hasn't included you in his plans, has he?* Frank thought. "Tell you what, Kyle. Go and look at your mother's yearbook. You'll see that I'm telling the truth. Look at what I wrote in her book."

"Can I go?" Kyle wiped his tears with his coat sleeve.

Frank softened again. "Your father is tricking you, son. You better check out what I'm saying before it's too late."

◆ ◆ ◆

There was a faint knock at the back door.

Jake looked at Sharon. "Must be Kyle. I thought I unlocked it."

"I'll get it." Sharon walked from the kitchen and opened the door.

Standing there was Todd Gifford. Right behind him, with her hand on his shoulder, stood his mother. "Hi."

Sharon looked at their serious expressions. "Hi. Come on in. Is something wrong?"

Jake walked up. "Where's Kyle?"

"He's not here," Mrs. Gifford reported solemnly. "It seems Todd here agreed to cover for him while Kyle went out on his bike."

"Where is he, Todd?" Jake asked with rising alarm.

Todd's mother pushed him forward. "I don't know," he responded slowly.

Jake and Sharon stared at the boy.

"Tell them what you told me. Where do you think he might be?"

"He's been talking about finding some guy named Frank Grimsted." Todd rolled his eyes. "He didn't want me to tell."

His mother prompted him again. "Todd . . ."

"I really don't know where he is. He went looking for this Frank guy. He wanted me to go down to check the old jailhouse, but I didn't want to." He shrugged. "He's seemed pretty upset lately about this whole candy wrapper and fire thing. He thinks everyone is accusing him. He thinks he needs to clear himself."

"What did he tell you about this Frank?" Jake asked as he scratched his head. This was the first time Jake had ever heard Grimsted's first name.

"Nothing much. He has his address. He thinks he's someone who had some obsession with his mother or something."

Jake muttered the name. "Frank . . . Frank." He put his hand to his mouth. "Oh, God, help us." His face paled.

"What's wrong, Jake?"

"I think I do know who this Frank Grimsted is."

Mrs. Gifford was anxious to get out. "I'm so sorry if we've caused any trouble," she said. "I see you've got your hands full. We'll leave you alone."

She grabbed Todd and nudged him firmly toward the door. "I'm coming," he whined.

The Giffords disappeared, and Jake ran to Kyle's room. He quickly located Kyle's memory box and retrieved Sarah's old yearbook. When he turned to the G's, his hand returned to his mouth again. "Oh, no."

"What is it?" Sharon had followed him upstairs.

"Frank Grimsted," he said, slapping the picture with the back of his hand. "I should have known. He's Sarah's old boyfriend!"

Jake sighed. "We've got to find Kyle. This guy is a nut. He's potentially very violent." He shook his head. "I can't believe this!"

"I don't get it," Sharon replied. "An old boyfriend?"

"It's a long story, Sharon. He's the father of the baby she aborted."

"Oh, no."

"We've got to find Kyle! There's no telling what this guy will do." He shook his head and turned to go down the stairs. "I thought this guy was locked up long ago."

The situation started to dawn on Sharon. "And this guy lives across from me?" She wrinkled her nose.

"I'll take my car and head over to your house. Maybe I'll find Kyle on a road between here and there."

"I'll drive over to the jailhouse."

Jake looked at Sharon. "Are you sure you want to do that? I told Kyle not to go there. He's not likely to disobey."

"You heard Todd. He's been trying to convince him to go there." She sighed. "Maybe he just got desperate."

"Don't you think you should go with me?"

"We've got a better chance of finding him if we split up. Besides, I won't go inside that creepy old place. I'll just look around outside for his bike."

Jake grabbed his coat and opened the back door. "Be careful."

Sharon turned off the stove and quickly followed.

This was turning out to be an interesting night after all.

◆ ◆ ◆

Kyle crossed the street and turned up a side road. He didn't want to be on the streets his father traveled, just in case he hadn't gotten home yet.

His head spun. What if Frank Grimsted was telling the truth? What if his dad really was out for revenge?

I've got to look at Mom's yearbook again. I've got to know whether Frank and Mom were really friends. He wanted to cry again. Fear made him pump faster. *I need to get home before Dad finds out I'm not there.*

He pushed his hand into his jacket pocket and retrieved the syringe. *Does this really prove that Dad killed Mom like Frank Grimsted says?*

◆ ◆ ◆

Jake drove up the street, looking carefully for Kyle or his bicycle.

"Great," he muttered. "No sign of him anywhere."

Jake strained to remember what Kyle had told him about Frank. *Boy, I wish I'd paid more attention to his detective schemes now.*

He could see Abington Apartments ahead. *There's Sharon's apartment. The windows are dark. Those other windows must be Frank's,* he deduced as he slowed the Trooper to a crawl. There was no sign of Kyle.

He thought for a moment about going up to Frank's door, but it didn't look like anyone was home there either.

What had Sharon said? That he works at McDonald's? He looked across the street to the golden arches. Kyle's bike wasn't there.

Maybe I should go over there and see if this Frank guy is working today.

◆ ◆ ◆

Sharon crossed the railroad track and shifted on her high beams. The old jail structure loomed in the dim moonlight. She drove around the building, surrounded on three sides with pavement. She strained to see the windows, then inspected the bushes on the three sides of the building she could drive around. She did not see Kyle or his bike.

At least I can walk around the outside, she figured. *But there's no way I'm going in there.*

Leaving her Honda running, she walked toward the far side of the building, the side that had the most shrubbery. "Kyle," she called timidly. "Kyle."

What is that? She looked up at a second-floor window. A faint glow was coming from one of the windows. Was it a light. Kyle?

"Kyle!"

The light in the window immediately darkened. Sharon squinted. Now all the windows looked the same. *Maybe it was just my imagination.* She walked over next to the building where a few windows opened into the basement at ground level. *Hmmm. I'll bet this is how Kyle got in.*

◆ ◆ ◆

Kyle arrived home before Jake. He skidded his bike to a halt in the driveway. *Great! I beat Dad!*

He thought momentarily about going back to Todd's, but he was anxious to look at the yearbook.

Quickly he ran in and up to his bedroom. The yearbook was already opened to his mother's picture and was lying on his bed. He knew he hadn't left it this way. *Had Dad been home?*

He traced his finger past Fields, Filbert, Goings, Grange, Green . . . Grimsted. There!

Slowly he read the inscription written in his mom's yearbook: "To my one and only love, Sarah."

Kyle sank onto the bed.

"Oh, no," he muttered. "Frank was telling the truth!"

◆ ◆ ◆

Jake circled the McDonald's, trying to get a glimpse of Kyle or of Frank. *It's no use*, he realized. *I can't see well enough from here.*

He pulled the Trooper into the first available spot and walked in. He scanned the tables. No Kyle. He couldn't see very well into the kitchen area.

"May I help you, sir?" The voice came from a teenager behind the counter.

"Uh, sure. I'll just have coffee."

"Will that be all?"

"That's all." Jake craned his neck to see if anyone was in the back. Two people were there, both women.

"Cream and sugar with that?"

"No, thanks. Just black."

Jake tapped his fingers on the counter. He thought about walking out without his coffee but decided to wait since he'd already paid.

Maybe I should call Mom, he thought. *It would be just like Kyle to go there.*

◆ ◆ ◆

Sharon couldn't shake the feeling that someone was in the jailhouse. She'd seen a light, hadn't she?

She spent a few moments looking around behind the taller bushes. This would be a perfect place to stash a bicycle, she figured. She looked for a moment longer before turning back to head for her car.

Snap.

She spun around, sure she had heard a noise. "Kyle?"

No response. She looked back up at the windows on the second floor. Everything was dark. *This place is giving me the creeps!*

She listened carefully for a moment. All she could hear was the gentle throbbing of her Honda in the parking lot.

She suddenly wanted very badly to be back with Jake . . . anywhere but here alone in the dim light of the half-moon.

She ran to her car and slipped behind the steering wheel.

Frank sat up in the backseat.

"Drive!"

Sharon gasped for breath. Fear gripped her voice, and she was unable to scream.

Frank pointed the tip of a cold metal barrel in her direction. "Nice of you to come to me, Ms. Isaacs. It makes it so much easier this way."

CHAPTER
33

KYLE stuffed the syringe and the old yearbook in his backpack. Then, having a second thought, he grabbed his toothbrush and pajamas and added them to the pack as well.

In a moment he was back on the road, taking back streets to his grandmother's. *She'll know what to do*, he figured. *Certainly she isn't in on this conspiracy.*

His breath frosted the air as he pumped faster and faster. Twice he squelched a sob.

I sure hope Grandma knows what to do.

◆ ◆ ◆

Silently Sharon prayed a simple prayer. *Help!*

"Pull over there, next to the dirt road."

Sharon obeyed.

"Get out."

Frank ripped the keys from her hand.

"Let's go."

"Where are you taking me?"

Frank motioned ahead.

A barn loomed at the edge of a field. Frank knew the place. He had been there with Sarah.

"You thought you would get away with it, didn't you?"

"Get away with what?"

Frank laughed, a low guttural response.

"Murder."

"Murder!"

"You and Jake are in this together. My Sarah's dead, and you thought he would walk away scot-free, didn't you?" Frank motioned toward the tall grass. "Through there. I've seen it so clearly lately."

"I didn't kill anyone."

"Jake did."

"That's only what the media implied," Sharon spoke up again.

"Shut up."

Sharon cast a hopeful glance at a nearby farmhouse. The lights were on. *He'll probably shoot me if I scream*, she realized.

"Dr. D told me that Jake brought her the medicine. Besides . . ." He paused, then added, "I saw him."

Sharon stumbled, twisting her ankle on the irregular ground. "Ow!"

"Quiet."

Silently she prayed again. *Help me know what to say. He seems to want to talk.*

He opened the door to an old barn. It appeared unused. He shoved Sharon forward onto the floor.

"You've been watching me. I've seen you . . . you and Jake . . . even Jake's son, Kyle." He stopped and chuckled. "I've straightened him out though," he added with a thin smile.

"What have you done with Kyle?"

"Nothing. I just told him the truth."

"Nobody is watching you, Frank. Certainly not Jake. He doesn't even know you!"

"You're lying." He started to pace. "Dr. D told me I would know when the time to fulfill my destiny had arrived," he stated flatly as he raised the pistol in the air.

"What does Dr. D have to do with this?"

"He's the only one who knows me." He paused. "He gives me my medicine . . . until recently." He stared at her. "He stopped it so I could understand who was after me . . . so I could act without any mental hesitation."

So Dr. D is behind this. Sharon tried to think of what to say next.

Obviously her captor wasn't thinking rationally. "Why do you go all the way to Ocean Sands? Dr. Willie is right here in town."

Frank laughed and momentarily put down the gun. "You don't understand, do you? Dr. Willie is Dr. D." Frank shook his head incredulously.

The words hit Sharon like a runaway locomotive. "What?"

"He just won't let anyone here call him that because it's his wife's nickname too. At least that's one reason." He raised the gun again.

"Wait!" Sharon pleaded. "The same doctor that treated Sarah hired Jake?"

Frank thought about it for a second. "Yeah."

"Don't you find that a little strange?"

Frank nodded numbly. "Never really thought about it. I think Dr. D just needed some help. Jake must have realized how good a doctor D was after seeing what he did for his wife."

"Come on, Frank. Sarah was dying of breast cancer."

"You're lying! I saw her on TV. She was cured by Dr. D."

Frank raised the gun again. "Jake killed her, and she was mine. Now I'm going to kill you 'cause you are his."

Sharon decided it was time to scream. It looked like he was going to shoot anyway.

A shrill scream pierced the night.

A pistol shot followed as a bullet ripped into Sharon's right chest.

She fell immediately to the dusty floor. Frank felt for a pulse at her wrist. He stood over her for a moment and gloated, then fled through the tall, damp grass to the dirt road beyond.

◆ ◆ ◆

Ezra and Betsy Berger were watching *Wheel of Fortune* when Betsy heard Sharon scream.

"Pick a T, pick a T," Ezra coached the contestant.

The contestant asked for an R.

A shot rang out.

"Oooh!" Ezra slapped his knee.

Betsy pulled back the drapes from the front window. "Did you hear something, Ez?"

He pointed to the screen. "This fella's never gonna make it." He looked at Betsy. "He picked an R."

"No, I mean, did you hear a scream and a shot?"

"Probably just old Henry sighting his rifle again."

"In the dark?"

"Pick a T. Pick a T."

Betsy went out onto the front porch. She strained to see a dark figure moving quickly down the lane.

"Ezra, I think there's been trouble! Some man just went running down our lane."

"Probably just high-schoolers, Betsy. They've been sneakin' 'round our barn for years."

"Ezra, I heard a shot! Go out to the barn and see!" Getting no response, Betsy picked up her wool coat. "I'll go myself," she grumbled.

"Don't you go out there, woman. You'll slip." He glanced back at the TV as a contestant asked for an M. "Come on!" He shook his head and stood up. "I could probably go to the barn and back before Mr. Big Shot here solves this puzzle."

"He's probably nervous, Ez." She handed him his coat.

"Where's my flashlight?"

"Above the kitchen sink in the cupboard," she answered. When he was out of sight, she added, "Just where it always is."

A moment later Ezra walked out with his coat and flashlight. As he walked to the door, he pointed to the screen. "Tell that guy to ask for a T."

Betsy looked concerned. "Be careful."

Ezra disappeared into the darkness, heading for the barn. After a few minutes he was winded, with his breath making small clouds of visible mist. He pushed open the door with his foot and swung the flashlight around in a slow arc. He almost missed her. Then on the floor he saw a shoe . . . no, a body!

He rushed to her, pushing her onto her back. Blood had spilled out on her shirt and was dripping from the corner of her mouth.

He felt for a pulse in her wrist. Nothing. He tilted her head back.

Sharon emitted a short gasp and took a shallow breath.

"Thank you, God, she's alive," Ezra proclaimed. He turned and ran for the house.

"Betsy! Call 9-1-1! Betsy, someone's been shot!"

Ezra slipped in the mud and caught his footing just before colliding with a board fence.

"Betsy! A girl is dying!"

◆ ◆ ◆

"Hello, Mom. It's Jake. You haven't seen Kyle, have you?"

"No." Phyllis Hampton looked outside. "Don't you know where he is?"

"He went out on his bike from a friend's house. He's not back yet."

"Have you called the emergency room? Maybe he's been in an accident."

"I don't think so, Mom, although it's worth a try, I guess."

"Where are you?"

"I'm at a pay phone outside McDonald's. I had a hunch he might have been here, so I came out to check."

"Oh, dear. Kyle could freeze out there. It must only be 15 or 20 degrees."

"Look, could you page me if he happens to come there? I'll call you when I get home."

Phyllis wrung her hands. "Sure."

"Bye."

"Bye." Phyllis put down the phone and folded her hands.

"Dear Father," she began, "watch over my grandson, Kyle . . ."

◆ ◆ ◆

Ezra tracked mud through the living room on the way to the phone. "Betsy!"

His wife opened the bathroom door.

"A girl's been shot! Take some blankets to the barn!"

Ezra grabbed the phone and punched 9-1-1.

"9-1-1 emergency. How may I help you?"

"A girl's been shot. She may be dead. Out on Route 6, just past the Stoney Brook Dairy, first lane to the right, back in the barn."

"Are you with her now?"

"No. She's out in the barn."

The 9-1-1 dispatch operator typed in the information as quickly as Ezra gave it. "I have a unit on the way, sir. Is she breathing?"

"I'm not with her now."

"Do you know CPR?"

"I've seen it on TV. Look, ma'am, I'd better go. Do you know the way?"

"First lane on the right on route 6 past the Stoney Brook Dairy," she repeated.

"Good."

Ezra slammed down the phone and headed for the door. Betsy was right behind him with an armload of quilts.

◆ ◆ ◆

Jake was just getting in the Trooper when the rescue squad rushed by with its siren blaring. For a moment he decided to follow. He was sure after talking to his fretful mother that Kyle was bleeding on the road somewhere. He watched the unit for a moment and realized it was heading out of town at a rapid pace.

Naaah, he told himself, *Kyle wouldn't go out there*.

He shook his head and jumped in his Isuzu. *I guess I'll just head back to the house. Maybe Kyle has come home, or maybe Sharon has found him.*

◆ ◆ ◆

By the time the paramedic unit arrived, Sharon was covered with blankets except for her feet, which Ezra held in his hands as he stood over her. He vaguely remembered an old Boy Scout adage: "If the face is pale, lift the tail. If the face is red, lift the head."

Sharon was definitely pale, so he had hoisted her feet into the air.

Paramedic Gil Cunningham knelt by her side. He put his ear to her lips. Her breathing was extremely shallow. He put his fingers on her carotid artery. "I've got a weak carotid pulse," he reported.

Diana Hibert cut away the shirt. An entrance wound just to the right of the sternum could be seen. Bubbles and blood were coming from the wound. "Get me some petroleum gauze. We've got to seal this wound."

Peg Johnson handed her the dressings as Gil put an oxygen mask on.

Peg looked at Gil. "I'm gonna start an IV. We're going to need access before she loses too much blood." She put a tourniquet on Sharon's right arm and swabbed it with alcohol. She then pushed an IV needle into a vein. She advanced the catheter and pulled out the needle. "There."

Gil stepped back and talked to Ezra and Betsy. No one knew who she was or what she was doing there. "Is that your car at the end of the lane?"

Ezra looked at Betsy and then back at Gil and shook his head. "My truck's up by the house," he responded. "Betsy don't drive."

"It might be the girl's."

"The dispatcher called the police. Be sure to show it to them."

Peg looked up. "All set?"

They loaded the victim onto a stretcher and began carrying her toward the house. The rescue vehicle was parked in the driveway, unable to get closer because of the mud.

Fifteen minutes after they arrived, the team left again.

Gil picked up the two-way radio. "Rescue One to Taylorville Hospital emergency room."

"Taylorville E.R. Go ahead, Rescue One."

"Be advised we are en route with an unresponsive, unidentified female approximately thirty years of age who has sustained a gunshot wound to the right chest. Blood pressure 60. Respirations 36 and shallow."

"Do you have IV access?"

"One peripheral sixteen gauge."

"Roger, Rescue One."

"We'll be at your facility in seven minutes."

◆ ◆ ◆

Jake arrived home just as his beeper sounded. He looked at the kitchen. The table was set. The food was cold. The house was quiet. There was no sign of Kyle.

He looked at his beeper. "Not now," he groaned, looking at the number at the top—4393.

"Great," he muttered. "E.R."

He dialed the number. "Dr. Hampton here. I was paged." Just then his pager sounded again. He recognized his mother's number.

"Dr. Hampton, we have a trauma alert situation here. Young adult female with a gunshot wound to the right chest with unstable vital signs coming in by squad, five minutes away."

"I'll be right there."

He jotted a quick note for Sharon. "At the hospital for emergency. Please take Kyle to his grandmother's."

He would call his mother from the car phone. He ran to his Trooper.

He sped north toward Main Street, dialing his mother as he went.

"Mom, what's up?"

"Kyle's here. He's safe."

"Thank God." He heaved a sigh of relief. "Can he stay with you for a few hours? I'm on my way to the hospital for an emergency."

"Why don't you let him spend the night? He came prepared."

"Sure, but . . . What do you mean, 'prepared'?"

"He's confused, Jake," she said, lowering her voice. "He's been talking to some man named Frank Grimsted. This Grimsted's been telling him about you. He's gotten Kyle pretty worked up."

"Frank Grimsted is crazy. I thought he'd been institutionalized."

"It sounds as if he should be, from what I've heard. Listen . . . don't worry about Kyle. I'll talk to him. I'll call you in the morning."

"Thanks, Mom. I owe you one."

"Only one?"

"No, Mom, a whole lot more than one," Jake said smiling.

"I know. I'll see you tomorrow."

"Bye."

Jake hung up the phone and raced to beat the rescue squad. He arrived in the E.R. just as they were bringing the stretcher through the doors.

"What've you got, Gil?" Dr. Hampton asked.

"Female, single gunshot wound to the right chest," he reported as they pushed the stretcher against the E.R. bed. "Let's move on three. One, two, three."

Jake helped hoist the back-board over onto the E.R. bed. He looked at the patient's face. "Oh, God, no—it's Sharon!"

Gil looked at Jake. "You know her?"

"Yes," Jake responded numbly. "Yes, I do."

He leaned close to her face. "Sharon?" He put his ear to her lips. "Sharon, it's Jake. Speak to me!"

There was no response.

Jake looked around. He needed to collect himself but had little time. He was the surgeon on call. He would have to deal with it.

He put his face up to hers again. "She's breathing. What's her pressure?" He looked at a nurse.

"Pressure 45 systolic."

Jake put his stethoscope to her chest. There were no breath sounds on the right. "She's got a tension pneumothorax. Set up a chest tube tray."

He quickly painted her chest with betadine and made a small incision in the fifth intercostal space. Sharon didn't flinch. He spread a clamp in the soft tissue just beneath the skin, then turned the clamp around and swiftly pushed it through the muscles above the rib into the chest.

There was a rush as the trapped air exploded from the chest. He then inserted a chest tube and secured it with a number zero nylon suture. He connected the tube to a collecting chamber, which immediately began filling with dark blood.

"Pressure's a little better," the nurse reported. "Sixty."

"We need to go to the O.R. for an emergency thoracotomy. We need ten units of packed red cells typed and crossed STAT."

"She's really clamped down," a young female nurse reported. "I can't get the blood for the crossmatch."

"Have them bring down O negative blood." Jake looked at the nurse. "Here, I'll do a femoral stick. I can get the labs drawn for you."

He took a syringe and a twenty gauge needle and felt for her femoral pulse. It was barely palpable. He inserted the needle just medial to the femoral artery pulse.

As he did, Jake's world seemed to slow. He saw himself drawing the blood. Rich, dark, poorly oxygenated blood characteristic of someone close to death . . . just like Sarah's. He looked at the syringe. The syringe! The syringe from the dream!

The room seemed to darken as the memory flooded back. *I was drawing her blood for a test! I wasn't giving a lethal injection! The syringe was for drawing Sarah's blood! The blood was drawn from a femoral stick just like this one!*

Jake pulled the needle from the vein. The syringe was full of blood. He handed it to the nurse and backed away. He wanted to sit down, but there wasn't time.

"Are you OK?" The nurse squinted at Dr. Hampton.

"Yes," Jake responded slowly. "I haven't been this good in a long time," he said nodding.

"The O.R.'s preparing room 3, Dr. Hampton," Tiffany Edwards, the E.R. coordinator, reported.

"Thanks." He surveyed the scene. "I sure could use an extra set of experienced hands for this case. Has anyone seen Dr. Willie?"

"He walked through about fifteen minutes ago, looking like he needed a long weekend," Laurie, the clerk, responded. "I'll have the operator page him."

"Ask her to try paging him overhead. I'm carrying the on-call beeper."

A moment later the hospital intercom sounded. "Dr. Dansford to the emergency room. Dr. Dansford to the emergency room."

Two minutes later Jake looked up to see Dr. Willie plodding in. He was already wearing his winter hat and coat. "What's up, Jake?"

"It's Sharon. She's been shot."

"Shot?" Willie paled. "Here in Taylorville?"

"It's a chest wound with lots of dark blood. Might be pulmonary artery. Could be superior vena cava. I could sure use some good hands."

"Shouldn't you ship her to Grantsville?"

"No time. I'm afraid she'll bleed out."

Willie nodded. "OK," he responded. "I'll go change."

The nurses started a second large bore IV in Sharon's other arm and infused a unit of O negative blood.

"Her pressure's coming up, Dr. Hampton."

They quickly wheeled her to the operating room while Jake and Willie donned their scrubs. Jake came into the O.R. first, just as Sharon began regaining consciousness.

"Oooh," Sharon moaned, flailing her arms in the air.

"Are you ready, Jake?" the anesthesiologist called.

"Wait. She seems to be coming around a little." He looked at the monitor. "Must be her pressure. Eighty systolic is the highest we've seen yet."

"Jake," Sharon gasped. "Jake . . ."

"She's trying to say something, Dr. Hampton," Mary Lancaster, the circulating nurse, stated.

Jake leaned over her. "Don't worry, Sharon. I'm here. We're going to take good care of you."

"Jake," she gasped, "it was Frank."

"Frank Grimsted?"

Sharon nodded. "But he's not the one control—" A coughing spasm interrupted her sentence, spraying blood onto the sheet beside her.

"Don't try to talk. We can talk later." Jake leaned close to her face.

"It's Dr. D," Sharon whispered.

Jake squinted.

"Dr. D controls him."

Just then Dr. Willie walked into the room. His eyes met with Sharon's.

Sharon's eyes widened. Raising her hand in the air, she tried to sit up. "It's Dr. D!"

The anesthesiologist injected a dose of Pentothal, scrambling Sharon's words and sending her into blissful but ill-timed coma.

Jake looked at Willie. "Let's scrub up."

At the scrub sink, Willie turned to Jake. "What was that all about?"

"She was telling me who shot her. It was her neighbor, Frank Grimsted. I'm not sure about the rest, but I think she was trying to say that Dr. D is behind it all."

Willie coughed. He tried to speak calmly. "That sounds pretty bizarre."

"I don't know," Jake responded. "I wouldn't want to be in that guy's shoes when they review his patient records." He shook his head. "I doubt this guy Frank is doing this all by himself."

Willie stayed quiet and nodded his head. *Frank!* he thought, *my "bullet." You weren't supposed to be aiming at Sharon!* His thoughts began to race as Jake walked into the operating room.

Willie watched him go and stayed at the scrub sink a moment longer. *I've got to destroy my office records! If they start listening to Jake, they might search my records and see that I've changed Frank's medication.* He cursed under his breath and recounted exactly who knew about Frank and his association with him.

Hmmm, Willie reasoned, *only Sharon and Jake. Sharon won't be too hard to deal with since she's in the hospital, but Jake . . . Hopefully Frank won't miss when it comes to him. But first I've got to get to my office records!*

Dr. D walked into the O.R. and observed Jake in action as he put sterile towels around Sharon's right chest. Willie put on a sterile gown and gloves.

Jake made an incision bordering the fifth intercostal space. After using a knife on the skin, he began dividing the muscle and the fascia with an electrocautery pencil. Soon he was in and inserted a retractor to spread the ribs.

"OK," Jake instructed the anesthesiologist, "deflate the right lung."

The anesthesiologist, who had inserted a tube with access to both the right and left mainstem bronchi, stopped ventilating the right lung.

Dark blood welled up from the floor of the chest. "Suction."

Dr. D shoved the tip of the sucker into the pool of blood.

"Careful."

Jake clamped the hilum. The bleeding continued.

"Packs."

Jake shoved a handful of absorbent sponges into the chest.

"How's the pressure?"

"Eighty systolic."

"Better give more blood."

"She's had eight units. Call the blood bank. Tell them to stay five ahead."

The circulating nurse responded and picked up the phone.

"Here's the problem," Jake reported, taking his finger off of a one-centimeter hole in the superior vena cava. Blood oozed through the opening before Jake quickly pushed his finger back over the hole.

D shoved the suction tip under Jake's finger, ripping the vena cava even further.

"Careful!" Jake looked into Willie's eyes. There he saw fear . . . or was it hatred? Jake didn't have time to decide.

"Sponge sticks!" Jake took one sponge stick from the scrub nurse and placed it on the vena cava below the tear. Then he carefully removed his finger from the injury and placed another sponge stick above the injury. He looked up at Willie again. "You'll have to hold these down so I can repair the injury. Don't let up or air could get into the vein. An air embolis through a hole this big could be lethal!"

Dr. D's hands trembled slightly as he took the sticks from Jake.

"Five-O Prolene suture."

The nurse handed Jake a stitch. Deftly, he began to sew.

Dr. D's pressure became irregular, and blood began flowing from the vein.

"Tighter, Willie. She's bleeding."

Dr. D lifted one sponge stick. The field filled with blood. Jake shoved his finger back over the opening in the vein.

"Jake, I—" Dr. D stammered.

"What's wrong?" Jake demanded. "She's going to die if we don't stop this."

"I—I can't help you," Dr. D responded, staggering back from the table. "I'm not feeling so well." He pushed open the swinging door and rushed into the central sterile hallway.

Jake looked at Mary Lancaster. "Gown up. Forget the scrub. I need some hands . . . now!"

Mary looked at the swinging door. "What's with Dr. Willie?"

Jake shrugged. He didn't want to think about that right now. He looked back into the chest. The bleeding was controlled as long as he had his finger on the hole.

Mary edged up to the table.

"Hold this here . . . and this here," Jake said as he positioned her hands. He looked at the scrub nurse running the back table. "Come on in, Jackie. I'll need you to suck."

Meticulously, Jake repaired the vena cava. He then took off the clamp near the hilum of the right lung. "No bleeding," he reported. "It was only the cava. The lung's not bleeding."

"Pressure 90 systolic."

"Good. I doubt she runs much higher than that normally. She's an avid athlete."

The team relaxed a notch as the patient stabilized.

"Now we can only pray that her head is OK," the anesthesiologist commented. "She seemed pretty delirious before going to sleep."

Jake smiled behind his mask and verbalized a prayer. "Thank you, God."

◆ ◆ ◆

Dr. D stumbled like a madman into the locker room. He didn't bother to change his clothes. All he wanted was to get to his office records. No one was going to pin a murder on him!

He grabbed his coat and headed for the door. In another three minutes he was on his way to the office.

He turned right into the parking lot and parked behind the building close to the dumpster. He fumbled for his keys in the dim light and opened the door. He stepped into the hallway, striking his foot on a discarded box on the floor.

He cursed the cleaning staff and searched the wall for the light switch.

"Why can't anyone put something away around—"

A blast interrupted his last complaint.

Dr. William Dansford lost consciousness as a projectile bisected his torso.

CHAPTER
34

OVER the next few days Taylorville buzzed with news as a story of greed, manipulation, and murder unfolded. Acting on a tip by a recovering Sharon Isaacs, the police quickly apprehended a delusional Frank Grimsted in the old jailhouse.

Although the back half of Jake's office had been destroyed, the front portion, including the record room, remained intact, along with F. Grimsted's record that detailed his paranoid delusions, his homicidal obsessions about Jake Hampton, and his predictable violent outbursts while off medication. Jake himself reviewed the records and shuddered as he saw each note with its scribbled signature: "Dr. D."

After a thorough search of Grimsted's apartment turned up ample evidence of Frank's fascination with Sarah Hampton, the police turned their attention to the old jailhouse, where they discovered a stash of explosives and Frank's .38. After the search, Don Rawlings personally apologized to Kyle, who smiled at the recovery of his tarnished reputation.

It wasn't until Sunday afternoon that Jake Hampton had a chance to reflect on it all. His memory of drawing blood from Sarah, along with the syringe that Kyle had retrieved from Frank's apartment, confirmed that he hadn't helped Sarah die after all.

Now he sat on the edge of his bed and stroked the stain on his jeans pocket. The pants, the ones he had worn on the night of Sarah's death, provided the final key to unlocking his memory of that lethal night. The bloodstain was indeed Sarah's! He was sure of that now. He ran his fingers over the stain, noting that it was much darker on the torn pocket liner than on the denim material itself. The blood had come from something in his pocket, not from his own skin! He ran his fingers into the pocket and retrieved the rubber stopper from a vacutainer blood sample tube.

Jake nodded his head in understanding as a new peace settled over his mind. Of course! The stain came from a sample tube of blood that Jake had drawn to have tested for evidence that Sarah was receiving more than just health food at Ocean Sands. The tube must have shattered in Jake's fall.

Jake shrugged. There were some things he would never have answers for. How exactly was Sarah overdosed? Obviously she had died at the direction, or directly from the hands of, the one person who acted to keep Jake off the track—William Dansford/Dr. D.

Just what was it she was receiving? That answer wouldn't come for another month, after Jake sent a sample of the jeans with her blood saturated in it to a forensic laboratory. It was Mitomycin, a chemotherapeutic notable for one characteristic side effect. It turns the patient's urine blue.

And what exactly did happen on the night of Sarah's death? Frank Grimsted had been present. That much Jake understood from Frank's own admission to Kyle. How else could he have gotten the syringe? But had he intervened and pushed Jake from the balcony? Jake sighed and rubbed his eyes with his fingers. He had a vague memory of the fall . . . of a sensation of being pushed. He had thought about talking to Frank himself but quickly decided against that option since Frank was delusional. *Some things might be better remembered on my own,* Jake mused.

Jake folded the pair of pants and placed them on the bed beside him. He grabbed his coat and headed for the Trooper. Kyle was staying with Phyllis, so Jake could go back to the hospital.

This time he would go as a friend, not as a doctor.

In a few minutes Jake knocked gently at Sharon's door.

"Come in."

Sharon smiled when she saw him.

"More flowers?"

Jake held up the roses. "I'll put them on the windowsill with the others." He leaned down and kissed her forehead. "How do you feel?"

Sharon wrinkled her nose. "A little sore, and I need to wash my hair, but otherwise I've never been so glad to be alive."

Jake smiled and took her hand. "It's been a wild couple of days."

Sharon nodded. "I've never been so afraid. I remember being shot . . . Then I remember seeing you and feeling like everything would be OK . . . and then . . ." Sharon's voice choked. "I remember seeing Dr. Willie." She shook her head. "I knew you didn't know he was Dr. D. I thought he would kill me . . . I tried to tell you . . ." She paused. "That's the last thing I remember until after the operation."

"He had it planned so perfectly. I would have looked like a fool to bring a suit against someone whom I'd just decided to work for."

"It was more than that, Jake. He brought you here, knowing that Frank could be manipulated into killing you."

"What an alibi! No one would have ever expected the one who had reached out to me like he did. When I think of how he treated me . . . how he treated Kyle . . ." Jake shook his head again.

"He was sick—an evil man, Jake."

Jake nodded. "I'm just glad it's over."

"Me, too."

They sat for a moment in silence as Jake stroked her hand. His eyes met hers. His were the ones that were brimming with tears. He hadn't allowed himself to show his emotions when he was the surgeon, but now as her friend he couldn't hold back.

"I thought I'd lost you."

She squeezed his hand.

"I was so afraid," Jake admitted.

"God wanted me to live," she responded. "And he watched out for me."

Jake thought for a moment, then spoke in a soft voice. "You know, I can't help thinking that it wasn't only Dr. D who wanted me here."

Sharon wrinkled her nose in a question.

Jake continued, "As strange as the events all seemed, I can see the hand of God in this whole thing." He paused and stroked her hand. "Who else but God could have arranged the circumstances that sparked the return of my memory? How else could he have brought light into my darkest hour? How else could he have brought me to you?"

Sharon bit her quivering lower lip.

They held hands for a few minutes, resting comfortably in a quiet understanding that communicated volumes without their saying a word.

Finally Jake slipped out and returned with a plastic basin and a towel. "Now, how about letting me wash your hair?"

The thought of finally getting rid of all the clotted blood and betadine was music to Sharon's ears. She brightened. "I must be a sight."

Jake laughed. "A beautiful sight."

She was a living, beautiful sight indeed.

Acknowledgments

NAMING the ones who have helped with this project is certain to be fraught with omissions. Nonetheless, I must acknowledge a few people who have been so generous with information and advice.

Thanks so much to Jen Martin, the registered dietician who specializes in counseling our oncology patients. The wealth of information about alternative cancer treatments was invaluable in this project.

Thanks to Dr. John Eagle, a psychiatrist and my friend, who allowed me to witness electroshock therapy and provided the insight into the history of E.C.T.

Thanks to the oncology team of Dr. Brian Robinson and Dr. John Barton, who answered my questions regarding breast cancer chemotherapy.

Thanks to my wife, Kris, for her faithful support and to my boys for their enthusiasm.

Thanks especially to the entire Crossway Books family. It has been a blessing to work with you again.

Of course, to acknowledge men without giving God our Father the credit is shortsighted. He is the source of everything good. Thanks to Him always!